GOOD DAYS BAD DAYS

OTHER TITLES BY EMILY BLEEKER

Wreckage

When I'm Gone

Working Fire

The Waiting Room

What It Seems

What's Left Unsaid

When We Were Enemies

When We Chased the Light

GOOD DAYS BAD DAYS

A NOVEL

EMILY BLEEKER

LAKE UNION PUBLISHING

This is a work of fiction. Names, characters, organizations, places, events, and incidents are either products of the author's imagination or are used fictitiously.

Published by Lake Union Publishing, Seattle

www.apub.com

EU product safety contact:
Amazon Media EU S.à r.l.
38, avenue John F. Kennedy, L-1855 Luxembourg
amazonpublishing-gpsr@amazon.com

ISBN-13: 9781662531248 (paperback)
ISBN-13: 9781662531255 (digital)

Cover design by Shasti O'Leary-Soudant
Cover image: © Zbynek Pospisil, © Westend61 / Getty

Printed in the United States of America

GOOD DAYS BAD DAYS

CHAPTER 1

CHARLIE

Present Day

GREETINGS FROM LAKE GENEVA.

The mural is new.

The impressive ten-foot-tall image covers the side of a wall just off Main Street. It looks like a vintage postcard from some fancy tropical vacation destination instead of the small Midwestern resort town of my youth. Right next to it—a Starbucks. Also new.

The smart, trendy mural contrasts the original welcome sign I just drove past half a mile up the road. I remember it from childhood—hand-carved brown slats with gold lettering surrounded by token-like circles representing organizations like the Kiwanis, the Lions, and the Masonic lodge. Back then, it was the official welcome for summer vacationers headed to the beach or winter travelers seeking the closest thing to skiing the Midwest can offer.

I haven't been back here since Child Protective Services pulled me out of my parents' house at fifteen. And sure, parts of the town look strangely new, but the view down Broad Street hasn't changed. A cloudy sheet of ice covers the lake, and a light dusting of snow blows across the frozen surface, reminding me how I'd walk home from school across the ice directly into my backyard.

Even with the lingering winter gloom replacing the beachy summer vibes, there's a nostalgic pull to this place. The mansions around the lake, the boat club, the country club, the resorts and spas are all remnants of a once-booming resort town for affluent Chicago families. Over the years, it's transformed into a playground that's easily accessible to the average person. No wonder people love it here.

When I was placed in foster care during the fall of my sophomore year of high school, I thought I'd be back home by the time the summer crowd trickled in. I thought my dad would drive up with Mom sitting in the front seat, fling the Subaru's door open, and we'd go back to the house on the lake together. With our home cleaned up, I'd be able to use the shower like a normal kid instead of having to sneak one in the locker room at school, and I'd be able to put my clothes in my own closet or dresser. We'd sit on the couch in the living room and watch the nightly news and then go into town and get a scoop of pistachio ice cream.

But my dad never came.

I saw him a few times during visitations, but not my mom. When I went to college, I made a choice—I decided never to come back here, at least not until my mom got treatment for her hoarding and my dad stopped ignoring the problem. I gave up hoping for anything to do with my parents decades ago.

Then last week my father called my assistant trying to get through to me. She looked at me with a crinkled forehead when she said, "I think it's your dad."

I never talk about my parents. Why should I? Just because they raised me for fifteen years doesn't mean I owe them a special mention in the acknowledgments section of my life. I've allowed occasional calls from my father through the years, though in my opinion, he's just as guilty as my mother for my parentless existence. I'd always told Dad to stand up to her, let me help clean the house, give her an ultimatum, or leave her. I was really saying, *Choose me, Daddy. Please, choose me.*

He'd make excuse after excuse until I'd eventually hang up, more hurt by the conversation than the lack of contact.

That's why this most recent call took me by surprise. His voice sounded old and trembly. He told me Mom had been sent to a long-term care facility after a neighbor called senior services about the state of the house. He said he had three months to get the place cleaned or it'd be condemned. He asked me to help. He also asked me to see Mom one more time.

For some reason, I didn't know how to say no when my father finally made the call I'd been waiting decades to receive. And that's why I'm here in Lake Geneva.

I pull into the large asphalt parking lot of the memory care center. It's been well shoveled and salted after a recent snowstorm. Weather in Wisconsin at the end of February can be intense, especially when your house backs up to a large body of water, like my childhood home. If summers reside in my memory in a playful haze of ice cream on my fingers and sand between my toes, winters dwell in a stuffy room with walls that seem to press in on me as each cold day passes.

I shiver as I exit the car, pulling my coat's lined hood in closer. I approach the front entrance of the Victorian-style facility with white siding and green shingles. A ramp leads to a spindled porch with modern sliding glass doors.

The doors to Shore Path Memory Care Center swoosh open, followed by another set after a large nonslip mat with the memory center's name embedded in it. Inside, a twentysomething receptionist in a green polo sits behind a large wooden desk facing a comfortable-looking cluster of padded armchairs and couches.

"Hello! Welcome to Shore Path. Who are you here to visit today?" she asks, her eyes widening as I push my hood off. "Oh!"

"Hi. I'm looking for Betty Laramie." I answer as though I don't notice she's recognized me from my Home and Family Network show *Second Chance Renovation*.

I was only stopped twice at the airport for a selfie and once on the plane for an autograph. It's easier to blend in when I'm alone. When I'm with my six-foot-two husband and costar, Ian, with his rich brown eyes, strong jaw, broad shoulders, and neatly trimmed beard, we can hardly go an hour without being noticed. If he's wearing any flannel—forget it.

"Oh, wow. Charlie McFadden. Hi." She waves. Her cheeks flush pink as she clicks her mouse while watching her computer screen until she stops and clears her throat. "Um, Betty Laramie? Yes, there's a note here. I'll call back to the nurses' station."

"That's great. Thanks."

The receptionist dials a number and pauses, nervously clearing her throat as it rings.

"I have to say I'm a huge fan. My mom and I have seen every episode of *Second Chance Renovation*. We have your book—"

"Thank you. You're too kind," I say warmly, cutting her off. Thankfully, someone picks up on the other end of the line and I successfully dodge any discussion of my book. Our book. Mine and Ian's book: *Our Second Chance*. It was published immediately after the episode featuring our wedding aired, and it spent six weeks on *The New York Times* nonfiction bestsellers list. It told our love story, how we took what we learned from our "failed" first marriages and turned it into a home renovation empire. Too bad it might be more fiction than I first thought.

It's been a week since I've spoken to my husband, other than a few texts and one awkward conference call with the production team to discuss the upcoming season of our home remodeling show.

When I found the messages from a female fan on his social media account, I wasn't shocked at first. We're in the public eye. We've had a hit show for eight years and counting. We've been on every morning show and a few late-night ones. We have a home decorating line at Target, bestselling coffee-table books, and one very popular memoir that earned out our high six-figure advance years ago.

I get hundreds of messages a week, and I leave the majority of them unopened. But the DMs I found on Ian's Instagram were not unopened. They were not hidden either. The profile picture was of a gorgeous blond woman in a revealing top, at least ten years younger than me with a smile that still pops into my mind when I let my guard down. The messages were flirtatious, inappropriate, heartbreaking.

And though I felt like a jealous teen looking through his DMs, I'm glad I did. I'd never distrusted Ian before. He's my business partner and TV cohost, and until a week ago, he was my best friend. He swears it was a silly mistake, that there was nothing physical, that this was the first and only time. I can't bear to linger on his excuses long enough to decide if they are true.

He calls at least five times a day and texts me even more. When I decided to visit my parents, I broke my silence and texted him back. I asked if he'd take my carpool day and keep my stepsons, ten-year-old twins, Mack and Bradley, connected with their older sister, my nineteen-year-old daughter, Olivia, from my first marriage. He agreed, and I left the next day.

I'm not ready to talk. I'm not prepared to ask myself if I want to play detective and figure out if I've been married to a stranger or if I want to walk away before he can hurt me again. Which might be another reason I'm here in Lake Geneva, waiting to talk to my mom after I'd vowed to never speak to her again.

The receptionist hangs up the phone and gives a big smile.

"Nurse Mitchell will be out in a minute. You can wait over there if you like."

She points to the sitting area with a fire burning in a large gas fireplace. I thank her and find a comfortable spot to wait. The whole room smells of campfire and cinnamon, with the ever-so-faint scent of bleach underneath it all. For a nursing home, it's welcoming and homey, which I'm sure is essential for the fifty-two residents with severe cognitive impairments like dementia or Alzheimer's.

Dad said it's the best facility in the area. It looks like one of the old mansions that skirt the lakeshore, carefully restored to transform it into a functional care facility. Still, I can tell this is new construction. The grand cathedral ceiling in the foyer has a more modern look, for one. The halls on either side of the desk lead to a key-card-controlled entry with low ceilings, closer to eight feet, which would've been unfashionable for an aristocratic family from the nineteenth century. The floors appear to be distressed oak, but it only takes two echoey steps to discover that it's tile.

New construction, for sure. It's similar to some of our city remodels with modern architecture—more Ian's thing than mine. I like the old stuff with a story behind it, wood that's been distressed by feet and time rather than in a factory or with a hammer and dark stain in a workshop.

"Hello, Lottie." Greg Laramie's voice pulls me out of my "work mind," and I suddenly find myself on my feet.

"Hey, Dad. How are you?" I ask as though we see each other regularly on holidays and birthdays like most normal families. Those normal families would hug now, but I don't want to embrace this stranger who vaguely resembles my dad.

"I'm fine. I'm glad you made it. I was afraid you might have problems with the roads after the storm." He makes small talk. I chat back with simple details of my trip, noting everything that's the same and everything different about him. His hair is gray and thinning, and the skin under his eyes sags. He's tall as before, well over six feet, but his shoulders are stooped, making him appear shorter. He's skinny everywhere except for a slight paunch that protrudes above his belt. He looks tired and old, a visual reminder of how many years have passed.

We get to an awkward pause in our conversation when we run out of weather- and transportation-related questions. I could ask about my mom, but I wish he'd ask about his grandkids, my husband, or my real life in any way.

He speaks again, starting and stopping a few times out of apparent nerves.

"You l-look just . . . like . . ."

I'm dying to know what comparison popped into his mind. Do I look just like I did on my first day of school? The last time he saw me? My mom when she was younger?

". . . you do on your show," he finally mumbles, and my hope drops a touch. It's meaningful to me that he watches *Second Chance Renovation*, but I'm far more interested in knowing where I came from, how he remembers me. Betty and Greg Laramie are the memory keepers of my early life. Since our estrangement, I've always felt like there are gaps in my childhood I can't fully understand without their input.

"Oh, you watch?" I continue the small talk.

"I've caught a few episodes here or there." I can tell by the shuffle in his stance that it was more than an accidental channel switch that brought him to my show.

"And Mom?" I ask, finally finding the courage to mention the reason we're both here.

He shakes his head and stares at the floor. It hurts but it's not a surprise. Betty Laramie, the caring mother who loved her daughter more than anything and then slowly turned into a woman who protected her belongings over all else, blames me for the school's call to CPS thirty-one years ago.

I know hoarding disorder is a real, complex, and difficult-to-treat mental health condition. I know her urge to collect, save, and protect her belongings is a compulsion linked to OCD and possibly PTSD that has nothing to do with her love for me. I know that for her, the cocoon of belongings feels safe, and the thought of losing them, panic inducing. I know all these things, but I still can't understand how she essentially gave away her one and only child without a fight and then ended up mad at me.

"Are you positive she wants to see me, Dad? I mean, it's been a long time . . ."

"She does love you, you know," Dad says, offering an olive branch.

I want to say, *I don't think she knows what love is* or *I'm a mother and I could never imagine choosing junk over my child,* but I'm not here to confront my parents. I'm here for closure, distraction, and maybe to get answers to questions about my past. I stop my bitter response and take a breath instead.

A tall, middle-aged woman in green scrubs with a name tag reading "Mitchell" pinned to her left breast approaches us, and my heartbeat travels to my ears. This must be the nurse who'll take us to my cold, judgmental, distant mom, who somehow thinks it's my fault she's not in my life after all she's done.

"Hello, Mr. Laramie. Is this the daughter I've heard so much about?"

"Yes. This is our daughter, Charlotte."

My God, it's been forever since anyone called me that. I have to pull back on the reins of my emotions as I shake Nurse Mitchell's hand.

"Wonderful to meet you. Your parents have told me all about you."

I smile and thank her, though I can't imagine what they've told the staff here. It's likely a mix of truth and imaginings about my life.

She continues, "So, Betty is ready for your visit, but I must warn you—she's having a bit of a bad day today. Your dad has probably told you—with RPD, rapidly progressive dementia, or really any major neurocognitive disorder, there are good days and bad days. It's what we call fluctuating cognition. Sometimes it can make our residents feel a little unstuck in time. So, don't be discouraged if she's confused today and doesn't remember what year it is. She might not recognize you or your dad at times. It's to be expected but not exactly predictable, right, Greg?"

My dad gives a polite chuckle, and I nod as if I know what they're talking about.

"A few tips. We suggest on these harder days to let your mom have the reality she's in at the moment. Arguing is not really productive and can actually prolong or exacerbate the situation. Distraction is great. Your dad's found that playing cards or working on a puzzle helps focus your mom. Music, too. I'll give you a printout with some tips, but it's understandable if you end up feeling overwhelmed and need to step away. This isn't easy for anyone."

"Sounds good," I agree.

We go through a locked door Nurse Mitchell opens with a key card and then pass a living room–like area where a few residents are watching a blaring morning show while another pair seems to be playing a game of checkers in the corner. It's a happy place, or so it seems. The elderly men and women look engaged and well tended. I'm sure my mother is in better condition here than when she lived at home, and even with all the hurt from my childhood, I'm glad she's being cared for.

When we reach room 184, I see my mom's name written on a nameplate under the room number. She has a sun sticker on one side of her name and a bright pink flower on the other, which seems awfully cheerful for the Betty Laramie I know.

"You ready?" Nurse Mitchell asks. I nod and my dad gives my shoulder an unexpected squeeze. I flash back to my childhood, how he'd say goodbye with a loving pat each day as he headed out to open our family store. It's strange how memories can be both exquisite and excruciating at the same time.

Nurse Mitchell gives a double knock on the partially open door and then steps inside, gesturing for me to follow her.

It's been thirty-one years, five months, two weeks, and three days since they took me out of my parents' home. Thirty-one years since I was taken out of my school and the town that was helping to raise me. Thirty-one years since my mom and I exchanged our last words.

Our last words—until today.

CHAPTER 2

Greg

April 3, 1969
Ike's Diner
Janesville, Wisconsin

"That might be the most beautiful woman I've ever seen," Mark Lucian says, a little louder than I'm comfortable with in the middle of Ike's Diner. "Look. Look."

"Would you knock it off?" I growl, staring at my empty coffee cup until the diner's door chimes, signaling her impending exit. I refuse to try to get a better look at her, hoping to make Mark's blatant drooling less obvious.

"Oh, man. You missed her." He tosses his last sliver of bacon into his mouth and wipes his mustache with a napkin. "Well, your loss."

I'd caught a brief glimpse of the pretty young lady when she first approached the counter before being seated several booths away from our table. She was wearing a figure-hugging red dress and a hat that likely cost more than I make in a week. Her medium-length hair had an unnatural platinum hue, root to curled ends. She was out of Mark's league and definitely out of mine.

"Don't you get enough of gawking at women over at that place in Darien? Leave the hometown girls alone."

Mark's a real ladies' man, who I personally know keeps a pack of nudie cards in his desk and visits the Vegas Club at least once a week. I know he doesn't think the same of me. I haven't had a date in half a year. At twenty-five, I've gotten to know all the eligible ladies in Janesville and watched most of them get married. A lot of them have at least one or two in their brood now.

"That was no hometown girl. You'd know that if you'd looked when I told you to." Mark sniffs and tugs his belt up over his slim abdomen. When I say Mark is a ladies' man, I don't mean that only he thinks of himself as one. He picks up women easily at any bar we go to. When I talk to women, especially beautiful ones, I get nervous and tongue-tied, my palms wet like I've dipped them in the Rock River.

"I don't like ogling women."

"I know. I remember you at the club. I was embarrassed for weeks at how you fell all over yourself around those gals. I don't know what's the matter with you . . ."

"What's the matter with him?" Lucy, our regular waitress and Ike's daughter, asks. Her husband went to Vietnam a few years ago and didn't come back. It's happening more and more lately, and when Mrs. Morris, my mother's neighbor and best friend, called me last June, I knew as soon as I heard sobs in the background that my family had been touched by this same kind of tragedy. "This man here is one of the last true gentlemen, unlike you, Mark Lucian."

I dip my last bite of pancake in an amber pool of syrup, blushing. Lucy is tall, blond, and constantly warding off Mark's advances. I have a particular softness for Lucy, knowing we share some of the same flavor of grief, and I'm easily irritated at Mark's childish flirtations. I think Mark has always been in love with Lucy. I suspect he would've proposed as soon as it was socially acceptable after her loss, but he's not the kind of man to ask a question he doesn't already know the answer to. It's not that I have a romantic inclination toward the young widow, I just wish Mark would leave her alone if he isn't going to go about things in a respectful manner.

"Hey, Luce, who was that woman that just walked out?" Mark asks as Lucy places the bill on the table and collects our empty plates. She shrugs, not seeming annoyed or jealous, which I'm assuming she would be if Mark had any chance with her.

"The fancy one from table three? No idea. Never seen her before. Must be passing through."

"Huh, that's what I thought."

"I'm sure that's not all you were thinking," Lucy says, giving him a look filled with innuendo.

"Who, me?" he asks flirtatiously. "What? I'm not the gentlemanly type, too?"

"Not one tiny bit," she quips and heads to the kitchen with our dishes. Mark watches her the entire way and then leans in.

"Maybe she's on her way to the Playboy Club in Lake Geneva. That blond girl, I mean. I'm thinking of getting a club key. Wanna come? Heard it's a happening place."

"I don't know," I say feebly, reading the check and pulling out my wallet to pay my half of the bill. I toss a dollar on the table for Lucy's tip. Mark searches his wallet and does the same.

"Can you settle up for me? I have a meeting with the new guy—Mr. Hollinger. Not sure what about. Unless he's calling me in to fire me. I wouldn't put it past that guy."

"You're not gonna get fired, Mark," I reassure him, and I hope I'm right. Mark hired me as a cameraman at WQRX TV four years ago when I was fresh out of college. He's an account executive now, one of the upper management people I normally would try to hide from by staying in the studio, but we've become friends. I'm pretty sure if he gets fired, I'll be next. "You know we'd be lost without you. Mr. Hollinger will figure that out, too."

Donald Hollinger is the new station manager at WQRX. From what I've heard, he appears to be a pleasant enough man, even though no one seems to like him. I suppose that's how things go when you're the one making changes.

Until now, WQRX has been under the same management since it went on the airwaves in '53. With new management comes new staff, programming, and rules. As long as I keep my job, I doubt much will change for me. A cameraman goes where the director or producer tells him to, and there's not much big news in southern Wisconsin these days. Recently we had a news segment all about the size of old Mrs. Tiller's greenhouse tomatoes and little Bobby Craig's lemonade stand.

"Yeah. You assholes wouldn't make it a day without me. Don't forget it." Mark claps a heavy hand on my shoulder. "When am I gonna get you to go out with me again, old man?" he asks as we move toward the exit.

"Soon." I push his nagging off for another week at least.

"I'll hold you to it."

"You better."

Mark leaves and I stand by the register. Lucy is nowhere to be seen. I could tap the little bell on the counter, but I don't want to rush her. She already has so much to deal with. I can wait a few extra minutes.

The door chime rings again, signaling a new customer. I fiddle with the bill and keep an eye on the kitchen, but there's still no sign of life. As I wait, determined to be patient, a small white hand dashes across me and taps the bell. It's a woman's hand, ivory skin, long red nails and a gold watch at her wrist. She's close enough that I can smell her expensive perfume through the grease-soaked diner air.

"I'm sorry to butt in, but I lost my keys and I have an interview in ten minutes."

"No problem," I say, facing the visitor. My mouth goes dry.

It's the woman in the red dress that Mark declared Janesville's version of Helen of Troy. I hate to admit it, but Mark was right. This woman is breathtaking, like a movie star—her lips carefully lined with red lipstick, lashes thick above her sky-blue eyes.

I try not to notice her figure, but even a glance reveals she's well shaped, and her dress definitely highlights her feminine form. My neck is suddenly hot, and I wish I could loosen my tie and grab a little fresh air.

"You're too sweet," she says, and I can tell I'm blushing. "I searched the booth where I was sitting and retraced my steps so many times I think I have blisters." Her voice is stronger than I expected, not light and wispy like Marilyn Monroe, whom she closely resembles.

"I can help, if you like," I offer, fighting my nerves. Mark and I were the only two left in the diner after the lunch rush, and I'm worried Lucy forgot about us and took a smoke break with Leo, the cook. We might be waiting a while.

"Would you? Thank you so much," she says with such overwhelming gratitude that I idiotically feel like a knight rushing in on his trusty steed to save the damsel in distress.

"What do they look like?"

She twists up her ruby red lips. "Metal, pointy, make a clanking sound when they crash together."

"Of course," I say, hiding my embarrassment by placing my bill on the counter with my payment.

"Only joking, hon. Two keys, one silver and one gold. The key chain is a small statue of the Eiffel Tower."

Silent, I go to the booth where she ate her lunch and run my fingers around the edges of the vinyl seats, realizing after a few moments that she might wonder how I knew where she sat without asking.

Smooth, Greg. Smooth. I chastise myself, but if she notices, she doesn't care. She rings the bell again and I consider going back to the kitchen to find Lucy myself.

"Wait! I see them!" the woman shouts. My head cracks on the underside of the table and I scramble to my feet, the stabbing pain dulling as the blood drains.

"I can't reach. Could you?" she asks, leaning over the counter, kicking her heels up and reaching for a spot under the cash register where Lucy must've stashed the keys after cleaning the table.

I'm a gangly six foot five, and though I've always hated that my height makes it impossible to blend in with a crowd, it does have its strong points. Without much effort, I reach my long arm to the little compartment behind the counter and snag the cluster of keys. They make a quiet tinkling sound as I place them on the woman's soft-looking palm.

"You're my hero. Thank you so much," she says, touching my sleeve ever so lightly, my head spinning at the simple motion.

"You're welcome." I overcome my tongue-tied nature temporarily.

"Well, thank you again. Have a good day."

"You too," I say with a nod, a smile tugging at the corners of my mouth.

I can hear Lucy and Leo talking in the back now, and the breeze pushes the faint scent of cigarette smoke through the swinging door. As Lucy returns from the kitchen, apologizing for making me wait, the woman in red pauses at the threshold like she's overlooked something else.

"Hey there, hero guy," she calls to get my attention, which hasn't actually left her. Lucy raises her eyebrows at me as though she knows she missed something important. "I forgot to ask—what's your name?"

"Greg," I say back, adding, "Laramie."

"Well, nice to meet you, Greg Laramie."

"Nice to meet you, too . . ." I leave a space for her name, too nervous to ask outright. She doesn't make me. A broad, enchanting smile spreads across her face.

"I'm Betty," she says.

It's the prettiest name I've ever heard. I know my cheeks must give away the effect she has on me.

"Nice to meet you, Betty."

"You too, Greg."

At that, she flits out of my day like a rare bird escaping its cage for the unwelcoming chill of the Midwest, and I'm left flushed and distracted, propped against the counter by one arm, wondering how any single human creature could move me so completely.

"Well, look at you, Greg Laramie. I'm impressed." Lucy smirks at me, elbows on the counter.

"I don't know what you're talking about," I say, passing her my payment, finally. I'll be late getting back to work.

"Sure you don't." The change plinks cheerfully as she drops the coins into the cash register. "You don't give yourself enough credit, Greg. Break out of that shell a little and you'd be surprised what'd happen for you." She shoves the cash tray back in and sighs. "Guess that's why you're behind the camera and not in front of it, huh? Well, makes sense, but you'd make some girl really happy, Greg. I'm sure of it."

I shrug and push my hands into my pants pockets. She wishes me a good day, and I walk outside into a revitalizing spring breeze that whips through my thin cotton shirt and tickles my scalp as it tangles in my hair.

As the door clinks shut behind me, a fancy red Corvette speeds down East Milwaukee in the opposite direction in a flash of color and exhaust. A slender white hand waves at me as the car revs past. I rush to return the gesture but can't get my hand out of my pocket until she's too far away to see my response.

By the time I run up the back stairwell to Studio C, I'm almost myself again, other than a smile that won't go away. And though no one can see it, it's there, behind the camera every time I think of the beautiful stranger who left me with only one of her names.

CHAPTER 3

Charlie

Present Day

"Good morning, Betty. Look who I have here for you. Visitors!" The nurse's tone is cheerful and bright, reminding me of how the elementary school teachers speak in my kids' classrooms. I clasp my hands together to keep them from shaking.

We duck around the half-closed privacy curtain and step into a sunny room with a hospital bed in the back corner, covered in a stitched blanket tucked neatly around each edge. There are two small side tables with pictures of my mom and dad, their house, and a picture of me when I was young. There's another table on rollers covered in a nearly finished puzzle. The Game Show Network plays on the TV with the volume turned all the way down. In the corner is an overstuffed green armchair that looks like it came from my father's shop. It is definitely antique and well preserved.

That's where she sits—my mom.

She's holding a cup of coffee, dressed in a loose pair of tan slacks and an untucked green blouse. Her hair is a light gray, nearly white, thinning at the top and sides. She looks as though she's had a trip to the hairdresser recently. Her cheeks are overly rouged and her lipstick a touch askew, but she seems ready for guests. Her skin is pale and so thin I can see the veins running up her arms and neck where exposed. Like my father, she is very slender and looks so frail that a single slip on the ice might snap her in half. She's like a dried-out rose that's still beautiful but could crumble to dust with one touch.

"Well, hello," she says warmly to all three of us, looking confused but bright eyed. She sets down her mug and gazes at us expectantly as if she's waiting for an introduction. I anticipate a flicker of recognition from her, but none comes. A wave of relief washes over me.

"Betty, Greg and Charlotte are here to visit you today." Dad and I hang our coats and stand a few feet away waiting to assess her mood.

"Oh, hi! Lovely to meet you," she says, smoothing her pants. I'm not surprised Betty doesn't recognize me, but I find the blank look she gives my father a little unnerving. There's something else new about my mother, a lightness in her expression that makes it seem like I'm meeting her all over again.

"Hello, Betty. This is Charlotte, your daughter."

"My daughter?" she asks, bemused, eyeing me skeptically. "I don't have a daughter."

She says it like it's a fact, not a bitter reference to our falling out. Nurse Mitchell gives me an empathetic look. I'm sure most visitors find it difficult to be forgotten by their loved ones, but strangely, it doesn't faze me. It's fascinating being in the same room as my mother without the undercurrent of negativity that always fed the electric fence around her.

"It's Lottie, hon. She's come to visit," Dad says, using my childhood nickname, stepping toward Mom's chair. She rolls her eyes like an annoyed teen and then zones in on me.

"Your hair is very shiny," she says with a friendly smile. I can't remember my mother saying something positive about my appearance since I reached puberty. Though our house was a mess, or maybe because of it, she insisted I always looked perfect when I went out in public. One of our last fights was when I tried to go to school in stylish ripped jeans that my friend Lacey gave me.

"You look unkempt," she said. "Plus, it shows your thick thighs. Skirts are far more flattering until you lose a few pounds."

I ran out of the house, causing several of her treasures to crash behind me, which always set her nerves on edge. I slammed the door as hard as I could. That day at school I talked to my counselor about it all. She already knew something of the hoarding. It's impossible to keep that kind of thing under wraps in a town filled with mansions and millionaires for very long. She saw me run into school late, crying, and pulled me into her office.

She was the first one I'd ever confided in about my parents' house, but the truth poured out of me that morning, and two days later, Mrs. Lavarito from Child Protective Services showed up on our doorstep. After her home visit, I was removed, carrying one garbage bag of belongings and my school backpack. It was supposed to be temporary. Mrs. Lavarito comforted me with promises of support from social services and mental health professionals. But I never saw my school counselor again, my mom or my house. I had no idea a pair of jeans would change my life so drastically, bringing me to this moment over thirty years later.

"Uh, thank you," I say to this friendly version of my mom and then offer back, "I like the color of your lipstick."

"Oh, thanks. I'm going to a dance later and it matches the dress I got from Gimbels."

"A dance? That sounds fun," Nurse Mitchell replies while writing a note on the whiteboard. I can tell from the look on her face that there's no such dance here at Shore Path Memory Center.

Unstuck in time, that's what the nurse said before we headed back to see Mom. This person I'm talking to is technically my mother, but I think she's reliving a moment from years before I was born.

"I guess. I'm going with Nicky Sheridan, so I don't know if it will be fun, but my dress has a crinoline, and"—she leans in and whispers—"it's a full inch shorter than the dress code."

"Whoa, Betty, you're a rebel," Nurse Mitchell responds, meeting my mom in her own reality.

She giggles, which is an odd sound from my mother.

"Wanna try it?" She holds the tube of lipstick up and squints to read the label. "Defiant Coral. It sounds sassy and I like that."

She gives her shoulders a little shake. I try to stop my laugh, but it puffs out. My dad holds back a smirk.

"I rarely turn down sassy," I say with a shrug.

She points to an aluminum and plastic chair across the room. Nurse Mitchell drags it over, saying something about how we're doing just fine. She excuses herself.

My mom takes the cap off her lipstick and gestures for me to sit, insisting on applying the color herself. I follow her instructions and give her a slight pucker as she uses her shaky hand to smooth it on.

"Press them together, hon," she says, and I comply. She makes a sweet cooing sound. "Perfect! That's a great color on you."

I have no idea what the color actually looks like since there's no mirror handy, but I don't care if I look like a clown.

"Wanna play gin rummy?" She reaches for a pack of cards sitting on the short table beside her.

When I was little my mom would play game after game of solitaire, but we never played games together as a family. My throat is thick and sticky.

I take a deep breath and answer, "Yes, I'd love to play."

My dad brings a side table over and puts it between us, and my mom starts passing out the cards. Dad does that shoulder squeeze thing again as he sits beside me, which doesn't exactly make it easier to keep my feelings under control. She picks up her cards and looks at me long and hard, as if she remembers something. I hope she's not remembering who I really am.

After a long pause, I look at my dad. He puts down the first card, starting the game. Immediately, Mom engages in the activity, and I play with both of my parents for the first time in my entire life.

As the game progresses, I watch my mother suspiciously and wait for her charming facade to drop. As the hour goes on, I find myself relaxing, enjoying myself, even. When it's time to go, my mom puts her arms out as though asking for a hug.

"I've missed you so much," she says, her eyes misty and sincere. I know I should respond in like and tell her I've missed her as well, but I can't.

The Betty I met today is the kind of mom I always wished I'd had. I'd missed out on that mom—the "I'll do your makeup" mom, the "let's play gin rummy" mom. But this coral-lipped, friendly woman isn't my mom. I silently lean into the embrace. She smells of coffee, peppermints, and baby powder.

She whispers, "Where have you been for so long, Laura?"

I pull back without an answer.

Laura? Another random memory, but I don't mind. I think I'd rather be Laura right now, whoever she is.

"See you again soon?" she asks. And though it's likely a lie, I tell her I will.

Dad walks me out, past Nurse Mitchell, past the front desk girl who asks for a selfie, and back into the cold. Now we'll visit the house. We have a meeting scheduled with the social worker and a city official for tomorrow morning, and I told my dad I needed to know what the situation looked like before I agreed to help.

"I looked Lake Geneva up. Sounds like a cool place. We should come visit . . ." Olivia, my college freshman, says on the other end of the line as I drive across town to my parents' house.

We. I loved it when she started saying "we" when referring to our little family.

She was twelve when I met Ian, and for a while we were a perfect modern family, at least when we weren't off shooting *Second Chance*

Renovation in some out-of-state locale. It all went sideways after we moved into a big house in LA and she had to get used to the little four-year-old twins that came along with her new stepdad. With Olivia in middle school, we had to leave her at home with her dad during our work trips, and because they were still so little, we'd take the boys all over the country with us for weeks at a time.

Eventually, Olivia asked to live at her dad's since it was closer to her school, and I forced myself to understand, to accept her decision. We still have epic summer vacations and holidays together and overnights whenever possible, but a distance has grown between Olivia and me that comes from a sense of abandonment on both sides, though we definitely don't talk about it.

Now that her dad has moved back to the East Coast, we see her more often. She comes home from Stanford every few weeks or so to do her laundry and see the boys. She's a good big stepsister, but I know she's always felt replaced by the twins.

"It's nothing spectacular, really. You've been swimming with the dolphins in the Galápagos; I think Lake Geneva, Wisconsin, would be a snore for you." The idea of having Olivia anywhere near this place gives me anxiety. Lake Geneva isn't a vacation location to me; it's more like a haunted house packed with unpredictable jump scares.

"Jeez, Mom. You make me sound spoiled," she grumbles through the phone like I'm the most annoying human that's ever existed. "I'd love to see where you grew up. I have a break in a few weeks. I could come out and help."

"Oh, God, no. I should be home by spring break. Besides, there's really not much to see."

Silence on the other side of the call, and I know I've pissed her off, again. God, I make all the mistakes. But she doesn't realize I'm saving her from a genuinely unpleasant experience. My mom was interesting and innocent today, but what will she be like tomorrow or the next day? And the house—I haven't even seen the house yet. No. This isn't a bonding opportunity for me and Olivia. I will spare her what I wasn't spared.

"We can go to Cabo for break, if you like. Or how about we go back to Venice this summer?"

Olivia sighs and changes the subject.

"Sorry, Mom. I gotta go. I have a study thing in a few minutes."

"All right, honey. Sounds good. I love you."

"I love you, too," she says, but not with feeling—more like it's a sentence she's practiced so many times that it's become automatic. "Oh, and Mom . . ." she calls out as I'm about to hit the end button.

"Yeah?" I wait, hoping she says she understands why she can't visit.

"Call Ian," she blurts out and hangs up before I can say anything.

Heat rushes up my neck.

So, he's got Olivia working for him now. I hate that he's gotten her involved in this. When Olivia's father and I divorced, we were cordial, friendly, could be in the same room without slinging accusations. She was three years old at that time, but still—we never put Olivia in the middle. Just because she's technically an adult doesn't mean that should change this time around. Ian knows how I feel about keeping the kids out of our disagreements. What an asshole. I know I have to talk to him eventually, yell, curse, cry and then listen to his apologies and promises, but I flew halfway across the country to escape that confrontation—I definitely won't be inviting it today.

I drop my phone on the seat beside me as I turn onto Main Street. Another rush of nostalgia washes away the flash of anger brought up by the mention of my husband's name. The snow-trimmed storefronts, the neon signs that speak to another era, the lake peeking through each lane like it's calling to anyone driving past. Even in the winter I can almost understand Olivia's desire to visit this town. Anytime a tourist kid found out I stayed in town year-round they'd give their parents a look, disappointed to have to go home to some boring Chicago suburb.

I allowed them to think my world was as perfect as it seemed.

Even if my house didn't feel like home back then, the town did—especially in the summer. I'd walk with my dad to his antique shop every morning and do my daily dusting while imagining who might have used the ancient treasures that filled his store. Around lunch, I'd pop into Annie's for a half-price cone and then linger at the bookstore until closing, where Mr. Tom would let me read the newest books without paying a dime.

In some ways it feels like I only left a week ago, especially when I pull up to the detached two-car garage on Lake Shore Drive.

Though the house is an inanimate building, it's hard not to have complicated emotions about the thing my parents chose over me, their own child. Dad says we can clean it out now, that we have to—thirty-one years, five months, two weeks, and three days too late. It still hurts. I can't imagine it ever not hurting, but curiously, as I climb out of my rental car, it seems a fragment of the bitterness sitting in my chest like a lump of poisonous lead has been lightened.

Today, for one hour, I had a mom.

This mom is funny, friendly, and encouraging. I've never experienced this kind of mom. I know today's Betty may not be the same as tomorrow's Betty, but I thought I was coming here to face a firing squad, to get closure and to say goodbye forever. What I never expected was to see my mom and actually like her—even if she can't remember my name.

CHAPTER 4

Greg

April 9, 1969
WQRX Studios
Janesville, Wisconsin

"Give a warm welcome to Donald Hollinger, our new station manager," Mark says, standing at the front of the conference room filled with our small cast and crew from WQRX. The employees erupt in aggressive applause, and it takes me a tick to join.

Don Hollinger takes Mark's spot, hands clasped in front of him in a sign of gratitude. He's young, a few years older than I am. Not a traditional-looking "bigwig." Though he wears a suit and fancy silk tie, he also has a dense beard and hair that touches his ears.

We all know Don isn't our friend. He's from the new Epistle Broadcasting Network. EBN is a television network that intersperses nationally broadcast content with locally sourced news and programming. EBN bought out WQRX with the promise of taking us into the future of television, but we know this change will inevitably lead to layoffs and replacing the old guard with the new.

Yet, here we all are, cheering him on like he's a returning hero.

Mr. Hollinger quiets the room before I can get more than a couple of claps in.

"Thank you. Thank you. What a warm welcome. I'm honored to be here officially at the helm of a ship you all have built and captained for a decade. We'd not be where we are at WQRX if it weren't for the fine work you've all done here." More applause. Don stops us and adds, "Yet more must be done. We are facing a new decade. Ninety-five percent of Americans now have a television in their home and look to their local stations for their news before a newspaper. We, my friends, carry that remarkable responsibility."

If I were in a private room with Mark, I'd roll my eyes and we'd talk about what a blowhard this guy sounds like, coming from a national news network and lecturing us on our station's importance. But I keep my head down like always.

Don continues.

"But we aren't just here for news. We also want to provide entertainment. We'll start some new special programming. For now, keep doing what you're doing and keep focused on growth and change. Sound good?" Everyone claps gratefully, again. I join them briefly before Mark excuses us.

I follow my coworkers out of the conference room. Larry Torrence, our head anchor who thinks himself a local celebrity, is chatting with Don like they're old friends. Mark gives me a brief look that I know means he's dying to get away from both of them. I nod emphatically, glad that I'm not in a position requiring that I do all that hand shaking and fake friend kind of BS.

"Gosh, this is exciting," Martha Smith says to me. Martha's a bright, ambitious production assistant who started here before I did. If she were a man, she'd be at least an associate producer by now. I think Mark keeps assuming she'll get married and leave the station to have kids, but Martha's a staunch feminist, determined to have a career even if she has a family one day. I don't know how we'd get on without her and her level head, so I'm glad she's avoided Mark's predictions.

"Uh, yeah," I say to Martha, tongue-tied as usual.

"I heard Mr. Hollinger is taking pitches for new programming." Martha's eyes sparkle with excitement. Though she's not beautiful in a traditional way like the women Mark drools over, when she's alive with a new idea, she's as beautiful as any woman I've laid eyes on.

"I . . . I heard that, too."

I push my hands into my pockets and keep walking toward the stairs, where she'll go up to her office and I'll go down to the studio where I have my locker.

"I think I'm gonna do it. Pitch, I mean. What do you think? Am I crazy?" I shake my head, confident in her abilities. "Oh, good. 'Cause I'm dying to try something new. To be honest, I was considering applying to KSTP-TV in Minnesota. They have an open producer position there and I was thinking I'd put my hat in the ring . . ."

At the door to the stairwell, she stops to face me. I hate the idea of Martha leaving WQRX. Mark used to tell me I should ask her out, that he thought Martha had a "thing" for me, but it felt strange. I'd be asking out my own boss. Besides, what do I have to offer her? What would she see in me? I can't imagine.

"So, what do ya think?" she asks, looking up at me. All I want to say is *I think you should stay,* but do I have any right to tell her what to do?

"I think . . . I think they'd be lucky to have you."

Martha's eyebrow raises, and she tilts her head to the side as if she's confused and a little hurt. I think she wanted me to tell her to stay. It's possible Mark was right after all. Maybe I made a big mistake. My mouth goes dry like it always does in tense situations.

"Wait. So, you think I should go for the Minnesota job?"

"No," I correct myself, stuttering, "I . . . I think you'll be great at whatever you try."

"Ah. OK. Well, I think I'll try to pitch a project here first." She runs the toe of her pointed brown shoe over the lines in the linoleum and then adds, "Would you want to work on it with me? Like, pitch it together?"

"Me?" The question explodes out, unlike most of my responses.

"Yeah, you." She looks up at me from under her curled brown bangs. We've worked together on multiple projects; one took us out in the field to cover the aftermath of a tornado in Whitewater. The piece was nominated for a Midwest Broadcasters Association award, but not because of anything special on my part. I followed her directions and so did the reporter who was the face of the segment.

"I . . . I'm not sure what good I'd be."

"Well, I *am* sure, so that'll have to do." She checks her watch. "Dang. I've gotta run to my next meeting, but let's chat soon."

"All right," I say as she dashes up the stairs. I head in the opposite direction, stunned. I've never really aimed for a job outside of the safety of the camera. I mean, I have plenty of ideas, millions of them, really, but I gave up a long time ago on trying to say them aloud without having a heart attack.

Six hours later, her offer is still on my mind as I walk across the glossy marble floors of the lobby, the sound of my footsteps bouncing off the old walls of the repurposed bank like they're being released from the abandoned vaults. I have nearly nothing in my cupboards in my little apartment on Court Street, so I take a left toward the diner. I've been back to Ike's nearly every day since my run-in with the pretty girl who lost her keys. It's not like I'm hoping she'll show up, or at least that's what I tell myself.

The curbs are lined with parked cars, and the street is nearly as packed with moving vehicles filled with every type of worker, but mostly those from the General Motors factory anxious to get home to their families after a long shift. I have no such urgency. All that waits for me at home is a fern named Jerry and the Steinway upright piano that's kept me company since I was a quiet child growing up in a loud family. My mom used to say the piano was my voice.

"Hey, Greg. Slow down, man," Mark calls from behind me. I consider pretending I don't hear him, but he'll catch up with me as soon as we reach the diner anyway. Although we have plenty to discuss from the morning meeting, I was kind of hoping to avoid a conversation with my talkative friend tonight. Mark is a nice guy, but sometimes I appreciate being alone with my thoughts, especially when they involve things I'm not ready to share yet, like Martha's pitch and her invitation to join her.

"Hi. Sorry." I slow my pace, which is a challenge with my long stride.

"Damn, you walk fast." Mark is huffing and puffing when he reaches my side.

"Guess I'm hungry." I attempt a joke.

"Good. You could use a few dozen hearty meals. Put some meat on those scrawny bones."

"Oof." He pokes at my ribs, and I dodge his second jab. Mark isn't exactly fit, but he's healthy looking, with large shoulders. He plays basketball at the YMCA a few times a week, and his charm completes the image. On the other hand, I am awkwardly tall and lanky. As much as I wish to fade into the background, I stand out like a stooped and slender sore thumb.

"So, what do you think of the new boss man?" Mark asks, bringing up a topic adjacent to the one I'd like to avoid.

"He seems . . . motivated."

"Motivated. Yes," Mark says with a negative undertone. "Motivated to get rid of half of us at least."

"Half?"

"Yeah, I mean, don't spread it around, but EBN wants to cut as many of us as possible and bring in their own crew. I think that's what those BS pitch things are about. It's their way of assessing the talent pool here so they can make cuts."

My mind immediately shifts to Martha and her hopeful eyes looking up at me.

"What if . . . what if someone were to pitch and not get picked up?"

Mark hikes his thumb over his shoulder.

"Gone. No way am I gonna be stupid enough to put my neck on the line with one of those proposal things. Keep your head down and do your best. I'm sure you'll be safe. That's my plan at least."

Keep my head down.

Usually, I'm good at that. My mom used to say, "Greg, stand up straight. You look like a candy cane all hunched over like that. You're a handsome boy. Let everyone see it." But what my mom never seemed to understand was, I didn't want everyone to see me.

But—I can't say no to Martha.

The door chimes as we walk in, and Lucy leads us to our regular table. I don't need to look at the menu. It's a Wednesday night so I'll have the pea soup and a club sandwich. Mark flips through the plastic pages, reading every one like he's a first-time patron. Eventually, he'll decide on the pot roast and a bottle of Old Milwaukee, which is what he does when Lucy gets around to taking our orders. I join him in his choice of beverage for once.

We sip on our beers as we wait for our meals. The television is on in the corner, the volume turned all the way down. The national news is playing images of men in green uniforms, thick jungles, and helicopters.

"I can't believe they're showing that in here while people are eating," Mark says, shaking his head. "It's a total shit show over there, from what I've heard."

"Yeah" is all I can say, knowing what it's like to lose someone to that shit show.

"I've heard there's a need for journalists and cameramen willing to be on the front lines. Pays real good, but you couldn't pay me a million dollars to get me anywhere near that fiasco."

Mark is an army vet who has strong opinions on the war in Vietnam, the draft, and the way the American media is covering the conflict. I learn a lot from him but mostly I listen. Though this time, I'm not sure I agree. The idea of being behind a camera, recording these horrific but significant scenes, standing as a voice for people like my brother who didn't get to come home, fascinates me in a way that frightens me almost as much as the rows of pinewood coffins shown on the screen. Anyway, I'd much rather hold a camera than a gun.

As Mark goes on about Walter Cronkite taking a stand against the war and Nixon's inauguration, a flash of red catches my eye outside the diner's fingerprint-smudged window. A red Corvette speeds down East Milwaukee and pulls up to the curb in front of WQRX. I strain to see, my heart racing faster than the car's engine a second ago.

The car door opens, and a lean, stockinged leg appears like it's part of a magic trick. Her heels are dark. The dress that quickly follows is navy blue with polka dots and a pristine white collar. Her sunglasses are two dark ovals with bone-white frames, and her little white gloves button at her wrists, her lips the same crimson as her car. Mark's commentary fades into nothing as I hold my breath, waiting to see which direction she'll go, hoping it's toward Ike's.

"Right?" Mark asks some question about Nixon.

"Uh, sure," I respond, completely distracted by Betty's potential destination.

"Sure? You think Nixon should use nukes? I mean, I'm no hippie, but do you really think that's a good idea?" His voice trails away as he follows my distracted, darting gaze and catches a look at Betty as the front door of WQRX Studios swallows her up.

"Now I see," he says like a sage reading tea leaves. "She sure does make an impression, doesn't she?" He takes a swig of beer. I fiddle with the condensation on my bottle, hunching over another six inches out of embarrassment.

"I don't know what you're talking about . . ."

"Yeah, right, you don't. Bet you've thought about that girl once a day at least since she did that little 'I lost my keys' job on you."

I told Mark the story about finding her keys when I saw him at work the next day, and he laughed his ass off. He asked if she was wearing a ring, and when I said I didn't know, he said he wished he'd been there to ask for her number since I didn't think of it.

I'm glad Mark wasn't around when Betty introduced herself and called me a hero. Most of the time I'm grateful for my gregarious friend. When he's running his mouth I'm not expected to speak up as often, but with this girl, this beautiful woman with a flashing smile and playful eyes, I'm glad I got her to myself for a few moments. And he's right—I've replayed that interaction more than once a day at least.

"I . . . I wonder what she's doing back in town," I say, taking quick side glimpses of her car in case she runs out and drives away when I'm not looking.

Before Mark can make his inevitably sardonic response, Lucy brings our dinners. I watch her in the reflection of the window.

"That girl?" she asks as she slides the chipped white ceramic plate in front of me. "Yeah, I heard she's moving into the apartments in the old Stevens place off Janesville Avenue."

My head whips around to check Lucy's expression. Her forehead is smooth, lips straight. I think, to my own shock and awe, she's telling the truth.

With his mouth half full of pot roast, Mark raps his knuckles on the table and confirms her statement.

"Yes! I forgot to tell you. She's moving here."

"What? I mean, why?" I stumble over my questions. She'd said she was going to an interview when I met her last week. I didn't guess it was for something here in town—in my town.

"I heard she got a job here," Lucy adds.

"What job?" I ask, clearing my throat and fiddling with my dinner so I don't look too curious.

Mark responds with one eyebrow up. "WQRX. Well, EBN, but still—basically WQRX."

My heartbeat whooshes in my ears, and I'm sure my face turns red. I'm mortified knowing it must be obvious to Lucy. But instead of teasing me, she crosses her arms like she's impressed.

"For real? That's crazy. So, you two met her here last week and now she's working at the station? That's gotta be . . . what do they call it when two things happen at the same time that have something to do with one another?"

"Coincidence?" Mark says.

Lucy gives him a playful slap on the arm.

"No. Not that. Like, the two things come together to make something good happen."

"I don't know, fate?" Mark adds, more seriously this time, focused on Lucy's profile as she continues to run through a mental list of words in her mind.

"Serendipity?" I suggest as I catch a glimpse of Betty as she runs out of WQRX and gets into her car. In a handful of seconds, she's halfway down the road, leaving only a poof of exhaust behind.

Serendipity. I recall the term from my English composition class in my junior year of high school. I like the idea of the word more than I believe in the reality of it. Serendipity is a combination of events that happen at the same time to create a good or wonderful outcome. There doesn't seem to be a whole lot of that kind of magic in the world anymore, but wouldn't it be nice if that's precisely what our meeting was—serendipity.

"I don't know what that is," Lucy adds, her nose wrinkling as she puts the pencil in her mouth to think. "Um, destiny?"

"Destiny?" Mark rolls his eyes this time, breaking out of his infatuation. "What, is she going to save the world or something?"

"Eh, screw you," she says and then looks at me. "Not you, Greg, just Mark." She winks, places her pencil back behind her ear, and walks away muttering. Mark watches her the whole way back to her spot behind the counter like he always does.

I reach for a spoon, fill it with soup, and take a sip of the now cold liquid.

Mark finally returns his attention to me.

"'Destiny.' What a weird thing to say." He shakes his head.

"Well, you said 'fate,' so . . ." I remind him.

"Eh, I got caught up in the whole thing." He dismisses it and takes another bite of his dinner, grumbling when he realizes his second beer is already empty. "Hey, I'm sorry I forgot to tell you about her getting a job. I found out today."

"No big deal," I say, hoping he'll add more information without me asking.

"She's a beautiful woman, but I wouldn't get too excited if I were you. No way she's single, not with a car like that, you know?"

"Nah, of course not." I shrug and take several spoonsful of soup in a row, Mark's warning sinking in.

Mark goes back to talking about Nixon, and we finish our meal. He heads to his car, and I walk a few blocks to my apartment, intentionally avoiding where her car was parked half an hour ago, ashamed of my earlier burst of excitement.

Rushing home, I settle onto my creaking piano bench and lift the key lid, desperate for a break from my buzzing thoughts. And as my fingers move freely, the music releases tension in my joints and thoughts, bringing my mind to a comfortable blank.

CHAPTER 5

Charlie

Present Day

"Welcome home," my dad says as I get out of the car in front of the oversized detached two-car garage. The driveway is unshoveled other than two long tire paths where my father just parked his car.

"I'll get this side for you, hon. Give me a minute." He reaches for a large gardening shovel and starts digging out a spot for me on the other side of the driveway.

"No. Let me do it." I take the shovel out of his hands as he tries to protest but acquiesces quickly. My dad doesn't have much fight in him, never really has. It's something I appreciated as a child when I needed a soft side to curl into or someone to play games in the lake with me, but it also failed me a lot. The older I got, the more I wished he knew how to be both my friend and a protective father.

"Well, thank you, hon. I'll head in, if you don't mind."

"I don't mind," I say, tugging my hood around my ears as my dad stomps through shin-deep snow to the front door. I finish one side of the drive quickly, pull my car in, and then move to the front path. It's not easy with the gardening shovel, but there's a nostalgia to it that brings back positive memories.

Clearing the driveway was always my chore when I lived here, and there are still odd cracks in the cement I swear I recognize even after thirty years. Something about the cold air in my lungs and the echoey solitude of the repetitive chore is satisfying. I only wish I'd worn snow boots rather than my heeled Coach boots because by the time I get to the front door, my socks are soaked and I don't think the suede will ever be the same.

I carefully place the shovel on a pile of snow next to the house and make a note to find a real one before it snows again. The steps are pure ice. I can't believe my eighty-one-year-old father made it up them without slipping. Salt. We will also need salt.

The storm door is opened a crack and the screen on the front has several holes from wear and tear. There should be glass there, but my parents stopped switching it out years before I left the house. Behind it is the door to my childhood home, green peeling paint with what looks like oak peeking out from underneath. In my line of work, people would pay good money for an artistically done version of this kind of decorative weathering, but this finish isn't intentional.

I touch the paint. It flakes off, showing more wood underneath. Definitely oak. I crossed this threshold a million times in my childhood. When I'd leave to meet my friends at the beach, walk into town to see Dad, catch the bus, jump in my boyfriend's car, or when I left forever. I reach for the doorknob instinctively but pull back like the metal gave me a shock. What am I doing? This isn't my house anymore.

I knock.

I can hear my dad moving around inside. The door finally opens, and he stands in the two-foot gap, his coat off and his blue-and-gray flannel shirt neatly tucked over his slight belly bulge.

"Hey, you don't have to knock. Come in. Come in." He backs up so I can enter. When I go to push the door open further, it doesn't move, so I turn my body sideways and slip into the house. My father reaches over my head to close the door behind me.

It's nearly pitch dark inside, and I hold back a gasp.

We stand on a small piece of parquet flooring that used to act as the home's entryway. To my right and left are literal walls of boxes, papers, and bags. There's a strong, musty mildew smell that makes it difficult to breathe, and a wave of claustrophobia overwhelms me.

I reach for my phone and turn on the flashlight function.

My dad looks at the floor. "Things may have gotten a bit hard to manage the past few years."

There's shame in his voice. I hear it. It's the same shame I heard when he visited me in foster care and told me I couldn't come home yet because the house "wasn't ready." I was placed at a small ranch house in Honey Lake. I'd been told my parents had been given six weeks and lots of support to help them clean the house. I could go home after some safety issues were addressed and resolved. When my dad finally pulled up to visitation in the family car, I had my garbage bag of belongings neatly packed. I was lucky, I know. My first placement was fine enough, but I was ready to leave the small, unfamiliar house and town and go home.

My father's head hung low that day. As a parent, I know it couldn't have been easy to look me in the eye and say, "It's going to be a bit longer."

But "a bit longer" turned into "a lot longer." Soon, a spot opened at a teen group home in Allouez near Green Bay. It was lonely and had a lot of rules, but I was a rule follower. I finished high school there, and tuition waivers and scholarships helped pay for my college education. My father came to my high school graduation, making excuses for my mother, who stayed behind either from shame or anger that I'd "caused this whole mess," but I didn't invite him to my college graduation. By then, I'd been on my own for nearly seven years. It hurt a lot less to stop reaching out than to have my offers for connection rejected.

"Dad, you can't live here. This is dangerous."

"Oh, no. No. We store things up here. I'm fine. I have all I need," he explains, but I don't believe him.

"Where do you sleep?" I ask, dumbfounded.

"In the den. After a while, your mother wasn't good with the stairs, so we moved down there."

"Show me, please."

"Yes, yes. This way." He takes me through a narrow footpath, and I have to navigate carefully, as though I'm walking a high wire. At one time I knew this house like the back of my hand, but this landscape is new and confusing. The house was a disaster when I was a kid, but we still had living spaces, even if they were surrounded by invading clutter. In this new world—I'm lost. I follow my father like he's a tour guide who knows the language and landmarks.

We pass the kitchen and I have to look away. No path even leads in there—it's so full of garbage and packaging materials. Even with my mother's acquiring, stacking, and storing when I lived here, the one room of the house she left clear was the kitchen. She made dinner every night, which used to be my reasoning for why things weren't as bad as they could be. But as I spent more time in foster homes, group houses, and then my own home, the uncluttered kitchen of my youth became a sticking point for my bitterness. If she could keep that one room clean and organized, that meant she knew how, it meant all the rest of the mess was her choice. But now even that bastion of normalcy is sealed off in her cocoon.

Every few steps, I hear the thump of an object crashing to the ground. I flinch and fight the urge to cover my head. I should be wearing a hard hat like we do on set when working on potentially dangerous construction sites. But this isn't a gutted house halfway through a total renovation—it's where my parents have lived for decades.

When we reach the den, I hold in my horror. All four walls are blocked by stacks of boxes and collections of folders and papers that are at least a foot thick. Two layers of bookshelves filled with books, photo albums, and some kitchen supplies keep the potential avalanche dammed.

There is a walking path around three out of four sides of the bed. Half of the ornate antique wooden headboard is mostly covered with my father's shirts and slacks, the other half empty where my mother's belongings must've recently hung. The bed is neatly made. A TV stands on one of the shelves facing the foot of the bed. There's a small wood-and-wicker ceiling fan that has accumulated an inch of thick gray dust on its edges.

This room was clearly the core of their life before Mom was placed in the memory center. They lived in this suffocating small space carved out of a whole house, four bedrooms, a full basement, a two-car garage, a half acre out back sloping down to the lake, and a long dock that would leave any vacationer or real estate investor drooling. Alone. Without their daughter or grandchildren or friends of any kind.

I place my hand over my aching heart. My dad shuffles around to his side of the bed and tugs at the comforter like he's trying to tidy the room for me. It's sweet but sad to see him trying to make a dent in a home that's taken thirty years to nearly destroy.

"Dad, this isn't safe," I say, assessing the bookshelves' stability and contents. As far as I can tell, this is the only semilivable room in the whole house. I'm already itchy from all the dust from the decades' worth of belongings. "And how do you eat or bathe or anything?"

"Oh, hon, it's not all that bad. I've been making some headway with tidying up . . ." He gestures to a bare shelf and a few less-dense spots in the room.

"Dad, this is way beyond tidying up. We need to hire a crew."

"Do you really think?"

"I don't think you see this clearly. This room alone would take at least a month to clean out on our own. You have a whole house—and the yard. And that's just to get things cleared out. I'm sure there's plenty of structural, plumbing, and mold issues we have to deal with."

"Well, hon, I don't know about all that. It seems like a bit much. I don't know if your mother would like that." The mention of my mother makes hot words burn on the tip of my tongue. The memory of the sweet old lady from the nursing home evaporates. Mother. How can he still worry about what she might say?

"To be honest, I don't really care what she thinks. I care what you think, Dad. Can't you see how bad things are in here—how dangerous they are?"

"Well, not . . . not really. It always served me and your momma well." His tone is infuriatingly calm.

"This has served you well?" I ask, gesturing to the room and the hall full of junk. I knock into a tower of papers, and it cascades onto the bed and floor. "Damn it."

Heat flashes up my neck and cheeks, bringing angry tears. I try to hide them as I go to collect the pages, but as I crouch, I see bulging black garbage bags stuffed under the bed. It never ends. I toss the last few pages I can separate from the clutter on the floor onto the bed with the rest of the papers.

"I can't do this," I sniff and say mostly to myself as I make a stack at the foot of the bed.

"I understand, sweetheart. I know it can be overwhelming."

"No, Dad. No. It's not because it's overwhelming. It's because you want to pass everything by Mom, and I didn't sign on for that. On the 'good days,' she'll say no to everything, and on the 'bad ones,' she won't even remember us." A ball of stress in my chest grows with every word. I'm starting to wonder why I'm even here. "This is serious. We have people from the county coming here *tomorrow*. We need a plan or you're going to lose the house. What do you think Mom will think about that?"

"I hadn't thought of it that way," he says, sitting on an empty spot by the pillows propped against the headboard.

I take a deep breath and remind myself I made my dad a promise—if he's willing to clean out the house, I'm willing to help him. He might not see how messed up the situation is, but I know how to work with demanding clients and sell them on my vision.

I don't want to bring up all the abandonment issues I've struggled with, and I don't want to fight. I only want to help free my dad of the burden of this house. Maybe then I'll ask him why he let Mom keep him from me for so long.

"How about this?" I say. "We'll start in here and I'll get information about hiring a cleanup team. I'll have a better idea of what's required when we talk to the social worker tomorrow." I talk to him like he's one of my clients and there's a whole TV crew here.

He picks at the cuticle on his left thumb. He has a cut; it's brownish red with dried blood. His nail is yellowed, and his hands look nothing like the ones that pushed me on the tire swing in the backyard or held my hand as we walked the lakeshore path to his antique shop a block off Main Street.

"You always have good ideas, hon," he says, avoiding eye contact.

By "always," he must mean on *Second Chance Renovation* since he has no way of knowing how good or bad my decision-making skills are as an adult.

"All right, well then, should we get started?"

"Sure thing," Dad says, leaping off the bed like I asked him to go for a swim off the dock on a hot summer night. He brings over a collection of grocery-style boxes and plastic bags as though they'll be sufficient for the tons of clutter and garbage surrounding us. It's a start.

He digs in on the other side of the room and I take the stack of books at the end of the bed, place them in the box, and then grab another.

My third trip to the bookshelf leads to another scattering of paperwork. I can identify some of the items: my birth certificate, my mom's social security card, a ribbonlike name tag with her name printed on it in faded gold lettering, a driver's license with my mom's maiden name and an address in Janesville, Wisconsin. At the bottom of the pile is a picture of a dark-haired woman holding a small baby that I think is me. On the white border in my mother's handwriting is a name—Laura.

"Dad," I call out to him as he goes through a pile of ancient newspapers on the opposite side of the room. "Did Mom live in Janesville? I thought she grew up in Madison."

"Oh, yeah. I think so." His response is vague and distant.

"Should I keep it? The license?" I ask, his slow and incomplete replies filling me with anxiety.

"I think so. That's where your mom keeps all the important things. We can ask her the next time we visit."

The next time we visit. With my back turned to my father, I roll my eyes. I enjoyed my visit with my mother today, which is super weird to admit to myself, but I don't know if I'll be making that trip again. If we have to run every decision past Betty, I'll be in Lake Geneva for an eternity.

"What about this picture? Mom called me Laura when we left. Is this her? And this award here, too. Has mom's name on it. Is it also important?" I hold out the black-and-white photo and black-and-gold ribbon. He puts on the bifocals hanging from his shirt collar and takes them off almost immediately.

"Yes. That's your mom's roommate from college." He steps back with a shrug. "I didn't know her well."

I inspect the picture again, but when I attempt to ask why she might remember Laura but not me, I realize he's moved into another room. I gather the interesting belongings and put them in an empty box, already gaining more insight on my enigmatic parents from a quick dig into their hoard. I don't know, maybe I'll visit Betty again and bring the box. It'd be more effective than my father showing her the items, plus, it's unlikely he'd even tell me if she remembered anything after looking at them.

My dad is a quiet man, a shy man, the kind of person who nowadays would've been prescribed medication for social anxiety, like my oldest, Olivia. Could that mean I get my outgoing personality from my mom? What do I get from my father, I wonder? What brought two such opposites into this strange, unhealthy symbiotic relationship that's led to this overloaded house and parentless daughter? My father surely won't tell me, and my mother can't.

If it meant a clean house and a new start, I'd throw out every item in this place without a second thought. But if I must indulge my mother's illness and my father's infuriating codependence, then I suppose learning more about them is an unintended bonus. I take in the walls of belongings surrounding me, towering above my head, encompassing me like an embrace. Perhaps the only answers are within these walls, waiting for me to find them.

CHAPTER 6

Greg

June 10, 1969
WQRX Studios
Janesville, Wisconsin

"Ready?" Martha asks when she meets me in the hall outside of Hollinger's office. She has a thick poster board under her left arm and a leather satchel over her right. Her hair is curled and sprayed in place, her cheeks flushed pink either from rouge or anxiety. She's wearing a loose pencil skirt that goes below her knees and a slightly crumpled polyester shirt. To a style expert she might seem frumpy or out of touch with fashion, but to me she looks pretty. Her nervous smile only adds to her charm.

"I'm ready," I say, holding up the portable projector and film canister. Martha wrote the script, and I was behind the camera. We both edited, and the finished product left us with a ten-minute sample of the locally focused variety show *Janesville Presents*. . . It's a working title, but the idea for the show is fun and timely. Variety shows are all the rage during prime time, and featuring local talent will keep our ratings up.

Watching Martha produce a show is impressive. She's brilliant, sure of herself, and I'm lucky she asked me to partner with her. I'm still puzzled why she chose me out of all the other talented people at WQRX, but I won't ask.

"Oh, gosh darn it. I forgot my note cards in my office. Can I leave this with you?" She holds out the supplies and I take them. "Why don't you go in so we're not both late."

She takes off running down the hall, her low heels making an echoing clip-clop on the freshly waxed linoleum. My hands and arms full, I face the office door. I've been avoiding this place, and the reason is more pathetic than being wary of the new station manager. Inside, sitting behind a desk outside Hollinger's inner office, is his personal secretary. She takes calls, keeps track of mail and meetings, and happens to be the one woman I haven't stopped thinking about since I met her. Betty.

The day after seeing her on the street, Mark showed up on set to tell me the news.

"She's Hollinger's secretary," he whispered, his eyebrows waggling. "Betty Wilkens. I was in there for a meeting this morning, and she was perched outside like a little bird. You should stop by and say hi. Make her feel welcome, if you know what I mean."

I did know what he meant, and though I wanted to reconnect with her, I hadn't forgotten Mark's other warning. There's no doubt in my mind that she likely has lines of men ready to make their move. It makes my stomach turn thinking about it. It's not like I know her any better than they do, but I'd at least spent a few minutes in the same room, felt the brightness of her personality, held her Parisian key chain dreams in my hand. The last thing I wanted was to be one of those drooling cads. So, I stayed away. I avoided Mr. Hollinger's office and the whole third floor to be safe.

But today, I have a legitimate reason to be here, on the third floor, in Don Hollinger's office, to talk to Betty. I could barely choke down my toast and jam this morning, and suddenly, my nerves about the presentation were overshadowed by my excitement and anxiety at seeing Betty again.

I step into the office, my arms full of supplies for the presentation. I keep my eyes down, knowing how ridiculous I must look, but once inside it's clear she's too distracted to notice my clumsy entry. She's on the phone frantically scribbling notes, her back to me. Being Mr. Hollinger's secretary can't be easy. In the short time he's been here, he's caused many controversies. Betty is the front line. I understand why. She's charismatic, warm, and genial. She knows how to bring calm to a tense situation. I heard that when Mick Olmstead got laid off, he nearly skipped out of the office after he spent a few minutes chatting with her. Perhaps this is part of the role she plays here. Perhaps there is nothing special about our interactions.

Today, she wears a Kelly-green dress. Her hair is stick straight with a white headband wedged in front of a stylish bump, giving volume to the back of her head. She's wearing the same perfume from the day we met; it's a light floral scent that tickles the back of my throat in a pleasant way that reminds me of walking under a crabapple tree's white blossoms in April.

I sit awkwardly in one of the upholstered chairs with exposed wooden armrests. Nothing much has changed in here since I was hired as a new college grad. The biggest change is Betty, and I only allow myself little glances at her as I arrange the supplies Martha left behind.

I haven't heard Betty's voice since our first interaction, so listening to her talk on the phone makes me smile, even though she's discussing the number of pencils and the size of paperweights to order. I've read and reread the same line of my proposal without understanding it for the seventh or eighth time when she hangs up the phone.

"What are you smiling at over there?" she asks, and it takes me a moment to realize she's talking to me. "How is that reading, Mr. Hero Man?"

My neck is hot and I wish I could loosen my tie. She remembers our encounter in the diner. I've felt like such a schoolboy at how often that interaction replayed in my mind, but Betty's comment confirms she remembers it, too, and the rush of hearing her call me a hero is as delightful as it was in the diner.

Don't act like an idiot, I scold myself, knowing my nerves have a way of getting the best of me. I scooch back in my chair, straighten my spine, fighting against my natural inclination to slouch.

I clear my throat.

"I . . . I'm trying to memorize this thing, that's all."

"And that's humorous?"

"Not humorous, per se, but I sometimes laugh at myself and my inability to remember anything significant." I clear my throat again, my airway tightening. I cover my struggle with a breathy chuckle. "Insignificant, sure. But give me something important to remember and it'll drop right out of my mind like there's a hole in it."

"Oh no. Well then, perhaps you forgot who I am. I remember your name—do you remember mine?"

I peek up from the page. Playful blue eyes stare back at me. Her lips are a pale coral today, and her smile makes her look like a master comedian, holding in all of her punch lines. This delightful creature remembers my name? Impossible.

"Well, I think I do remember." Her name hovers on the tip of my tongue, but I hold back. It could be unsettling for her if my memory is too good, so I glance at the nameplate on her desk. "I don't think I've given you a proper welcome to WQRX, Miss—" I almost say her last name, Wilkens, as to not be too familiar, but she scolds me.

"Betty, Greg. My name is Betty." She wiggles her red-nailed fingers at me. "It's OK you forgot. Lots of new faces around these days."

I want to tell her I remembered her name, but before I can explain, the hall door opens and Martha bursts in holding a stack of cards. The frizz to her curly hair has pumped up the volume so much that the ends stick to her sweat-dotted face.

"You weren't called in yet. Thank goodness!"

"No, no. Not yet," I say as she sits in the seat next to me, organizing her notes.

"Should I let Mr. Hollinger know you're here?" Betty asks, her grin just as vivid as before but with a tautness that reminds me this is part of her job.

"Yes, please," Martha says, using the cards as a fan. She raises her eyebrows at me as Betty buzzes through to the back office. "Are you ready?"

"I think so."

"That doesn't sound very confident."

I shrug, as I always do. I'm not confident. I might not have a job after this meeting, or at least that's what Mark said. I could move forward in my career or get kicked out of it. I believe in Martha, she's hardworking and so innovative, but Don Hollinger doesn't seem like an easy-to-please kind of a guy. He seems like a man's man. Like a commanding officer who wants to be lauded by his superiors but wants to scare the shit out of the new recruits. I'm no Mark. I'm not gregarious, I'm not into sports or the Playboy Club. Beautiful women make me nearly as frightened as when I had to climb the rope in the gym, and my closest friends are plants and a piano.

"He'll see you now," Betty says, standing with a notepad and gesturing to Hollinger's office. Martha and I collect our presentation supplies. She swings the door open, and I let Martha enter first. She's the brains behind our presentation, and beyond that, my mama taught me that gentlemen let ladies go first.

As I pass Betty on my way into Don's smoke-filled office, where I can hear him greeting Martha with a booming "Hello," I get one last sniff of her perfume as she whispers, "You got this."

Her reassurance lifts my spirits.

I shake Don Hollinger's hand, not intimidated by his dry-clean-only suit and Pepsodent smile. I sit tall and proud in my seat as Martha and I present our proposal, and I only need to glance at the papers in front of me once. Martha is the shining star of the *Janesville Presents . . .* production team, but I can sense Betty's gaze from where she's been taking notes in the chair to the left of Don's desk.

"Well, here's what I think," Don says, and both Martha and I tense up, bracing ourselves to discover our fate. "This idea is great. Very timely, popular, very palatable to our viewership. Plus, Larry Torrence is already well liked in the community. I'll give you the Monday nine o'clock slot for a month and see what you make of it. But . . ." he says, sucking the excitement out of his offer. Whatever is on the other side of that "but" is not more good news. Martha must sense it, too, because she stiffens. "I want you to produce a daytime segment for me as well. Something I've been trying to make happen, think it'll be popular with the housewives who want something other than soap operas and news programs, you know? And I think you'd be perfect for it, Miss Smith."

He looks only at Martha after mentioning housewives, and I can sense her irritation as he continues his pitch.

"It's a 'happy housekeeping' kind of a show with tips on how to make your bread rise or polishing the floors and such. It is a popular topic for a daytime slot and will give us plenty of ad revenue since we could use sponsored products on air. What do ya think? Two shows for the price of one?"

"I . . . I have no background in that sort of programming," she replies politely, pushing a few unruly strands of hair away from her flushed face. "I fear it would spread us too thin."

"Oh, no. No. Not at all. This is a little thing but great for advertising dollars. How much time could a few soapsuds and sparkling windows take?"

"Well, it's a whole other show, sir. So . . . as much as any other—"

He cuts her off and pushes a folder across his desk.

"It's all laid out here. The set would be in Studio C and have a working kitchen, tile floor, et cetera. Set up like a good ole American home. I think it's what we need right now. A return to the values that made this country great."

Martha looks like she wants to speak but the words are stuck inside her mouth. The battle that must be going on internally I can only guess at. Say no to the midday fluff show and lose the *Janesville Presents* . . .

opportunity and potentially our jobs altogether. Say yes and we have double the work and very little reward, at least when it comes to the housekeeping show. As the assistant producer and Martha's tagalong, I don't think I'm even invited to the conversation. I take the offered folder, and Hollinger continues. Inside I find a sketch of a cozy modern kitchen with curtains, a round table large enough for a family of six, a counter with a four-burner range built in, a fancy modern refrigerator, and cabinets lining the walls.

"You'd have a six-person team. Laramie," he says, "would be with you, but you can hand pick the rest of the crew. And of course you'll both be compensated for your additional time."

A promotion. Well, a double promotion. Two assistant producer credits for me. A bigger paycheck. More possibilities for the future. Less time at home, alone in my little one-bedroom apartment playing the piano to numb myself. Nothing about this show appeals to me—it's old-fashioned and sounds like something my mom would've kept on when she did her Tuesday afternoon ironing, but we'd still get *Janesville Presents* . . . and we'd get to keep our jobs.

I pass Martha the proposal. She scans through the plans, flipping the stiff manila folder closed.

"I'd like some time to talk this through with Greg."

Betty is watching me again. Hollinger stares at both of us one at a time, his nicotine-stained fingers templed.

"That's fine. Take a day. I'll have legal draw up the paperwork for both shows and we can move forward next week."

"And we'll brainstorm our crew and get a short list of some names for potential hosts for the daytime show," Martha adds. She's so self-assured, so professional. I know a lot of the men find her outspoken personality annoying and unattractive, but I find myself learning from her and studying her boldness, hoping some rubs off on me.

We're immediately on our feet. Hollinger rises slowly from his squeaky desk chair, offering a hand across the tidy workspace.

"There's a list of potential hosts in the packet. If you want to add a few more, go ahead, but I think I have some good ideas there. We'll hold auditions as soon as the ink is dry."

We both agree and shake a farewell. Betty, who's been silent the whole time other than the scratching of her pencil, follows us out of the office.

"Congrats," Betty says in her bright, friendly way. I say goodbye but don't use her name in front of Martha, afraid the familiarity would spark too many questions.

We are only two steps away from the frosted glass of Hollinger's office when Martha grabs my attention.

"What was that?" Her heels clatter against the waxed tile floor, the proposal clutched in her hand like she wants to crumple it. "He can't be serious."

"I know it's a lot, but at least—" I begin to console her, but she keeps talking.

"It's too much! *It's easy because it's a woman's show,* that's what I heard."

I shrug. She's not wrong. I lengthen my strides to keep up with her frenzied walk.

"Yeah, he . . . he did say that."

"Ugh." She shoves open the door to the stairwell and then flops down on the cement stairs, forehead pressed against the metal railing. "This is so unfair. You know he's doing this 'cause I'm the only woman on the production team."

She drops the papers on the ground, sending them everywhere. She's right. It *is* unfair. And it is definitely because of her gender. I don't know what to say, so I collect the scattered pages and take a seat next to Martha, taming them into a straightened pile.

"I know. It's backward."

"And now we're neck deep in this mess, and if we don't say yes, then . . ."

"We're finished," I complete her sentence, and she nods.

"Getting fired wouldn't be terrible. I have that offer at KSTP still out there. I could try to get them to sign you on, too. Ever consider moving to Minneapolis?" She laughs a little but doesn't wait for a reply. "Then again, he basically greenlit the Janesville show. And he's so invested in this antifeminist piece of garbage that we'd have more freedom. Ugh. It's such a catch-22. What do you think?"

"Hmmm," I say, pondering the situation. *Catch-22*, an eye-opening satirical novel I read in Comparative Literature at Beloit College, was one of the first cracks in my thoughts about the war. The concept fit too well in this modern world. The government says that to have peace, there must be war, but with war, there is no peace. In this situation, supporting the only woman on the production team to help her keep her job and retain hopes of upward mobility means also supporting backward "keep women in the kitchen" programming. And if I truly back Martha's decisions that also means I have to be okay with losing my job if she rejects this offer. She's right—it's a catch-22.

Martha peeks at me through the crook of her arm, watching me nervously fuss with the papers, stacking and restacking them to give me a few more seconds to think. People usually get used to my silence, even take advantage of it. I find Martha's interest in my internal thoughts exciting but also nerve racking. I like to think before I speak, think a lot, which can make it seem like I have nothing to say, but it's often the opposite. When I do speak, it's because I'm sure of what I'm saying.

"I trust you either way," I say, handing over the file, our fingers brushing. She takes the stuffed manila folder with the handwritten "Happy Homemaker" label on the tab and lays it in her lap like a sleeping baby. We both stare at it.

"What the hell," she nearly shouts, raising the file to her chest and holding it tightly. "Let's give it a shot. I mean, how bad can it be?"

The phrase echoes ominously down the stairwell as she opens the proposal to the first page.

"Yeah," I lean in to read over her shoulder, swallowing down an unexpected wave of unease. "How bad can it be?"

CHAPTER 7

Charlie

Present Day

"Thumbs tonight at eight. You promise?" Lacey, my childhood BFF, asks through the car's speaker as I wind my way through a back street on my way to the memory center. Lacey and her parents, Mr. and Mrs. Perkowski, visited me once a month when I went into foster care. Her mom bought my prom dress, and her dad gave me flowers when I graduated from high school.

They moved to Florida a few months after Lacey married and have lived there ever since. We drifted apart over time, but Ian and I had dinner with the Perkowskis a few years ago while working on a house in Hollywood, Florida. Lacey and I catch up through occasional texts.

But today, I get to see her in person, along with friends from Badger High School who still live in the area. Thumbs Up is a popular local bar I've never been in because I was too young when I lived in town. But even back then, it was always a busy place. Not as busy as Sugar Shack, the co-ed strip club a few miles west of town, but that's still a little outside my comfort zone even at forty-seven.

"Yes, yes. I promise. I could use a drink."

"I'm sure. How are things going with the cleanup?"

"Slow. Insanely slow. It took a harsh inspection and threats from the city to get Dad to let any of the junk places give us a quote. Then he thought the quote was too expensive, didn't want to let me help pay, and then insisted we could do it ourselves, which—we can't. But he's on the verge of losing guardianship of my mom, so he's starting to listen to some options."

I park my car in a spot right in front of the center that I've claimed as my own. I've been here three times in the past seven days. Dad came with me the first time I returned. He and Betty held hands like teenagers dating. Mom hasn't recognized me even once, which I'm not complaining about, though Nurse Mitchell looks brokenhearted for me every time Betty calls me Laura. I'm too ashamed to admit that I prefer it.

"No. You certainly can't do it yourself. Finn had to go in there a year or two ago because of a burst pipe. He said it was . . . intense." Lacey's husband, Finn, is a plumber. She's already told me this embarrassing story twice, so I shift away from it before she can get to the part where my mom chased him out of the house, accusing him of theft.

"Well, I've got a crew coming next week whether my dad likes it or not." I grab a cardboard box of my mom's belongings from the car's front seat, balancing the phone as I head into the memory center. "We've made plenty of progress in the bedroom, but even after a week's worth of work, it's barely a dent. Oh, shit."

I curse as I fish my foot out of an icy puddle. I still haven't gotten decent boots, but I hope an early spring thaw is around the corner. The freezing gray water soaks into my socks immediately.

"You good?" Lacey asks.

"Yeah. Just trying to balance too many things." I shake my booted foot to drain as much water as possible. "I better get inside. I'll see you tonight, though. OK?"

"Yeah, for sure. Get inside. It's cold as balls out there. And don't you dare try to cancel again. I need this."

"Believe me. I need it too," I say, rearranging the box to grab the phone off my shoulder.

"All right. And if you don't show up, we're gonna hunt you down."

"I know. I know. I'll be there. I promise."

"Yay! See you tonight. Bye!"

"Bye."

We end our call as I step onto the plastic mat in the foyer of Shore Path Memory Center. The faux fire is lit in the fireplace, and the room smells of pine and bleach. No one is behind the counter, so I sit in one of the armchairs facing the red-and-orange LED flames and remove a layer of outerwear.

All of my social interactions from the past week have taken place here. I've been dodging spending time with Lacey and a few other friends from the good old days, but at this point, I think I need peer interaction. My dad is a quiet man, and Nurse Mitchell is all business all the time.

I still haven't picked up any of Ian's calls, and the boys have very little to say about their days. Olivia has been distant since our last call. I've been researching all-inclusive vacation packages, hoping we can reconnect over a few oceanside sunsets.

Strangely, my closest friend right now is my mom.

Sure, she thinks my name is Laura and wants to talk about boys and fashion while playing cards or working on her puzzle, but I don't mind. Betty and I are buds; she makes me laugh and feel important.

Walking into my mom's room at the center is like walking into a time machine. I don't know anything about Betty Laramie outside of her easy-to-spark temper during my teen years and her obsession with our home's belongings. I never met grandparents, aunts, or uncles. She had no friends or visitors. She didn't go to church or belong to any clubs or organizations. It's like she married Dad, had me, moved into our house, and then disappeared like a hermit crab retreating into its safe shell.

Dad and I have thrown out fifty-six bags of papers, garbage, and broken items from my parents' room, and this box holds the most exciting discoveries thus far. The first items I found were a set of keys to a Corvette with an Eiffel Tower key chain, her driver's license from '67 with her maiden name, a formal bridal photograph of her in a delicate lace veil, the strange ribbon with her name on it, and an ID badge from WQRX.

Every item in this brown box filled me with a massive dose of curiosity when I uncovered it in their bedroom. I learned a long time ago not to ask Dad too many questions. He answers them but with brief, generic responses. But when the social worker assigned to my parents' case mentioned it might be good for my mom to get some physical reminders of her past, I brought them to Betty.

Some items she looked at blankly, but others elicited a story or reaction. She thought the picture of her wedding was from a magazine, told me the keys were to her first car and the ID badge was from her favorite job, and she fumbled with the pin on the back of the black ribbon, trying to fasten it to the hem of her shirt, thanking me for bringing it.

Once we got it in place, she picked up her ID and lingered on the blurry picture of young Betty. Her hair was long and blond, her face smooth and her smiling red lips beguiling. I instantly knew this was the Betty I'd been talking to, who I brought treasures to and who I snuck caramels to from KC's Sweets.

"I didn't know you lived in Janesville," I said during that visit, looking at the address on the small, tattered white rectangle when I first showed her the badge. "I thought you grew up in Madison."

She handed the card back to me and shook her head.

"I met my husband in Janesville. We worked together," she said. She didn't sound like she was lingering on the memory of a shimmering romance. She sounded sad.

"Dad worked in Janesville?" I asked and realized my mistake when I noticed the confused look on her face. "I mean, what did you do there at WQRX?"

"Oh, goodness. Let me see. What didn't I do there?" she said, fussing with some puzzle pieces in front of her. I could tell she was getting confused by too many questions. "Mama doesn't think I should go to college. Says I should settle down and make a home."

Suddenly, she was talking about a grandmother I'd never heard of. I sat in awe as she spoke of her childhood bedroom and its tragic lack of curtains. We didn't get back to talking about Janesville, the TV studio, or how she met my dad. I left that day wanting to know more.

Sitting in the lobby, the feeling in my toes returning, I take out one of the black-and-white pictures from the box. The photo on top is the one of a woman holding me as a baby with the name Laura written on it. I've stared at it for way too long trying to figure out why my mom could possibly confuse us. The real Laura looks nothing like me. She's a tall, thin woman with long black hair parted down the middle, dark eyes, and tan skin. There must be something more to their connection that I haven't stumbled on yet.

"Hey, lady! Here to see your mom?" Kelsey, the bubbly receptionist, calls to me from behind the counter. We're now best friends though I've seen her only two of my three visits. It's all right—people think they know me because of the show, our TV appearances, and social media. Olivia finds it annoying, but I take it as part of my job. That was until one of those strangers slid into my husband's DMs and ruined my marriage, but I'm guessing Kelsey isn't nearly so nefarious.

"Yeah. Thought I'd show her a few more things from the house."

"Oh, that's fun. I'll buzz you through. You know the way, right?"

"Sure do." I collect my belongings and stand at the locked door, waiting for the signal to sound.

"Well, have a nice time!" She pushes the button and the door opens slowly. As I thank her and walk through to the residential area, she adds, "I heard she's having a good day today."

I stumble and nearly drop the cardboard box as the door swings closed behind me.

A good day.

Is it a day when my friend Betty is happily sitting in her room doing puzzles, lost in time, and unable to recognize her own daughter? Or does it mean she's back to the mom I grew up with, the one who found fault easily, who chose her house of garbage over me?

A small, panicked voice inside tells me to leave and return another day—but Nurse Mitchell approaches and I don't have a choice. I follow her and nod and answer her friendly questions, but under my calm exterior, my nerves are fraying, my mind racing a million miles a minute.

She's having a good day. A *good* day.

Well, what the hell could that possibly look like?

The box of Betty's belongings starts to slip, and Nurse Mitchell reaches out for it.

"Hey, you look a little overloaded there. Let me help."

I let her take it, rearranging the puffy coat slung over my arm.

"Thanks," I manage to say, my voice barely a whisper. I follow her past the living area and the OT room where several residents work on a craft project. Who will I meet today? Betty? My mom from my childhood? The elderly mother who is still angry I never returned home? Someone else entirely?

"I found a few more interesting things," I explain in reference to the box, trying to act normal.

"Well, that's just great. It's beneficial for the residents to have physical reminders of their life stories. Very grounding." Nurse Mitchell says, her voice a soothing balm to my ragged nerves. "I'm sure your mom will love them."

I nod and slow down as we get to Betty's room. I'm like a child again, or a teen who snuck out and was returned home by the police.

Nurse Mitchell's knock is followed by a faint "Come in." My mouth is sticky, and I might be more anxious than on my first visit.

"Betty, look who's here! It's your daughter," Nurse Mitchell declares as she bursts into the room. The overhead fluorescents are off, the only source of light coming from an uncovered window. No music is playing today, and I notice paper plates in the sink as though she plans to keep them. I shiver, a chill running up my arms and down my legs.

By the window sits my mother, with her freshly curled white hair, staring at her puzzle, a frown tugging at the corners of her mouth. Her lips are bare and pale, and her cheeks are, too. She doesn't look up.

"I don't have a daughter," Betty says, her voice a touch deeper than during my previous visits. It's a voice I recognize. It's my mother's voice.

Nurse Mitchell glances at me with pitying eyes as if she thinks my mom doesn't remember me, which is an understandable mistake. Every time I've visited, my mom has said she doesn't have a daughter, but today, the phrase has a different meaning. I glance at my mom, hoping her deeper, raspy tones are all in my imagination.

"Sorry, dear," Nurse Mitchell whispers to me after writing a few numbers on Betty's whiteboard. She takes my coat and hangs it on a hook next to the closet. "She had a great morning. Thought it would last longer. You good?" she asks, always so caring, like she's my nurse as much as my mother's.

What would she think if I up and left? On my first day here, she told me she'd understand if I needed a break. She told me I could step out whenever I wanted. I'm sure she'd let me go, but would she really *get* it?

Probably not. Not many people do—it's why I let everyone outside of my family believe my parents passed away during my teen years. It was easier to lie than to explain the whole situation over and over again. Ian knows a bit of the truth, the foster care and hoarding bits, and I've shared a story or two with Olivia over the years, but what they know more than any details of my past is that I don't like talking about it.

"Yeah, I'm fine," I say, though I don't mean it. Nurse Mitchell smiles softly and nods.

"All right then. I'll leave you two on your own for a bit. Looks like you've got some fun things to look through," she says, backing out of the room. "Bye, Betty. Enjoy your visit."

"Thank you, dear," Betty says cordially, preoccupied with sorting her puzzle pieces on the rolling table in front of her. As soon as Nurse Mitchell shuts the door behind her, Betty addresses me directly, all the brightness leaving her voice. "What are you doing here? Was this your father's doing?"

She speaks of my loyal father as though he's committed high treason. Even when Betty doesn't remember Dad, she has a sweet spot for him, she sometimes holds his hand and often enjoys his arm around her when they sit on one of the great-room couches. This hostility, toward him at least, is new.

"Kinda," I say, stuttering, frozen in place near the entrance. She sighs and rearranges a few oddly shaped puzzle pieces of the same color, eyes never leaving the tabletop.

"I never would've guessed he'd do such a thing. But I bet you're happy to see me locked up in a place like this."

"No," I say honestly. "No, I'm not."

Her hand trembles as she clicks a puzzle piece in place.

"Well, you got what you wanted. You got your hands on my house."

"That's never what I wanted." I've never tried to take her house away. She must mean when I was made a ward of the state. Back then the house wasn't nearly as bad, the kitchen mostly usable, a working bathroom, but she and Dad faced similar threats to what they do now. Clean the house—or else. They must've done enough to get the authorities off their backs but not enough to get me out of foster care.

I start to devise a comeback but then I remember Nurse Mitchell's advice from my first visit—don't argue. Try to redirect. I hold up the box of belongings. "I brought you some things."

"I don't want your fancy gift, whatever it is." She brushes me away with a flip of her hand. I sit on the edge of the mattress and pull out the items we've already reviewed together, setting a few more on the comforter.

"It's not a gift. It's some things from the house." I pick up the picture of Laura holding me as a baby and walk across the room to her green chair. The photo trembles as I place it on the table next to the puzzle. She glances at it and shoves it away.

"Where did you get that?"

"The house, like I said." I almost mention cleaning out her room, but I know it'll trigger "good day" mom even though it wouldn't phase "bad day" Betty.

"You have no right to be in that house." Her voice rises. "The day you walked out that door, I told you that you'd never be welcome again."

So, *this* is a good day. She remembers everything. And she remembers it from her skewed, blame-filled perspective. I didn't come here to fight, but a response slips out, lubricated by my outrage.

"I was a kid," I remind her, old resentment flaring inside me. "I didn't have a choice. CPS took me away because of your junk." I sound like I did when I was fifteen, arguing with my mom about the mess in the house, pushing back on all her control and rules.

She ignores my response as though I didn't speak at all.

"And now I bet you're throwing out all my stuff, aren't you? I didn't give you permission to do that. I didn't sign anything that said you could. Tell your father I need to see him. There's a lot in there that's valuable. But I'm sure you know that with your fancy TV show."

She pushes the wheeled table with both of her spotted, arthritic hands. It coasts a foot across the tile floor, half of the nearly completed puzzle slipping off and clattering onto the ground along with the photograph. I step back, hands up as though she'd tried to assault me.

"I'm sorry. I thought you'd like to see these . . ." I say with an attitude, picking up the photograph and collecting the puzzle pieces off the floor in handfuls. Once I've retrieved as many as I can see, I let my gaze lift from the floor. My mother is watching me. It's hard to believe this is the same woman who told me I was beautiful last Sunday and asked if she could brush my hair—the one who wanted me to paint her nails and gossip about boys. Today she looks sad, as if her anger is sorrow that's smoldered for so long it's caught fire. I don't recognize her, but at the same time I do.

I remember moments of kindness and love from my mom when I was a little girl. She was creative and beautiful; she'd sew my dresses and make cookies on Sunday afternoons. The clutter in the house seemed normal then. It was organized in spare bedrooms or unused corners. As I grew, I came to loathe the encroaching towers of boxes and papers, but any effort I made to gain control of my own living space was met with panic and disdain from my mom.

As a teen, my strained relationship with my mother went beyond her hyperfocus on her house and belongings. It was like the more independent I grew, the more fearful she became that I'd leave her—as if she wished she could box me up and put me into one of her piles like I was a belonging rather than an independent person. She didn't want a single item removed from her house without her permission—including her own child.

Don't argue, I tell myself as tears rise in my eyes. Heaviness fills my chest with all the unshed tears from the past thirty-one years.

"This was a bad idea. I'm sorry. I should go," I say, putting on my coat and taking the box. I can't stay here. I don't care if she's unwell, if part of her disdain is misplaced or from confusion; I can detect enough of the mom I swore I'd never see again that I don't feel safe here.

"Goodbye, Charlotte," my mother says as I walk out of her room.

Rushing down the hall, my eyes are blurred with tears. I know it's crazy to come back here and face her again, hoping she'll be the mom who calls me Laura instead of Charlotte, the jovial, friendly girl still inside of my mother somewhere who wants to play cards and holds all the answers to my questions. The version of my mother that might be able to love me. But as I rush past the front desk, waving goodbye to Kelsey with my damp face turned away, I know I'll be back—because I miss her.

I miss Betty.

I miss my mom.

CHAPTER 8

Greg

October 13, 1969
WQRX, Studio C
Janesville, Wisconsin

"And that's all for today. Time to get that vacuum running and dinner cooking. But first, take a moment to put on a little touch of lipstick. And don't forget, a smile goes a long way. Tomorrow: how to keep your roast delectably moist without breaking a sweat. Until then, I'm Betty Wilkens. Keep your home happy and your homemaking classy."

I watch through the small camera viewfinder and zoom in on Betty's bright unbroken smile. Her hair is a little shorter now, curled under her chin, and she wears a tidy light-blue cotton dress with an apron tied around her waist. It's ironed crisp and starched till it could almost stand up on its own. And white, of course. Brilliantly white.

She is the perfect vision of American domesticity, standing in her spotless kitchen, a spread of finger sandwiches laid out on large ceramic Noritake platters with white and yellow daisies around the perimeter. When the floor manager calls "Cut," I take off my headphones, click off the camera, and step away, reorienting to the real world after the idyllic vision Betty has transported us into for the past half hour. Martha initially wanted me in the booth to manage the mixing of the show like I do with *Janesville Presents . . .*, but I requested to be behind a camera for *The Classy Homemaker*.

This half hour is my favorite part of each weekday. I know the show drives Martha crazy and I can't blame her. She's a hardworking unmarried woman who fights every day for equal footing in an industry run almost entirely by men. She's damn good at what she does. When Betty was officially cast as the host of the show after all the bigwigs saw the auditions, Martha lost it once we were in private.

"She's a secretary!" Martha exploded behind the door of our shared office. She angrily packed her over-the-shoulder attaché. It was already two hours past my normal clock-out time, and we'd been waiting on pins and needles for the final casting decisions. "How is she now suddenly some journalist?"

She tossed herself into her wheeled green vinyl chair, and it rolled a few feet to the desk behind her. She covered her face, and I could tell she was crying. I knew I should do something, comfort her, make these men change their minds and listen to the voice of reason, but I also knew they were unlikely to listen when the voice of reason sounds like a woman.

"I'm sorry," I said, patting her back, unsettled by the way she was shaking.

"I need a minute, OK?" she said between gasps for air.

"OK." I took a step back, overcome with guilt for my failure to manage the situation, but also for another more shameful reason. I was excited when Betty was announced as the show's host. As soon as I saw her name on the short list of candidates auditioning, I knew they'd choose her, and I suspected that Hollinger created the show with Betty in mind.

Though I'm sure Hollinger's intentions had little to do with his secretary's qualifications, I learned a lot about Betty during the casting process. She wasn't some girl who'd wandered in off the street. She'd recently graduated with honors from UW-Madison with a degree in journalism and she had a little on-air experience. She tested well and seemed to have the exact look desired by the higher-ups at EBN. But no matter her résumé or GPA or waist size, the choice was out of our hands.

And now, in the month and a half since the show first aired, viewership has exploded, nearly doubling every week. Our sponsors are ecstatic, and local businesses have started reaching out to the station asking to be featured on the show.

Truly, Martha and I should be overjoyed. We have a successful show. We're being lauded by the executives and praised at every meeting. But *The Classy Homemaker* has never felt like our own show, and our cherished *Janesville Presents . . .* is struggling.

Though Hollinger extended our monthlong trial period, the *Janesville Presents . . .* numbers seem to diminish as *The Classy Homemaker*'s numbers skyrocket. In the Monday nine o'clock slot, we're up against the likes of Carol Burnett, *Love, American Style*, or *Monday Night at the Movies*. A quaint local variety show during prime time brings in abysmal viewership.

Hollinger has given us till the end of the quarter to "pick things up," but at this point, neither of us has a brilliant idea of how to save our precious brainchild. Instead, we spend the majority of our days discussing segment ideas for Betty's show like "How to keep your hair from going flat without wearing curlers to the grocery store" or "Basting—your roast's best friend!"

But even with those frustrations, the half hour I spend in the clean and inviting world Betty creates makes me happier than I've felt in a long time. The set looks exactly how Hollinger presented it to us. Rows of high-end vinyl cabinets, sparkling laminate countertops, a brand-new GE appliance tucked into every useful-looking cranny. I can't help but wish my childhood home looked similar, that I could pull up a stool to a bleached countertop and enjoy a warm chocolate chip cookie made out of love for me.

Perhaps that's what's being sold here, why the sponsors are so greedy for airtime and so willing to invest their dollars. It's a fantasy. It's a fantasy everyone thinks is accessible but is really just out of reach. If they only found the right detergent or newfangled appliance or "a color that really brings out their eyes," then they might find their own version of this domestic heaven. I get it. But I'm not sure I believe it. And I definitely don't trust it.

Martha is at my side before I've finished shutting down my TK-42 four-tube camera and pulling the shot list. She's holding a yellow "missed call" slip.

"Well, it looks like Alderman Grant canceled for tonight. The St. John's children's choir can do three songs instead of two. But we need some substance in tonight's show—something political would be best. Something that really gets the mind turning, you know? Larry shines in those circumstances."

I remove my headphones and flip off the speaker that connects us to the control room. No one else needs to be in on this discussion. We have some version of it every week. We need more content. We need something that really will make viewers tune in. We need. We need. We need. But we don't have. How do we acquire the talent we need? How do we get people to tune in when our advertising budget is the lowest of all the programs on WQRX? Martha is reluctant to raise the white flag, and I'm willing to do whatever I can to support her.

"I think Mark is in Knights of Columbus with the comptroller," I offer.

"Comptroller? Oh, my Lord, Greg. We're trying to get more viewers, not offer a new sleep aid."

"A segment on natural sleeping aids doesn't sound too terrible," Betty says, meeting Martha and me next to the camera.

Martha, dressed in a forest-green blouse and brown skirt, bristles. She has no reason to actively dislike Betty; the charismatic TV host has done nothing wrong. She's never been rude or diva-like in her time here on *The Classy Homemaker*. But something definitely irritates Martha about Betty, and there's something somewhat needy about Betty's desire to be respected and liked by her female boss.

Whenever Martha grows cold, I try to compensate. As a result, my friendship with Betty has grown over the past few weeks. I still consider her the most beautiful woman I've ever met, and every time I see her, it takes effort to straighten my thoughts and not act like a bumbling schoolboy.

I've learned she's funny. She'll blurt out a joke during rehearsal that sends the whole crew into laughter. She's not as worldly as Martha, who always has at least two books in her satchel. I rarely see the same one twice because she reads them so fast. But Betty is quick witted, learns nearly instantaneously, and adapts seamlessly.

I keep thinking she won't be here long. She's not a small-town girl. She's one of those rare people you're certain one day you'll point to and say, "I knew her when." I could say the same thing about Martha.

Unlike the two women I work with, I have no idea what my own future holds. Possibly a family and some of the domesticity shown on this stage kitchen every day. Sure wouldn't mind that.

No, it's fake, I remind myself. Falling for my own fantasy, now wouldn't that be wild?

Martha brings me back to reality, saying sarcastically, "Oh, yes. Natural sleep aids. Like some of 'mother's little helper'?" Then she refocuses on me, picking up our conversation where we left off. "Let's meet after this. Ike's? We might have to go with the comptroller."

"Yeah. For sure," I agree, even though I already had my lunch. I won't be eating anyway, stress ruining my appetite.

Martha stomps off in a hurry, stopping the sound engineer and having a lively conversation. Betty unties her apron, pulls it around her styled hair, and drapes it carefully over her arm.

"My goodness, that seems stressful," she says with an empathetic smile.

"You know how it goes."

And she does, in fact, know. Betty's started to pitch her own ideas for segments and has helped us plan and brainstorm others during our weekly production meetings. It's not producing, but her job isn't the same as an anchor like Larry, hosting the nightly news, reading off cue cards he's never seen before. Betty has opinions. She has something to say. She's an active part of the team, even if it drives Martha crazy.

"I don't know, what you two do seems impossible to me. I feel nice and safe here behind my little kitchen counter. I could never do what you do." So many "I could nevers" come out of Betty's mouth on a regular basis. I think it's another reason Martha finds her irritating. Clearly *The Classy Homemaker* host is fully capable of every single "never" she proclaims.

After our first production meeting where Betty presented a fully illustrated and scripted proposal, Martha said to me, "It's like she thinks if she says she's good at something it will intimidate the men in charge. It's the pussyfooting way women have been taught to weasel into any position of power. I hate it." And I get why it bothers her. It's definitely not one of Betty's stronger traits, though I have to imagine she has a reason for her approach. Martha's willing to make waves; Betty tries to ride them out.

I reassure Betty. "I think you're doing fine at your own job. The ratings are—"

"Looking all right. I know. It's what Don keeps saying. And I appreciate it, but . . ." She stares at the stage and then back at me and then at the tips of her polished black shoes. "I feel like I keep upsetting Martha."

This is the first I've heard of any dissatisfaction from the star of our show, and the fact that it's because of Martha is fair, though unexpected. I stop fussing with the camera's power supply and give Betty a worried look. If Betty jumps ship and *Janesville Presents . . .* continues on its downward spiral—Martha and I would be out of a job.

"I think you have great ideas. We both do," I say, remembering Hollinger's push to sign Betty as our host despite her single status.

"Every girl is a homemaker in the making," he said, shoving her headshot across the conference table to the EBN executive sitting at the head, smoking a cigarette. "And Betty's the kind of homemaker every girl wants to be and every man wants to marry. And here's the bonus—this is who she really is. She was made for this part."

Even Martha agrees that it's hard to argue against the ratings or the piles of fan mail we get each week. I tell Betty that, hoping it will address her insecurities.

"That's kind of you," she says like it's a line in a script.

"That's kind of you, but . . . There's clearly more to that sentence," I say.

She twists the apron string around her pointer finger and then lets it unravel in a spiral that looks like the funnel of the tornado Martha and I filmed in our award-winning segment. "But clearly she hates me."

I am searching my thoughts for the right response to comfort Betty when Don Hollinger approaches from the rear of the studio.

"You about ready to go? The meeting's in fifteen minutes," he scolds Betty, sounding impatient. He's dressed in a pressed suit with a Paisley tie and a three-button vest. His beard is neatly trimmed, and his hair is crisply parted on one side and sprayed down with enough hair spray to make the hair-and-makeup department envious.

"Oh, I'm sorry, I still need to change and touch up a little," Betty says, looking up at him with wide, apologetic eyes. Hollinger has expected Betty to manage both of her positions while he finds a new assistant.

He glances at his wristwatch stiffly and then gives her permission to take a few minutes to change into her office attire, mumbling a little something to me about how silly women can be with their makeup and dresses as he watches her sway out of sight down the hallway to the dressing rooms.

"I heard you had a guest drop out from *Janesville Presents* . . . Seems like that's happening a lot more lately, huh?" Hollinger says, now that Betty's left us alone. Martha is still nowhere to be seen.

"Yeah, the alderman stepped out this morning. We have a few leads. I'm gonna be meeting with Martha in a few minutes to see what we can come up with."

Hollinger nods stoically, running his tongue over his teeth and then making a little smacking sound.

"I don't think I need to tell you this, Laramie, but it's looking like we're gonna need to pull out of *Janesville Presents* . . . I know it's Miss Smith's baby. Looks like it didn't take the teat, if you know what I mean."

Mark is better at this kind of business talk. I hate it when I get sucked into the men's world of all knowingness. I hate that he's coming to me about the dying program instead of Martha, but I won't let him accept its death so easily.

"We have a few ideas for the second half of the season . . ." I run through some of them, promised guest spots including Tim Davis and the Steve Miller Band, but Hollinger doesn't seem to care, stopping me after only a few examples of what we have lined up.

"That's great. Keep working on those, but if I'm being honest, there's not gonna be a whole lot of funding for that kind of programming. EBN has some plans for the slot unless we can get some advertising dollars in." Martha is going to crumble. She's worked so hard. It's not her fault. This town is too small for her big ideas. "But don't worry—I've got your back. We'll turn this little beauty here into a full hour. You'll have one show instead of two. Simplify your life a little. What do you think?"

Simplify. Is it really simplifying to lose something that sparks creativity inside of you? Hurting a dear friend and colleague in the process, is that simplifying?

"Martha won't—" I don't get the chance to finish the sentence because Hollinger cuts me off.

"Martha's not in charge here. If she wants to stay at WQRX, she'll do what she's told. Right?" He crushes my shoulder in his grip, and it comes off as a message not only for Martha, but also for me.

I nod. He drops his hand.

"Good. Don't worry, Laramie. There's lots of opportunities for a guy like you at EBN. Don't let Smith hold you back, all right?"

"All right," I say to get out of the conversation, but even that's a major betrayal.

When Betty returns wearing a burnt-orange jacket over a professional-looking knee-length pencil skirt, Hollinger acts like our discussion never happened. It reminds me of how I've learned to put away bad things like a half-finished casserole to be taken out later and reheated or tossed out in tomorrow's trash.

"Ready for lunch?" Martha asks, back from wherever she'd wandered off to, after Betty and Don exit the studio. "Sorry I left you alone with Mr. Hollinger. He's such a creep. I can't stand being around him when I don't have to be."

"Eh, it's OK." I call over one of the other camera operators and leave him with a few instructions so Martha and I can get to work on finding a new guest for *Janesville Presents . . .* , no matter how futile the effort.

"So, what did that asshole have to say?" Martha asks as we exit the studio together.

I consider telling her everything—Betty's confession, Hollinger's thinly veiled threats, the new one-hour format of *The Classy Homemaker* that might push Martha past her patience point, chasing her away from WQRX entirely. Instead, I do what I do best.

"Nothing," I say, hands in my pockets and my stomach twisting, uncomfortable knowing too much but even more uncomfortable sharing it. "Nothing at all."

CHAPTER 9

Charlie

Present Day

"That'll have to do," I say to my reflection. After the confrontation with my mom, I dried my tears, picked up an iced coffee from the new Starbucks on Main Street and Center. Then I stopped at the Ross Dress for Less off the highway, where I grabbed discounted Calvin Klein jeans and a flowy, though likely polyester, white top. It shows a bit of what my producer calls "tasteful cleavage," and the pants hug my ass, making me grateful I've done all those squats my trainer insists on. I look my age but in a "good for your age" way with the help of weekly facials and only enough Botox to keep the higher-ups at HFN happy.

I tweak my three-tiered gold necklace and then fluff my shoulder-length hair, and the diamond on my solitaire gets caught in the hair spray–coated strands.

"Damn it." I work to detangle the ring. I should've fixed the loose prong on the setting long ago, but I keep putting it off. Finally I free it and I examine the setting. A few pieces of golden hair remain stuck in the prongs.

As I remove them, my phone buzzes on the bathroom counter. In my gut I know who it is before I even look. The name Ian McFadden stares up at me, confirming my suspicions.

It's been weeks since I've responded to his pleading texts other than essential confirmations of safety. When I found those Instagram messages, when I confronted him and he tearfully confessed, he swore it was a mistake, that it was an isolated incident, that he never, repeat, never met the woman in person, or any others for that matter. I tried to believe him. I wanted to give him some space to be human, to make a mistake, but then the questions started to build in my mind.

What if he's lying? What if he's making a fool of me? What if he's telling another woman he loves her? What if he's pretending to love me because of the show, the image, the fame? What if . . .

Damn it. Today was already hard enough with Mom's supposed "good day" that turned my day into a depressing fog. I finish lining my lips and applying a nude gloss with flecks of gold that match my eyeshadow. Then, I shove all my makeup back into the large zippered travel bag. There are so many what-ifs, and I'm too exhausted to dig into every single one. When I asked for a separation to think it all through, Ian reluctantly agreed, saying he'd do anything necessary. And then I left for the airport.

I think he thought I'd be gone for a weekend, possibly a week, but I'm not ready to go home and face the unsolved questions. *Second Chance Renovation* is on a filming break, Olivia is thriving at Stanford, and the boys are in school and well taken care of by Ian and Layla, their regular babysitter, and they spend every other week at their mom's house.

I'm "only" the stepmom, but I love the twins like they're my own. When I travel, we try to FaceTime as often as possible. Some days, the ten-year-olds are bubbling with stories, questions, or requests, and other days they want me to sit on the phone while they play a video game and narrate. But no matter what, our calls help us stay connected.

Some people might call me a bad parent or wife for not always being at home with after-school snacks. They did when Olivia was little; God, even her father accused me of being too career focused—but no one says a CEO dad is neglectful or selfish for spending two weeks in Japan to work out a merger. I work, then I'm home, then I work again, and then I come home. I always come home, and when I'm home—I'm home. I'm really home—I'm "read to the boys in bed" home. I'm "let's go to the pool" home. I'm "I love you no matter what" home.

So now I'm gone for not-work. I'm gone for family reasons, personal reasons, broken-heart reasons. And I don't know when I'll be ready to go back. The inspector gave us a month to show some progress. "It doesn't have to be perfect, but we need to see some good faith effort," said the man with the clipboard, wearing a neatly tucked polo shirt and the hard hat I'd longed for when I first walked through the house.

I don't need his report to know my parents' house is potentially irreparable. And I don't need a social worker to tell me my relationship with my parents is perhaps in even worse condition. But I'd rather work on these nearly hopeless situations than even consider what's next with Ian. That being said, I can't avoid him forever. My parents' house is a perfect example of what happens when avoidance is taken to the extreme.

As I wipe down the counter and retrieve the cheap pair of snow boots from the box on the bed, the phone buzzes again, reminding me of Ian's text. I could've turned off Ian's notifications a long time ago, but I didn't. I think I need them. I need to know he cares enough to continue to reach out. I take a deep breath, pick up the phone, and read his long message.

Ian: I hope you had a productive day. You've been on my mind tons. Let me know if I can help you with anything out there. I don't want to drive you crazy with my calls but please know I'd love to hear your voice. I love you.

Tears rise in my eyes and I reread his message three or four times. An unexpected urge to call him swells inside of me. I check my watch. I'm supposed to meet Lacey at Thumbs Up in fifteen minutes. It's freezing outside, but I've decided to walk, hoping the steps will clear out some of my pent-up emotions so I can actually have fun.

I could call Ian on the way. We could talk, and now that we're at a safe distance, I could let him in. He could build up trust, and maybe I could remember what it was like when we first started dating in secret after meeting on set, both single parents trying to figure out the modern world of dating.

My finger trembles as it hovers over his name, his smiling contact picture tempting me to hit the call button.

I can't.

Not yet. Letting Ian in so soon after taking my big stand and asking for time away would make me a pushover, like I'm telling him he can mess around behind my back. I'd be one of those wives who looks the other way to preserve the marriage. But I miss my husband. I miss the security of our relationship, the stability of our family life, and the comfort of the safe space I thought we'd created together.

A long time ago, on the frozen lake behind the house on Lake Shore Drive, I learned not to trust cracked ice. You don't walk on the broken surface expecting it'll be fine. Death lies only a few inches beneath you—cold, heart-stopping death. It requires inspection, it demands caution one step at a time, and I'm not going to rush out onto cracked ice and fall through when I know better.

The first step is not a call—it's a text. I type a simple response.

Charlie: Long day. Meeting friends for drinks. Tell the boys I love them.

I hit send, and bubbles representing Ian's typing almost immediately appear on the screen. I watch, a tickling excitement matching the pace of the gyrating bubbles.

Ian: Hey! That's great. Anyone I know?

Ian doesn't know any of my childhood friends. Gosh, I barely know them. I don't answer, but I don't put my phone away. Pulling on my boots and coat, I watch as one more message comes through.

Ian: And the boys say I love you, too.

I heart his last response and then mute my phone, slipping it in my purse. I'm not ready for a back-and-forth. I took one step, one dangerous, frightening step. That's all I can afford for tonight.

Before pulling on my gloves, I stare at the ring and the hairs caught in the loose prong. Then, I slip it off and place it on the marble kitchen countertop just across from the photograph of my mother in her wedding dress held to the door of the refrigerator with a magnet. Young Betty in her gorgeous lacy gown and cathedral-length veil stares at it judgmentally, but I don't put the ring back on. I won't let her shame me. It's not like her nearly fifty-year marriage is without flaws. I turn my back, slip on my gloves, and walk out the door. I need to spend one night away from all . . . this.

The short walk to Thumbs Up, or Thumbs, as the locals always call it, is a cold and uneventful mile. As I hoped, the fresh air pinching my cheeks and cooling my lungs is invigorating. I'm early when I turn on Broad Street, the thump of bass leaking into the street from the glass bar door. The facade of the bar is styled like an Old West saloon, including the carved wooden sign that reads "Thumbs Up" in large saloon typeface and below it in smaller lettering—"A Drinking and Dancing Establishment."

Thumbs has been here since I can remember, a few blocks away from Dad's shop. I've been inside only once—when my friend Stacey Sherman crashed her bike outside and skinned her knee so badly she couldn't walk home and I ran inside to ask for help.

I remember that cigarette smoke hung in the air and I recognized a few vaguely familiar faces sitting at a spot along the bar. One of them kindly called Stacey's mom to come get us.

Stepping inside Thumbs today, it looks both different and the same. No more cigarette smoke, though the air still seems cloudy. The original wooden bar is there, but the rest of the room has been renovated, with video games, gambling, and a pool table. But the biggest change is the patrons. Instead of older men with mustaches drinking steins of Miller Light, the place is packed with kids—well, not kids, but young people closer to Olivia's age than mine.

The men are in loungewear and silk smoking jackets or bathrobes, and the women are dressed in tight corsets, bunny ears, tights, and heels like the Playboy Bunnies in the grainy photographs on the wall.

Lacey, what the hell have you gotten me into?

"Excuse me." I tap a girl on her bare glitter-coated arm. She spins around with a glare that softens when she sees I'm not some creepy guy trying to hit on her. "Sorry. I'm from out of town and I was wondering what all this"—I gesture at the blue velvet of her Bunny suit and the tall satin ears—"is about."

"It's Playboy night. You dress up and drinks are half price." She says "half price" as though that's the interesting part of the sentence. I shout a follow-up question in her ear.

"Playboy night? 'Cause of the Playboy Club-Hotel?"

When I was a kid it was the Americana and it's now the Grand Geneva, but we all knew the origin of the massive hotel, golf course, and ski resort. As salacious as the Playboy name has become over the years, the resort didn't have the same reputation, and I remember the Perkowskis talking about how it was common for families to spend their holidays there. Clearly I'm not the only one who remembers the long-rebranded hotel.

"I don't know." She shrugs, and a blond girl in a red Bunny suit passes over a shot, pointing at me and leaning in so closely I can smell her Sol de Janeiro perfume and the tequila on her breath.

"I know you," she says, finger in my face. "Where do I know you from?"

Great. Just what I need, to be recognized at a Playboy party full of barely legal adults. I lean away, thinking quickly.

"Yeah, I think I know your mom. She told me to keep an eye on you tonight . . ."

"You know my mom?" The girl looks me up and down and seems to decide not to pursue the nagging little voice in her mind telling her that we've met before, though really she's only seen me on TV. "Whatever."

As they walk away, I order a simple cocktail from the bar and push my way through the crowd toward the only empty table I can spot in the whole joint. Lacey will have to find me instead of the other way around. On the wall above the wobbly circular table where I place my drink are photographs of girls dressed very similarly to the kids in Thumbs tonight. Some of the Bunnies hold shovels with a tiny sprinkle of dirt on the point, others are inside the VIP Room carrying trays with a little ribbon pinned at their hips.

The ribbon looks familiar. I think of the black ribbon I'd tossed into the box and brought to Shore Path, the one with my mom's name on it that she fastened to her hip, the one she seemed relieved to have back in her hands. I'd thought it was a prize or award of some kind, but maybe not. I click a picture with my phone to compare later and move to the next framed image, a black-and-white shot of Bunnies in black satin with a banner above their smiling faces that reads **Grand Opening 1968**.

I inspect each face, each figure, going on a hunch, a wonder, a premonition. There, in the front row, a woman wearing her hair in a beehive, her hip tilted out, her smile possibly familiar. I snap another picture, questioning my own sanity. My strict mother a Playboy Bunny? Just because I found a ribbon that looks similar to the ones in the picture. No. Not possible. Right?

"Is that Lottie? Lottie Laramie?" I jump and spin around at the sound of my maiden name. An auburn-haired middle-aged man wearing a shocked expression as well as a flannel shirt with a white undershirt, dark jeans, and heavy tan hiking boots stands in front of me. I cock my head to the side, taking in the hints of gray in his hair, the wrinkles around his eyes, stubble on the chin, and let myself return to an era I've worked hard to banish to the darkest corners of my mind.

Then he smiles, and an old memory flutters to life. Freshman year, the lead in *The Music Man*, my first kiss onstage, my first boyfriend offstage. Someone else I lost when I was escorted from my house and put into foster care.

"Cameron. Cameron Stokes. Hi!" He comes in for a hug like we're old friends, even though he's basically a stranger to me now. His shirt is soft and his arms far more substantial than when we first dated. His closely trimmed beard brushes against my cheek, making me think of Ian for half a second.

"You haven't changed," he says, shaking his head and running his free hand through his thick-for-forty-seven hair.

"Take that back," I joke. Hell, I hope I've changed.

"No, no. You're right. You've changed but like—you've aged down or something. God. I knew it was you. What have you been up to?"

What have I been up to? So much, Cameron. So much.

It's not like I'm so full of myself that I think everyone I've ever met is aware of my career, my books, and my very public marriage. But clearly my first boyfriend hasn't been keeping up with my life, and I kind of like that.

"Oh, you know. Work. Kids. All that jazz," I say generally. That should cover everything.

"'All that jazz,' ha! You still say that? It's such a classic Lottie-ism. You used to say that all the time."

"And you'd do jazz hands like Mrs. Bernstein taught you for 'Ya Got Trouble.'"

"Me and those jazz hands." Cameron covers his face, rolling his eyes at himself. I laugh at the memory of his explosive, hilarious, playful personality. I always thought he'd go on to do comedy in Chicago, possibly *SNL* or something one day. "I don't think I learned how fiercely uncool we were until I hit college."

"Uncool? You? Me? Never." We both laugh, and I remember how we'd sneak onto a private peninsula three miles up the shore path, lie in the hammock hung between two silver maples, and try to spot constellations between the branches.

"You, never. Me—always." He takes a deep breath and then a drink from the glass in his hand. "You know you were the first to break my heart."

A glimpse of that boy I once loved peeks out as his cheeks flush at his admission. I spin my cocktail straw, wishing I had something witty to say back, some coy denial. But I know it's true. He was also my first tragic romance.

Our first kiss was onstage, but our last kiss was in that hammock the night before I was taken away. We talked on the phone once I got to my first foster home in Honey Lake and made plans to see each other when I came home, when he got his license, when summer came. But I broke up with him a week later, finding it easier to be alone than to think of him kissing Debbie Marcus in the fall play now that I wasn't there. It was a heartbreak I chose but a heartbreak nonetheless.

"What are *you* up to nowadays?" I ask, changing the subject to something less incriminating. He slants his eyes like he's acknowledging he's letting me get away with something.

"Same as you, it sounds like. Work, kids. All that—"

"Jazz," I say, completing the sentence.

"Exactly."

"And what is 'work'?" I ask, not letting him off as easily as he did with me.

"God, you're gonna think I'm so boring."

"Cameron, I'm sure a lot has changed, but there's no way you're boring now."

"Oh, just wait. I'll give you an oh-so-exciting summary. Hi. I'm Cameron Stokes. I'm a dentist in Janesville. I'm a fairly recent single dad to two boys, one getting his MBA at Loyola and the other a junior at UW. I'm into biking, D&D, and watching documentaries," he says, eyebrows raised, deep into his point, "*and* I need at least a week of listening to potential songs on YouTube before attending any form of karaoke night."

I cover my mouth to hold in my laughter, letting it linger inside my lungs before releasing it.

"What? Does my patheticness entertain you?"

"Pathetic? You sound like you have life figured out, Mr. Stokes. I'm sorry, Dr. Stokes. I always knew you'd turn out all right."

His shoulders rise and fall; a sweet, reflective smile lingers after our playful exchange. I focus on the ice in my drink when long-dormant butterflies twitch their wings in my belly.

"So, what's brought you back to the lake, Lottie?" He asks sincerely. The humor has left his voice. "I heard you said you'd never set foot in town again."

"Lacey clearly has a big mouth," I say, raising my eyebrows before continuing. "What I think I said was 'I'd never so much as drive through even if my life depended on it.'" I risk looking at him again, and the vodka and soda or the butterflies or good old-fashioned loneliness weakens my defensive walls. "My mom isn't doing great, and my dad moved her into Shore Path."

"Oh, man. I'm sorry, Lottie. I know things with your mom were . . . complicated."

"You could say that." I chuckle sardonically, recalling my mom's cutting accusations this morning and then Betty's tender "I love yous." "All this time I've always told Dad I'd help him with the house if he wanted it. I thought it might take a week or two, a month at most, before I came back. Turned out it only took thirty-one years." I finish my drink with a dramatic slurp through the straw. "But when he called—I came. Talk about pathetic."

Cameron's head tilts to the side. He touches my back lightly.

"Not pathetic. Not pathetic in the slightest."

He hasn't seen or talked to me since we were both fifteen, he doesn't seem to know about any of my biggest triumphs, yet he knew me when

I was most transparently myself. How do I tell him how much his generous evaluation means to me?

"Hey! There you are." A familiar voice makes me jump. Cameron removes his hand. "I swear we lapped the bar two times looking for you!"

Lacey is here, finally, and I'm flooded with conflicting emotions—relief that I have a reason to escape the weight of this serious conversation, disappointment that my time reconnecting with Cam is over.

She's out of breath, carrying a drink in one hand and a long winter coat in her arm like an unruly toddler. Her off-the-shoulder sheer blouse reveals her spray-tan and black bra strap. Her hair is dyed and highlighted, but other than that it looks very similar to her permed and hair-sprayed look of the early nineties.

Next to Lacey stands Connie Perry, face filled out around the jawline, hair updated in a short bob, wearing her thick puffer jacket over an oversized sweatshirt and jeans. And taking up the rear is Michael Willards, Connie's high school boyfriend who, according to Lacey, came out in college and now lives with his partner and two kids in a northern Illinois suburb.

"I'm sorry, I should've texted, but look who I ran into!" I give a round of hugs to each of my now-old old friends, and they gather around the table.

"Cam! I thought you moved to Janesville. You visiting John and Sue?" Cameron's parents, John and Sue—so Midwestern, so welcoming—the kind of parents any kid wants or needs, the kind who make sure you take your shoes off at the front door and get home before curfew but also find you a tutor for calculus when your grade drops and hug you after a big loss instead of telling you all the ways you could've done better. God, I worshipped John and Sue. I think sometimes I still model them when parenting my own children.

"Yeah. They're moving down to the Villages in Florida and turning the house into a rental property, so I'm out here whenever I have some free time. Came out with Bongo and Luke, you know, the Wagner brothers." He points to two older men sitting at the bar, clearly annoyed at the bustling twentysomethings in their ridiculous outfits dancing around them. We're all almost shouting over the thumping music, the voices of the crowd joining in the chorus, jumping in unison. I know the song and the words, and part of me wishes I could join in. "We did not expect to walk into Bunny night or whatever."

"Yeah, sorry. Thumbs was my call. Haven't been here in forever. I didn't know they were doing this Playboy thing tonight," Michael apologizes, his long-sleeve button-up clearly not meant for a night of wild partying.

"We could go to Champs," Connie shouts, referencing the sports bar less than a block away on Main Street. "See if the vibe is a little less—"

"Corset-centric?" Cameron suggests, and we all agree, even though a tiny part of me wishes we could stay, that I could get lost in the mob, drink a little too much, and let the music move my body without my mind shouting reasons I should act proper, why I should act my age, why I should worry someone will recognize me.

We finish our drinks, take a selfie to memorialize the meeting, and bundle up for the walk. Lacey invites Cameron to join us, but when he checks on the already half-wasted Wagner brothers, he declines, explaining he's their designated driver. That same conflicting emotion hits me again, disappointment and relief.

At the door, I give Cameron a side hug and tell him to keep in touch even though I know he won't be able to find "Lottie Laramie" anywhere on the internet.

"See you in another thirty years?" he says as I pull up my hood.

"I'll try to make it closer to twenty this time," I say, waving. It takes two of us to open the door, pushing on the glass with the wind driving biting snow crystals against it, stinging any exposed skin once we stumble out into the street.

Michael and Connie huddle together, skipping through the snow, laughing like two kids on the playground. I watch them like I watch the twins when they chase each other around our backyard. It's good to do this every so often, act like children, access that dormant part of our spirits that climbed trees, made gourmet meals out of mud, and believed in forevers and happily ever afters.

"This feels right," Lacey says, slipping her arm through mine, our synchronized breaths tossing great clouds of vapor in front of us.

"It really does."

"I've missed you, girl." She squeezes my arm against her side in a friendly embrace.

"You too."

"Was it weird seeing Cameron again? I know you, like, ghosted him before that was even a thing."

"It was fine—nice, even. I think bygones are officially bygones. We were kids back then," I say, as though I've convinced myself that everything that happens before you turn eighteen can be blamed on immaturity.

Ahead of us, Michael stumbles and nearly falls. Connie holds him up, her feet slipping around on the icy cement. Their laughter bounces off the brick and asphalt and up into the clear, black, star-cast sky.

"Yeah, *were* kids." We both giggle at their struggle, then she returns to our conversation about Cam. "I'm glad you feel that way."

"Wait," I say, sensing her comment means more than she's letting on, "what does that mean? Why are you glad?"

"'Cause I gave him your number," she says, her eyebrows wiggling. She's the only one I've told about my issues with Ian. She can't possibly be playing matchmaker so soon after finding out my world might be falling apart. Before I can say any curse words, she lets go of my arm and rushes to meet Michael and Connie standing at the entry to Champs.

"Lacey!!!" I call after her, swearing under my breath and then rushing to catch up.

We don't talk of Cameron again the rest of the night because any discussion of Cameron would inevitably lead to Ian. So I let it go, reminding myself to tell Lacey fewer secrets, and we end up closing Champs. When Lacey drops me off at my rental at 2:30 a.m., I'm drunk on shots and nostalgia. I lock up, yank off my snow gear, peel off my tight jeans and Ross shirt, and slip into my robe.

Crawling into bed, shivering, I finally look at my phone, something I've avoided all night. There I see three texts from Ian and one call past midnight, and two below it from a new number, one a text and the other the picture of our whole group, staring up at the camera, smiling. Cam's directly behind me wearing a big, cheesy smile, and I'm surprised to see my expression matches his.

The message reads:

Great seeing you tonight. Let's make a habit of it. Drinks before you leave town?

And then one more.

Oh, this is Cameron.

"Shit," I say, dropping the device on the empty pillow next to me, burrowing into the flannel sheets and pillow-top mattress. "Oh, shit."

CHAPTER 10

Greg

November 7, 1969
Playboy Club-Hotel
Lake Geneva, Wisconsin

"I can't believe we're getting paid to go to the Playboy Club," Mark says, clutching the wheel of his burgundy Impala driving away from the setting sun as it projects warm shadows across the barren harvested fields.

"Sure," I say, shifting in my seat, smoothing the stiff fabric of my trousers. "It's not exactly how I planned on spending my Friday night."

"Are you kidding me? We get to go to the Playboy Club for work, spend the night, and don't have to pay a cent. And I heard Hollinger got a key. You know what that means, right?"

I don't know what it means. At least, not exactly. Everybody in the area has been talking about the Playboy Club-Hotel since it opened. Supposed to be like Vegas but nestled in some bucolic corner of Lake Geneva, a resort town an hour away from Janesville.

It opened in May of last year, and the golf courses and women in bunny suits aren't the only draw to the club. There are multiple bars, pools, and—once snow starts to fall—artificial ski hills. You can go to any show you want to if you have enough money to pay the 130 bucks for a three-day weekend.

And the Playboy Club key, well that's the modern myth of the lunchrooms and watercoolers in most of the offices within a one-hundred-mile radius of this hotel. In order to get into the club, a key is required. As exclusive as it sounds, Mark says it's only a twenty-five-dollar-a-year membership fee. Some guys get the key just so they can say they have one, but I doubt Don Hollinger is one of those kinds of men.

When Hollinger spread the word about the overnight business trip to the Playboy Club-Hotel in Lake Geneva, it was supposed to be hush-hush. Each producer and advertiser got the invitation directly from Mr. Hollinger, bypassing secretaries, assistants, wives, and any other potential sources of gossip. EBN is supposedly a family-centered place with wholesome traditional values. So, spending twenty-four hours at a resort named after a pornographic magazine featuring scantily clad women dressed as bunnies seemed a little out of character.

"It's all look but don't touch," he explained in a closed meeting with the production team. "Plus, this isn't for us—it's for our sponsors, and *Classy Homemaker* is going to be an important part of this weekend. We get more sponsorship dollars from that half hour than any other show currently running on WQRX. Oil that locked jaw of yours, Tin Man."

I hate the *Wizard of Oz* reference he uses for me lately: Tin Man. I see why he chose it. It's clearly obvious how awkward I am in my body, gangly and stumbling and stiff. I have too many emotions and too little gumption. But when he says it in front of everyone else on the production board, including Martha, I wish I could melt away like the cackling green witch from that same film.

"I don't know about this," Martha said. Hollinger tried to keep Martha out of the clandestine meeting, inviting only me. But I knew it wasn't right. Martha produces two WQRX shows, and one of them is the admitted cash cow of the station. I told Mark I'd only go if Martha was invited, too. He looked at me with some pride at my flash of courage and said, "Message received. I'll pass it on." A few hours later, Martha received the go-ahead, unaware that she had almost been excluded.

"You don't have to come if you don't want to," Hollinger said, almost too quickly, clearly eager to keep Martha home, where I'm sure he believes she belongs. "Greg can step up for you. Might make everybody more comfortable anyway."

"I don't know what that's supposed to mean," she said, a number two pencil clutched in her fist.

"Yeah, neither do I," Hollinger replied with a rude chuckle and an edge to his voice. "Listen, one of you needs to be there. I don't care who."

Martha insisted we both go, and I didn't want to let down Martha so—that was that.

As Mark and I follow Highway 50 into Lake Geneva, the distance between the houses begins to shrink. It truly is beautiful here. Rolling hills that lend their stature to the ski area during the winter. Clean, spring-fed lake that provides entertainment and excitement for the summer months. And now the Playboy Club-Hotel, a 320-room resort set a mile off the main road, with its own airfield where the likes of Frank Sinatra and Bob Hope arrive weekly to perform on the cabaret stage.

"Here it is!" Mark says like he's bringing me home to meet his family. Though Mark has never been to the club, he's well known around Lake Geneva. As a thirtysomething single man, he comes down here every few weeks to enjoy the nightlife, bars, and on some very lonely nights, the strip clubs. Perhaps that's why he's so interested in the Playboy Club. It's not a strip club, though. In fact, as we pull up under the covered entrance, I notice a family with two school-aged kids retrieving matching hardside suitcases from the back of their wood-paneled station wagon. There's something classy about this place, and in Mark's mind, far more respectable than his regular strip joint. And now he gets to go into the inner sanctum of "the club." We both do.

And I'm dreading it.

A valet stands behind a podium at the apex of the curved driveway. Mark passes his keys over like he's a millionaire who's done this countless times throughout his fancy life. He's wearing a black suit with a white button-up shirt underneath and a thin black tie. His shoes are polished, and though I know they're the same ones he wears nearly every single day to work, they look brand new.

As he rips off his sunglasses, envy rises inside me. Mark knows how to fit in. He looks like he belongs here. Six foot one, tall, but not too tall, his appendages slender but with enough muscle to give him some definition. As I slink out of the car, unfolding my lanky limbs like an accordion being unstretched, I'm like an oddity from the circus sideshow. My button-up shirt is crumpled around the waist, and the fabric of my tweed jacket looks like it's been brushed one too many times.

Buy a new suit, I think to myself. My new position came with a raise. So far, I've put the excess in my savings account, but I could afford a hundred smackers to look presentable at meetings like this.

"Hurry up, slowpoke!" Mark says like a kid anxiously awaiting the opening of a toy store. I'm glad I'm the only one with him. It's a little embarrassing.

As we walk through the glass entryway, I spot Kev and Darryl, the producers of the nightly news. There's Don, of course, and our anchor Larry, and a few other familiar faces. Then, interspersed, a few unfamiliar faces, four in total, all wearing some variation of gray or black business suits.

One of the men has his back to me, leaning against the lobby bar, but when he shifts to one side, I can see who he's been talking to. Martha. She's dressed in a formfitting green cocktail dress with thick straps that cover most of her shoulders and a straight knee-length skirt. A string of dainty pearls circles her neck, and a glittering gold watch glints on her right wrist. Her hair, unlike every other day I've seen her, has been tamed, curled, and sprayed into a stylish bouffant. It's modern, chic. She looks beautiful, and I'm not the only one who thinks so. Mark elbows me in the ribs.

"Well, who would've ever guessed that?" he asks, running his eyes up and down Martha's newly revealed figure in a way that makes me cringe.

"Knock it off," I say under my breath. Instead of waiting for her to join me and Mark and Mark's hungry eyes, I meet her at the step that elevates the bar, bringing Martha nearly to my same height.

"I'm so glad you're here. I would've died if you didn't show up."

"Did you really think I'd abandon you?"

"Not abandon me, but find some good reason to not show up? Yes. I definitely worried about that. Promise me you'll stay close tonight. OK?" she asks, making me feel needed and useful.

"Of course. We're a team."

"Yes, we're a team," she says, and I notice her eyes, framed by mascara and eyeliner, are the same green as her dress. "These are the guys from Parker Pen, and over there are the guys from GM."

Her transition into work talk is a good reminder. Unlike Mark, we're not here for a fancy night out in nice clothes. Martha and I are here to get sponsors for our two shows—one that is thriving and one on the verge of cancellation. I'm not sure if we can save *Janesville Presents . . .*, but I'm determined to try.

"Listen, I need to go powder my nose and you need to check into your room. Dinner reservation is in fifteen minutes or so. If you're not back, I'll save you a seat."

I agree, straightening the overnight bag slung over my shoulder. She sways up the main staircase toward her room, and Mark comes up from behind with a giant growl that makes me jump.

"Hey, I got us checked in. Here's your key. I don't mind sharing, but if I need the room tonight, you're gonna have to make yourself scarce, if you know what I mean."

Of course I know what he means. I have no desire to be anywhere close to Mark and his escapades once he's had a few drinks in him.

As we follow a slightly confusing interior map to our accommodations, Mark runs through the itinerary for the rest of the night. Once in our room, he claims the bathroom, and I hang my bag on a hook by the door in case I need to grab it and leave quickly if Mark brings someone back later tonight.

Mark comes out of the bathroom smelling heavily of aftershave.

"Don't even try smoking in here or you might blow the place up," I call out to him once I get a turn in front of the wall-size mirror over the sink. I splash some water on my face and put a discreet amount of the provided aftershave on my neck. Face dripping, eyebrows coated in droplets of water, and a nick on my Adam's apple burning where it came into contact with the aftershave, I stare at this awkward version of myself, wondering how the hell I've gotten into this situation.

"Hey, we gotta go," Mark says, pounding on the door.

I don't know how, and I don't know why, but as we make our way to the VIP Room, I'm fairly certain of one thing—this night will be important, monumental, memorable, in some unforeseen way. I've had this sort of prophetic tingle before, like when I boarded the bus to Beloit College with a bag packed with all my belongings, or when I said goodbye to my brother, Jim, after he was drafted, or when I left my mother crying on her couch after Thanksgiving dinner last year, or when I saw Betty for the first time. This prickly, uneasy, skin-crawling sensation has happened before both the best and worst moments of my life. It's yet to be determined which sort it will be tonight.

CHAPTER 11

Charlie

Present Day

"Seven hundred seventy-six. Seven hundred seventy-seven. Seven hundred seventy-eight." I tie up the red plastic strings of a garbage bag filled with stiff crystalized sugar packets like the ones set out on the table of any diner. I know counting is a time waster, as Dino Flanders would call it. He's the professional cleaner/organizer featured on another popular HFN program from Clinton, Mississippi. I finally convinced Dad to let me hire him after a local crew backed out, scared off by the intensity of the project and the potential dangers of unloading a house that'd been jam-packed for so long.

"Can't start at the bottom," one of the local guys said after touring the house. "Only reason the upstairs hasn't collapsed is all this junk holding it up." He motioned to the floor-to-ceiling boxes, and I felt my dad stiffen at the mention of "junk" when referring to my parents' belongings.

"What do you think?" I asked Dino over the phone last week after acquiring his number from a colleague at HFN and sharing a highly embarrassing but completely accurate video of the state of my parents' house. I waited patiently for another terminal diagnosis, another "tear it down, garbage and all" but instead Dino grumbled, cleared his throat, and spoke, his gruff voice softened by the elongated vowels of his southern accent.

"We've seen better and we've seen worse. I'll be there on Monday with my crew."

Monday morning, he drove up with a line of cars behind him, a group of ten, all wearing matching coveralls like on his show. Dino and his team are experts when it comes to working with individuals with hoarding disorder and their families. He insists it's important we all be involved, even my mother from a distance when possible. The incidence of suicide in those with hoarding disorder is high after a rushed mandatory deep clean. I trust him, and I think my dad is starting to trust him, too.

First, he met with me and Dad to set the ground rules for the crew. Anything outside of my parents' room with mold or animal damage or droppings could be tossed immediately. Broken furniture should be assessed by Dad in case he could restore it and sell it in his shop. And a request from my mother: All pictures, books, and official documents should be approved by my father. Upon some negotiating, he added me to the reviewer list.

The final and most important of my father's rules pertained to the 778 sugar packets that I'd found under my mother's bed in a series of rotting shoeboxes. No one—not Dino, his crew, or even me—is allowed to remove even one item from my parents' room without my father's permission.

"Your mother's most prized possessions are in there," Dad explained to both me and Dino when he refused to budge on the one caveat. He pushed his hand in and out of his jeans pocket, nervously, like he was looking for evidence that he wasn't being unreasonable but kept coming up empty. "What if she asks for something and I can't find it?"

"She can barely remember who you are, Dad. I don't think she'll care," I said, siding with Dino, even though I knew it wasn't as black and white as that. Nurse Mitchell says as the RPD progresses, my mom's memory is like Swiss cheese—there are holes but there's also a lot of cheese. Eventually, the holes will grow, her memory retention will lessen until there's little substance and mostly holes. The last memories to go are the ones that've been there the longest.

My dad's shoulders hunched at my indelicate reminder of his wife's deteriorating condition. I know it's already painful enough how she often calls him one of her old boyfriends' names or shoos him out of the room like a stranger.

I felt like shit almost immediately, and when he kept his fists buried in his pockets and pleaded, "It's just one room," I told Dino I was fine with making this one exception for my dad.

In exchange for my flexibility, Dad added me to the list of people allowed inside the room, and we've been slowly but surely making a dent in the ten-foot-thick wall of hoard that surrounds my parents' bed in carefully crafted layers, like a wasp's nest.

"Dad. Sugar packets. Can I toss them?" I call to him from across the room from behind a white KN95 mask that's supposed to keep dust and mold and other irritants out. He's on the other side of one of the now-empty shelving units, digging into a fresh line of boxes. There are two layers, at least that's the number my father remembers. Two sets of floor-to-ceiling shelves arranged with so little walking room between them that I wonder how my mother ever expected to access the belongings she'd basically walled off with each additional strata of storage.

"Let me look," he calls, his voice muffled by boxes and books and clothing no one will ever wear again. I sigh, annoyed that he has to look at every single item I uncover.

"It's just sugar, Dad. Let me toss it. I have to throw out garbage or else we're gonna be here forever." He peeks through the empty shelving as I display a handful of packets, letting them rain down into the overflowing bag.

"I think your mother was saving those for the food drive at the lodge."

"These are hard as a rock." I demonstrate their petrified nature by snapping one of the packets in half. It makes a cracking sound that should be enough to convince him. "No one wants this in their coffee."

"All right, all right. Fine. Throw them out." He gives the approval, and I grab that bag along with four others he's OK'd throughout the day. It's nearly quitting time and I'm dying to go back to my little rental house, take a long shower, pour a glass of wine, and unwind.

My back aches from endless hours hunched over boxes and bags, sorting and counting, finding more and more creative storage solutions for the items my father insists on keeping. Four bags to toss? That's huge.

"Thank youuuuu," I say, squeezing through the doorway with my hard-won bounty before he can change his mind. It's clear that though my father isn't the hoarder in the family, he's still complicit in the state of this home and the state of his life. I keep thinking about what I'd do if Ian had such a grand and damaging obsession, one he wasn't willing to address. I mean, I'm still unable to get past a couple of salacious texts.

You're a quitter. You've always been a quitter. My mother's voice rings in my mind as I wind my way through the footpath in the dining room. I was twelve, and after coming in dead last at each and every cross-country meet, I decided running was not my talent. Auditions for the fall play were the next week, but rehearsals conflicted with cross-country practice. So, I quit and auditioned for *Alice in Wonderland* and somehow got the lead. When I told my mom, she said I couldn't accept the part. I'd made a commitment to cross-country and I had to stick it out.

"You're a quitter," she said again, and I stared at the wall where the wallpaper in the dining room didn't match up quite right.

I turned down the role and stuck with track until I hurt myself two weeks later and had to sit out the rest of the season. Mrs. Robins, the director of the play, let me take a small part once she heard what happened, and then I landed the lead in the spring musical. I never ran again, and my mom has pointed to that as evidence of my "lack of drive" ever since. I'm sure she found my first divorce quite satisfying.

"Here. Four more," I say from the porch to the small crew in the yard, holding up the bags like a prizewinning fish I'd pulled out of the lake. Tina, Dino's wife of thirty years and business partner, claps her gloved hands, and Will, one of their assistants, barely acknowledges my declaration.

"We're up to sixty for today," Will says dully, stacking items on a folding table under one of the six blue canopies used as sorting stations. "I need approval here," he adds, stepping back from the spread in front of him.

"Let me toss these and I'll be by."

My wrists ache from the weight of the bags, and as I pass Tina on my way to the dumpster, she adds, "I have some items for you to check, too," with a southern drawl as charming as her husband's.

She stands by a folding table covered with papers, books, and a few photographs, along with a pair of baby shoes and two unopened boxes with mailing labels on them and yellowed tape peeling up on the corners. I'll need to look through and decide the fate of these objects—garbage or storage. I lean heavily toward garbage in my decision-making, especially when I'm lucky enough to give approval when Dad is busy inside. I've found that what he doesn't know is thrown away doesn't hurt him.

I'd like to think I'd be fine with shoveling nearly everything from this house into one of the portable garbage bins sitting in the driveway, but that's not totally true. Sugar packets, yes. Broken frames and melted candles, most definitely. But little pieces of my mother still linger in this house, pieces I've never seen or known or understood. Those items I do want, I desperately want.

It's been a week since I've seen her, a week since she was lucid and accusatory, since she remembered who I was and how deeply she hated me. Nurse Mitchell called me a few days ago, saying Betty was asking for me. Every day I wake up thinking I'll stop by for a cup of coffee or at lunch or before dinnertime or . . . but I haven't. Every time I pull into the Shore Path Memory Care parking lot and reach for the box I keep in my back seat with the items I want to show my mother, I think about her telling Mitchell "I have no daughter" and how much it hurt when I knew she remembered me.

I want to go back. I will go back.

Tomorrow.

Maybe.

Or maybe not.

It takes four tries to get the first bag into the overfilled metal dumpster, but the last three fly in no problem. I remove my mask and take a few deep breaths of clean, unfiltered air as I walk back to the sorting area, where the other team members, including Dino, are transporting another load out of the house. No wonder Will thought my measly four bags were pitiful.

Will takes me through his pile. I end up approving the disposal of 90 percent of the papers, all the *Reader's Digest* magazines with corners of pages turned down in each one. Part of me would love to check what stories my mom found interesting, spend a few days or weeks reading them to understand who she was without the risk of another confrontation. But we realize rodents have clearly been snacking on the pages, and that's an automatic toss. And when I smell the stench of animal urine, I remember I'm not wearing my mask and snap it back into place.

I take the photographs with me; two are of me as a little girl, and one is simply a view of the lake from our back porch at sunrise. Nothing special, but I still want to keep them. My kids have never seen a picture of me as a little girl, and I can't help but notice how much I resemble Olivia when she was a toddler. I snap a photo of all three pictures with my phone and send them to Olivia with a text: Guess who looks like her mom after all?

"Here, hon. A few more to look through." Tina gestures to a pile of photographs with a headshot of my mother in black and white on top. She looks young, late teens, early twenties, hair teased toward the sky in an impressive bouffant that looks to be held up by someone as grand as God himself. She's downright stunning, and if it wasn't for a handwritten note on the back of the eight-by-ten photograph labeling it "Betty Laramie-headshot proof," I would've thought it was a picture that came with a frame. The other photos are less telling, more images of random landscapes, houses, a barn, a farmhouse, a kitchen, artfully taken but giving me no clues to why they were taken at all.

"Dad!" I call to my father as he walks out of the house, his hands empty. My curiosity is temporarily displaced by a hot flash of annoyance. How does he have nothing to throw away?

"Hey, honey. It got quiet inside. Thought everyone called it quits for the day."

"Sun is setting so we'll be out of here soon. Charlie was just looking through some things, if you'd like to help." Tina focuses both me and my dad with her comment.

"Yeah, sorry. Found this headshot of Mom." I hold up the photo with a question in my voice. He takes it with a smile without giving any detail about its origin. "And a bunch of these," I continue, passing him the small landscape images, keeping the two grainy photos of myself in a white dress and bonnet, playing in the grass on a summer afternoon. I wait for him to take a hint and explain the pictures, but instead, he tosses all of them into the garbage pile.

"Whoa, wait. Why are you throwing those away?"

"Eh. A silly old hobby."

"Photography?"

He nods and I fish the pictures out of the garbage.

"Why did Mom have a headshot? Was she an actress or something?"

"Or something," he says vaguely. "But she won't want this. You can throw them out."

"What about these?" Tina points to the sealed boxes. Up close, I can see the corner of one box has lifted, showing stacks of papers inside.

"Those can go, too," he says. Tina nods and places them in the "throw away" side of her station, praising my dad for tossing two whole boxes without picking through them.

"What do you mean, 'Or something'?" I ask. "And you didn't even look in these. What are they?" I read the label. "Betty Laramie at WQRX" and an address in Janesville, Wisconsin. Janesville, again. That station, again.

"Nothing important, honey."

"I showed Mom her ID from WQRX last week and she said you worked there, too. You never told me that."

"It was a long time ago—before the shop—before you were born." He tugs on my ponytail and walks away to another sorting area. I follow him.

"I didn't know you were both in television. So, what did you do there? What about Mom?"

"I was a camera operator and your mom was kind of a Renaissance woman, you could say." He releases another pile of belongings into the garbage pile and then moves back toward the house.

"Like, in what way? In front of the camera, crew, or more like production?" It's a link to my parents I didn't expect, like those identical twins separated at birth who each had become nurses, had three children, and married a man named Bob.

"You make it sound so official. It was a tiny local station," he says, heading up the front steps, not answering the question. I had already Googled WQRX and learned everything Wikipedia could tell me about it, which was one paragraph and a link to the parent network Epistle Broadcasting Network that ended up rebranding in the mid-seventies and moving to Texas, leaving WQRX to a small public access station. The Wikipedia page had a few names and dates, and so I found as many people as I could, former producers mostly, and sent them emails, but they all bounced back.

I think I could ask my dad a million questions and they'd get me nowhere. He doesn't want to tell me about his past, my mom's past, the roots of my nearly rotted-out family tree. Why??

I let him leave without asking more questions, not willing to have an all-out confrontation with my dad in front of my professional colleagues, who I'm sure see me more as Charlie McFadden than Lottie Laramie, daughter of a hoarder. He's off the hook for now but not forever, that's for sure.

My phone buzzes. I step away from the sorting area and glance at the screen. It's a text from Cam. We've exchanged a few messages every day since we ran into each other at Thumbs. He asks if he can buy me dinner at least once in each conversation, and every time I nearly say yes. As I peel off my gloves to open my phone, Tina calls me back for one last query, pointing to the sealed boxes I'd been questioning my father about.

"So, these boxes. Toss 'em for sure?"

"Probably. Let me look." Out of curiosity and a little stubbornness, I rip off the decaying tape in one tug and the flaps gape open. Lifting one side with the tip of my ungloved finger, a familiar set of eyes meet mine. They're my mother's eyes—my eyes. I spread the beleaguered flaps wide, and now four sets of eyes look back at me. My mother's headshots. Hundreds of them. There's only one reason someone would have this many headshots—the same reason I've had stacks of similar shots in front of me with a black Sharpie in my right hand. She had fans, and those fans wanted her autograph.

"I'll throw these out," I say, balancing the stack of boxes in my arms. As I pass Dino, I tell him there's a new exception to the auto-toss rule—anything with the name Betty Laramie or the call letters WQRX needs to come to me immediately. Not my dad, not the garbage, not a pile to be sorted—me.

"Yes ma'am," he says, touching the tip of his baseball cap before digging another armful of clothing from the laundry trolly. I say my goodbyes and rush away from the chaos of my parents' front yard.

However, I don't stop at the industrial-sized garbage bin as I'd promised Tina. Instead, after making sure no one is watching and seeing that the coast is clear, I use my knee to prop the boxes open and pop the trunk of my car by pressing a button. I cringe at the beeping sound, but thankfully, no one is close enough to hear it. I shove aside two other cardboard boxes containing my mother's belongings and drop in the new boxes. My mother's stiff smile and sparkling eyes seem to peek back at me through the unfastened flaps of the box.

I know where I can get answers without reaching into my father's throat and forcing them out. I can't put it off anymore. I have to go see my mother.

CHAPTER 12

Greg

November 7, 1969
Playboy Club-Hotel, VIP Room
Lake Geneva, Wisconsin

Mark and I are escorted to the table by a curvaceous woman in a black satin corset, a white collar with a black tie, wrists encased in shirt cuffs, a grapefruit-sized white poof on her perky rear end, and a pair of drooping bunny ears on her head. Mark raises his eyebrows and whispers something untoward, which I pretend not to hear. The petite brunette wears a ribbon name tag pinned at her hip at the top curve of her high-cut leotard that reads "Jessica." A warmth floods through me that makes me keep my eyes to the floor.

"Where are you from, sweetheart?" Mark asks her as we dodge between tables filled with mostly middle-aged men and a few younger guys who likely think the Bunnies will ignore the strict rules and hand over their number if they show up enough or tip well.

"You know, around," she says, and I can tell it's a question she answers often.

"Well, that's fun. I'm from around, too."

Jessica giggles demurely, and I think he actually caught her off guard with his humor. "Maybe I'll see you there next time I'm in town," she teases.

"Sure hope so," Mark says, approaching the table of seven men and one woman.

"You two get settled and I'll send Tammy over to get your drink order, OK, hon?" she asks as she wiggles her Bunny tail back to her hostess station.

"My God, I love my job right now," Mark says, eyes locked on Jessica until she disappears into the dim, crowded room.

"Behave yourself," I say, pulling out the chair next to Martha where she'd saved me a seat.

"I'll do my best, but no promises," Mark agrees, locating his seat on the opposite side of the large round table, next to Hollinger, a representative from the EBN head office, and another man in a boss suit too busy chain-smoking to say anything.

Martha doesn't acknowledge my arrival at first. She's already in conversation with Jerry Bartholomew from Jerry's Shoes. He's in his fifties and his bloodshot eyes and reddened cheeks make it clear that the drink in front of him isn't his first. Martha is laughing, tossing her head back like she's learned how to be a socialite overnight. A twinge hits between my shoulder blades when I watch her interact with the businessmen.

To my left is Tony Caveola, owner of a chain of Italian restaurants. He's already a sponsor for *The Classy Homemaker*. It's on me to get him to expand his advertising dollars to the sinking ship of *Janesville Presents* . . .

"My God, these women are gorgeous," he says, taking a sip of his whiskey neat. His voice sounds raspy, like he smokes more than a few packs a day. I try to follow his eyeline to see which of the Bunnies he's staring at, but the air is thick with cigarette smoke, and the dim lights turn every Bunny into a runway model. "Ever been before?"

"To the club? No. I . . ." I don't tell him the truth—that I've never enjoyed this kind of joint. "It's a bit of a trek."

"What, an hour from Janesville? You're a single guy. What do you have keeping you at home?"

I'm happily a homebody, but that image won't do for impressing the men here tonight. I glance at Martha, sipping on a glass of pink champagne and looking nearly as lovely as the Bunnies. If she can play a part tonight, so can I.

"Mark and I have been meaning to take a trip. He's thinking of applying for a key."

"That's great. Why not, you know? My wife would *kill* me, otherwise I'd be right there with you two. But as for tonight—what she doesn't know won't hurt her, right?"

A new Bunny in a blue satin corset and matching ears drops off my drink. The busty auburn-haired waitress takes Tony's order for the next round with a slight southern accent that leaves him tittering.

"That accent," he says, shaking his head like he's heard the voice of God. I take a sip of my scotch and the nip hits me almost instantly. I'll need it tonight. I take a deep breath and ask the first question that comes to mind.

"How do you like WQRX's programming this fall?"

Tony raises his eyebrows and gulps down a mouthful of whiskey.

"It's all right. Local TV is its own breed. No one hustles to get home in time for local news, or what is that show with all the losers from the town? My wife and I saw it the other night and laughed our guts out."

My shoulders stiffen and I take another drink, knowing he's talking about *Janesville Presents* . . . I hold still, hoping Tony won't notice my irritation. My God, I hope Martha didn't hear that.

"But there's one show she won't shut up about. The one with the hot blonde making food and cleaning house. I saw it when I got the flu last month and had to stay home from work. My wife loves that girl, and I gotta say—I didn't mind watching her on the TV either. Sweet thing. Was hoping she'd be here tonight . . ."

"She's just talent," I say, a protective twinge hitting my shoulders again, this time over Betty. Behind us a jazz trio starts to play their version of Patsy Cline's waltzy "She's Got You." Some of the men from the other tables wander onto the parquet floor with their companions.

"Yeah, makes sense. She's definitely too sophisticated to be in a place like this. Was already surprised the one next to you was here. Is she someone's younger sister?"

"Martha is my producer, actually." When I say her name, she turns in my direction. She's smiling and seems to be pleased to see me.

"Greg! There you are. We were just talking about you."

"So were we," I say, gesturing to asshole Tony.

"Well, look at that," she says, putting out her slender hand. "I might as well introduce myself since I already know who you are, Mr. Caveola. I'm Martha Smith. Greg and I produce *The Classy Homemaker* and *Janesville Presents . . .*"

Tony's eyes widen as he realizes he's been shit talking my show right to my face, and then he laughs and hits me in the shoulder as though I'm in on the joke.

"Damn fine shows you've got going on."

"Why, thank you, Mr. Caveola."

"Tony. You should call me Tony," he says, taking Martha's hand and squeezing it. "Wanna take this conversation onto the dance floor?" Tony asks Martha as she's trying to tell him about all the changes we're making on *Janesville Presents . . .*

Martha looks at me like she's asking my advice. I'd rather choke on my drink garnish than dance with that asshole, but I get why she's considering it. Dancing with Tony could get him on our side. Then, the other advertisers might consider sponsoring us, too.

"Why you looking at this guy? Is he your boyfriend or something?"

"No," we both say in unison. "No," she says again.

"Then what do you say?" Caveola puts out his hand, the song changing in the background. She takes it and doesn't look at me this time. Damn. This is unfair to Martha.

I finish my drink and watch as Martha sways to the rhythm of the band's rendition of "I've Been Loving You Too Long" while Tony shuffles from foot to foot. I glance around the room at the half-toasted businessmen in various levels of formal dress and the few tagalong women who came with husbands or lovers.

At our table, Mark looks bored but locked into a conversation with Hollinger and Quinton Florence from EBN. I'm sure he wishes he was on the dance floor or trying to flirt with one of the Bunnies. The room has a different vibe than I expected. The Bunnies are friendly and beautiful but nothing more than that.

A short blond Bunny in a pink satin corset catches my eye. She has her back to me, taking orders from a table in the far corner of the dim room. A man wearing a dark suit keeps taking advantage of his seated position, her Bunny tail right at eye level. He flicks it every time she looks away and then winks at the man to his side. She stays professional and cool, ignoring his behavior as she makes notes on a napkin. Then, when she turns away, the older man grabs her ass cheek with a rough squeeze, the flash of an expensive golden watch peeking out from under his shirtsleeve.

The Bunny doesn't yelp like I expect her to, which is telling in and of itself. How often must she put up with this sort of violation? The rules must be strict on keeping quiet and not insulting the patrons. Though she doesn't verbally protest, she does move away smoothly and swiftly, like it's a step in a well-practiced choreography.

The two men elbow each other, and the older one reenacts the grab in midair as the woman walks away. She seems cool and collected, but maybe it's a sign of her nerves that she drops her pen. She bends at the knees and dips to the ground, snagging it, then stands, smoothing the fabric at her abdomen and scanning the room to see if anyone noticed.

I should avert my gaze, look away so she doesn't think I'm ogling her like the rest of the men, but I'm so far across the room and it's dark, so it's not likely she can see me. But then she tilts her head over her bare shoulder, revealing her face. She looks directly at me, as though I'm the only man in the entire room.

My heart stops.

I know that girl.

The lashes and blue eyeshadow are different, the ears and the black tights as well. But her eyes, those I can't forget, literally cannot no matter how hard I've tried.

"Betty?" I whisper to myself, half rising from my seat, wondering if I'm seeing things. She rushes through a curtained exit, leaving me in a state of puzzlement.

"You owe me a dance," Martha says, tugging at my bicep. Tony is back at the table with another drink in hand. Hollinger orders another round as the music slows.

"I'm not much of a dancer," I say, looking past Martha toward the mystic partition where the girl who looks like Betty disappeared.

"I don't really care," she says, yanking on my arm.

"You gonna make her drag you?" Tony looks at me as though something's wrong with me.

"No, no. I . . . I would love to." I offer Martha my arm as we make our way onto the dance floor. I try to keep my feet in time with the beat, enjoying the playful rhythm of the pianist.

Even the liberal strain of improvised jazz gives the musician no more than eighty-eight keys on the piano, twenty-four musical keys, three or four instruments playing together in an attempt to make something not only good but also worthwhile. In jazz there are rules and then freedom within those rules. But not so with the rest of life. Don't murder, but go to war. Don't lust, but don't be a prude. Protect women, but also hunt them. Money isn't everything, only it absolutely is.

Martha knows how to dance, and though as a man I should be the one leading, I follow her guiding movements. Even in her heels, her head reaches no higher than my chest, and my long, gangly arms awkwardly encircle her waist. She's not shaped like the women who work here, but she has a womanliness to her figure, pliable and enticing, especially when she leans in closer to whisper in my ear.

"That man has hands like an octopus. My lord."

"Are you kidding me?" I whip around, my mind flooded with hot words heated not only by Tony's brazen womanizing but also by what I saw happen to the girl I'm fairly sure is Betty.

"Shhh. It's OK," Martha says, regaining my attention, her lightly boozy breath caressing my neck. "Not sure what kind of business will get done here tonight. It's all so . . . distracting." She gestures to the dolled-up women in the room. "They seem to forget I'm not one of these laughably desperate girls, shaking my ass for attention. But I'm not. I'm a producer, dammit."

I think of Betty, that man's hand, how she looked like a wild creature stuck in a trap rather than a woman in a costume. But Betty isn't desperate, or at least she doesn't seem to be when I watch her through the camera's lens at work.

Martha can't know about Betty. She already despises our daytime show, and to find out our host is a Playboy Bunny . . . I'm not sure she'd recover from it. Does Hollinger know? Is that why we came here tonight?

I check the rear table again and see the outline of a Bunny. She's not standing anywhere as close to the old man as before, a wise decision no doubt. But is it Betty?

"You OK?" Martha checks my line of focus. The Bunny turns her head, laughing at something one of the men at the table said.

It's not her. It's not Betty. Was the whole thing a trick of the shadows and scotch?

Then the velvet curtain to the kitchen sways for a moment before a redheaded Bunny explodes out from behind it. A form stands in the darkness, blond, wearing pink satin. Then, the figure is gone.

Martha glares in the redheaded Bunny's direction, noticing my preoccupation with the back of the room.

"Ugh. Men." She huffs and rolls her eyes, and as the song ends, she rushes back to her seat, where she gulps down a full glass of freshly poured champagne.

The rest of the night she has no interest in talking to me. The men at either side of us have swapped positions, and we both dive into the same conversations we had earlier. *Where are you from? What show are you working on? Oh, the cooking one? That little blond girl—she's great.*

As the night rolls on and Martha starts to slouch beside me, the room blurs with each drink. And it becomes clear—and no one, not even Martha can deny it—that Betty is our star. She's the reason WQRX is making a dime. She's the pure, charming model of what a woman should be like.

And as Mark and I escort Martha to her room, keeping her upright as she trips up the wide-set stairs, my arm around her waist for the second time this night, she stares up at me while Mark works her lock.

"We have to give them what they want, don't we?"

"Yeah, I think we do," I say, hoping she remembers at least some of what she's saying in the morning because Martha has to bury her resentment toward Betty if we're going to find a way to move forward.

"Damn it," she says, her green eyes glistening from a gathering of tears. A drop escapes and slides down her cheek. I catch it with my fingertips and brush it away, wishing I could do the same for all of the problems with our show—her show.

"Got it," Mark says as the door pops open.

I attempt to help Martha over the threshold, but she pats my chest, slips her feet out of her dressy shoes, and picks them up. Stepping into her room, she retrieves her key from Mark, thanks us both, and promptly slams the door in our faces.

"Well, that wasn't exactly how I thought the night would go," Mark says, blinking rapidly, staring at the closed door.

"Me either," I say, unsure if any good came from sharing a table with those men tonight.

As we get to the end of the hallway, Mark hesitates, checking his watch. "Wanna go to a strip club? I know some of the girls in town. They'd go bananas over you."

"Nah, I'm gonna crash," I say, following the number signs in the direction of our room. "Don't drive, though. They have a disco downstairs."

"Yeah, full of couples and old men and Bunnies who can't even say whether they're married or not. No thank you." Mark trails me to our room. I let myself in and he reminds me of his earlier warning. "And if I come home with someone tonight, you're sleeping in the bathtub."

"I'm gonna be asleep, so good luck making me." I chuckle at the idea of Mark trying to carry all six feet five inches of me to the bathroom as he stumbles off down the hall, so clearly drunk that I'm sure the valet will refuse to get his car.

Inside, the smell of aftershave still lingers in the air. I slip out of my suit, hanging each piece carefully so it'll be presentable for our meetings tomorrow.

In bed at long last, my mind returns to Betty. Could that woman have been her? Does our wholesome homemaker have a secret life? If it's her, do I keep my mouth shut? It's not like the side job gets in the way of her work at the station. But then again—what happens when the housewives and young mothers and matronly grandmothers find out their respected figure of wholesome womanhood is a Playboy Bunny? What happens when Martha finds out, or Hollinger or Quinton Florence?

Nothing good, that's for sure.

CHAPTER 13

CHARLIE

Present Day

"Charlie! So good to see you," Nurse Mitchell in her pink scrubs greets me from a desk down the hall. "Just in time for dessert."

I wave back but don't linger for a chat, and she doesn't try to stop me. I basically just got off the phone with her. I dialed the memory center when I pulled onto Main Street, hoping to assess my mom's mental state before seeing her.

"She's a little lost today," the nurse said over the phone, with a note of compassion. "But she's in a good mood overall. Made bracelets for half the memory care unit at arts and crafts. I know she'd like to see you."

I tried not to snort at the idea of my mom wanting to see me. Either she remembers me and hates me, or she's forgotten me and loves me. Kind of a messed-up dynamic, that's for sure. I thanked Nurse Mitchell and told her I'd be there soon.

The memory care halls are decorated with pastel eggs for Easter, and none of the employees try to stop me now that I'm a fairly common face around Shore Path. I haven't been asked for a selfie or an autograph in two weeks, which usually means the novelty of having a television personality walk around their place of work has worn off.

I take a right and a left and then another right, and when I'm only a few doors away from Betty's room, the sound of *Abbey Road* trickles down the hall, and the tension in my shoulders releases. She won't remember me today. Today, I'll listen to records and have dessert with Betty instead of my mom.

I knock on the door. It's ajar, so I push it open slowly. I didn't bring the whole box of items from the house today, only the headshot and a few pictures. Also, I brought a new pack of cards from Dollar General as a peace offering.

Inside, Betty stands in the center of the room, shuffling her feet in a circular motion with her eyes closed. She holds a long, translucent scarf that flutters around her like it's dancing, too. Her hair is styled into a chic white-platinum poof that frames her face, and her eyeliner is smudged up the side of her right eye. Her cobalt-blue eyeshadow, the same color she used to buy from the makeup counter at Waals Department Store in Walworth, is slathered on her eyelids all the way up to her eyebrows. She wears a soft pink dress with a sash around her middle and slippers on her feet.

"Oh, you're finally here!" she says, opening her eyes when I walk past her to place the items I brought onto her puzzle table. Betty is glad I'm here, even if she doesn't remember I'm her daughter—or more likely *because* she doesn't remember.

"Sorry I've been gone a bit. Work got busy," I say, turning the headshot face down so I can share it when the timing seems right.

"Oh, my goodness, yes." She drops the scarf and it falls into a lifeless pool on the ground. "I have to get to work. I forgot." She looks down at her dress and then presses her face close to the mirror mounted on the wall above the sink. "I can't go like this. My boss will kill me."

She reaches for a bar of amber-colored Neutrogena soap and a damp washcloth. Her panic reminds me of my stress dreams about being back in school and suddenly realizing I have a test but haven't studied.

"You look lovely," I reassure Betty, crossing to the sink. Steam rises from the faucet, the hot water turned on full blast. I imagine her thin, fragile skin assaulted by the heated stream pouring out of the spout and move quickly to turn the temperature down.

"Here, let me help," I say, rubbing the soap against the washcloth until suds appear. Betty closes her eyes and tilts her face to me. It's the same face from those photographs, but now it looks like the image has been distorted, melted, or altered with a filter. Wrinkles, yes, at her eyes, around her mouth, across her forehead, and at her neck. I trace them all with the cloth, wiping off the black liner, blue shadow, orange-tinted base, and electric pink blush until her skin is fresh and pink.

"There—all clean." I pass her a dry towel, and she drapes it over her face.

"Peekaboo," she says, yanking it off like we're playing a game, her urgent need to get to work on time forgotten. Her age-bleached eyes are a silvery blue, nearly as gray as her black-and-white headshot. They twinkle with mischief, and I remember when I was little, we'd go to the blueberry patch in Woodstock, just over the border in Illinois. My mom used to make preserves to sell at the shop, and I'd help her pick whatever fruit was in season.

Blueberries were my favorite, the bushes low enough to the ground for me to reach. I loved the plunk, plunk, plunk of the juicy blue globes as they hit the bottom of the bucket my mom tied around my waist. When she filled her own bucket, she'd take aim, and I'd hold perfectly still while she tossed a few perfectly ripe berries into my collection. We were a team. We'd laugh when she'd miss or when she'd catch me gobbling down a secret snack.

"What happened to you?" I whisper to myself as Betty once again applies the towel to her face and pulls it off playfully. She must hear me because she stops her little game and raises her nearly invisible eyebrows.

"What do you mean? Is there something wrong with me?" She touches her face, her neck, leans over to check the mirror again, gasping. "My makeup. It's gone . . ."

"Oh, shhh. It's OK. I can do it for you." I beckon her to the green chair by the window. As I gather the scattered beauty supplies from her nightstand, I remember the headshot. "I have something for you."

I place the print in front of her, hoping for another distraction, moving the smaller, plastic visitor's chair into position so I can reapply her makeup. Betty picks up the image and stares at it, the photo paper trembling in her creased fingers.

"Who is this?" she asks.

"It's you," I say, arranging the tubes of makeup on the tray.

"Me?" She checks the picture again. "Are you sure?"

"Yes. It's you. Betty Laramie."

"Oh, yes. Yes," she says like a thought is coming back to her. "I'm supposed to sign them, I think." Then, looking confused, she lets the picture fall into her lap. "I think I'll do it later."

Bare faced and anxious, she seems overwhelmed at her fictional work demands. A ripple of compassion rolls through my conscience. I set the headshot aside and pick up the liquid concealer.

"Hey, Betty? Let's not worry about that now. We've got more important things to think about. Still want me to fix your makeup?" She looks up at me with trust I've never received from my mother.

"Oh, yes. Please. I can't show up like this. Less liner this time," she says as if I'm her makeup artist. She closes her eyes while I apply the concealer and pat it into an even coat under her eyes. Her breath is steady and calming as I apply a light-colored foundation with a fresh sponge wedge, placing dots of makeup across her crepey skin and blending them into a uniform base.

I work silently, my mom's record player still running in the background. Asking questions now wouldn't do any good. Besides, this is different than any of my other fact-finding missions. I thought this kind of synchronicity with my mother was beyond my reach. But isn't this how it's supposed to be? A mother sharing with her daughter, and the daughter caring for her mother? The service she is allowing me to provide fills some of the battery inside of me that's been out of energy for so long.

My mother can't love me, but it's possible Betty can.

"Did you want one? A headshot, I mean?" Betty asks out of nowhere when I finish lining her right eye.

"I . . . I'd love one," I start the second line of black eye makeup, surprised that she's returned to the previous topic of conversation without my interference.

"I'll make sure my producer gets you one before you leave."

Producer? I hesitate as I reach for the blush compact. It's a job title I'm familiar with in my profession. She must have been on-air talent. I wasn't going to push for more, but if she's initiating, I'd be a fool to pass on the opportunity.

"What kind of a producer?" I ask, acting casual, fluffing a dusting of pink on her high, defined cheekbones.

"Stop messing around with silly questions," she scolds, opening her eyes. "We can talk shop later at Ike's."

"Ike? Is that your boss?" I apply mascara to her translucent lashes.

"Is that a joke?" Betty asks, blinking rapidly, the lines between her brows deepening. "You know Ike's Diner. Jeez Louise. Call is in five minutes. Pass the red lipstick, please, hon." I snag the silver tube and place it in her waiting palm, taking note of the information.

She applies the color with three deft swipes, her muscle memory more precise than her mind. She presses her lips together to distribute the creamy red tint and smiles at her reflection. She looks confident and beautiful.

Why didn't I grow up with this version of my mother?

Tears tingle at the corners of my eyes and I snap up a tissue, turning my face to dry them without giving myself away to Betty.

"Do you have a pen handy?" Betty asks as I keep my back to her. "Never mind. I found one."

When I regain my composure enough to look at her again, Betty's holding a pen above her headshot. She scribbles a message that I can't read from where I stand and adds a swirling signature underneath before handing it over.

I thank her and slip the photograph into my bag, about to ask another question, when a knock sounds at the door. A nursing assistant pushing a meal cart rumbles in with sugar-free cake and fresh raspberries.

"Dessert!" he calls. At the mention of sweets, Betty forgets her call time, Ike's Diner, and her mysterious producer, and I let go of the questions on the tip of my tongue. We dine on artificially sweetened vanilla pound cake and play cards until the night nurse brings Betty her evening medications.

I say good night to my mom, as well as the other residents, nurses, and staff as I leave. Outside, the night air is nearly freezing, and while I let my car warm up, I turn on the dome light to retrieve my mother's headshot. My breath clouds around me like the exhaust pouring out from the rear pipe as I examine the barely legible writing on the black-and-white glossy paper. The yellow light isn't bright enough, so I turn on the flashlight function on my phone and hold it up, following the lines of writing with the intense beam.

Thanks for watching!

Love, Betty

Thanks for watching? Thanks for watching—what?

That's when I notice—below her signature there's another line. The black ink is nearly invisible against the image of Betty's black off-the-shoulder dress. I struggle to decipher my mother's handwriting, shaky and jagged like my nerves every time I walk into her room. I blink, and finally I make the words out.

The Classy Homemaker

I read the whole message again.

Love, Betty

The Classy Homemaker

My mom—the hoarder, the recluse, the woman who gave me up for her house full of junk—was formerly known as the Classy Homemaker?

What the actual fuck?

CHAPTER 14

Greg

April 15, 1970
WQRX, Studio C
Janesville, Wisconsin

I lower the bulky TK-42 to the lowest position on its pedestal and open the side panel in an attempt to fix some of the camera's focus issues. The grayish-beige metal casing drops down on hinges with a crash, echoing through the empty studio dimly lit by a few base lights.

Martha said she'd put in a work order. "They have enough money for this damn show to get us a new camera. Don't you dare fix it," she directed, but I snuck back after having dinner with Mark at Ike's. I was hoping to fix the camera as a surprise. I like showing that I'm good at something, even if it's not business or advertising or programming or saving *Janesville Presents* . . . from getting canceled.

I'm still trying to make it up to Martha. In those last tumultuous weeks when the writing was on the wall, we'd spend hours on the phone each night. Those calls became a routine, and even after the axe finally came down and cut our show, I still find myself ending most nights listening to Martha's voice through my receiver.

At first it was to plan our new hour-long *Classy Homemaker* programming, but eventually, we got around to other topics, worldly things like the war or music or television shows on other networks. I like listening to her talk about jazz and tell the story of going to Newport for the jazz festival and seeing Louis Armstrong perform. She's not just passionate about music, she's also passionate about social issues, she's anti-war and pro-woman. I like to listen. I can't help remembering my premonition when we started this whole fiasco together. Whether it's Minnesota or Milwaukee or even Chicago—Martha Smith is playing big league on a little league field.

Hollinger sees it too and I think he's jealous. That's why he tried to relegate her to the homemaking show. But little did he know that *The Classy Homemaker* would be so popular. Hollinger would say it's because of Betty. And he's right in a way. Enigmatic Betty is great on-screen, she can read copy off cue cards better than any of the anchors or reporters I've ever worked with, and she even comes with her own programming ideas. But Martha is the reason the show is fresh and snappy and just modern enough to hold viewers. We've heard rumors of syndication to bigger local markets, which should numb the wound from the cancellation of *Janesville Presents . . .*, but it doesn't. Not yet.

The memory of how things went down at the end of our pet project sends a flash of frustration through me, and I dig my screwdriver under the lip of the access panel to the auxiliary fan and pry the broken connector out of its position. It crashes onto the metal plate, sending an ear-rattling clank through the echoey room and denting the casing.

"Damn it," I curse out loud.

"Well, good evening to you, too," a familiar feminine voice says from the shadowy set. Betty stands behind the long L-shaped laminate counter with a collection of supplies in her arms. She unloads them one at a time, starting with a spiral notebook she has balanced on the top of the pile. My stomach does that thing it always does when I see her.

I've gotten used to her beauty, I've learned to expect it, too, but this reaction is about more than Betty's looks. I've seen her in curlers, without makeup, and on one particularly messy broadcast, I've seen what she looks like covered in vanilla pudding. That doesn't stop the butterflies, though. In fact, I think it's only made them grow larger, like bats or great winged birds of prey.

"Sorry about that." I put down my screwdriver and pick up the new part, sliding it into place.

"Don't worry. I've heard much worse." Her voice projects across the room. "Say as many *damns* and *shits* as you find necessary. I won't judge."

I can't help but snicker. Hearing seemingly perfect Betty swear makes the butterfly-bats go wild.

"Well, thank you." I try to double-check my repair while watching her from the corner of my eye. I secure the metal plate, plug the camera in, and look through the monitor. With a few adjustments, the familiar sight of Betty working comes into focus.

She lays out a line of provisions. Some look to be ingredients, others cleaning supplies. Her uncolored lips move as she makes notes on the paper in front of her, her hair pulled up in a smooth ponytail, partially covered with a folded bandanna. She wears cotton slacks and a loose blouse tucked into the waistband.

It's intimate, being in the same room as this version of Betty. I imagine this must be what she's like at home. I let myself pretend this is our house and I've walked in after a long day at work. She's lost in her project and doesn't notice me enter. I watch her, eager to ask about her day, what she's doing with the supplies in front of her, wishing that I'd been there for everything I'd missed. She'd look up and catch me observing, perhaps rebuke me playfully, invitingly. I'd drop my bag and remove my shoes, because it's Wednesday and she always washes the floor on Wednesdays, and I'd take her in my arms and kiss her—first her forehead, then her cheeks one at a time, and finally her inviting lips.

I'm glad you're home, she'd whisper.

And I'd respond, *I wish I'd never left.*

"Is it working?" Betty asks, looking right at me through the camera, breaking the fourth wall.

This is not fantasy Betty, this is real-life Betty who now has her hands coated in a mucusy white substance and is talking to me through the camera. I jump back, blushing. She can't possibly know what I've been thinking about, but it feels like I've been discovered.

"Uh, yeah. I think so." I shut down the camera and collect my tools as she continues to ask questions while submerging various items in the off-white goo and placing them onto a sheet of wax paper to the left of the bowl.

"Did you go to school for that, or are you a natural with mechanical things?"

"A little of both." I shrug, not wanting to sound too cocky, though it's true. Ever since I was a child I've been good with my hands, whether playing piano or fixing Ma's vacuum or helping Pop with the Oldsmobile. Ma used to say I had an eye for beauty, an ear for poetry, and a hand for fixing things. Pop didn't agree. When he was still around, he said I was a bumbling idiot, a mama's boy, a kiss up, a sissy boy. It's always been easier to believe my father's criticisms than my mother's glowing report.

"What school did you go to?"

"Beloit."

"Oh, that's fun. My friend went there."

"Yeah, it's a good school," I say, loading the tools onto a work cart on the far side of the studio.

"She got married after her first year. Got her MRS degree, as they say. She and her husband live in Boston now. I think she had a baby not too long ago."

"Fairly common," I say, wiping my greasy fingers on an already dirty terrycloth towel on the cart.

"I guess." She blows at a lock of hair that's escaped from under her headscarf. "I mean, I get why they do it. I paid my own way through school working two jobs the whole time. That's hard. Getting married looks easy compared to all that."

"So, you don't want to be a 'classy homemaker' after all?"

"I'm not saying that," she says, turning on the faucet with her elbows. "It's just—I have a family back home to take care of, and this gig pays better than being a real homemaker." She rinses her hands before aggressively rubbing a bar of soap between them, and changes the subject. "Come here. You're next."

Her hands are coated in suds as she beckons me over. I have black grease embedded in my fingernails. I'm embarrassed, but I do her bidding. It's hard not to.

Once I'm at the sink she orders me to roll up my sleeves. Obediently, I unbutton my cuffs and fold them up.

"Good. Now, in the water." She urges my hands into the running water. It's cold and I remember we decided to only run one pipe through to the stage. Just as I'm getting used to the bone-aching chill of the tap water, her hands take mine, luxuriously warm, smooth as silk, and slippery with soap. I flinch, but she keeps them in place with a light tug as she scrubs.

"They want us to use that Ivory soap on air, but Lava is the only kind that really works."

The bubbles turn dusky gray and then the color of storm clouds. It's a strange and delightful closeness after keeping a measured distance. Now I can smell the baby powder scent of her hair and notice the fine lines around her eyes, along with the way her face powder rests lightly on her skin. My heart rate rises and I become increasingly aware of each brush of her palms, her nails dragging against the fine hairs on the back of my hand, and how her hips sway into my side with each stroke.

"And now rinse." She shoves our joined limbs under the spout. The freezing water does little to cool my boiling skin and take down my exploding body heat. But then she lets go, drying her hands on a dish towel as I finish rinsing. Hands dry, she leaps up onto the counter, her legs dangling, Keds sneakers crossed and swinging.

"You're a kinda quiet guy, aren't you?" She watches me intently, making my heart race like I've walked up ten flights of stairs.

"Not really," I say, knowing I'm lying. I turn off the water and take the towel she offers me. "I like to think things through."

"It's not a bad thing," she says. "I think the world could use a few more shy guys."

Shy. I hate that label. It's been my moniker since I was a little boy who'd rather hide behind his mama's skirt than go play with the other kids. It's taken a lot of effort to muscle past those inborn anxieties that kept me silent as a child. I feel exposed by her use of the term.

"I don't know about that." I shrug, wiping down the chrome on the sink and then starting in on the linoleum.

"I do. Most men talk too much and think too little. I like that I can, I don't know, breathe a little when you're around. Like, I can hear myself think, you know?"

She says it like we spend hours together every day, which we do, but it's in a room with a dozen other people. It's not like this. To know her opinions on me and my personality sends pinpricks of electricity across my flesh and into my joints.

"And when you do have something to say, I really listen 'cause you must mean it. I like that. It's more honest, like, no BS."

"I . . . I'm glad you feel that way."

"Well, I do." She hops off the counter and takes the damp dish cloth out of my hands. "Like, how you brought up the idea for a new opening song. It's so catchy." She hums a few bars of the new theme song as she arranges the drying flowers in rows. "Where in the world did you guys find that tune?"

"I . . . I wrote it." I know I'm blushing.

"You did?" She looks at me with wide sapphire eyes like I've admitted to being the president of the United States. "It's so good. I didn't know you were musical. What instruments do you play?"

"Piano. Since I was five or six. My mom was a piano teacher."

"So she taught you?"

"Yeah, and my brother and both of my cousins."

"So you were like the von Trapp family?" she asks, putting the now-empty sticky, dirty metal bowl to the side. I place it in the sink, filling it with water and adding soap.

"No, no. Not even close." I laugh a little easier this time. "I'm the only one who really took to it. My cousins stopped taking lessons after grade school, and my brother . . ."

My brother. I don't talk about my brother, not since that call and definitely not since his funeral two months later.

"Your brother quit, too?" she asks, laughing. I turn off the water and start drying the bowl, the ache in my chest as monumental as the day I tossed dirt on his grave.

"No. He died, actually. Two years ago." I blink away tears. Crying in front of Betty is completely unacceptable.

"Oh, my gosh. I'm so sorry." She touches my arm. No butterflies this time.

"It's the way it goes sometimes." I put the bowl on the counter, my empty hands cold and damp.

"It is, but it shouldn't be. We lost my youngest sister, Eliza, when she was only four. My mom made a carrot cake with cream cheese frosting, Eliza's favorite, on her birthday for years after she died. We'd gather round and sing 'Happy Birthday' and blow out the candles for our baby sister. It was nice and all for a while, but at some point I think I came to dread it, you know? It was like I was watching the rest of us grow, which only reminded me of all she missed." She slips the loose lock of hair under her scarf, untying her apron and folding it on the counter. "Then we lost Mama, and that year we let Eliza's birthday come and go with no cake. I thought it'd feel better to let her go, to let her birthday become just another day, but I felt like I was betraying her and my mother. So, the next year, I made Eliza's carrot cake, put a candle in it, and sang 'Happy Birthday' all by myself."

"That's really sweet." Somehow, I've been leaning against the counter and watching her without a touch of anxiety. "I wonder how many cakes I'd be making by the end of it all." My father, my brother and—my mother.

"That's true. We all are gonna die one day. Can't make cakes for everyone," she jokes ruefully. "Not unless you want to gain twenty pounds."

She grows quiet and lets out a little sigh. I don't know what it means, but I want to ask. I think of touching her shoulder comfortingly, letting her know she's not alone. But as I try to will my hand forward, grappling for the right words, the silence expands between us and she finishes her arrangement.

"By the way, I know you saw me," Betty says, rinsing out a paintbrush covered in Mod Podge. She picks at the bristles with her long nails, staring at the column of water pouring over them. "At the club."

I blink, her unexpected confession hitting me like a sucker punch. I'd nearly convinced myself I'd been hallucinating that night.

"I didn't tell anyone . . ."

"I know. Thank you," she says, shaking out the brush. "I didn't know they were coming, and if Don had seen me . . ."

She looks at me with worry in her eyes.

"I know," I say empathetically. I know her job is on the line.

Without letting on why, I'd casually questioned Mark about the club, how they treated the women who worked there, and what would happen if one of the Bunnies tried to get a job here in Janesville. After winking and grunting and making all kinds of jokes, he confirmed what I already knew—the men of EBN and WQRX could happily visit the club, but there's no possible way they'd allow a woman who'd worked there to join their self-righteous and clearly hypocritical staff.

She frowns and starts to gather supplies in her arms.

"Look at me going on and on. Thanks for keeping me company and trying out the Lava soap. You made my prep fly by."

It's felt like a wonder, this conversation, this moment in time where I could talk freely and listen comfortably. I have a lot more I'd like to say, especially about her unexpected gratitude. And she's unlocked a lot of thoughts inside of me as well. I open my mouth to try and put some of them into words, when the studio door opens with a clank.

Don Hollinger's deep booming voice interrupts before I can tell her how much I've appreciated this conversation, too. He's wearing a white dress shirt with no tie, the top button undone, a cigarette in one hand and a briefcase in the other.

"Not ready yet? I gave you an extra twenty minutes. I'm starving."

Betty slings the bowl onto her hip.

"Sorry, Don. Almost done. Let me put a few things in the back."

"All right," he says with an annoyed sigh.

Hollinger's entrance is even more unexpected than Betty's earlier appearance. When we moved to a full hour show, Martha petitioned Don to release Betty from her secretarial duties. And Hollinger finally hired a new girl from the technical college.

I move from the lights of the stage area to tidy my workstation. The unavoidable clanking of tools draws Hollinger's notice.

"Tin Man! Hey! Didn't know you were here."

I give him a friendly greeting, hoping it's unfriendly enough to keep him from engaging me any further, but I'm not that lucky. I toss my Bucheimer leather bag across my body and head toward the exit. He stops me as I try to squeeze past him in the doorway.

"You working late?" he asks.

"Yeah. Camera three had a busted connection."

"You fixed it?"

"Yup. Found the part in the workshop. Patched it up."

"Damn. Didn't know you were so handy."

I shrug, wanting to leave. His compliments mean little to me. Don Hollinger knows nothing about cinematography or journalism. He's a businessman who was hired to make this station profitable. I'm sure once he succeeds or gives up, finding his task impossible, he'll move on to bigger and better things. He doesn't care about Janesville or WQRX or even EBN. As far as I can see, he's nothing more than a mercenary, a hired gun with zero loyalty and very little integrity.

"You should come out with me and Mark sometime. We've been going to Pub Cellar. It's a shithole, but the waitresses are nice, if you know what I mean."

Mark's been trying to get me to go out with them for weeks now. He insists Hollinger isn't that bad, that he's a guy's guy. They go to the YMCA together, play basketball once a week, head to the local clubs to pick up girls.

"Sure," I say, knowing I likely never will. According to Mark, getting in with the man in charge would help my career, but I can think of about a million things I'd rather do than watch Mark and Hollinger scam on girls in smoky clubs with bad music and even worse drinks.

Hollinger looks at me with a raised eyebrow like he knows I'm BS-ing him.

"What? You got a girl already or something?"

"No. I'm just not into the bar scene."

"You don't have to drink. It's one thing to live without alcohol. It's another to live without women." He winks. I snicker like I've learned to around other men, even though it makes me feel disgusting.

"I think Martha Smith would go for you, if you like that kind of girl. A little mousy for my tastes but some nice curves if you can put up with her mouth." He makes his hand holding his cigarette look like a puppet and rapidly flaps it open and closed. A flash of indignation strikes me between the shoulder blades. Martha keeps the lights on in this place. She should've left forever ago for a bigger market where she might actually be appreciated.

"Martha's a talented producer," I say protectively as Betty finally emerges from the back room. She's let her hair down and tied up her shirt, exposing a small triangle of her translucently white abdomen. She's slipped on heels, lined and colored her lips, and looks like a runway model swaying our way.

"Oh, so you do have a soft spot for her," Hollinger says, referring to Martha. "I thought so. Hey, man. To each his own. Go for it." He smacks my shoulder.

"I . . . I . . ." I'm grappling for a way to defend Martha but also put an end to his matchmaking when Betty reaches us, blushing and a little out of breath. She looks at me first, her smile familiar and welcoming, like we're now friends who keep each other's secrets.

"Look at you all prettied up. Aren't you a sight for sore eyes?" Hollinger says, crushing the nub of his cigarette into the cement floor and wrapping his arm around Betty's waist. A knife of outrage stabs through me at least ten times more intense than when he mocked Martha, and I want to tear his grubby hands off Betty like he's some guy at the Playboy Club breaking the "no touching" rule.

I expect Betty to recoil from his touch, look at me with panic and embarrassment, signaling me to save her from the lascivious boss man taking advantage of her, but she doesn't. Instead, she leans in, giggling, putting her arm on his shoulder, placing a light kiss on his cheek, which he rubs at like he's trying to remove a lipstick stain.

"Sorry, sweetie. I needed to prep for tomorrow's crafting segment, and it takes twelve hours for the flowers to dry properly . . ."

"Blah, blah, blah. You know that stuff goes right over my head. But seriously, you should use production assistants for that kind of thing. Right, Tin Man?"

I feel more like a rusted-out character than ever. My jaw is locked shut and my limbs are frozen as I begin to understand what I'm witnessing.

Don Hollinger is dating Betty Wilkens. It's a common enough thing, a man dating his secretary or at least his former secretary. And it's not uncommon for a man of power to give preferential treatment to the woman he's seducing, something special like giving her a show. I never expected it to happen with Don but especially not Betty.

"Uh-huh," I manage to grunt. Hollinger smacks me on the back as he and Betty walk away. He embraces her waist, his thumb tracing a sultry line on her bare skin. I shudder, bile rising in my throat as I recall her soft hands caressing mine as she scrubbed them, and I wonder how delicate her back, her sides, and her belly must feel under Hollinger's touch.

"You got the lights?" Hollinger asks over his shoulder. I clear my throat and steady my reply.

"Yup," I shout back, the *p* bouncing off the cinderblock walls in an eerie echo that sounds like I'm chasing them down the hall.

"Bye, Greg," Betty calls out, and I watch as she walks off with a man she's keeping secrets from and leaves behind the man she's asked to hold them.

CHAPTER 15

Charlie

Present Day

"And she wrote a book," I tell Olivia through the phone's screen, holding up the blue-and-white hardcover. *The Classy Homemaker* is in playful lettering across the front, with drawings of a perfect-looking housewife in a tidy skirt and low heels doing various chores by each line of the title. "Tina, Dino's wife, she found it in a pile of books and, God bless her, remembered that I'd asked her to set aside items with Betty's name on them."

It was basically a miracle she saved anything coming out of the house at this point. The upstairs is nearly cleared, and after a weekend off, the crew will start on the main floor, pending an inspection from the city.

"My God, that's wild," Olivia says, squinting at the cover. It's good to see her face and listen to her voice at the same time. It's been a month since I got here, and though I've seen the boys on FaceTime, with Ian looming in the background, I've had inconsistent communication with Olivia since our disagreement.

To keep the questions about my relationship with Ian at bay, I've been sharing little tidbits about my mother and the enigma of her past.

Only a picture or detail here or there until tonight. We've been on the phone for two hours already, catching up.

"I know, right?"

"I can't believe she had her own show, too. Does that mean I have to take up the family business? I'm not really up for being any kind of on-screen guru."

"You don't choose the guru life, Livy, it chooses you," I say, taking a sip out of my wineglass, more settled than I have been in weeks, maybe even years. "From what I can tell, it was this Holly Homemaker kind of a show. Like, how to be a perfect housewife kind of a thing. And the book looks like it's about that same old misogynistic stuff like 'Do your hair before your husband comes home' and 'Never, ever show any emotion other than joy at cleaning toilets and changing diapers,' and that's just the first two chapters."

"Written by your mom—who is a hoarder. That's crazy," Olivia says and then immediately covers her mouth. "Sorry. I didn't mean to call her crazy. I know it's more nuanced than that . . ."

I swallow the last bite of my dinner and smile into the phone so she knows I'm not upset. Olivia's had her own struggles with anxiety that she manages with medication and therapy, so I know she meant no harm. I'm far more worried about how she's handling all of this on top of her first year of college.

"It's OK, honey," I say and then check the clock on the microwave. It's nearly 10:00 p.m. As much as I've enjoyed our conversation, I know I've kept her too long. It's the night before spring break and she told me two hours ago about an impending deadline. "I should probably let you go, though. You said you had your project due tonight, right?"

"I almost forgot. It has to be in by midnight. Shit. Sorry. Shoot," Olivia says, checking her watch and then slapping her bedspread.

"You're fine!" I chuckle at her attempts to hide her cursing, though it doesn't really bother me at all.

"Oh, God. I feel like an idiot. I'm gonna go."

I reach for the phone, ready to sign off, when Olivia stops me. "Wait, Mom."

"Yeah?"

"Thanks for sharing all that stuff with me. It's super interesting. You never really talk about your past or anything. It's always felt, like, off limits or something."

Her comment strikes me in a strange way, like it smacked my funny bone. Olivia wants to know about my history as urgently as I'd like to know about my mother's. I've vowed to be nothing like my mother, yet I continue to discover more ways we are alike.

"You're . . . you're welcome," I say, taking a deep, wine-flavored breath in before adding, "I can keep you updated."

"I'd like that," she says, her eyes the same blue as her grandmother's.

"Sounds like a plan," I say, waving at the screen. "Now, get to work, young lady. That's an order."

"Yes, ma'am," she says with a little salute, then, breaking from her act, adds, "Love you, Mom."

We used to say it all the time when she was little, easily, no effort. Every night when she went to bed, in the morning before school, sometimes even randomly while hanging around the house. But during her teen years it became more and more rare, and even then it sounded forced, hesitant, insincere.

But not tonight. Tonight, it sounds like she means it.

"Love you, too, honey."

I drop the phone and click on the TV, refilling my glass and settling into the leather couch with my mom's book next to me. I flip through the stations, pausing at a few late-night-show monologues.

I keep flipping till I speed past HFN, where I see a familiar face. Dino. I click backward, sipping on my freshly poured glass as Dino's warm southern drawl fills the room. He's helping a family of four who have triplets on the way maximize storage options in their small three-bedroom ranch-style home. I turn down the volume until I can't make out each word he's saying but still get the calming benefits of his self-assured tone.

I pick up *The Classy Homemaker* and open it to the next chapter, bookmarked with a photograph of the view of the lake from the land where our house now stands, my father and mother holding a shovel between them. My father has a large grin on his face, and my mother wears a formfitting top and bell-bottomed jeans that accentuate her waist.

I put the photo on the armrest and start to read.

Chapter 3

D. I. D.

A Recipe for Success

As a child, I decided to prepare a fancy dinner for my family to celebrate my father's promotion. I saved my babysitting dimes for weeks leading up to the big event and went to the store to buy all the necessary ingredients from the recipe I had copied from a fancy French cookbook I found at the library. At the store, I carefully selected the ingredients and then brought them home to create the much-anticipated meal.

I placed every item into a bowl and swirled them together and then poured them into a large pan. The meal cooked into a thick, mushy paste that looked nothing like the image I remembered from the cookbook. My father pushed away his plate and my younger sister spit out her first bite, and I found myself crying on the back porch after dumping my hard-earned dinner into the pig's trough.

I had the recipe, I had the ingredients, I had the pure desire to make a meal for my family. What went wrong?

I'll tell you. When I wrote down the recipe, I only wrote down the ingredients I needed and their amounts, I didn't think to read the instructions explaining how to use them. So, instead of dipping the chicken into the egg whites and then coating them in flour to be fried in the oil, I mixed everything together at the same time with no thought to order or timing.

We've discussed having a desire to be a joyful homemaker and the reasons for taking your responsibilities as a wife and mother as seriously as your husband takes his role in the boardroom. But now it's time to get to the nitty-gritty. It's time for the "how" of housewifery. And it starts with three simple letters: D I D.

Disposition, Image, and Drive.

This chapter will cover the first step in our recipe—Disposition.

A man comes home from work to a tidy house, a beautiful dinner, and clean and respectful children, but his wife is angry, perhaps bitter about the time and effort she's put into the home while he's off at work. Does this make a happy husband? No.

Having a joyful attitude is your first step toward success in your role in the home. Do you have a headache? Take an aspirin and then move on with your day. Have you received bad news? Wipe away those tears and find a new project to put your energy into. Never, ever allow your children or your husband to know you are having a hard time of things. This is your business and your business alone. Your husband doesn't come home and tell you all the details of his workday, does he? No. And neither should you.

My God, I think, head in hand as I let my mother's written words sink in. Perfection, that's what she's talking about. An image of happy perfection. What a load of bullshit. Is this who she used to be, my Classy Homemaker mother? Her headshot certainly looks that way. But is TV homemaker Betty really who she was, or was that an act, an act supported by a show and a station that hired her to look, act, and speak a certain way? My God, I hope this isn't how I'm perceived by viewers.

I've started reading again when I hear my own voice coming from the TV. I look up and recognize the outfit I wore during a promo shoot before Christmas. It'd been a cold day in Southern Indiana and so I'd rushed to get my jacket back on between takes. My cheeks are pink and my breath puffs out with each extended vowel.

"Will the Wilsons choose to relocate to this newly constructed two-story Craftsman?"

Then, the camera cuts to Ian, standing a foot to my left with his neatly trimmed (secretly dyed) black beard, warm brown eyes, and salt-and-pepper hair, parted on the side and trimmed close in a crew cut. His broad chest pushes against his buttoned red-and-blue flannel shirt, and my heart flip-flops at his deep baritone voice.

"Or will they choose to let us help give their home a . . . second chance on . . ."

"*Second Chance Renovation*," our voices mingle together as the title card expands into the screen with details on dates and times. I reach for the remote and click the TV off.

I stare at the dark, blank screen.

I don't know how to watch the two of us now that I know what he did, that in December he was flirting with a stranger while filming with me, while kissing me, while holding me in his arms as we made love, while I snuggled into him and let his breathing lull me into a deep, blissfully ignorant sleep.

My phone buzzes. Was he watching at home right now, remembering that cold fall day when our marriage still felt like a fairy tale? I can hardly stand to look at the screen.

Cameron: Dinner? Next week?

Cameron—again. I curse Lacey every time he makes this request, not because I don't like the guy or find him creepy, but because I do like him, and I don't know how to feel about that. But why should I keep dodging him? Why shouldn't I give Cam a chance when I can't seem to get myself to put my wedding ring back on? I find every reason to leave my finger bare—because of the gloves we have to wear during cleanup or the number of times I wash my hands. But really, it's because it's safer this way. Without the ring on, I have plenty of options instead of only one where I give in and forgive Ian.

The phone is cool and heavy after the tactile experience of holding my mom's book and turning its pages. I touch the screen and type a message and hit send before I can talk myself out of it.

Charlie: How about tomorrow?

I've never been to Janesville, Wisconsin, but the more I learn about my parents, the more significant this area seems to be to their history. Cam offered to make the hour drive to Lake Geneva, but I'm happy to have a reason to visit. I suggested meeting at Ike's Diner, the one Betty brought up during my last visit, after discovering it's still open, but Cam said it closes at three on weekends.

So instead, we're meeting at an upscale spot near the Rock River for an early dinner. It's a quarter of a mile from the address on my mom's ID for WQRX, where my parents met and fell in love. As strange as it is to think of my parents falling in love—it must be true. They've stayed together all these years despite my mother's complex personality and my dad's ghostlike nature. I mean, I couldn't make it past six years with Ricky and he's a totally stable, nice guy. Although a nice guy who didn't really want a wife with a career in the public eye.

"I want a quiet life with you and Olivia, a nice little house somewhere with a little land and possibly some animals . . ."

"A farm?" I shouted, slamming my hand against the table. "Like a *Green Acres* kind of a thing?"

Ricky shushed me. I'd just finished the nighttime routine with three-year-old Olivia—bath, singing songs, and one book to get her droopy eyed enough that I could sneak out of her toddler bed and meet my husband in the dining room for "a talk." That's what he called it—a talk—but I actually knew it was THE talk, the one that would change it all.

I'd been offered a segment on *The Today Show*. We'd have to move to New York, and Ricky would have to change jobs or stay home with Olivia so I could make the 5:30 a.m. call time.

He'd put up with my dreams and my ambition when they were still aspirational in nature, but when it came to red-eye flights, days or weeks away on business trips, and half the bed bare—his tune changed. He wanted no part of it all.

What should've been the best event of my life turned into the worst since I'd left my parents' house fifteen years earlier, and my hope of giving my daughter the family I never had died on the vine. I wasn't willing to give up my career, and Ricky wasn't willing to give up his kinda-out-of-nowhere farm dream either. So, Olivia learned how to move between houses, how to pack a bag, how to be independent and flexible—how to form her life around her parents' dreams.

Maybe all parents do the same thing to their children in their own way. That's why it's comforting to think of my parents as being deeply in love because people who are in love often have tunnel vision.

It's like the time I found my dad watching a news segment about the Gulf War, helicopters crossing the screen and tears in my dad's eyes. His brother died in Vietnam, my mom explained, pulling me away from the sight of my father crying on the couch. She gave me a glass of milk and one of the cookies she'd baked back when we still had a functional kitchen, and then left me there with a coloring book while she delivered the same treat to my dad.

When she didn't come back, I snuck into the den and found the television off, a record playing softly, and my mom's head lying sweetly in his lap as he ran his fingers through her hair. My dad peeked at me through half-opened lids and placed a finger over his lips. I dashed back into the kitchen, running away from witnessing my parents' humanness living just beneath the surface of their parental varnish. They seem to love each other, deeply. And maybe if they didn't love *me* passionately I could blame it on them loving each other passionately, or at least that's the narrative I prefer. I only wish there wasn't still a little child inside of me longing to be loved in the same protective way.

Another turn and I'm crossing over a wide latte-colored river on a long bridge with arched cutouts on the cement barrier rails trailing down each side. The next right takes me into the town of Janesville. The Ace Hardware sign looks original. Driving under an arch reading

"Festival Street," I spot three more bridges to my right, two for cars and one for pedestrians.

But the most breathtaking sight of all are the large murals decorating the sides of the brick buildings, bringing life to the worn and weathered storefronts. This had once been a bustling town, but now, empty stores and several bare lots are interspersed with businesses, restaurants, and specialty shops. I find myself wanting to know the history of each and every building, to step inside and imagine who first walked their halls.

After driving across another bridge and then past a large official-looking building and a community pavilion, I pull into a spot in front of the restaurant's large plate glass window. My phone rings. I check the name.

This is a call I can't ignore.

"Hey, Alex," I say. Alex McNamara. My boss. Everyone's boss. The head of HFN, the man who greenlit *Here's Hoping*, the show that led to my romance with Ian, and then *Second Chance Renovation.* I only hear from him on the best and worst of occasions. And he's calling my personal number on a Saturday—great.

"Hi, Charlie. Hope this isn't a bad time."

Well, yes it is, Alex, but I can't really say that, can I?

"Not at all. I always have time for you," I schmooze, because what else am I supposed to do with someone who holds my whole family's livelihood in his hands. He's so rich he owns a town in Montana along with an active silver mine where half of the residents work. The man is completely used to everyone telling him yes all the time. I hate these kinds of meetings.

"Good. Good. Well, now, I've heard you've had some family things going on, and I'm not trying to pry, but Karen and I have been talking . . ." Karen Terry, head of World Window, the production company for *Second Chance Renovation.* What the hell does Karen think she knows about my family life? Though it's possible Ian went to her about my lack of communication. A stone drops in my stomach. Did the tabloids catch wind of Ian's messages or even worse—TikTok? I realize I've lost track of what Alex is saying.

". . . Dino's been doing some work for ya and we were thinking—what about a crossover episode?"

"I'm sorry," I say, my catastrophizing brain so far down a "we're getting canceled" scenario that I can hardly catch up to reality. "A—what?"

"A crossover episode with *Squeaky Clean* and *Second Chance*. Karen came up with a great proposal, and we all think you and Ian with Dino and Tina, we think that'd be amazing. Plus, the family angle and the hoarding element—that'd be a ratings bonanza right there." The rock in my stomach turns slimy, like it's been sitting in the nearby Rock River for a century.

"No." The response bursts out of me. No one says no to Alex McNamara and yet here I am—saying no. This feels awful.

Alex is silent on the other side of the phone, and I see Cam walk into the restaurant without noticing me in the car. His hair is neatly combed, his beard trimmed close to his skin, and he's wearing a light spring jacket and dark jeans, washed out at the thighs and butt. He's perfectly on time, and I wish I'd gone inside and left my phone in the car and missed this call.

"No?" he repeats when I leave the refusal hanging between us. As a professional I think a special crossover with *Squeaky Clean* and *Second Chance Renovation* would be great—I love Dino and Tina, and I love the idea of restoring a house that's been ravaged by hoarding. And no matter what happens, Ian and I will have to find a way to maintain a work life. I think we both know that. It's why this space is so necessary for me to process what I need next, what our little family needs next.

But I don't like the idea of exposing my parents to the unforgiving glare of the public eye—of exposing our relationship to the judgments and comments of fans and critics who'd like nothing more than to spend hours on discussion boards or in comment sections talking about my past, a past I've spent my whole life running from.

"I'm sorry, Alex, but I'm not comfortable with it, and I don't think my parents would sign the participant agreement. Besides, Dino's more than halfway finished, and the house—the house might need to be torn down. We won't know until we get it cleared."

"Then we do a rebuild."

"That's not our brand," I argue, sticking to business-related issues Alex's fiercely capitalistic mind can grasp rather than personal ones he's likely to brush off. "Our brand is renovation—not new construction."

"Charlie," he says my name in a deeply condescending tone, "it'd be a crossover episode. Brand matters less with a crossover. Plus, the audiences of both shows will love how relatable you are. America is tired of the perfect family. They want the slightly messed-up family. I bet we could get you on the cover of *People* again, in a heartbeat. This is gold."

Gold. As though Ian and I sharing our first failed marriages and our now blended family isn't enough vulnerability—I have to bare my greatest traumas to the world? What the hell kind of business am I in?

"I'm sorry but—no. I can't," I state firmly, anger heating my neck, making me restless. Abandoning all effort at playing nice, I collect my purse, keys, and sunglasses to signal my impatience with this conversation. There's no wiggle room in my answer, and after years of working in this industry, I know it's clear—this is a hard no, a no that could lead to attorneys on both sides if it's not respected. Would I blow up my whole career for this no? Maybe. I really might.

Alex sighs, and after an annoyed pause continues his side of the conversation like I haven't drawn a line in the sand.

"I'm having Karen get some details together so we can really talk through what this would take and then I'll circle back around. Dino is in, and I'd like to see this happen sometime next week so we don't miss any more of the cleanup. Take the rest of the weekend to think on it." He doesn't wait for my response and hangs up.

I'm left with a silent phone in my hand and a ringing in my ears as a list of every single person I need to contact to shut this down filters into my consciousness, when a knock sounds at my window.

I yelp, placing a hand over my racing heart when I see a familiar face. "Cameron Stokes, you almost gave me a heart attack," I say, rolling down the window.

"Oh, gosh, I'm sorry Charlie." He leans low enough to make eye contact. "I stepped outside to call and check on you and saw you sitting in the car. I knew I was going to freak you out if I snuck up on you. I tried not to."

"No, no. I . . . hold on, I'll get out," I say, rolling up the window and tossing my bag over my shoulder. It's not snowy anymore, a slight warm-up over the past few days melting much of the spring snow into large, murky puddles, but I'm still wearing my cheap snow boots, preferring comfort and warmth to fashion while here in Wisconsin, and they hit the asphalt with a clomp.

Cam offers his hand, which is surprisingly smooth compared to Ian's calloused palms. He helps me out of the car, nonchalantly pushing the door shut behind me so we end up face to face, inches between us. He smells good, a rich, musky cologne with a slightly sweet undertone that for half a second makes me want to lean in for another sniff.

"I thought maybe you changed your mind," he says, staring down at me. He's taller than I remember, my head only reaches his shoulder, and in the daylight his hair looks lighter, a sandy blond and curled a bit at the roots. His smile is white and polished, which should be expected for a dentist. But his eyes—his eyes look the same as I remember. Green with brown spots—eye freckles, I used to call them.

"No, no." I break eye contact, blushing as an indulgent tingle travels over my arms and legs, settling into my chest. "Not at all. My work call went long. That's all."

"Ah, yes, the infamous work call. That explains everything." His reply is lighthearted, playful, as easygoing as when I told him I couldn't go to homecoming because my mom didn't want me dating until I was sixteen. He glances at the fancy facade of the restaurant and then back at me like he's picked up on the anxiety bouncing around inside me. "You look like you could use a walk. How about a quick tour of the town? Oh, and if you don't mind eating on the go, there's a stand not too far up the street that's said to cure all work-related stress in one burger or less."

"In one burger or less?" I ask, a giggle tickling the back of my throat. A walk with Cam is exactly what I need to clear my head. "How can I resist that kind of guarantee?"

He tugs on my hand, the one I'd nearly forgotten he's still holding, leaning in the direction of the pedestrian bridge. My bare ring finger feels strange wrapped up in another man's grip, no matter how familiar he might be. I give his hand a squeeze and let go.

"Hold on one sec." I dive back into my car, locate my phone, shut it down, and place it inside the storage area under the center console just in case Alex or one of his bots tries to call me again.

"Ready?" he asks, his hands shoved into his coat pockets as though he's showing me he has no intention of rushing things.

"Ready," I say, slamming and locking the door.

"Then let me be the first to say—welcome to Janesville."

CHAPTER 16

Greg

September 5, 1970
Janesville YMCA

"She's coming to your place?" Mark asks as he wraps a towel around his waist in the YMCA locker room. "That's a date."

"It's not a date. It's work."

"Just the two of you at your apartment? That's a date." Facing the open locker, he takes off his towel and tosses it into a canvas bag, exposing his bare ass. It's not a new sight. Plenty of exhibitionism here, and Mark definitely isn't the only one.

"Two adults of different genders can be in the same apartment together and have it not be about sex."

"Whoa. You're the one making it about sex. I said 'date.'"

"My God, you're annoying," I say, tossing my towel at him once I have my boxers back in place.

"Ugh. Yuck. That touched your dick."

"You're sitting on a wooden bench in a men's locker room naked. Don't tell me you're worried about my towel."

Mark mimics a vomiting sound, which I ignore. I've taken him up on the offer to get together a few times a week, sometimes for basketball or tennis or even to swim a lap or two. Thankfully, Hollinger has only joined us twice, and both times he talked of nothing but football and work, not his girlfriend, who we all know about but don't talk about.

Betty seems to be taking the same approach. She's been joining me at Ike's more and more often lately. She doesn't talk to me about Hollinger or even much about her part-time work as a Bunny, though she does insist she's getting ready to quit. Hollinger has a key, and though she's good about finding out his schedule ahead of time, she's had a few close calls recently that've left her with an urgency to leave for good.

She said she's finding it so hard to get out because of how much the money helps her family. Now that her parents have both passed, she feels responsible for her sister and her nieces and nephew who still live in her childhood home. She speaks of her past in vagaries that zoom in and out like a camera's lenses.

"Learned most of the things I talk about on TV in my parents' house. I grew up reading books on how to eat for a week off one chicken and how to stretch a grocery budget. I taught myself to sew so I could turn my sister's skirts into pants for my brother Adam and then into a layette for little Eliza. Necessity is a harsh but precise teacher."

She sounds so wise sometimes, so experienced. Then other times I question her thought processes, mostly how she talks about Hollinger like he's some kind of Greek god who will save not only her but the world. I'm fully aware of my jealousy, but it's not like I'm trying to be with Betty. I want the best for her, and she can do better than Don Hollinger. I only wish she knew it.

Martha and Mark join us for a lot of our diner meals. Lucy calls us the Cleanup Crew—mostly because of our work on *The Classy Homemaker*, especially Betty, who gets recognized more and more often, but also because we've been known to stay late enough to close out the restaurant on a weeknight. Most of the time we don't talk about serious topics at all. Betty insists the Beatles are superior to the Rolling Stones, and Martha thinks we're both sellouts. We talk about books and laugh about old *I Love Lucy* episodes.

It's nice having this kind of camaraderie. Martha is softening to Betty, offering her feminist books like *The Feminine Mystique* and *Sexual Politics*. I think she's hoping to challenge the traditional female mores Betty leans into so often around men. And Mark is learning to keep his chauvinistic side to himself to avoid a smackdown from Martha and occasionally Betty.

Despite our closeness I haven't told a single one of them about Betty's secret, and I don't plan to. I know it'd change how they all see her. Martha would return to her self-righteous coldness, Mark wouldn't be able to stop himself from seeing her as a sex object, and who knows if either of them could keep the truth from the one person who really matters to Betty—Don Hollinger.

Tonight it's Martha, not Betty, I'm inviting into my apartment for a "totally not a date" date. Dressed in my casual jeans and white cotton T-shirt I'd worn to the gym, I run a comb through my hair and check my watch. Six thirty-five. I have less than half an hour to make it home, change, and tidy my apartment before Martha arrives. No more time for pep talks or locker-room banter.

"Gotta run, man," I say, slamming my locker door and clicking the lock. I quickly tie my shoelaces, and Mark gives me a shirtless salute.

"Good luck! And don't do that quiet-guy shit. Speak up."

"Yeah, yeah, yeah," I say, waving him off lightheartedly, heading for the swinging exit door.

"And for God's sake, if you get the chance—kiss her!" Mark shouts his last bit of advice as I break into a run. The YMCA is three blocks from my apartment, and I make it there in a few minutes, undoing all the work of my postgame shower.

Tonight is a work meeting, like I said to Mark, but it's definitely the first time I've ever had a woman in my apartment. I sprint up the stairs, get the door unlocked, and run into my room to change into my least faded slacks and a slightly wrinkled button-up shirt, then there's a knock at my front door.

I look around my bachelor pad—the sink is clear of dishes; my overgrown fern, Jerry, is leaning toward the front window like he's trying to soak up the last rays of the evening sun; and my Steinway is nestled against the wall on the opposite side of the room like it's hiding from the same light that feeds Jerry. My brown couch with orange flowers has a dented cushion where I usually sit at night to read and listen to the radio or occasionally bring out my portable television set to catch the news or a rerun of *Classy Homemaker* when it replays overnight.

It's not much, but it's tidy, and though some dust catches my eye, it's too late. I know Martha will give me a pass because not much is expected of a bachelor. That's technically why I should be in search of a wife. Then I'd have someone to look after me, the apartment—I note my rumpled shirtsleeves—my ironing.

But I'm also proud I manage myself for the most part. I don't know if it's because I gave up on the idea of a wife when I haven't even had a girlfriend yet, or if seeing Jim's fiancée cry at his funeral and then walk down the aisle with another man a few months later reminded me of how quickly life can change on you. I don't want to marry to get a maid or a cook or a babysitter. I want to marry because that person makes me happy and I make them happy. I want to marry because I can't imagine living a life without them in it.

There's a second knock. I can't stall anymore.

When the door swings open I remember I'm barefoot, which seems like an incredibly informal way to greet a guest. A delicious scent rushes in, and I realize that I haven't eaten since my egg salad sandwich and a cup of stale coffee at lunch. There on the other side stands Martha, a paper grocery bag in one arm and a cardboard box with a burnt-orange pot in the other. She wears bright blue jeans and a formfitting maroon sweater with a comb holding back one side of her curly hair. She has a splash of color on her cheeks and a clear gloss on her lips.

"I brought you some chili," she says, rushing inside like she's visited a million times before. She puts the pot on one of the burners and spills a block of cheese and a loaf of bread out of a cloth bag. "I think I burned it a little."

"My mom always said that it gives chili extra flavor," I say, even though as a kid I knew it was her way of getting us to eat our dinner after she'd been distracted teaching piano or ironing piles of clothes for Mrs. Green to help make ends meet.

"Well, God bless your mother," she says, wiping at her forehead with a friendly titter. Martha is standing in my kitchen, cheeks flushed, eyes dancing, and the intimate nature of having a woman in my apartment make my nerves rise, and a warmth comes over me.

Keep talking, Greg.

"Thank you for cooking. I haven't had a home-cooked meal in . . . forever."

"A girl's gotta eat, and I usually make chili on Saturday, so I thought I'd share. I probably should've mentioned it, though. Did you already have dinner?"

"No, no. I just got back from the gym so I'm starving. Would you like a drink?" I consider what I have to offer. Beer and a few bottles of Coke in the fridge. Something stronger in the cupboard. And always, coffee.

"You got a beer?"

"Yup!" I say, relieved. "Old Milwaukee?"

"Obviously," she says, watching me as I retrieve two cans from the top shelf in the refrigerator. I offer her a glass, but she turns it down, cracking the tab and taking a sip directly from the container. I find myself observing her again, the way she dabs the foam with the back of her hand after taking a long drink. She raises her eyebrows and cocks her head, snapping me out of it.

We both start talking at the same time.

"The chili needs to warm up . . ."

"Should we sit down . . ."

We both laugh. She lets me start again and we agree to work at the coffee table rather than the small kitchen counter. We're presenting the next season of programming to EBN's executive board and Hollinger on Tuesday when we get back from the Labor Day break. Betty submitted her ideas, Hollinger pushed a few of his, and Martha has her own strong vision for what she wants to happen in the next six months of *The Classy Homemaker*.

"I'd like to get away from this vapid shit. Like, we both know Betty, she's not a brainless blonde. Why are we making her seem orgasmic over using baking soda and vinegar to make stainless steel sparkle?"

"What would that look like?" Don Hollinger isn't eager for a feminist homemaker, no matter how liberated Betty is or becomes.

"I don't know. Something outside of cleaning and decorating. Like, we could have a segment where women can send in their poetry or other creative projects or accomplishments. And we could teach how to clear a clogged sink or . . . or how to change a tire. You know, something to help women become more independent."

I like the idea, but Martha is stepping outside of what WQRX and Hollinger want for the program. I try to pussyfoot around the issue.

"Have you talked to Betty about these concepts? Because her proposals seem more traditional in nature."

"I think she's trying to keep Mr. Hollinger and the executives happy. She can do that, but I don't want to sit around and keep playing into this 'women belong in the kitchen' kind of a thing. It's so old-fashioned."

"EBN is old-fashioned."

"And Mr. Hollinger is old-fashioned and Betty is old-fashioned. I know. So what? We shouldn't even try?"

"I don't think Betty's old-fashioned." I think of Betty dressed in her Bunny uniform, working a second job that would get her fired. Betty doesn't show all sides of herself.

"You don't like saying no to her," she says, clearly annoyed. I redden. Am I that obvious?

"It . . . it's not that . . ." I stutter.

"It *is* that. Everyone stumbles over themselves to be that girl's savior. She knows what she's doing, don't fool yourself." She points at me with her pen, and in some ways I know she's right. Betty knows she's beautiful and she knows men treat her differently as a result, but I don't think she wields her beauty as a weapon or manipulation.

It's simple. The two women have opposing viewpoints. Betty is willing to be the picture-perfect image of the ideal woman, knowing it's a facade. Martha wants to shatter the facade of perfection, proclaiming it impossible to attain. Betty is the face of the show, but Martha is the boss and I will always defer to her.

"I think we should try it," I say, leaving the Betty debate out of my response. "The creative segment thing. Call it 'Creative Corner' or something. We could interview people on the show occasionally. Reminiscent of *Janesville Presents* . . ."

She sniffs and writes something on the legal pad on her lap. "I like that. We can sandwich it in between the 'Cooking like Mom' segment and 'Homemade Solutions.' Sneak it in." She scratches at her pad one more time. "And we'll leave the oil changes for next season."

I nod and we move on to the next subject on our agenda. The conversation ebbs and flows at a very natural pace, and I find myself more comfortable speaking up as the meeting continues. Eventually, our discussion turns to a more casual tone, when the sound of bubbling chili hitting the hot grate interrupts a dialog on homemade dishwashing detergent.

Martha's green eyes bulge as she notices the light smoky haze quickly filling the apartment.

"I totally forgot about dinner!" She bolts out of her seat and into the kitchen, turns off the heat, pulls off the lid, and stirs the gurgling liquid. "My God. This might not be salvageable."

"I'm willing to risk it," I say, taking out two mugs from my cupboard. "Sorry, I only have one bowl. Will these do?"

"Only one bowl? So it looks like it's true what they say about bachelors. Do you have more than one spoon?"

"Of course. What am I, a heathen?" In truth, I only have a small collection of cutlery, but I sneak the spoons out of the drawer and

Martha doesn't seem to notice. She fills our mugs, uses a serrated knife to cut the bread into hunks, and then uses the same knife to scrape cheese from the block since my kitchen is "horribly lacking."

I put on Marion Brown's *Porto Novo*, and we lean against the counter drinking cold Coca-Cola while eating our less than gourmet dinner, the work talk on hold for the time being. She tells me about a folk concert she went to last weekend with her sister, and I tell her about going to Summerfest in Milwaukee last year. We talk about Nixon and the war and an upcoming protest at UW. She invites me along.

I don't tell her about my brother's death or about my mother's suicide or my guilt over somehow escaping the draft. I listen to her speak of grand things, change, revolution, a way out of the chaos of our present that brings a comforting buzz into my apartment.

When the record ends and our conversation lulls, I glance at the clock and realize we've lost track of time. The sun has set, and the one light in the sitting room casts a yellow glow in a semicircle that reaches only to the edge of the sofa, leaving us in the dim kitchen.

"I can take that," I say. We both reach for her empty mug, and my hand lands on her long, slender fingers. Her skin is silky, and my touch lingers. She notices but doesn't pull away. Her stare meets mine, the light from the sitting room reflecting off her eyes, giving them the look of polished glass. Her lower lip seems to pout, and I wonder if the rest of her skin is as smooth as her hand. An undeniable desire to kiss her rolls over my body like an invisible switch flipped on inside me. I want to touch her face, run my fingers down her neck, wrap my arms around her waist, and pull her into me. I'd blame the beer, but we both only had one and that was two hours ago.

She shuffles closer to me and caresses my arm, eyes on mine. I stand over her, watching her upturned face, knowing this is the moment. I can kiss her. She wants me to. My body is letting me, my mind is sitting mute.

The phone trills.

My longing is strong enough that the first ring doesn't break the spell. But as I lean toward her welcoming lips, the second ring makes her flinch, and by the third she's moved her hand from my arm.

"You should probably get that," she says, taking our dirty dishes to the sink.

The opportunity has passed, and the emotions and hormones numbing my overthinking mind are also gone. Damn it. What an idiot I am. She invited herself to my home, made me dinner, flirted and shared with me, and then basically asked me to kiss her, and I messed it up.

The phone rings again. If it's Mark I'm gonna kill him.

"Hello?" I let my irritation show a little, expecting Mark's voice in response, asking something obnoxious about my evening with Martha.

"Greg? Greg Laramie. Is that you?" It's a woman's voice, small, hard to hear.

"This is Greg." Who could be asking for me this late?

"Oh, thank God." I hold the phone closer to my ear, straining to take in her halted speech. Sounds like she's catching her breath or crying.

"I'm sorry—who is this?"

Martha raises her eyebrows. I shrug.

"It's me." She raises her voice a little, but it doesn't help.

Martha, drying her hands on a towel, stands close to me, listening in. My thoughts start to wander back to our almost kiss.

"I'm sorry. I don't know . . ." I admit. Martha shakes her head. A muffled sob comes through the line and a sniffle.

"It's me, Greg. It's Betty."

"Betty?" I blurt.

Martha repeats the name to confirm, and I nod. Her features harden at the revelation, and she steps away like she's no longer interested in the conversation.

She must think it's a normal thing, Betty calling me, especially since Martha and I talk on the phone into the wee hours of the morning several times a week. She must think this is just something I do with women.

But I doubt Martha can hear the crying from where she's standing, the fear in Betty's voice. She doesn't know what I know—something is very wrong.

I turn away from Martha and lower my voice.

"Are you all right?"

"No. Everything is wrong. I was in the VIP Room, working and . . ." She sniffs again and takes a shaky breath. "I'm stranded here. C-can you come get me?"

"Get you?"

"Yeah, can you pick me up? I need a ride."

"From, uh, from work?" I stumble over my attempt to keep her secret from Martha, who is splashing water around in the sink, washing the mugs and silverware and scrubbing where the chili bubbled over onto the range.

"I know it's a lot to ask but . . ." She pauses, and I pause too, considering the hour drive to the Playboy Club-Hotel in Lake Geneva and how in the world I'll explain all this to Martha if I say yes. I'm about to suggest she call a cab or stay the night at the hotel when she finishes her sentence. "You're the only one I trust."

The only one I trust.

My God, that phrase coming out of her mouth nearly knocks my knees out, and I feel like I'd tear through a brick wall filled with dynamite to help her. I check on Martha. She folds the washcloth, watching me with her mouth quirked up to one side. I should stay. I should finish our meeting. I should see if we can recreate the moment in the kitchen. I should take a risk, and I should kiss her.

"Greg?" Betty calls my name through the phone. "Can you help me?"

I turn away from Martha and shove the receiver against my mouth and give the answer squeezing at the back of my throat, begging to get out.

"I'll see you soon."

CHAPTER 17

Charlie

Present Day

"It looks like you're moving," Cam says as he tries to shift the boxes in the trunk of my car into a Tetris-like pattern. We need to make space for three more large containers at his feet labeled "Hedberg Public Library" and the black faux-leather-covered rectangular case waiting on the sidewalk with a barcode on one side and library stickers on the other.

"Hoarding must run in the family." I try to make a joke of the collection of memorabilia I've accumulated in the back of my car. I could easily bring them into my rental house—there's a whole second bedroom I've barely even examined—but something about keeping them in my car makes them seem like a puzzle I'm on the verge of finishing.

"This whole thing blows my mind. It's like you're getting to know your mom before she became your mom, it's like . . . like time travel–level stuff," Cam says, finding room for one more box and slipping it into place.

The sun is setting on the other side of the Rock River. We stopped at the Janesville library after I'd spilled every single detail of my low-key investigation during our walk.

"It's not a foolproof method," I admit, stacking an additional box on two others in the back seat. "I've been sitting with Betty playing cards and then *bam*, my mom calls me Lottie and tells me my nails are too long or something. Or accuses me of putting her in 'this place,' or in the worst of times, she thinks I'm a kidnapper holding her prisoner."

"Not painless but you're still making the most out of a difficult situation, maybe?"

"You are one 'glass is half full' SOB, Dr. Stokes," I say, stepping back to assess my completely stuffed vehicle and shaking my head. "I took too many canisters, what do you think?"

"No way. They would've let you take the whole library if you asked them. I don't think they let just anyone stick around after closing. Being famous has some perks."

He'd admitted at the beginning of our date, or whatever the hell this is, that he'd only recently found out about my television persona but still claims he's never seen an actual episode of *Second Chance Renovation*. I'm sure he has plenty of questions since the whole focus of the show is my relationship with my cohost/husband, but he didn't push after I told him Ian and I are separated. I really like that about Cam—he doesn't push me, which is exactly the energy I needed after the call with CEO asshole Alex.

He doesn't push, but he does encourage. Like, when I brought out my mom's book at dinner, it was Cam who questioned how much of it was written by my mother and how much came from the perspective of the trademarked Classy Homemaker. He pointed out that by the time I came around, we weren't a traditional home, with all Mom's collections, nor did we have a traditional family structure, with Mom calling the shots more than my dad. And in my head I had to admit he might be right.

Then it was Cam's idea to walk a few yards away to visit the library and search for archived copies of my mother's show. *The Classy Homemaker* ran from 1969 to 1974 on WQRX, ending four years before I was born. We found five years' worth of episodes available as kinescopes on 16 mm film. Well, not all five years' worth. The librarian explained that the collection wasn't complete due to some water damage ruining nearly half of it, but once she started showing us all the remaining metal film tins, it didn't seem like a huge loss. And though I'm getting damn good at taking care of myself and others, I like having Cam with me on this leg of my investigation.

The setting sun has turned the world to pink and orange, the sky filled with creamsicle-colored pulled taffy clouds, and inviting an aching chill that cuts through my light leather jacket. I fight off a shiver, but Cam seems to pick up on my discomfort.

"That's it. I'm calling an audible. The rest of these are going in my car. I'll follow you back and drop them at your place. Then you'll be free of me, I swear," he says, stacking the last three boxes and carrying them to the rear of his SUV.

"That's two hours round trip. I can't ask you to do that. I can rearrange some things . . ." He slams the rear door before I can finish my protest. Clapping his hands together like he's dusting them off, he places them lightly on my shoulders, the last few sunrays illuminating the golds and greens in his eyes so the tiny brown flecks embedded in his iris stand out.

"You're not asking me to do it—I'm offering." He brushes a strand of hair from my forehead, his fingertips somehow blazing hot in the rapidly chilling evening air. I breathe in his natural scent still discernible beneath his fading cologne and shiver again, this time for an entirely different reason.

"All right, if you insist."

"I insist," he says, running his hands down my arms, warming my frozen fingers with his fiery ones. I linger there, indulging in the electric current running into my body from his skin. I break our connection, reaching into my jacket pocket for my keys.

"I'm staying on Center Street. Across from Josh Dunleavy's house."

"Got it," he says, watching me walk away, then calling after me, "Drive safely."

I volley the sentiment and climb into my car, grateful for the solitude but also missing him almost immediately. I flick on the radio, crack the windows to help with the mildewy scent invading the car's interior, and intentionally leave my phone turned off and stowed away, hiding from all my future problems a little bit longer.

I pull into my rental's driveway almost exactly an hour later, my skin cool and fresh from the breeze, the tip of my nose numb. Cam parks at the curb. We meet on the cement walkway that leads to the front door, just outside the half circle of yellow porch light.

"My God, I haven't been out this way in years. I'm having flashbacks," Cam says, examining the Cape Cod–style house across the street that used to belong to his best friend, Josh. "Remember the huge oak out back? The tree house?"

"The one that got struck by lightning?" It'd been the biggest shock of our freshman year. Sparks from the blaze blew onto the roof of Josh's house and burned enough of it to make the family homeless for the next six months. The town held bake sales and clothing drives to help the Dunleavy family get back on their feet.

"Not struck by lightning, actually. You wouldn't know that, though. It came out after you left that Josh was smoking cigarettes in the tree house. He caused the fire. Got probation or something like that. The town kinda turned on the whole family after that, and they moved to Illinois."

"I had no idea. That's wild." Hearing Josh's sad story, I think about how people must tell my family's tragic tale. *The mom is psycho. CPS took that poor girl away. Never saw her again. Someone should do something about that house, though. It's an eyesore.* "Did you keep in touch with him?"

"Yeah. He's an electrical engineer now, three kids." Cam chuckles, still staring at the perfectly rebuilt house.

"Bet they don't know about his run-in with the law." I think of all the stories from my formative years I've kept from Olivia, giving her the edited version of my childhood. It's like those photo filters she likes to play around with that can erase wrinkles, blemishes, and dark circles or even raise cheekbones and sharpen jawlines.

"That's a parent's prerogative," he says, his gaze running up and down my face like he's scanning it into memory or updating an old one. "Did you ever tell your daughter about . . ."

He doesn't finish but I can tell he wants to ask if I've ever talked about him, about my first love, about the boy who kissed me with his eyes closed, who left me flowers in my backyard on the shore path so my parents wouldn't see them, who I still dreamed of for years after leaving this town.

"No, I kinda left all this behind me." I motion to the town, but I think we both know it includes him. I've always felt justified in cutting off the dead limb of my childhood, my parents, my hometown, and burying it in a shallow grave I avoid at all costs. But the past month has unearthed the unmourned remains, and I'm often the one holding the shovel.

"Until now," he reminds me, holding up a finger and sliding his feet a few inches closer, causing a soft whooshing sound in my ears. The unreleased electricity from our connection in Janesville tingles at the tips of my toes and fingers.

"Until now," I repeat.

Cam touches my cheek and then digs his fingers into the hair at the nape of my neck, sending a tremor down my spine. If I don't move, if I keep staring up into his eyes and letting the loaded silence expand between us—he's going to kiss me. If he kisses me, this is a date. If I kiss him back, I'm dating a man that isn't my husband. If I'm dating someone other than Ian, does that mean my marriage is over?

I inhale sharply. His eyes fly open and he's about to speak when a bluish-white beam of light cuts through our bubble of reminiscence, making us blink. A car pulls halfway into the space behind my rented

Audi. I expect it to back up immediately, likely a tourist realizing their mistake while looking for their own vacation rental, but instead the engine clicks off and the sound of two doors opening and slamming follows.

Cam angles his body toward the intruders as though he might need to protect my honor, which is totally endearing.

"Can we help you?" he asks, the blinding lights on the dark SUV making silhouettes of the two approaching figures. The beep of the car's security system engaging is immediately followed by the headlights going dark. It takes a second to clear the spots from my eyes, but I soon recognize the voice that calls out from the darkness.

"Mom!!!" Olivia breaks into the porch light's circumference at full speed, slamming into my body like she's trying to merge our molecules. She hugs me more aggressively than she has since reaching puberty.

"Olivia," I gasp once I catch my breath, dazed from the impact, confused to find my child suddenly standing in front of me in a town I've intentionally shielded her from for her entire life. "How . . . where . . . why?" I stutter, when from behind my daughter, the second figure comes into focus.

"Hi, Charlie."

It's Ian, hands in the pockets of his green Columbia jacket, wearing a canvas burnt-orange cap with a frayed bill, his dark hair curling up around the edges by his ears. His beard is a bit longer than I'm used to, and dark circles are clearly visible under his brown eyes. It feels like every organ inside of my body flips at the same time, reminding me this is the man I love and the resulting nausea reminding me he's also the man who hurt me. And now he's here, standing in front of me.

"Don't be mad at Ian. It was my idea," Olivia says. "I told him I was coming and begged him to join me."

"She's very convincing." Ian smiles his heartthrob TV smile but with a touch of a hard edge, eyes darting between me and Cam, who I'd nearly forgotten was standing next to me. "I'm sorry, we haven't met," he says directly to Cam, who's no longer in his defensive position.

"Oh, this is Cameron Stokes. My . . ." I search for the right description and decide to be as general as possible. "We grew up together. This is my daughter, Olivia, and . . ."

"I'm Ian, Charlie's husband. Nice to meet you," Ian says, shaking Cam's hand, pumping once before dropping it and folding his arms across his chest, his tungsten wedding ring with redwood inlay standing out on his left ring finger as a stronger statement of our union than his self-introduction. Cam makes some generic, friendly greetings as my head spins, recalibrating my plans for the night, week, month.

Cam touches my elbow, drawing Ian's gaze.

"I should go," he says with a stiff grin that looks more like a grimace. "I'll call you later."

I'm about to apologize and thank him for dinner and a beautiful evening when he walks off without waiting for my response. All three of us watch as he gets in the car and pulls away, the Wisconsin license plate receding as he turns onto the main road.

"I'll get your bags," Ian says to Olivia, the stormy heaviness hanging over him fading a bit with Cam's departure.

"Seriously, Mom, don't be mad," Olivia says as Ian wrestles her luggage from the trunk and I unlock the deadbolt with the code from the property manager.

"I'm not mad, I'm just surprised. I wish I'd known you were coming."

"I tried calling you from the airport, but your phone was off. Besides, if I'd told you any earlier, you wouldn't have let me come."

"I told you we could go to Cabo. Why come here rather than the beach?"

"I've already been to Cabo. I've never been here. I want to know about this stuff, Mom. I want to know where you came from."

Where you came from. That phrase hits me as we cross into the dark living room just like it did when she brought up her interest in our call last night. That's exactly what I'm doing digging through my parents' house and with my visit to Janesville and my trips to Shore Path to talk to Betty. I don't know where I came from, and as a result, Olivia is missing a piece of her history, too.

"You sure you won't stay? We have snacks," Olivia asks Ian as he drops her luggage by the door, holding up a bag of cheddar popcorn she found in one of my cabinets.

I add a half-hearted offer for him to stay on the couch and am relieved when he turns it down.

"Tempting but I'm wiped. I'll let you two have some girl time." He reaches for the doorknob, assuring us both he has accommodations in town. Standing on the welcome mat, something in the kitchen catches his eye, and he shakes his head. I follow his stare and see my sparkling three-carat solitaire and white gold band blinking back at me from the island counter.

Compassion rises inside me, thinking what it must've looked like seeing me and Cam on the porch, how excruciating it is to sense you're losing the person you love.

Then I remember—Ian is the reason I'm so intimately acquainted with that sensation. This isn't the same. I'm not sneaking around behind his back. We are separated. He knows that.

My empathy dial clicks back a few levels.

"Hey," I call out as he opens the door. "Thanks for bringing her."

"Bringing me?" Olivia chimes in. "Remember? I brought him." She tosses a kernel in her mouth, talking as she chews.

"More like a willing hostage," he says, still avoiding eye contact. I've never seen Ian so jittery, anxious, lost. "Good night, sweetheart," he says to Olivia as he heads out. And when his headlights disappear from the front window, I turn to my daughter, suddenly realizing her motivation for this surprise visit.

"Olivia Grace. What are you up to?"

"What? Who, me?" she asks with an exaggerated air of innocence, licking her cheddar-coated fingers. "I don't know what you're talking about."

"Olivia," I scold, an accusation tickling the tip of my tongue, "I know what you're doing."

As a little girl, Olivia was obsessed with the 1961 Hayley Mills classic, *The Parent Trap*. I considered it a phase, and eventually, she grew out of it when her father and I both remarried other people.

We watched the film a few years back with the twins for nostalgic fun and to see if it'd held up over the years. When the boys got bored, Olivia and I snuggled up just the two of us, hating Vicky, the evil stepmother wannabe. We sang along with the random musical number and laughed at the psychotic lengths the twins go to to reunite their parents.

"Why did you ever like this movie? Those girls are sociopaths."

Olivia laughed, "I don't know. Maybe it's a child-of-divorce thing."

"I knew it. You wanted to *Parent Trap* me and your dad, didn't you?"

"At first," she admitted. "But then I realized things were different for me."

"Different how?"

"Different 'cause you and Dad married nice people. Dad's happy with Natalie and you're happy with Ian. Now they're part of my family, too."

I remember fighting through my emotions at her stunningly mature perspective—we are a family and that family is worth preserving.

Was worth preserving, I think, watching Olivia staring at the picture of her grandmother in her wedding dress that still hangs on the fridge. Maybe still is. But I don't know, yet. I can't know, yet. The last thing I need is some little plan inspired by a Disney movie.

"Don't try to *Parent Trap* me and Ian." I say the ridiculous phrase firmly. "I have my reasons." She doesn't know the whole story, and I'd rather let her think I'm a coldhearted bitch than let her read those Instagram messages.

"Ew. It's not that deep, Mom," she says, rolling her eyes and opening the refrigerator to search for more snacks. I sense a whole vault of previously unreleased animosity loaded into how she says "Mom," letting me know it absolutely is that deep. It's probably so deep that it's a part of her foundation, and if I push too hard or dig in unthinkingly, it could crack, and our connection could crumble.

So, I drop the topic of Ian and ask about school instead. Eventually, I end up sharing some of the clues I'd collected from my parents' house. Olivia reads long segments of *The Classy Homemaker* out loud and does a Google image search on the ribbonlike name tag I'd found. The internet agrees it came from a Playboy Club, which by 3:00 a.m. makes both of us fall into a giggle fit.

After dozing on the couch for a few hours, she wakes me up with Ian on speaker, asking him to meet us at my parents' house. She's doing it again, the *Parent Trap* plan. Grumbling, I turn over and cover my head with a knit throw blanket. Olivia is letting me in more than she has in years. I know what it's like to go through adulthood without my mother. The taste of connection I've gotten with Betty has made me crave a healthy connection with Olivia even more. How can I say no without being a total hypocrite?

"Fine," I give in. "Tell him to bring coffee."

CHAPTER 18

Greg

September 5, 1970
Playboy Club-Hotel
Lake Geneva, Wisconsin

The road to the Playboy Club-Hotel is well lit compared to the pitch-black Highway 50. I follow the winding route through a mile of manicured lawns and finally approach long, streamlined buildings with roughcast stone walls.

My blood pressure has been at an all-time high since I hung up the phone with Betty, and I have a pounding headache. Though Martha didn't know the specifics of Betty's call, she did know I ended our evening to help the "damsel in distress," as she called her.

"So, I take it you're leaving," she said as soon as I rested the phone in the cradle.

"Betty is having car problems and needs a hand." I distilled the truth down to one statement, editing out the less convenient details.

"Are you a car specialist?" she asked, placing her chili pot back in the cardboard box she'd brought it in.

"No. I . . . I think she needs a ride."

"And you own a taxicab?" She asked this snarky question while shoving her folders and notepad into her workbag.

"No. But . . ."

"But she needs you, so you run over and help her. Like I said earlier."

"I mean, I'd help anyone who was stranded," I said, knowing it was an almost truth rather than a total one.

"We were working, Greg. Sure, we stopped for dinner and . . ." She faltered, perhaps remembering the very non-work-like experience we'd had together. "And some conversation, but this was supposed to be a work meeting."

"I'm sorry. She sounded desperate," I said, stuck between two bad decisions.

If I left, I'd upset Martha. If I stayed, I'd abandon Betty, which seemed like the worst of the two options, especially since I'd already agreed to get her. It's not like I could call the front desk and ask them to give her a message behind building four next to the dumpster.

"A woman like Betty is never desperate for help. She could snap her fingers and ten men would come to the aid of a damsel in distress."

"It's not so simple," I said, grabbing my keys and checking for my wallet in my back pocket. Martha picked up her belongings while trying to balance the cardboard box with the stew pot inside on her hip. "Can I help you carry something?"

"No. Unlike some women, I can manage this myself, thanks."

I opened the door, and she rushed past as I muttered a thank-you for dinner. I caught up with her at the bottom of the stairs, where she was struggling to open the door, her arms full.

"I got it," I said, leaning past her to turn the knob, bringing us face-to-face in a tight spot with only the box between us.

"I'll call you tomorrow to finish up the proposal so we're ready for the meeting," she said, the fury in her eyes calming a bit, her forehead smoothing.

"Call anytime," I said, briefly wishing I hadn't answered my phone, wondering if Betty actually had an army of men she could call for help.

And then, for the shortest instant, I wished I'd never seen Betty's red Corvette parked down the street from Ike's, that she'd remembered her keys and hadn't gotten the job at WQRX. "I really am sorry."

Martha adjusted the box and studied my face.

"You're too nice, Greg Laramie," she finally said with a sigh. "It's gonna get you in trouble one of these days."

Then Martha turned on her heels and stormed off toward her car.

Too nice.

The phrase has been lumbering through my mind like a refrigerated truck speeding down Highway 12 since she said it. The closer I get to my destination, the more I worry she might be right.

Is this what Betty does? Find ways to convince men to take care of her, manipulate them with her sex appeal and the touch of innocence that follows her around like a spotlight? It's half past eleven. Martha should be home safe by now, not that I have any way of knowing. She's probably up and working on our proposal—all alone.

My life is quickly turning ridiculous. There are real issues in this world, and I should know—they destroyed my family. And here I am on a Saturday night running away from one woman while searching dark corners of a hotel parking lot for another one.

As I turn down the last lane of parked cars behind building four, my headlights rest on Betty's red Corvette. I shift into park and get out to see if perhaps she's waiting inside her vehicle, when something crunches under the sole of my shoe. I squint at the ground and in the dim light make out sparkling clusters of shattered glass.

"What in the world?" The hairs on my arm stand up as I creep close enough to the automobile to see through the windows, but I quickly realize there's no glass. Every window has been demolished, as though the car was used as target practice. I check the parked vehicles to the left and right, but they appear untouched.

"Betty!" I call out in a hushed whisper. There's no response.

I dig in my pockets for my keys, remembering the Swiss Army knife I'm carrying. Unfolding the one-inch blade, I lean into the driver's side through the shattered window, knife clutched in my right hand, and call her name again.

"Betty? Are you in here?"

There's nothing inside other than glass and debris. I carefully pull myself back out, avoiding the jagged edges, and examine the rest of the car. The door is pocked with dents, and the paint is gouged so deeply that the metal underneath is visible. What the hell happened here?

"Greg?" I hear my name. It's the same small, wobbly voice from the phone an hour ago asking me for help.

"Betty?" I narrow my eyes in the darkness, trying to see where her voice is coming from.

"Over here." A slight form moves toward me from behind the dumpster at the end of the line of parked cars. At first, I can't make out more than a pile of blond hair twisted on her head, but as she crosses through my high beams, her image comes into focus.

It's Betty and she's been crying.

She wears jeans, a white blouse, and a sweater around her shoulders that hangs askew like it's trying to escape. She's shaking.

"My God, what happened?" I fold up my less-than-helpful knife and leap over the glass-littered terrain to meet her at the front of my car. The headlights shine in her eyes. I examine her closely, like a mother checking a toddler for injury after a tumble. She appears unharmed, a little scratch at her cheek and some blood under her nails.

"I'm fine. I'm fine," she says, trembling as though she's caught a chill. "Though it doesn't look like my car is doing so great."

She takes a step forward and stumbles, and I notice she's only wearing one shoe; her other foot is bare and covered in crimson scratches.

"Don't move," I say. "There's glass everywhere." Working off an instinct I didn't know I had, I dip low, fling her arm around my neck, and steady her with a hand around her waist. "Lean on me."

"Thank you," she says, hopping through the battlefield on her one covered foot.

She smells of perfume and sweat and the faint odor of whiskey and feels frail, so easily breakable, like one false move could snap her in half. A shocking, boiling, bubbling, furious sensation builds inside me. What kind of selfish animal did this to her?

Anger is not an emotion I let inside often, not something I allow to overtake me after a childhood of dodging my father's indiscriminate ire. But this throbbing, vengeful rage refuses to relent, and by the time I get both of us into the car, I'm grasping at the steering wheel like I might fall out if I let go. My breathing is ragged, and the rush of perspiration on my forehead drips down my face.

"Where's the security office? We need to report this." I start driving toward the main building. Someone there will be able to help.

"No. We can't," she says, sitting up on the edge of the cracked vinyl, her macramé bag slipping off her lap.

"They'll call the cops. There's plenty of security in the club. No way they let this kind of thing happen to their employees." The curved drive of the main entrance is one turn away. I'll leave Betty in the car. I'll go in and get a security guard or tell them to call the police. I won't let my nerves or anxiety get in the way. I'll be a man, "for once," as my pop used to say.

"No. Don't. Please." She grabs the steering wheel as I'm about to make the turn, and I have to step on the brake to keep from running off the road onto a manicured lawn. Her pupils are dilated in fear. "I don't work here anymore."

"Oh," I say, looking her over again. Her hair is pinned up, styled and sprayed, and the blue eyeshadow, full red lips, and dark liner look similar to when I first saw her here at the VIP Room. "I'm sure they'd still call the police. Your car, that's not OK. Unless—" I consider a nefarious possibility. "Did they do this?"

I've heard gossip, dark rumors of Playboy's association with the Mafia. This seems like something from the whispered stories of mob violence in the big city, intimidation or retaliation, but how could a small-town girl like Betty be involved in such a thing?

"Heavens, no." She looks at me like I said Jesus Christ himself was the president of the United States. Then, she stares at the front doors of the lobby; the yellow lights lining the lane reflect off the moisture in her eyes like summer fireflies. "It's a long story. I just want to go home." She blinks away the rising tears and forces a smile. "Please."

I long to rush into that building, kick through the glass doors, and call in the cavalry. I wish I could build a wall around her so nothing like this can ever happen again. I want to fix it for now and forever, not run away like a coward with my tail between my legs. I want to fight; I want to dig my nails into my palms as I curl up a fist and let it fly against whoever stands in my way. But the one person I don't want to fight is *her*. And she's asking me to put her wants in front of my own, to let her make the decision about how to navigate this situation. And maybe the thing that Martha said about Betty earlier tonight is true—I don't know how to say no to her.

"Of course." I swerve back onto the main road, holding my tongue.

Betty clicks on the radio and flips through static until she finds a station playing "You Can't Always Get What You Want." She shifts in the seat over and over again, and by the time we get to 50, she seems to have found a position that works, with her forehead pressed against the window, arm propped on the armrest, and the seat belt strap flapping behind her, unused. I accelerate, watching the lines in the road, trying not to choke on my swallowed anger.

CHAPTER 19

Charlie

Present Day

"That was built in the thirties. Big names performed there in the upstairs hall, like Eartha Kitt and Frank Sinatra. Mail is delivered by boat during the summer to all the lake houses. And that's the public beach." I point to the large octagonal brick boathouse, the Riviera, and the strip of sandy beach to the right of it, digging into the part of my brain that holds all the bits of information I learned in my years of school trips and history reports.

Olivia asked if we could take the long way through town as we drive over to the paused worksite, where Ian is meeting us and Olivia will meet her grandfather for the first time. My eyes are scratchy from too little sleep after a long night of catching up, and I'm taking my time with the tour, avoiding what comes next.

"And that's the store," I say on our final loop through town before heading to the house. I point to the two-story red building a block off Main Street. "My parents bought it before I was born."

"Was it always an antique store?"

"I'm not sure," I say, turning around in the parking lot. "The previous owners also ran it as an antique shop. It was once just a house, I think."

I try to run through the very few memories of my father's business. The two-story house is one of the handful of antique shops in town, my father acquiring pieces through estate sales, auctions, and private sales all over the Midwest. It always seemed like he brought in more supply than the demand of our small town, but now that I've been in the home renovation circuit for some time, I know better.

Lake Geneva is not only a summer playground for middle-class Midwesterners, but also flush with well-to-do families who own the hundreds of mansions that line the shore of the lake. Not to mention the other nearby communities with residents who have money to spend on a piece of furniture with a story behind it. With wealthy clients, once money isn't a concern, it's the uniqueness of an item that gives it appeal, and my father sells rare, unique treasures.

"And that was my elementary school." I point to a brick building surrounded by fenced fields. "It was so close to the store, I'd sometimes walk there during lunch and eat my peanut butter sandwich at my dad's desk."

Olivia leans against the window, taking in the novelty, unaware of how many difficult memories these buildings evoke.

Dad's shop, though cluttered in its own way, was a haven for both me and my dad. I'd do my homework in the upstairs storage room on a velvet chaise lounge my father always intended to have reupholstered. Even with the springs poking at my bony legs through the thin fabric, it was more comfortable than my own room, which by third grade my mother had started to fill with boxes.

When I was removed from my parents' house, I imagined my dad moving us into his shop, me and him, clearing a few of the rooms so we could have a place to sleep. It seemed so easy to me, choosing to keep me instead of my mom and her belongings. And no matter how many books, photographs, or name tags I find in my mother's hoard, I don't think I'll ever fully understand his perspective.

"I can't believe you grew up here. It's so . . . sweet."

"It's a beautiful town," I acknowledge wistfully, attempting to view it all through my daughter's sheltered eyes, which grows more difficult the closer we get to the house on Lake Shore Drive.

When we finally arrive, Ian is standing in the driveway, holding two large disposable coffee cups, wearing the same coat and jeans combo as last night but with a different-colored flannel and a stocking hat instead of the baseball cap.

It's no wonder this man is on television. He's so ruggedly handsome, even with his somewhat obvious spray tan and bleached white teeth, that it's hard to blame the women in his Ian's Angels fan club. But I notice one difference between today's Ian and TV Ian—this Ian looks like he hasn't slept in a month, and his shoulders slump like they're carrying a crushing burden.

"Hey," I say to Ian when Olivia and I join him on the salted cement driveway. He holds out the drinks.

"Americano with oat milk and two pumps of hazelnut. And for you—a chai tea latte." I take his offering in my gloved hands. I still haven't put my ring back on.

"This looks like a"—he assesses the scene before him—"big project."

"That's an understatement. We've already removed six dumpsters full of junk."

"Six?" Olivia chokes slightly on her chai.

"And we still have the main floor and the basement to go. Not to mention the yard."

"Wow," Ian says, though it seems like what he's really saying is *You're bonkers to take this on.*

"Can we go inside?" Olivia asks, rising on her toes like she's trying to see through one of the many blocked windows.

"I don't know. It's a little sketchy in there." A familiar anxiety scratches at my throat, the same sort I felt as a kid when one of my friends would ask to come over. I don't want Olivia to see the house this way, to get a close-up of what my mother's dysfunction looks like, what my childhood looked like. Not yet at least. "I've been promised the inspector will be here by Monday morning, first thing. Then Dino will be back to help with the next phase."

I leave out Alex's offer for the crossover episode. I still need to check in with Ian about Alex's proposal and make sure we're both giving a firm no.

"And your dad, he still sleeps in there?" Ian asks, bewildered. "If it's that bad—no one should live here."

"He won't leave," I explain, making a tsking sound. I try every single day to convince my father to leave the house, spend a night in my spare bedroom, or let me check him into one of the hundreds of available hotel rooms in town, but he refuses every offer.

"I'm fine right here. I don't need much," he insists.

"I think he's afraid that if he leaves even for one night that we won't let him back in again." It's like he's a sentinel sworn to stand guard over my mother's belongings, the ones she remembers and even the ones she doesn't.

The screen door hinges squeak, announcing my father's arrival.

"Is that him?" Olivia bounces on her toes again in nervous excitement. I never intended to introduce my parents to anyone in my family, and the only reason it's happening now is because of Olivia's insistence and Ian's assistance. I'm annoyed but resigned.

"Hi, Dad," I say as he reaches the driveway. He looks anxious, picking at a loose thread on his denim belt loop. He's wearing one of his threadbare flannel shirts with an off-white T-shirt showing through the V of his unbuttoned collar.

"Hello, hello," he says, nodding in my direction and then acknowledging Ian, who I know he's seen by my side on TV. Ian shakes his hand, and I introduce them to one another using the terms *husband* and *father* even though neither feel completely accurate.

"And this is Olivia," I say, gesturing to his granddaughter but leaving out the unearned moniker this time. Olivia greets him graciously but doesn't reach out for any physical connection, which comes as a relief for some reason. He asks her a few general small-talk questions, and she answers warmly. Ian and I flank her on each side, and when their conversation comes to an end, Ian breaks the uncomfortable lull with an unexpected offer.

"Greg, would you mind if I came in and took a look at the house? I'd like to get your input on a few details so we can start drawing up plans for after the cleanup."

We. The word is so misleading. It makes it sound like I've agreed to his participation in the project, though I never asked for his help. I take a burning gulp from my coffee, and my dad looks at me for my guidance.

This is a massive undertaking, one I can't do alone. I brought on Dino and Tina and their whole crew, but the house needs more than cleaning. It needs restoration, and no one does that better than Ian. It'd be selfish to reject his offer out of spite.

"Ian's the best at what he does," I say plainly and honestly.

"If Lottie trusts you, I trust you." Greg claps and the dull-gold band on his left hand glints in the morning light.

"Sounds great. Should we get started now?" Ian asks, rubbing his hands together and finally meeting my eyes.

Unease fills my midsection. Ian will see the house. He'll see part of me that very few people have witnessed firsthand. Ian already knows so many parts of me intimately—he knows about the birthmark on my ribs, hidden by my right breast; he knows how to nibble at my ear as we make love to make me gasp; he knows how to tangle his fingers up into the hair at the base of my skull to calm my anxiety. That closeness used to make me feel safe, but now it makes me feel vulnerable.

"Will you girls be joining us?" Greg asks timidly, like he's also reluctant to let Olivia inside the house in its present state.

"Probably not. I'm thinking of taking Olivia to lunch at Lake Aire's."

"That's your mother's favorite," he reminds me, resurfacing memories of when I was younger and my mother would dress up and go out with us for dinner, her lipliner perfect, shoes nicely polished, looking like one of the rich housewives summering on the lake. I loved those dinners where we looked like a normal family.

"We could bring her lunch," Olivia suggests, and before I can rescind the offer, my father piles on.

"I think she'd love that. I can call the nurses' station and let them know, if you like."

"Well, I don't know—" I start to say, but Olivia overrides my protest. "Great!"

I don't want to fight, not in front of my dad, not in the same spot my mom and I had our last argument before our family fell apart, so I let him step away to make the call.

Olivia holds out a trembling hand for the car keys. "I'm going to wait in the car. I'm freezing."

"Of course. Warm up the car. I'll be there in a second." I pass her the keys and she hugs Ian, waving to her new grandfather cheerfully. Olivia is a friendly girl, but she's never been this friendly. I'm watching her navigate down the slippery driveway with suspicion when Ian steps close.

"Hey there," he says, his voice deep and gravelly in that sexy morning way I've always found irresistible. I clutch my coffee to my chest as though it can protect me from his innate charm.

"Hi."

"You OK with this?" I think he means am I OK with him going in the house, but I take the opportunity to share my thoughts about the whole surprise-visit situation.

"I really wish you'd given me a heads-up."

"I know but . . ." He shrugs and runs a hand over his beard. "Olivia thought you'd shut the whole thing down."

"And I probably would've. Since when do we let the monkeys run the circus?" We always laugh about how our life is like a three-ring circus with too many sideshows to count. Come see the incredible joined-at-the-hip couple who juggle meals, chores, TV shoots, and their relationship seamlessly; watch breathlessly as they traverse the dangerous tightrope of work, life, and family over a pit of sharks.

But what happens when the woman on the flying trapeze loses her grip and falls with no net?

"I know, but—" His Adam's apple bounces up and down, and I pick at the lid of my drink. "I wanted to see you, too," he says as he grips my forearm, turning me gently.

"I told you. I'm not ready." My eyelids quiver and I breathe in the scent of my coffee in an effort to keep calm.

"I'll do anything to make it better. What can I do? Please . . ."

The anguish in his voice infuriated me the night I discovered the messages, but something has changed, because now it doesn't seem like manipulation.

I let my gaze rise to meet his. The dark circles under his eyes are intensified by the redness of his lower lids, and I think about the last time he looked this way, when I had a devastating ectopic pregnancy in our first year of marriage, our one and only attempt at having a child together, something we'd wanted desperately. But that tragedy wasn't something either of us chose or made happen out of sneakiness or ego or lust.

"That's the problem, Ian. I don't know if you *can* make it better."

He takes in a long, unsteady breath. He's mad. Ian rarely loses his temper, but I know his tells. Who is he mad at? Me for not forgiving him instantly or himself for putting us in this situation? I don't know and I'm not up for asking. I want what I came to Lake Geneva to get—space.

I change the subject.

"Thanks for offering to help my dad. Maybe you can talk some sense into him."

He lets out a long breath like he's reluctant to drop the topic of possible reconciliation and then looks over his shoulder at the house. My dad is making his way back to where we're standing.

Ian presses his lips together till they turn white from the pressure. "I'll do my best."

"I talked with Nurse Mitchell, and you're cleared for a visit," my dad interjects, pushing his blocky phone into his shirt pocket, a big smile on his face like the cold and the stress of the ongoing renovations don't affect him.

"I'll stay here, then, and go through a few things with Greg, if that's all right," Ian says as though I'd invited him to meet my mother, which I definitely had not.

"Yeah, that sounds like a plan," I say, not wanting to call him out in front of my dad, who is beaming now.

"Your mother will be so pleased to see you and Olivia."

I try to muster a sincere smile. I should be happy, my parents are finally meeting my daughter, my dad is proud of me, proud of her, interested in my life, but I'm numb to it right now. Just like the way Ian's love and apologies come off as hollow, so does this. Or maybe I'm the one who is hollow, empty, unwilling to accept anyone's fallible love.

I join Olivia in the car, elbowing her out of the driver's seat where she'd pointed all of the heating vents when she started the engine. My dad shouts one last thing, but it's muffled by the car's engine revving. I pull out and point the car toward Shore Path Memory Center and ask Olivia if she understood what he said.

"I don't know," she says, readjusting the vents. "It sounded something like 'She's having a good day.'"

A good day. It's the phrase I've come to dread, the one that tells me my mom, the firing squad, the critic, the hoarder, is back. And we're on our way to see her.

Great.

CHAPTER 20

Greg

September 5, 1970
Highway 50

I slow my speed as we hit Main Street in Lake Geneva. The glowing neon makes me wish we could stop in one of these little cafés, have half a sandwich and a cup of soup and forget everything.

"I'm gonna miss this place. It's so magical here in the summer. I've always wanted to see some of the big houses up close. It must feel like a dream living in one of those," Betty says as we crawl past the Lake Geneva public beach with its tall white lifeguard towers. In the distance I spot the Riviera boathouse, where I saw Hal Iverson and danced with a cute girl from Appleton who gave me her number. I never called her, but every time I see the boathouse I think of Maggie Brady and wonder if she ever went back there looking for me.

"I once hiked the whole shore path with my scout troop." I add to the conversation as we glide through the town.

"I heard about that path. It goes all the way around the lake, right?" she says, squinting at the black waters reflecting the moonlight in wavy lines across its surface.

"Yup. I heard every couple of years the summerhouse people try to change the rules, stop the unwashed masses from walking through their yards. It's only twenty miles long, but our troop stopped at Camp Augustana overnight. It took us two days."

"Boys are so lucky," she says as we leave the glow of the resort town and are embraced by the darkness of the country roads. "In Girl Scouts all we did was press flowers, go on a few nature walks, and if we were lucky, learn a little basic first aid. So if you ever get a first-degree burn, give me a call. I know exactly what kind of ointment to use."

"Pressing flowers sounds nice. Boy Scouts could be a little more *Lord of the Flies*, if you know what I mean."

"Oh, yes. We read that in lit class." She slowly removes hairpins from her updo, placing them in the ashtray one at a time. "Listen, girls are just as cutthroat. We just hide it better, which makes me think we're more dangerous."

"I don't know about that."

Dangerous. The word evokes images of her car, torn up, dented, and scratched, and Betty only a little less damaged.

"What? You think because women haven't had the chance to start wars that they wouldn't if given the opening?" She shakes her hair out and runs her fingers through the stiff shoulder-length strands.

"You really want to start a war, don't you?"

"No. No," she snickers half-heartedly, working her hand free from a sizable tangle. "Don't get me wrong, I love being a girl. I love dresses and makeup and fancy shoes, but being a girl is more than that. Put us on a deserted island and I promise you we'd have many of the same problems as those *Lord of the Flies* boys."

"Is that who tore up your car? A rogue Girl Scout?" The question slips out, her hands drop to her lap, and her long, dark lashes flutter as she melts back against her seat.

"That's not nice."

"Sorry. It was only a joke . . ." I expect a sharp retort or bitter silence, but she looks resigned as she stares out the window.

"No, it's fine. You came all the way out here. It's natural for you to have questions." She curls her legs up on the seat and crosses them like a yogi at a retreat. Her bare feet peek out, and though we're speeding down the highway at fifty miles per hour, it's like we're sitting comfortably together in my living room.

"It began like any other workday there," she starts, and I split my focus between the road and catching glimpses of her expression. "I mean, I don't clock that many hours anymore since I moved off-site, but I come in on busy nights or when someone calls in sick. I can't complain—the money isn't terrible, especially on a weekend and especially in the VIP Room. I got tired of the grabby hands and the sexual advances a long time ago, and the smoke has started to really sting my eyes and I get this cough every so often . . . anyway . . . I'm ready to be done, so it's not like getting fired is a tragedy. But it's the money. My income at WQRX isn't exactly great, and my family still needs me to help out, you know?"

She checks in to see if I'm keeping up and maybe assess my level of compassion or judgment. I nod to let her know I'm on her side, and she continues.

"All I have of value is the car. It was a gift from my boyfriend." She clears her throat and corrects herself. "Ex-boyfriend. I met him at the club. He was a businessman from Milwaukee, handsome and really well established. He wasn't the kind of guy who looked down my top or grabbed my ass or anything like that. He was sweet and really kind of protective. When Harry was around, no one messed with me. But you're not supposed to date the men who come to the VIP Room unless they have this extra special key, and Harry didn't have one."

I memorize every detail in case I need to use it in a police report in the future: Harry. Milwaukee. Regular at the club.

"Anyway. We dated in secret, and he treated me like a queen. He'd tell me every time I saw him how it killed him to see men ogle me and how he wanted to marry me and get me out of this place. Blah. Blah. Blah." She waved her hand in the air and then smoothed a crease in her cotton pant leg. "But I didn't want to get married until I graduated. So, he got me the car instead of a ring. And then two weeks later, as I was walking into the locker room, this woman in a pretty gingham dress came up to me holding the hand of a cute little blond girl with pigtails. 'Please,' she said, grabbing at my arm with her dainty kid gloves, 'please stop.' I thought she might be a religious zealot trying to save my soul or something, but then I looked closer at the girl. She had Harry's eyes. Damn fool was married the whole time."

She stops talking and digs through her bag as though she's explained everything, when clearly she hasn't. She takes out a pack of gum and pops out a white rectangle, offering me one. I decline, choosing instead to ask my first question.

"So, Harry, he's the one who wrecked your car? 'Cause you stopped seeing him?"

"Oh, my God, no." She tosses the pack of gum back in her bag, her teeth crack through the hard candy surface, and the scent of peppermint fills the car. "We got in a fight that night and I told him I never wanted to see him again. He threatened to tell the Bunny mother about everything, but his wife must've gotten to him first, 'cause I never saw Harry again and that was over a year ago. No. It wasn't him. Sorry, I'll start again. Tonight I was filling in for my friend Larissa. She's one of the handful of girls that also has a day job, so we cover for each other lots. The night really picks up after dinner, at least in the VIP Room where Larissa is stationed, and that's when he walked in."

"He?" I prompt when she doesn't clarify.

"Don," she says, biting at her glossy red nail. "Hollinger."

"Shit."

"More like holy shit," she jokes somberly, and I feel sick. "As you well know, it's not the only time I've seen someone there I recognize," she said, referencing the night she nearly ran into not only me, but also Don and the whole executive team and potential advertisers.

I assumed she'd be more cautious or maybe even quit, but obviously she'd chosen to keep playing with fire or perhaps felt like she had no other choice. She tells me the rest of the story like she's lost in a dream, her delivery monotone, her eyes glazed over like she's watching the scene from a great distance.

"Usually when I recognize someone, I see them first, avoid the table, get one of the other Bunnies to swap with me or something, and that does the trick. Honestly, most of the time men don't even look at our faces, that's why you caught me by surprise that last time. I don't know"—she taps her thumbnail against her front teeth—"but this time I definitely didn't see him first. I was working at a table across the room when someone grabbed my elbow roughly but not rough enough to trigger the bouncer Eddie, who hangs out at the bar. My heart nearly stopped. He didn't yell, not in the lounge, but he did look at me like I was dirty and told me I'd better meet him in the hall in fifteen minutes or else."

The "or else" lingers ominously in the air. I could probably guess the rest of the story, but she continues, and I listen with rapt attention.

"I snuck out the side entrance to the stairwell that leads to the guest rooms, where Don was waiting for me. I've never seen him so . . . unglued."

I haven't seen him anything more than stern, but I can imagine what unfiltered Don Hollinger looks like because I know what my dad looked like when my mom burned his toast or forgot the celery in his chili. I follow the curve of the highway, nearly wild at the idea of Hollinger harming Betty.

"Bunnies aren't allowed back by the rooms ever—and I knew it. I knew the rules and I knew why. My Bunny mother told us on our first day of training: 'We're not a brothel and you girls are not strippers, remember that.' And so we were never, ever, ever to go anywhere close to the guest rooms. Well, it didn't take long for my security to show up after drunk Don started yelling. They forced him out, and within ten minutes I was out, too. Fired."

She makes a loud raspberry with her tongue, blinking her fake eyelashes rapidly, fighting off tears. "I didn't push back. I'd broken the rules and I knew it, and I couldn't even blame Don. I'm his girlfriend and I'd been lying to him for months. What man wouldn't feel betrayed?" she says with resignation.

She looks at me as though, as a man, she expects me to agree that Hollinger didn't have any other choice. But I can't agree with her or condone his explosive behavior. I've never had a serious girlfriend, but I'd like to think I could keep my head screwed on straight in a similar situation. I'd feel betrayed, sure, but would I raise my voice, get her fired, and single-handedly destroy her most prized possession? I hope not.

"Anyway, it took me a bit to change, turn in my uniform, and clean out my locker. I only got to say bye to a few of the girls before I was escorted out by Eddie. He looked like he could cry, I swear. He's always been such a sweetheart. His wife works in the laundry at the hotel, and I'd bring them some of the baked treats from the set when our schedules lined up. I gave him my number and he told me he'd pass it on to Naomi. He locked the door behind me, and I walked off into the parking lot with no problems other than a lack of tissues." She sniffles.

I offer her a clean, folded handkerchief from my back pocket, which only seems to make her cry more.

"Thank you." She dabs at her cheeks and under her nose. "You always seem to be there when I need you."

"Wish I'd been in that parking lot." Instantly, the image of my fist slamming into Hollinger's face flashes through my mind.

"What? So he could've beat you with that golf club as hard as he tore into my car. No."

"With a golf club?" I echo, imagining the shiny steel reflecting the yellow overhead lights with each swing, the glitter of glass splashing through the air, the sickening clank of metal against metal keeping time.

"He'd done most of the damage before I got there, slashed my tires and bashed out my head- and taillights. He was hacking at my windshield when I ran up and tried to stop him, but he kept going as though I wasn't even there. His friend was parked behind my car, hanging out the window, kinda like . . . cheering him on." She shakes her head a little like she knows how awful it sounds. "Finally, the two of them drove off and I . . . I didn't know what to do. So I found a public telephone and thank God you're listed 'cause I had only one dime left in my change purse."

Rage pulses and grows with every added detail until it burns like a molten ball of lava in my throat waiting for the right opportunity to spew out. But who could I direct my vitriol at? Betty? No, she's been through enough tonight already. I could find Hollinger's address in the phone book, go to his house, pull him out of bed, threaten him. But even though he's at least half a foot shorter than me, I'm sure all his time in the gym would mean I'd end up in the same shape as the car.

"We really should call the cops," I spout, clenching and unclenching my fingers around the steering wheel, craving some sort of immediate recourse.

"I told you. No police. You think WQRX will let me keep my job if I report him? I love our show. I can't lose it . . ." She sounds terrified.

I want to say "You won't!" but she's right. She'd lose the show, her only remaining job, all she's worked for and deserves.

Betty begs me again to "let her handle it."

And I respond with a muttered "Fine."

"Thank you," she says, and it's the first time those words coming from her mouth make me ill.

As I drive, counting the yellow dotted lines down the middle of the highway to keep my murderous thoughts at bay, she rolls down her window, letting in the cool night air. I hadn't realized how stuffy it'd gotten, and the fresh breeze is exactly what I need. I roll my window down, too, and inhale deeply, savoring the sweetness of the warm wind whipping through my hair.

Betty twists her legs up under her again and turns up the volume on the radio. We drive like that for a while, Betty's head against the headrest, hair lashing around her face, her lips occasionally moving along with the lyrics coming through the speakers.

We soon reach the turn that leads back to Janesville. I slow to a stop, clicking on my turn signal. Betty sits up, rod straight, and puts her hand on the wheel.

"Stop!" she shouts, shaking her head, staring deep into my eyes. "He might be there, at my place. I . . . can't go back there. Not yet."

We sit at the crossroads, exhaustion tugging at my limbs as the sweet saccharine lyrics of "Monday, Monday" play. My bed is only ten minutes away, fifteen if I count dragging my tired ass out of the car and up the stairs to my room. But as much as the comfort of my own home and my own bed calls to me, Betty's tearstained cheeks and fine lines of worry call to the part of me that only wants to be with her.

"All right," I hear myself say before I've even truly decided to give in. "Where to?"

"Kegonsa," she says, licking her nearly nude lips, leaving a natural shine that turns the bare part of them a little pink. Kegonsa is another forty minutes away, just off 90 and east of Madison. I've seen the exit at least a hundred times while driving back and forth to UW-Madison for football games. It's a tiny town in the middle of nowhere, corn fields and dairy farms with little else to brag about.

I flick off my turn signal. When the light flips to green, I shove my foot on the gas hard enough to make the engine rev and our heads whip back as we speed past Janesville.

"You maniac!" she shouts over the wind. I smash the pedal against the floor and she whoops, throwing her arm out the window, making me feel invincible.

"So," I yell, adrenaline chasing away the exhaustion and heaviness, feeling like a bad boy for once in my life, "what's in Kegonsa?"

She pulls her arm back inside, presses her head into the headrest, and closes her eyes like she's submitting to the chaos of sound and air inside the car.

"Home," she says. "We're going home."

CHAPTER 21

Charlie

Present Day

My father had alerted Shore Path that we were on our way, and Nurse Mitchell did a good job of preparing Betty for our arrival. She knows who I am as soon as I walk into the room, calling me Lottie in the same irritated tone she used the last time I saw her on a "good day."

But within a few seconds, Betty calls me Laura and refers to Olivia by my childhood nickname, making it clear that today is a bit different. Not exactly a good day but not fully a bad one either. I'm not sure if that's entirely positive, but I keep my mental fingers crossed as Nurse Mitchell excuses herself, leaving us alone with Betty.

I thought it'd be hard to explain to Olivia that my mother might be a little pricklier than her loving grandmothers on her father's side and Ian's side, but she seems unfazed, even when my mother sends a cutting barb my way every so often.

"I volunteered at Mountainview for my NHS community service hours, remember?" she reminded me when we got into the room. "They had a whole memory wing there."

"Aren't you a sweet thing," Betty declares from her armchair when I introduce her to her only grandchild. Olivia accepts the offered kiss on the cheek.

"You too. I like your green chair. It's so regal looking."

"Yes, my husband got it for me. He's a kind man. Are you married?" she asks Olivia, who seems to find the question funny.

"No, no. Not yet."

"You have time but might need a haircut and some rouge."

"Olivia is wonderful the way she is," I snap back, remembering how my mother's critiques had stuck with me over the years. "Besides, she's only nineteen."

"So, you're not going to school for your MRS, then?" She makes an old joke I heard several times as a kid.

"No. More like a bachelor's in arts," she banters back. "Grandma, how old were you when you got married?"

Betty's eyes roll upward like she's counting, but when she doesn't come up with a number, I fill in the little bit of information I know about my parents' marriage.

"Thirty-one. Well, thirty-one when I was born. So, a year before that I think."

"Is that right?" Betty asks as though we are talking about an old friend instead of her own history. I know it's part of her memory loss, the Swiss cheese, as Nurse Mitchell calls it. I have holes in my memory as well, but for very different reasons.

As Betty and Olivia chat, I pull out a deck of cards, shuffling them a dozen times, keeping an eye on the door for our food delivery and hoping it gets here before Betty remembers who I am again.

"I read your book last night when I got to town," Olivia adds, catching my interest, as I deal three hands in a clockwise order.

"My book?"

"Yes. *The Classy Homemaker.*" Olivia retrieves the book from the box we brought with us and lays it on the corner of the roll-away table. "I didn't know you wrote a book."

My mother glances at the weathered hardcover a few times and then stares daggers in my direction.

"I wish you'd all stop digging through my things, Lottie. The girl doesn't know better, but you should and so does your father," she scolds, as though my childhood mother just popped into the conversation from another room.

Her reprimand releases a flood of frustration inside me as I think about everything we're doing to clean up the mess she left behind—our time, our money, and the physical and mental effort we've put in. I open my mouth to respond, but Olivia stops me with a steady gaze.

"I'll go first," Olivia says, flipping the top card of the deck over.

I close my mouth with a click, which stops my retort but doesn't stop the resentment behind it. It's so hard not to engage when my mom's hardened edge returns on her more lucid days.

Olivia's redirection works, and we all ignore the book on the table, playing silently until our meal arrives.

"Ooo, this looks like a treat," Nurse Mitchell says as she brings in the brown paper bags of food.

"I hope you didn't let Mrs. Thompson near it," my mother bites. "She stole my brownie after dinner last night. I saw her chomping on it in her room." I cringe, filled with a familiar embarrassment at her sharp complaint.

The paranoia isn't new, though it's likely heightened by her illness and new location. But even when I lived at home, my mother's anxiety increased as her hoarding intensified. Eventually, she was sure anyone walking on the shore path was trying to peek into our house. To my mortification she'd often yell at them if they stopped for too long within her sight. She also insisted our house be removed from the boat tour's script and opted to have our mail delivered to a PO box in town rather than the box on the dock.

The one time her paranoia was merited was when CPS showed up and she blamed Miss Johnson, saying my teacher made the call, that she had it in for her. In that case, she was right.

The nurse leaves the brown paper sack, assuring us it's been in no hands but her own. I distribute the Styrofoam containers, the heavenly scent of homemade soup filling the room, distracting my mother from her suspicion.

"This is sinfully good," my mother says, taking a spoonful of cream of potato soup with a saturated lump of homemade sourdough bread. "I haven't had Lake Aire's in . . ." Her thought drifts off.

"Mmmm, so good," Olivia agrees. And I remain mute so I don't distract from their conversation.

"You are a pretty girl," she says to Olivia, who's wearing ripped jeans and an oversized sweater that would've triggered my mother in my younger years.

"Thank you. I like your nails. Did you just get them done?" Olivia returns the compliment. My mother stares at her cotton candy–pink fingernails.

"I . . . I think so."

"Well, that's a lovely color."

"Thank you. It's my favorite."

The idea that the soft pink of a baby's blanket could possibly be my mother's favorite color strikes me as odd. Pale pink is such a contrast to the dark cavern of our home.

"It's my favorite too," Olivia adds, which is true, though for a brief time in high school she shunned the color, calling it "demeaning" to her feminist values. But apparently she's realized she can be a feminist and wear pink.

"We should go shopping," Betty says to Olivia with a youthful verve, finishing the last bit of creamy broth. A long-lost grandmother shopping with her newly acquainted granddaughter—it's like a subplot from a Hallmark movie. It's sweet and it's something I never thought could possibly happen in my lifetime.

"Shopping?" Olivia looks to me to see if this is an odd request. I shrug.

"Yes. Shopping. I know a girl who works at JCPenney's. She lets me use her discount." She's slipping a little, teetering between two times, two realities. I don't know if my mom has ever left Shore Path, much less visited a department store. I peel a piece of crust off my roll and chew it slowly as I watch the interaction. "And we could go to Ike's for dinner. If you think this is good, wait until you try Ike's pot roast. But they only have it on Wednesday nights so we should go on a Wednesday."

My ears perk up and I risk an interruption. "Ike's Diner? In Janesville?"

"Yes, yes. Have you heard of it?" she asks us both politely. Olivia shakes her head as I nod mine.

"Olivia, that's where I was coming from yesterday. It's the town I was telling you about."

"When your phone was off?" Olivia asks with raised eyebrows, leaving out the handsome dentist companion. I roll my eyes as Betty claps her hands.

"We should go to Ike's," Betty says eagerly, sitting up in her chair as straight as her stiffened spine allows. Olivia seems nearly as worked up by the idea.

"When I volunteered at Mountainview, family could sign the residents out for the day. We could ask," Olivia says to both me and her grandmother, which enhances Betty's mood. She starts to list off places she'd like to take us, a park by her house, the ice cream shop, the studio.

While shopping sounds like torture, I'd love to take Betty back to the mysterious town where she met my dad and see if any of the sights trigger her memories. But I deflate internally as the voice of reason prevails. It's unrealistic.

"Let's not get her hopes up," I say under my breath to Olivia before the fantasy of a day trip can take hold any further. I read every pamphlet Nurse Mitchell gave me on my first day here, and one of the big rules, after the one about not arguing, is don't make any promises, especially false promises, to the dementia patient.

I stand up and start collecting the cards.

"Sorry, but we should probably get going," I say to both Olivia and Betty, cutting our visit short. The lack of sleep is catching up with me, a piercing headache developing in between my eyebrows. I've been the engaged mom, I've shown Olivia the town, introduced her to her grandparents, and even played nice with Ian, but I'm out of parental patience. I've had my oasis invaded and far too many of my choices hijacked. I need a long bath and maybe a nap before I can think clearly again.

Olivia must be able to tell I'm burned out, and after pushing her luck by showing up on my doorstep, she doesn't fight me. Betty says easy farewells, the sharp edge to her comments having dulled a bit.

"Ike's next week," she reminds us as I write in her visitor's log, detailing the visit with Olivia, our special lunch, and the card game, leaving out the proposed visit to Janesville, hoping she'll forget all about it.

Olivia disappears into her room when we return to the rental with promises of unpacking. I take the opportunity to run an insanely hot bath, soaking with the lights off and listening to a white noise app on my phone until the water grows tepid. Wearily, I work my fragrant argan oil shampoo through my hair and rinse by holding my head underwater, shaking the strands wildly till they tickle my shoulders and I run out of air.

I repeat with the conditioner, remembering when I was a little girl how my mom would sit on the edge of our pink porcelain tub in the upstairs hall bathroom, scrubbing my scalp and delicately rinsing it with a large plastic cup filled with bathwater.

Breaking through the surface of the water, I hear the doorbell ping through the static pouring out of my phone's speakers.

"Olivia!" I call out, but no one responds. The bell rings again. "Damn it," I grumble, slithering out of the tub. I quickly run a towel over my body and wrap it around my hair. After wiggling into a clean pair of underwear, I slip on silky blue pajama pants and a matching top, adding an oversized sweater to conceal my lack of a bra.

As I rush toward the front door, a flash of white-hot pain shoots through my shin when I bang it against the corner of the bed frame. I clutch my leg, trying to keep the towel on my head. As I stumble down the hall, deep voices come from the front room. One belongs to Ian. For some reason, he's standing in my open front door, leaning halfway out and talking to someone as if he lives here. Then, the second voice registers in my mind. It's Cam.

What the hell?

The discussion seems civil enough, and when Ian pivots back into the house, closing the door, he's holding a large box that matches the others we retrieved from the Janesville library basement yesterday afternoon. The textured projector container is already lined up against the wall alongside the other two boxes I'd forgotten in his car.

"Uh, hi?" I say to Ian, letting go of my tender shin, cocking my head with a *What is going on?* expression on my face. I know he can hear the confusion in my greeting, but he doesn't address it.

"Your friend said you forgot these." He puts the last box on the ground and looks me up and down in my postbath state.

"Why didn't you get me?" I ask, untwisting the towel from my hair and shaking it out with my fingers. I quickly retrieve my boots from the closet and force them on. Ian watches me with raised eyebrows, sitting on the back of the couch as I head for the door.

"Olivia is getting ready. I'm taking her to dinner, if you'd like to come. She said you were in the bath and I didn't want to disturb you, so I just . . . wait, are you going out there like that? You'll freeze."

"I'll be fine," I say, slamming the door behind me. As I walk, the cool air blasts against my damp skin and settles in my hair, giving me a deep chill. Cam's car is parked in the street parallel to the house, and he's halfway into the front seat when I call his name across the lawn.

"Cam!" I wave my arms wildly. I must look like an eccentric shut-in limping down the slight slope of the lawn in my boots and pajamas.

He seems to hesitate before coming around the front of the SUV. He's wearing a Brewers baseball cap, and the bill casts a shadow on his eyes so I can't see his expression. My fingers are numb when he meets me on the cracked cement of the driveway. I warm them under my armpits, crossing my arms to hide my lack of a bra.

"You should've let me know you were coming. I would've put on real clothes," I say, shaking my cold, damp hair away from my face.

"I texted. You didn't answer so I thought I'd stop by since I was around the corner at my parents' place. Clearly, I overstepped," he says, taking in my disheveled state. I suddenly realize how it must've looked when Ian opened the door while I was in the bath.

"No. You didn't overstep at all. I really appreciate it. I was telling Olivia about the films, and now that we have the projector, we can watch them. She'll be really excited." I fight off a tremor of shivers, clenching my jaw.

"Glad I could help," he says with a nod, spinning his keys. I get a peek at his eyes. They look disconnected, like he's trying to hide that he cares.

OK. So Ian got into his head. How can I blame Cam for feeling thrown off? We hadn't officially called our outing a date, but it was definitely heading in that direction until my estranged husband showed up and put a damper on things. I'm still relieved Cam and I didn't cross that line last night, but that doesn't mean I want him out of my life or that I'm ready to completely write off our connection.

"So, um," I start cautiously, "do you want to come in and we can watch a few episodes of *The Classy Homemaker*, order some Thai?"

"I don't think that's a good idea."

"You have other plans?"

Cam's shoulders flinch and he scratches his shoe against the raised edge of one of the cement fissures in the driveway. "No, but you haven't seen your family in a while. I . . . I don't want to interrupt."

"Cam," I say firmly, placing my hand on his forearm, not caring that Ian is probably watching. "Ian is staying at The Cove. He's here to pick up Olivia, so I'm free for the night."

I'll miss dinner with my daughter, but then I remember her as a little girl, with her chin propped up on her knees, singing along with the twins, Sharon and Susan, in *The Parent Trap*, and get suspicious. This is part of her plan.

"Ah." Even through his puffer jacket I can sense his body unclenching at the new information. He rests his warm hand over mine. "You're so cold."

"No. No. I'm fine."

"I think hypothermia is definitely setting in," he jokes sweetly, taking my other hand and sandwiching both between his, rubbing quickly to warm them up. He looks over my head at the house, like he's debating whether he's ready to confront Ian or if he'll have to let me freeze to death.

Oh man, I like Cam a lot. I like who he is now and the memories of who he was to me thirty years ago. I also like that he's apparently found a way to forgive me for the mistakes I made as a teenager. It's an impressive example, one I'm grateful for, one I want to understand, one I want to emulate. He was a refuge for me when I was younger, and so supportive on our semi-date last night. When I was a teen, Cam didn't think of me as the weird kid with the erratic mom, and he doesn't think of me now as an out-of-touch Hollywood type. He's always seen me for me. That sense of emotional safety is something I currently lack, especially compared to how I feel with Ian right now.

A door slams behind me. Cam backs away, and the cadence of the footsteps heading our way lets me know why. As Ian approaches, I brace myself for a potentially heated exchange, accusations, and questions about what happened while we were apart and where we stand as a couple. But Ian doesn't stop. He rushes past and climbs behind the wheel of his rental SUV.

Olivia pauses to explain. "We're going to Hogs and Kisses for a burger or something. You coming, Mom?" she asks, enunciating "Mom" to make it clear Cam is not invited. She has to know what my answer will be, standing on the front lawn wearing no makeup, pajamas, and my hair more frozen than dry.

"I think I'll pass," I say, kissing her cheek. "We might not have paparazzi here, but I'm still not sure anyone is ready for this look." Cam laughs, and Olivia seems to find it irritating.

"We'll be back in a little bit," she says to us both as though I'm a teenager being left at home with my boyfriend.

"We'll be good, Mom. I swear," I say, mocking her parental tone. Olivia rolls her eyes and joins Ian in the car. As they drive away, I raise my eyebrows at Cam.

"How about now? Dinner and a movie?" I ask again and then think of an additional offer to help make him more comfortable. "I'll invite Lacey."

Cam looks down the road and then back at me, shaking his head like I've tricked him into something. "How do I say no to that?"

"You don't. Come on. Let's go. I'm freezing."

"I knew it!" he says, following me as I run into the house. It doesn't take long to return to the safe, playful banter from our younger years. Cam sets up the film projector while I text Lacey, put on a bra, and order dinner. Lacey says she can grab the takeout once her kids are down for the night. And soon all three of us are seated on the couch staring at a white square on the wall.

"You ready for this?" Cam asks us both.

Lacey holds up her glass of wine and shouts, "Yeah!"

They both look to me for my approval. Am I ready? Probably not, but since when does that matter? Looking at my two old friends with a crooked grin, I pop off the lid of the can reading "Aug/1969, Pilot" and hand the film to him.

"Let's do this."

CHAPTER 22

Greg

September 6, 1970
Kegonsa, Wisconsin

When Betty shakes me awake, the sun is rising. The late summer sun lights up the cornstalks in shades of pink, gold, and red like they're on fire, giving Betty's face an ethereal glow. She's removed her false lashes and wiped away the majority of her makeup. She looks so different, still maintaining a level of beauty most women would covet, but with a raw simplicity that's like a miracle of nature rather than a painted-on facade.

Last night, Betty quickly fell into a deep sleep that I envied as we barreled through town after town. Struggling to keep my eyes open, I nearly missed the exit to Kegonsa, which only seemed apropos since the town was nearly as easy to miss. Not wanting to startle Betty, I pulled into an abandoned lot surrounded by tall, ready-to-harvest cornfields. I turned off my lights and engine and decided to close my eyes for a few minutes, hoping the halted movement would eventually wake her, but apparently we both overslept.

"Oh, my gosh. I'm sorry," I say. She flaps her hand at me.

"It's fine. Charlotte would've killed me if I'd shown up at three a.m., anyway. And this gave me a chance to freshen up a bit." She gestures to her clean face.

"You still don't have shoes," I remind her, but she laughs and wiggles her toes like it's no big deal.

"My sister and I wear the same size. I'll sneak some from the front closet when I get inside. The house is that way."

I follow her instructions, taking a series of turns I know I won't be able to remember on my way back out of here after I drop her off.

We finally turn down a long, wooded dirt path that twists for another half mile until the greenery parts to reveal a little white farmhouse set in a small clearing surrounded by maple trees. A screened-in porch skirts the front of the house, one of the panels with a hole big enough for a large dog to fit through. A barn, at least twice the size of the house, sits to one side, a small red shed on the other side, along with a chicken coop. Chickens mill around the yard, pecking at the ground.

Two vehicles are parked in the dirt driveway, an old truck and a slightly newer sedan with rust spots over the rear tires. A worn-down red trike is stranded next to the largest tree, where a tire swing hangs on a long, thick, moss-covered rope.

"Home again. Home again," Betty somberly chants as though the early morning vision in front of us brings up less-than-positive emotions.

"You grew up here?" The setting is both humble and picturesque. I'd never have guessed Betty, metropolitan, stylish, classy Betty, would come from such unassuming beginnings.

"Yup. And I couldn't wait to leave. Didn't get far though, did I?" She gathers her things, hops out of the car barefoot, slams the door, and leans back in through the open window. "Wanna come in for some coffee?"

I glance at my watch, remembering Martha's promised phone call. It's only a few minutes before seven so I have time. Plus, after the late night and long drive I could use some coffee and a bathroom break.

"Sure," I say, stumbling out of the car.

"Good. We gotta keep it down. Charlotte's got a baby and two other little ones. She'll kill me if we wake them."

Betty's already halfway to the house by the time I get my feet under me. With my long strides, I catch up to her quickly, immediately wishing I'd taken an extra second to tidy up before meeting her family.

"Watch me," she says from the porch stairs. She glides up the peeling wooden planks in a cautious dance, turns her body sideways and lithely slips through the screen door without disturbing the rusty springs. Not nearly as gracefully, I follow.

Inside, the house is quiet and dark, though there's the strong scent of fresh coffee. Someone must be awake.

"This way," Betty whispers. She threads her fingers between mine and guides me through the cluttered front room. It's filled with tidy decades-old furniture, dusty bookshelves, and not one sign of the children who live here. The wooden plank floors are covered in a series of worn and uncoordinated carpets, and the walls are filled with framed photographs I wish I could stop and study.

Truly, it's a miracle I notice anything in those minutes between the front door and the kitchen other than the smooth hand holding mine. I imagine what it'd be like to twist my wrist enough that I could thread my fingers between hers, nervous to meet my girlfriend's family.

Stop. I chastise myself. I can't pretend we'll ever be more than what we already are—friends.

We pass the dining room and push through a set of swinging white doors to the kitchen. On one side of the room stands a round oak table, piled high with mail and newspapers, except for a spot large enough for a single place setting that remains empty. It's nothing like the sterile kitchen on *The Classy Homemaker* set, but there's a hominess about it, a lived-in quality reminiscent of my childhood. The line of bacon spitting at us from an iron skillet on the stove and the percolating coffee pot make my stomach grumble.

"Betty?" A young woman, barely out of her teens, steps in from the back door holding a handful of blueberries. She's barefoot and dressed in an oversized housecoat with a scarf tied around her light-brown hair. Betty drops my hand, throwing her arms around the girl who I can only assume is her sister.

"Sorry, I let myself in. I didn't want to call and wake the kids."

"My gosh! The kids will go berserk. They ask about you all the time. I fed Lulu and put her back down, but Willie and Suzie are awake and playing in their room. I was trying to get breakfast going while I had a minute."

"Here, I'll make breakfast. You deserve a break." Betty holds her sister at arm's length, looking into her face. The dark crescents of motherhood stand out under her eyes, not matching the youthfulness of her frame and features.

"I mean, if you don't mind. I'd love to run upstairs and wash my hair," she responds, glancing at me quickly like she's wondering who I might be.

"Oh, sorry. This is Greg. We work together at the station. Greg, my baby sister, Charlotte."

"Nice to meet you," I say, offering my hand. She drops her collection of berries into a white cereal bowl.

"Nice to meet you, too." She shakes my hand, hers almost childlike in my grip. "Make yourself at home. There's some banana bread in the cupboard, and the apples started falling a bit early this year so we have too many to eat. Help yourself."

"Oh, he's not staying," Betty clarifies for her sister but also for me. Coffee, bathroom, and then I go. I guess Betty'll figure out what comes next with Hollinger without my input or assistance. "I was hoping I could stay here for a few days," Betty says. "I could help with the meals, the kids, finally get that upstairs bathroom repapered."

Charlotte's smile fades, and she glances at me again like she's uncomfortable having this conversation in front of a guest. I consider leaving, but I'd also like to know Betty's plans. If Hollinger decides to be petty, which seems likely given the condition of her car, Betty could lose her job. If that's the case, I need to know.

I could tell Martha. She's not afraid of Hollinger and would surely lose her mind if they cut Betty without any warning. We could go to the EBN executives and tell them what happened. If they choose Hollinger over Betty, I could quit and Martha would likely follow. While my resignation might not hold much weight, losing all three of us might make a difference. These plans began to form as I struggled to stay awake during my early-morning drive, although I haven't shared them with Betty yet.

"What? Why do you look like that?" Betty asks Charlotte with her head cocked. Unlike her sister, she must not care what I think because she pushes for a response. "Charlotte Eleanor. What's going on?"

Betty's sister crosses and uncrosses her bare toes, her face turning red as Betty's stare bores into her.

"Bill is back."

The color drains from Betty's face and she stumbles backward, crashing into me. I steady myself against the counter. I don't know who Bill is, but he's clearly another man in Betty's life who's bad news.

"Here?" She scans the kitchen, and I quickly see several clues that hint at a man living here. Men's boots by the kitchen door and a canvas jacket hung above it, an uncleaned pipe spilling tobacco into a crystal ashtray, a *Farmers' Almanac* left beside it with a bookmark peeking out the top.

"Where else?" Charlotte says flippantly, crossing her arms defiantly like a teenager. Betty's shaking.

"My God, Charlotte. You promised you wouldn't this time. I worked two jobs to make it so you didn't have to count on him anymore."

"He's their dad, Betty. It's not right to keep him away."

"It's not right? You know what's not right? What he did to us, that's not right. What happened with Mom . . ." Betty looks at me and stops herself from finishing whatever she was on the verge of saying. "Why the hell didn't you tell me?"

"'Cause I knew you'd be like this." Charlotte clicks off the burner and moves the skillet of perfectly cooked bacon away from the hot grate. "You can have some coffee, but then you'll have to leave. I need to check on the kids."

Charlotte moves to go upstairs, but Betty blocks her exit with an arm across the door, speaking with the kind of authority you'd normally hear from a parent.

"No. No, that's not it. Tell me. Why didn't you tell me?"

Charlotte's nostrils flare as she breathes heavily in and out, biting her lip where a piece of dead skin flaked up, leaving a crimson crack behind.

"He told me not to," she admits, her eyes dropping to the floor as though they're weighted with shame.

"Because of the money?" Betty asks almost sweetly, like she finally understands.

"Because of the money."

"How long?"

Charlotte, still as a statue, doesn't respond at first. Betty repeats her question, even more tenderly this time.

"Since right after Lulu was born."

"But I was here after Lulu. How . . . ?"

"He stayed in the shed. Made me promise not to say a word. You know how he is. I wanted to tell you, Bets, I swear."

Betty flattens her sister's hair under the pink and white scarf and kisses her forehead and cheek. Charlotte melts into her sister's arms, tucking her head under Betty's chin.

"Don't tell him I was here, OK? I'll keep sending you what I can."

Charlotte nods and sniffles. Betty came home for the comfort and safety she's now giving to her sister and nieces and nephew.

"Thank you, Bets," Charlotte says, pulling away and wiping her nose with her sleeve. "He's better now. I'll leave him if I'm wrong. I promise."

Betty smooths the tears off her sister's face, puts on her audience-pleasing smile, and proclaims everything will be all right. A creak upstairs makes both women freeze, and then Betty takes my hand again. She leads me out at double speed. We end up sprinting across the front yard shoeless, the dew soaking into my socks and clinging to the cuffs of my jeans.

"Go. Go," she says breathlessly once we're in the car. Turning the key, I slam on the gas, making the wheels spin in the dirt loudly enough to wake anyone.

"I'm sorry," I say, out of breath, my head spinning. "Her husband sounds terrible."

"Her husband?" Betty asks, craning her neck to look out the back window.

"Bill. Her husband. He sounds like a bad man."

"Oh, he is a bad man. Very bad. But he's not her husband."

"He's not?"

"No." She slams on the armrest, tears in her eyes. "Damn it." She drags her arm across her face, breathing heavy. "Bill's our stepdad."

I shudder, and nausea hits me as I reanalyze the sisters' conversation with the new perspective applied. "And those are his kids?"

"Yup. It's a real fairy tale, isn't it?" she says bitterly, settling into her seat once we're back on the paved road.

"Your mom—you said something about your mom . . ."

"They called it involuntary manslaughter, but I doubt there was anything involuntary about it." She digs through her bag, taking out tissues. The story I'm piecing together about Betty's past is starting to make my head spin. Poverty, abusive stepfather, loss of her mother, sister victimized by the same man.

"She lets him live there?"

"Apparently. I thought she'd never let him back in once he got out of county this last time, but . . ." She tosses her hand up and slaps her leg so hard I flinch.

"And your brother?" I think back to our discussion on the empty *Classy Homemaker* set. Her mother passed away, her little sister, too. All she had left were her two remaining siblings.

"Moved away at fifteen. Last I heard he joined the army. So, who the hell knows where he is now. Maybe dead for all I know." A memory of a red, white, and blue triangle folded on my brother's coffin flashes through my mind. I push it away as we fly through the small town, headed toward the highway.

"So you feel responsible for her, for Charlotte?" I ask, overwhelmed by the image of Betty Wilkens that has zoomed into uncomfortably detailed focus since her call last night.

"For all of them. Not dickhead Bill. But the rest of them. And if I don't give them money, I'm pretty sure he'll get her to cut me out entirely." She rummages through her macramé bag again, this time pulling out a collection of beauty supplies.

"She might leave. Doesn't hurt to hope."

"Actually," she says, no longer crying, "sometimes it hurts a ton."

Uncapping a silver tube, she spins up a column of red lipstick, which she applies while looking in a silver compact. She caps the tube and clicks the mirror closed.

She's right. Not many people would admit it, but hope hurts a whole lot if the situation is actually hopeless. I stop before the highway, tapping the steering wheel with my thumbs.

"So. Where should we go now?"

"Home," she says, powdering her nose, and unlike last night, home doesn't mean the little two-bedroom farmhouse we just ran from. She means Janesville. Poor Betty, always chasing home.

But at least we share Janesville.

"Let's go home," I say, pointing the car south and pressing the gas pedal to the floor mat before she changes her mind.

CHAPTER 23

Charlie

Present Day

Standing in a retro kitchen set, my mother speaks to the camera with poise and charisma. In each episode she wears a stiff white apron and is in flawless hair and makeup as she teaches women how to be the perfect housewife.

Lacey gasps and clenches my hand within the first five minutes of the show.

"Your mom was hot."

Lacey and Cam have only seen the scary version of my mom. She never let people inside our house when I was a kid and discouraged friendships with other children. Once I was removed from the house, the town was left dealing with her. Lacey hasn't been tactful in her retellings of my mother's interactions with the local police, the health department, and Code Enforcement. This view of Betty must be just as much of a shock for them as it is for me.

"Yeah. Yeah, she was," I agree, not as stunned as Lacey by my mother's beauty, but totally hypnotized by her camera presence. Although *The Classy Homemaker* book struck me as a hilarious irony, the films make me a believer. She's convincing, she's enthralling. And though she seems like a stranger to the three of us, I feel like I've been getting to know the woman on the screen—getting to know that Betty.

"She knows how to talk to a camera," Cam says as the film rewinds at the end of the episode. "Or like, through a camera. Reminds me of you on your show."

Lacey agrees, repeating his assessment but with more words. As much as I usually hate being compared to the woman who screwed up the first few decades of my life, I definitely don't hate being compared to Betty Wilkens.

"Wait." I look at Cam with a raised eyebrow. "How would you even know that? You supposedly haven't seen my show."

Cam shakes his head, grinning like he's been caught. "I mean, I hadn't seen it, but that's since changed," he admits.

"In like a day? You little stalker," I say, carefully removing the delicate film and replacing it with another one.

"A little friendly stalking is normal, I think," Lacey interjects, curling up under a fleece blanket. "Especially when you find out your high school ex is a full-on TV star." I squirm at the "star" label but let it go, knowing Cam probably streamed a couple episodes of *Second Chance Renovation* after meeting my costar in person yesterday.

"Fair," I say, flicking the projector's motor back on. It starts with a whir, and I hop into the open spot between my two friends, my knee lightly brushing Cam's every time one of us shifts positions.

That's where Olivia finds us when Ian drops her off without coming inside, much to Lacey's chagrin. She holds a Styrofoam to-go container, explaining it contains a dinner Ian bought in case I didn't have a chance to eat. In her other hand is a piece of carrot cake, my favorite. I put the meal in the fridge next to our Thai leftovers and bring the cake to the couch with four forks.

"Join us?" I ask, after introducing Lacey and Olivia, pointing to the makeshift movie screen. She glances at me and then at Cam and finally at the carrot cake.

"I think I'm good," she says, retreating to her room. I shrug at my friends, and Lacey says something about teenagers as she takes the first bite of the newly delivered dessert.

The rest of the night grows fuzzy as fatigue pulls at my eyelids. Soon, with Cam already snoring lightly next to me, Lacey excuses herself just past midnight, and almost immediately after, I also surrender to sleep.

Some unknown number of hours later, I awake to Cam sitting beside me, a gentle hand on my shoulder. As the fuzziness clears from my eyes and head, I squint at the glowing numbers on the microwave clock. It's 3:00 a.m. I gasp and sit up, pushing off the fleece blanket Lacey placed over me when she left.

"How long have I been asleep?"

Cam laughs. "Only a little longer than I have."

His hip presses into my side, and the light scent of his woody cologne lingers in the air between us. The ambient light from the projector hits his iris at an angle, highlighting the brown freckles. He rubs his lips together, and I half expect him to finish what we started on the front porch last night.

"You should stay over. It's too late to leave." I prop myself up and then clarify quickly, thinking of Olivia in the other room. "The couch is comfy."

"As tempting as that sounds," he says, giving me a small, rueful smile and shaking his head, "I have work in the morning, so I should go."

"I get it. You have important teeth business."

His head bobs, but he doesn't leave immediately. He has that look again from last night, like he wants to pull me to him and kiss me with the pent-up passion of a heartbreak that's been marinating for thirty-one years. His touch would be eager, his mouth hungry; we'd be back in the hammock on the peninsula, but this time as adults who know what comes after the thrill of a deep, meaningful kiss.

I shift in my seat and the moment passes—again.

He gathers his few belongings and starts tidying the room. I shoo him away, reminding him of the time. I don't stand, we don't embrace.

He leaves, and I collapse into the cushion, tossing the blanket over my head, imagining what could've happened if either one of us were slightly less pragmatic.

Emerging from my fleece bubble of shame once I'm sure he's gone, I collect the glasses and bowl of half-eaten popcorn, flicking on the last of the film already threaded in the projector.

Betty's voice fills the room, starting a new *Classy Homemaker* episode with her cheerful greeting to the audience and a wave to the camera, calling, "Welcome home!"

As she lists the topics for the day, I notice a theme: how to make old lace look new, the proper neckline and hemline for each age of bride and type of wedding, the rules of etiquette for who and who not to invite to your wedding, pine cone centerpieces, the must-have household items for your wedding registry, and a step-by-step guide to arranging silk flower bouquets.

I imagine what my parents' wedding must've looked like. I've only found the one picture of my mom in her wedding dress, and after showing it to her I put it on the fridge. I made ten copies and passed them out to the clearing crew with the hopes of finding the wedding dress among the hoard, but so far, no luck.

My mom once told me she and Dad were married in the backyard of our house, on the dock, with flower petals floating in the water. At one time I dreamed of a similar ceremony, maybe on an early summer night when the city had fireworks over the lake.

As Betty arranges white pine cones in circles large enough to fit tall pillar candles that she'd made on a previous episode, I wash the dishes, wipe down the counters, fold the throw blankets, and fluff the pillows.

Betty's hair is shorter in this episode. Her long red nails collect bits of the sparkles as she dusts them onto the wet pine cones, which makes me think of the twelve bins filled with sticks and rocks that we recently removed from the house. In an earlier episode she had used cardboard toilet paper rolls to make Halloween ghost party favors, which explained the twenty or so garbage bags of empty cardboard paper towel rolls and toilet paper tubes in one of the upstairs bedrooms.

It doesn't explain the whole hoard, that's for sure, but some part of my brain calms every time I find a clue to my mother's way of thinking. It's not completely unlike how my father saved and sold antiques, found value in the old or even ancient. Others often paid a hefty price for those treasures. My mother also valued old things, the difference being that no one else could see their worth. It's a little like what we do on my show with old houses, and if I try hard enough, I can find something noble about my mother's perspective, relatable.

"Ugh." I shudder at yet another similarity between me and my mother. I need to get to bed and away from the flattened image of Betty projected onto the living room wall.

I wipe down the sink and dry my hands on the dish towel, watching as *The Classy Homemaker* episode comes to a close. Betty holds up her finished project, and I'm impressed at how fashionable it looks, like evergreen trees covered in sparkling snow.

That's when I notice something. In every other episode I watched, Betty's small, nimble fingers were bare, but in this episode, she's wearing a large diamond ring on her left ring finger that I've never seen before. Hm. I rewind the film and play it again at a slower speed. The image isn't the best quality, but I'm fairly certain it isn't my mother's wedding ring, at least not the one she's worn my whole life—the one she wears now.

Surely it doesn't mean anything. This episode is from the second season, but my parents weren't married until 1976. The ring could be part of her wardrobe, a strategic decision to make her look like a married homemaker instead of a single girl playing house. But then again . . . I step closer to the projected image. There's something familiar about that ring. It sends an unsettled chill through me. I remember where I've seen it before.

I take down the wedding portrait from the freezer door and examine the details closely. Young Betty is wearing a lace and chiffon dress, her hair elegantly pinned in a twist, and her cathedral-length veil cascades down her back. Next to her, I now realize, is a silk flower arrangement like the one she's constructing in *The Classy Homemaker* episode. But . . . the ring. I bring the yellowed photograph over to the image on the wall and hold it up in the light.

The rings match.

I turn the photo over, looking for any clues I may have missed. Could this be a promotional photo from the show? But when Betty looked at it weeks ago she said it was a picture from her wedding day, which was supposedly in 1976, not 1971 when this episode was filmed. Maybe Betty remembered wrong, or they were engaged for longer than I'd been told or maybe were married a different year. Maybe she lost the ring or sold it. There are plenty of rational explanations, but all of them would mean my parents had lied about some part of their love story. Why would they lie?

The question reverberates through my mind as I shut down the projector for the night.

There's literally no reason to lie about their wedding date, I think over and over again as I climb into bed. Then again, if there's no reason to lie then there's also no harm in double-checking. I take out my phone, set an early alarm, and send one last text to Cam.

Charlie: I need you to do me another favor.

CHAPTER 24

Greg

April 1, 1971
WQRX Boardroom
Janesville, Wisconsin

"Sit, sit, sit." Don Hollinger, asshole Don Hollinger, stands at the front of the conference room. The large oval table is fully populated with producers and assistant producers, broadcast technicians, our main anchors, and Will Barnett, who does field reporting. Standing in the corners of the room are the crew, camera operators, gaffer, lighting assistant, and audio engineer. The meeting memo was labeled "MANDATORY," and no one is missing.

Mark sits at the table. He motioned at an empty seat beside him when I first came in the room, but I took a spot leaning against the back wall, understanding the risks of accidentally sitting in the hot seat.

I've avoided close contact with Hollinger at all costs since that night seven months ago when I left my meeting with Martha and rushed to Lake Geneva to help Betty. After speeding away from Betty's childhood home that Sunday morning, we drove back to Janesville in complete silence. When we pulled up to her apartment, she hopped out as if nothing had happened.

"Thanks for the ride," she said, tidying her hair and throwing her bag over her shoulder, starting to walk away and treating me like a friend who was simply dropping her off after a casual meetup for coffee and a half sandwich.

"Wait," I called out, confused and a bit hurt. I hadn't given up my time, sleep, and sanity to be her chauffeur—I helped her because I was her friend, 'cause I cared about her. "What are you gonna do about the car?"

She shrugged and glanced around the parking lot like she was hoping it'd appeared overnight.

"I think I'll be taking the bus," she said nonchalantly, as if she hadn't cried in my front seat or held my hand in her sister's kitchen. The wild change in her demeanor made my head spin.

"You're going back to work on Tuesday?" My mouth went dry with shock as I realized what was happening. There would be no police, no reports to EBN, no quitting, no consequences for that asshole Don Hollinger. She was going to pretend like nothing had happened and hope Don did the same.

"Show must go on," she said, retrieving keys from a pocket inside her bag. They jangled as she swung them around her pointer finger. Then she added with intensity, "I need to keep this job."

After her conversation with Charlotte about finances, I should've seen this coming. She'd decided to choose her job over justice.

"I . . . I could give you a ride." I offered to change my routine if it'd make her first day back easier after such a tumultuous breakup.

Palming her keys, she gave me a twisted look and then popped her head through my window, making me jump. Her breath touched my cheek, and her defenseless eyes told me she hadn't forgotten I'd been there when she needed me.

She leaned in a bit further, her full, soft breasts pushing against my forearm where it rested on the door. Immobilized, her lips brushed my stubbled cheek. Heat spread through my body, an energy that filled and swelled every cell with a startling ecstasy.

"You're a good man, Greg Laramie," she sighed into my ear before slipping away and heading into her apartment building. I watched to make sure she made it inside safely before driving home, more intoxicated from her kiss than I'd ever been off alcohol.

She didn't call me for a ride. And when I saw her on set on Tuesday after the Labor Day break, she'd fully retreated back into her false self, pretending I was only a cameraman and she was only the on-air talent. Two days later she drove up to WQRX in a new car—a black Plymouth Barracuda—as Martha and I were walking into the studio after grabbing lunch at Ike's.

"Looks like Betty got a new toy," Martha said, her eyes slanted in judgment. "Maybe she'll call whoever bought her that thing next time she needs help."

My stomach lurched. I had an idea who was behind Betty's new ride. If I were a braver man, I would have asked her why she would take back someone who treated her so terribly, like Hollinger did. I would have pointed out that she recognized her sister's poor choice in men but failed to see her own. Was it about money? Her job? I shook my head to get the idea of Betty as a gold-digging woman out of my mind.

"It's possible she bought it herself," I said defensively.

"Then we're not getting paid enough," she snipped back, taking my arm and urging me inside when Betty looked to be moving in our general direction. "Let's go before she sees us."

I followed, disappointed that our burgeoning friend group had fallen apart as a result of one phone call.

At least Martha and I reconciled quickly. When I'd talked to her that Sunday, I'd told her Betty's engine had locked up and my number was the only one she could find in the phone book. Martha made some snarky comment, which I ignored, and then we quickly moved to making plans to meet at the park on Labor Day to finish the proposal. I picked up sandwiches and slices of chocolate cake from Ike's, and we ate them on a blanket while listening to the community band play.

Like all time spent with Martha, it was calm, efficient, and enjoyable. When we walked to her car as the sun set over the Rock River, there was an opportunity to make up for the missed moment in the kitchen, but I couldn't bring myself to kiss her. Not while my head was still so completely consumed with thoughts of Betty.

I gritted my teeth through the production team meeting the next week and let Martha present our programming, advertising budget, and plans for the future. Hollinger sat across the desk from us, acting like he wasn't the son of a bitch who'd accosted the show's star, who also happened to be his secret girlfriend, destroyed her car, and then left her stranded at a job he'd gotten her fired from.

Betty. She's here at Hollinger's mandatory meeting, of course, sitting at the conference table, fresh off shooting. She's still wearing her stage makeup and a poofy *Classy Homemaker* skirt and formfitting blouse. The only thing missing is her iconic apron, which she hangs on a hook at the end of each show. It's washed, starched, and pressed every night, ready for a new day of cakes, grout, and floor wax.

Though I see her five days a week, somehow I miss her. My eyes find her in every room, and I memorize every detail through the camera's lens. She treats me with a distant kindness, and I don't know if that's out of concern that I'll tell someone her secrets or out of shame that she stayed with Hollinger. But what I do know with complete unsettling certainty is this: I'm stupidly, head over heels, unwaveringly, and illogically in love with Betty Wilkens.

Don Hollinger throws papers onto the table with a loud bang, like it's a gunshot starting a race, and every head in the room snaps to look at him.

"Those right there are our second quarter numbers, and let me tell you"—he pauses dramatically, making eye contact with several of the staff sitting at the table like he's about to ream them out for an abysmal report—"they're damn amazing. We're number two in our market. Number two. Way to go, boys."

He says "boys," though Martha is sitting to his right and Betty to his left. The women take it in stride, joining in with the roar of cheers. I watch, arms folded across my chest, unwilling to applaud anything, even good news, that Hollinger presents. He allows us a minute of celebration before rapping on the table with his knuckles.

"I knew we had something special when I started here, and it turns out Midwest Broadcasters Association agrees. I got word today that we have nine nominations this year." A rumble runs through the room, and murmured speculation. "Shhh. Hold on. I've got them here."

Hollinger clutches a sheet of paper. He reads off some minor nominations, some similar to the one Martha and I won in '68. We received a certificate and Martha put hers on her desk, but mine is in a folder somewhere in a box in the back of my closet.

When I hear Mark's name, my attention returns to Hollinger's announcement. Mark is nominated for Best Promotional Announcement in a Small Market. This is a major award that gets him an invitation to the MWBA ceremony, something Mark has coveted since I first met him.

"I wanna go. I don't give a shit if I win one of those stupid plaques, but I could meet Nicole Davenport and slip her my number," Mark said every year when the nominations came out. Then, when WQRX didn't get any significant nods, he'd tell everyone he'd have to wait until next year to meet his future bride. But it's not only his crush on Nicole Davenport that makes Mark want to stride into the MWBA wearing a black tie and cologne. He's worked here since he got out of the army. He craves, and I think deserves, the recognition.

The room lets out a big "woop," and I'm pulled back to the present by a slap on the back.

"Hey. Congrats," Will Barnett says, and one of the news producers shakes my hand. I've completely missed something. I hear Martha calling my name and I find her smiling at me with pink cheeks.

"Woo-hoo. Greg! Hello?"

"I think he's had the life shocked out of him," Mark jokes, and I laugh like he's right. I didn't catch the nomination, but it must be for something good, really good. Instead of admitting to being mentally checked out, I give Martha a thumbs-up as Hollinger announces the last two nominations, each one more monumental than the one before it.

"For Best Personality . . ." We all pause, expecting to hear Larry Torrence's name. Instead, he says, "Betty Wilkens."

Martha's eyes bulge, and Larry makes a very unattractive guttural sound of surprise. A woman has never been nominated in this category before, and we all know it. Betty covers her mouth like she's holding in a scream. The applause is delayed, but when Hollinger starts clapping, the rest of us join in. Betty blushes, and I have to look away when Hollinger squeezes her shoulder. He keeps his hand there as he announces the final Small Market nomination for WQRX: Best Station.

The meeting room door opens, and Hollinger's new secretary wheels in a cart filled with glasses of champagne. Stunned, head swirling already, I take a glass and hold the bubbling golden liquid up in the air along with the rest of my coworkers. Martha stands behind her chair, her eyes sparkling like she's intoxicated. Hollinger stays directly behind Betty, his hand holding her in her chair, while everyone else stands for a toast. Betty catches my eye as he gives a short speech.

"Congrats," she mouths to me, tipping her glass in my direction.

"You too," I say back as the rest of the crowd chants something about WQRX. We all drink in unison. Eyes locked, Betty takes a sip and I down my entire glass.

Across the room, I feel closer to her than I have in weeks.

"We must be doing something right," Martha says, beside me now, breaking my connection with Betty.

"You're doing something right. I'm just along for the ride—again," I say, referring to our other joint award nomination. But I understand her excitement.

Overall, this is a triumph. Even though *Janesville Presents . . .* failed, we are not failures.

"You know I wouldn't want to do this without you, right?" Martha says, her warm green eyes connected to mine like she's sending a secret message through ESP, though I don't know exactly what it is. Thankfully, I don't have to figure it out because Mark wraps both of us up in a giant bear hug, planting a sloppy kiss on my cheek first and then on Martha's, which she wipes away.

"You know what this means?" Mark asks, picking up someone's abandoned but nearly full glass of champagne. "We're going to MWBA and I get to meet . . ."

"We know, Mark. Nicole Davenport," I say, deadpan.

"Mrs. Mark Lucian, weather goddess, if you please."

"You're bonkers," Martha says, smacking his upper arm.

"I'm going stag, in case Miss Davenport needs a ride home. What about you two? Who you gonna bring for your plus one?" Mark subtly bumps my side, and Martha looks at me shyly, like a girl hoping to be asked to prom.

Over her shoulder, I spot Betty and Don whispering to one another in a corner. The magnetism between them hurts to see. The only woman I really want to be with is in love with another man, a man who did unspeakable things to her. Am I as much of a fool as she is? Chasing a love that hurts?

"We could, uh, we could go together," I say to Martha, my cheeks burning. Mark beams.

"Uh, yeah," Martha says, fidgeting with a button on her blouse, then smiling. "Yeah, that sounds like fun."

I don't know what to say after she accepts. Perhaps sensing my discomfort, Martha quickly excuses herself to check in with the rest of our team.

"Way to go, man. You did it! About time," Mark says, shaking my hand vigorously, his grip crushing my bones. "That girl has been into you for so long."

"You think?"

"Totally. Aren't you jazzed?"

"Yeah, super . . . jazzed," I say, trying to match my expression to my words, but Mark follows my eyeline and catches what really has my focus. It's Betty and Don slipping out the back door of the packed conference room, eliciting a pang of envy so strong I wince.

Mark speaks to me close in a low whisper. "She's with Hollinger, you know that, right? Like, they're an item."

I nod, putting my champagne glass on the table with the rest of the empties.

"Martha's a fine girl and she likes you. Plus, she's not dating our boss," he adds wryly, and I bob my head up and down again. I must seem like a fool to him, like I'm chasing butterflies instead of enjoying the meadow of flowers surrounding me.

Thankfully, Mark changes the subject to Nicole Davenport and how he plans to start up a conversation with her using meteorological puns. He's always known of my fondness for Betty, but he has no idea how deep our friendship has become—the shared secrets, the visit to her childhood home. It wouldn't help to tell him, anyway. Betty is taken. No, not taken, she's given herself willingly.

CHAPTER 25

Charlie

Present Day

When my alarm goes off at six this morning, I'm a woman on a mission. Despite having gone to bed late, I spring up, grab my phone, and scan my backlog of emails. There are plenty waiting for me: messages from my producer, Alex McNamara, the house inspector, and a friendly note from Dino confirming the next steps for the cleanup.

I move on to texts. There are no good-night messages from Ian, which sends a pang of regret through me, remembering the twisted, pained look on his face from last night as he and Olivia left me on the freezing lawn with Cam. On the other hand, I have three texts from Cam. I'd texted him with news of my ring discovery last night. His response this morning is an offer to go down to the Rock County clerk's office in Janesville at lunchtime to check out the marriage records. I reply with my decision to visit my mom and ask her about the ring, no matter what kind of day she is having.

Before leaving the house, I quietly get dressed, deciding to let Olivia sleep in. Within an hour, I'm waiting outside Shore Path for visiting hours with the picture in my pocket.

When the lobby doors open, I'm asked to wait in the common area while my mom finishes her occupational therapy session. I stare at the photograph, determining at least two explanations for every detail.

"What a beautiful picture," Nurse Mitchell says from behind me, making me jump.

"Yeah, Betty sure had a sense of style." I lay the image in my lap, not knowing enough about its origin to make small talk.

"Still does. I'd take fashion advice from her," Nurse Mitchell says jokingly. When I don't banter back, she grows more serious. "She asks to see you every day, you know."

"Me or Laura?" I ask in a way that comes off as bitter. Mitchell sits beside me on the floral love seat.

"Her 'friend,' which I'm assuming is you. Usually, it's when she's hungry."

"Probably because of the soup from our last visit." I chuckle a little, even though I know Betty's obsession with Ike's might also be to blame.

"Probably," she echoes, laughing softly before clearing her throat. "Listen, your dad told me a bit about what happened, uh, before, when you were a kid. And I know it's none of my business, but"—she pauses like she's measuring her words—"I think it's pretty impressive that you're here at all."

"Oh?" I say, taken aback, and search for an easy, appropriate reply. "I mean, I'm here for my dad. He never lets anyone help him, and now he's been forced into it."

"Yeah, I can see that. He's a kind man—codependent as anyone I've ever met, but a kind man."

"My God, he is tragically codependent, isn't he?" I laugh loudly at the nurse's spot-on analysis. My father, the grand enabler. It was definitely the topic of more than one session back in my postdivorce therapy days. Nurse Mitchell grows quiet as the OT room door opens, signaling the end of Betty's session.

"It's sweet that you're here for your dad and even for your mom, but I hope you're also here for yourself." She unfolds her arms and gives me a sincere smile. "This is hard stuff, Charlie, even without the baggage you're carrying. A common mistake caregivers make is not taking care of themselves."

I feel exposed by her statement. I'm not some selfless family member here out of the kindness of my heart, swooping in to save the day. I came seeking closure and to escape my real life, hoping to gather information about my childhood and the parents who let me go so long ago. I can't convince my dad to move out of his dangerous home, and the photograph in my lap reminds me that I can't seem to leave my mom and her secrets behind.

Before I can respond to Nurse Mitchell's far too generous assessment of my visits, my mom calls "Laura" from across the hall. Thank goodness. Today she is Betty.

I may not be in Wisconsin for entirely altruistic reasons, but the warmth in Betty's voice when she greets me on these days makes me think that the benefit isn't entirely one sided. My dad will have a safe house to live in, Betty has a friend to have soup with, and both of them have a granddaughter they, so far, are treating with appropriate care and attention. Maybe it's OK that I want to ask a few questions here and there, maybe it's OK if I prefer the days when my mom doesn't know me to the ones where she does.

With a knowing smile, Nurse Mitchell stands and suggests we take a walk in the garden. Betty loves the idea and slips her arm through mine as we return to her room for a jacket. She's smiling today, and the weight of her thin, frail arm threaded through mine makes me feel protective.

"This is nice," Betty says as we walk along the gravel path around the facility's garden. I inhale deeply, my lungs stretching out against my rib cage, the scent of wet dirt thick in the air.

"It finally feels like spring," I say, exhaling, the overnight change in the weather turning my breath invisible again.

The weather is warmer today, and I remember how exciting these glimpses of outdoor freedom were as a child. It meant summer was coming soon, where my world went from the tiny corner in my bedroom that'd been left untouched by my mother's belongings, to miles of houses, beaches, new friends, and plenty of ice cream. I think that's why I love living in California now; I don't have to stay locked inside for half the year.

"Look. Tulips." Betty points at the cheerful green sprouts peeking out from the rich brown soil. "I hope they're pink."

"We'll have to check again in a few days," I say. She won't remember this walk or these buds in a few hours, much less in a few days, but it's not an empty promise. If I'm still here, I'll take her to the garden to see if the tulips have blossomed.

See, I tell myself, *not totally selfish.*

We always had tulips in April, even after Mom stopped tending the flower beds. The bulbs kept coming up every spring, nature's timekeeper, "a little gift for surviving the winter," my dad used to say. I still claim tulips as my favorite flower even though I don't think I realized why until now.

Betty closes her eyes, trusting me fully to keep her safe.

"I'm a flower," she says, turning her face to the sun as we walk, and I let myself really look at the woman who I'd forced myself not to love anymore. She's wearing her coral lipstick and costume diamonds in her drooping pierced lobes, and there's an unmistakable glow to her cheeks. Something long dormant stirs inside of me, like those little green sprouts reaching for the sunlight after a deep winter freeze. It's a link stored inside my mind or DNA from when she carried me and cared for me. I have an urge I haven't felt in a while—to call her "Mom."

"Let's sit down," I say, patting her arm.

"Oh, yes. Yes." She opens her eyes and with some help settles into a spot on the cast-iron bench. I cover her legs with the quilt I've been carrying over my arm like a maître d'.

"Thank you." A perplexed look comes over her face as I sit beside her. "I'm sorry, I forgot your name."

"Charlie," I say, watching for a sign of recognition and glad when it doesn't come. I don't tell her I'm her daughter or use my nickname; that seems too risky.

"You are very pretty." It's a common comment from sweet Betty. She's always full of compliments my mother never would've given me.

"So are you. Like a flower."

"What a funny thing to say." She giggles, not remembering she's the author of the simile. "My husband brings me flowers."

"That's sweet." I think of the times my father would come home with armfuls of wildflowers he'd picked from the patch outside of his shop. My mother would bury her face in them and arrange bouquets that'd sit in clusters until they dried into stiff vestiges of their former beauty. She never threw them away, piling them in one of the spare bedrooms until the hall stunk of the sickly-sweet rotting corpses of flowers. At some point Dad stopped bringing home flowers, and eventually, the smell dissipated, and I wondered if my mom missed the surprise bouquets from her husband.

"Do you have a husband?" she asks me.

"Y-yes." I stutter as I answer, not sure if I really do after last night.

"That's nice. My husband isn't here today. He's probably at work," she says, smoothing the blanket over her legs, the plain wedding band on her left hand scratched and faded, reflecting the midmorning sun. Which reminds me . . .

I take the picture from my sweatshirt's large front pocket and hold it in front of Betty.

"Look what I found," I say, pointing at the smiling picture of my mom in her wedding dress. She saw it a few weeks ago but she treats the photograph as new.

"Oh, she's beautiful." She caresses the image.

"Do you know who that is?" I ask, slowly, kindly, trying not to be greedy or selfish.

"Do I know her?"

"Yes," I say, pointing to the young woman's face. "That's you."

"Me?" She laughs and covers her mouth. "Are you sure?"

"Yes. That's you on your wedding day."

"Oh?" she says, picking up the portrait and holding it close to her eyes.

"Do you remember that? Marrying Da—" I almost say "Dad" but stop myself. "Your husband?"

"Oh! Oh, yes." She runs her fingertips down the picture slowly and then again like she's tickling a deeply buried memory.

"I made my dress," she says.

"And your flowers?" I ask, pointing to the fabric flowers in the image, remembering the silk flower segment from *The Classy Homemaker* episode.

"Make flowers? I can't make flowers . . ."

"They're pretend—the flowers. You made the arrangement. Do you remember how you used to make things?"

"I think so," she says, the information prickling the edges of her mind. I wait, hoping more details will surface if I'm patient. "My husband didn't like them, though. So we threw them out."

Threw them out? I'd never seen my father throw out a single one of my mother's treasures before she moved into Shore Path. Maybe that's what she means, that he's throwing them out now. It must be part of hoarder Betty leaking through.

"Your ring is so pretty," I say, gesturing to the large diamond and thick gold band in the image.

"My ring?" She inspects the black-and-white photograph but can't seem to see it clearly. I take a picture with my phone and zoom it in so she can see it better. She holds up her hand and then gasps. "I . . . I lost it."

She leans over, inspecting the ground, and nearly loses her balance.

"Hey, no. It's not lost. Come here." I guide her back into a seated position and show her the band on her finger.

"The diamond is gone. My husband will be so mad."

"No, no, he won't. I'm sure Greg has it." I remember to use my dad's name this time.

Betty's eyelids flutter and she stares at me, puzzled.

"Greg? Who is he?"

She doesn't remember Dad. I've seen her forget him face to face. When it happens, my father doesn't even flinch. He'll remind Betty that he's her husband—sometimes she accepts the fact and other times she doesn't, and they let it go. I use the same strategy.

"Your husband. Greg. He's probably keeping it safe for you. But look, you still have this one . . ." I return the picture to my pocket and point to the dented gold band encircling her ring finger. It's the only one I've ever seen her wear. It looks nothing like the one in her wedding photograph or the one she wore on *The Classy Homemaker*, but it's the one she'll likely wear until the day she dies.

"That's not my ring," she says, tugging at the metal circle, but it becomes stuck on her swollen knuckle. "Who stole my ring?"

Her voice pitches up to a decibel that strains my eardrums as she claws at the ring on her hand like it's eating through her finger, her nails leaving long scratches on her paper-thin skin.

"Stop!" I say, throwing my hand over hers, taking the brunt of her self-attack.

"Who stole it? Who?" she wails, and I grasp her wrists, holding them up.

"Help!" I shout, but no one comes. The garden is empty and all the doors and windows closed.

"Betty. Betty." I chant her name as she attacks both herself and my protective restraint. "Betty!" I yell forcefully, and she zeros in on my steady stare, sniffling. "We should go look in your room. Perhaps it fell off there." Betty starts to argue, not noticing the blood pooling in the divots of her bony hands, insisting a theft had taken place, so I rush to add, "If not, we can call the police."

Her muscles relax, and though my heart is still racing, she returns to a less frantic state.

"Yes. We should call the police," she says steadily. "Tell them Mrs. Thompson took it. She takes everything," she says, blood dripping off her nails and into the gravel at her feet. I take off my sweatshirt and wrap it around her hand. Drops of red trail behind us as I urge her toward the garden exit.

As soon as I'm through the side door, I flag down a nursing assistant. By the time we get back to Betty's room, a member of the nursing staff is there with disinfectant and bandages, listening to the retelling of the incident, which I explain from an emotionally distant place so I don't break down. Betty's energy is low and she gets her wish—to have her ring removed.

"You'll visit me tomorrow? We'll go to Ike's?" she asks with eager eyes as I back out of the room, my stained sweatshirt tied around my waist, her blood under my fingernails, my hands shaking.

"Soon," I say, my throat tightening. I clasp my hands behind my back to still them. No one speaks to me on the way out, which is the only way I keep myself from losing it in front of the whole staff.

With my head resting against the steering wheel, I let it out, everything I've felt since walking into this parking lot, every sob I've stopped, every tear I've willed back inside. I think of Nurse Mitchell's kind words, calling me a caregiver, a good daughter, and feel like a fraud. What am I doing? Why am I trying to pry information out of my sick mother instead of facing my emotionally removed father with the same energy?

I slap at the steering wheel and start the car, knowing exactly where I'm going next.

Sure, there are times when my mother is painfully angry with me, opening old wounds. Some fester, but some are healing. There's someone else I need to talk to. Someone who is in his right mind. Someone who has the answers.

My father.

CHAPTER 26

Greg

May 8, 1971
Midwest Broadcasters Association Awards
The Venetian Club
Rockford, Illinois

"Damn, she really knows how to clean up," Mark says, staring at someone over my shoulder. He's already two drinks in, and we've located WQRX's banquet table. I rented a tux. Mark already had one but had to have the pants let out, claiming his dry cleaner shrunk them.

I've only worn a tuxedo once before, to an orchestra performance in Chicago. Mark tried to talk me into wearing a tux in powder blue or with a fancy silk lining, but I went with the classic look, hoping to blend in.

I turn around, expecting to see Nicole Davenport but instead spotting Martha in a floral-print dress with large, playful blue and green flowers, cinched at the waist with a long blue ribbon. Her dark hair has been professionally done and is piled on the top of her head, her skin is impeccably powdered, and she's added lashes on top of thick black liner. When I picked her up outside her apartment, I did my own version of

Mark's double take. She looks even more glamorous than she did at our ill-fated advertiser meeting at the Playboy Club-Hotel.

"Don't forget your manners," I scold Mark with a pointed finger, more forcefully than I typically speak to him. But I know him well enough to not trust him.

"Who, me? I'm a goddamned gentleman."

"Sure you are," I say as Martha reaches our table.

Mark politely kisses the air next to her cheek, and I think about taking her hand since she's my date, but I'm not as smooth as Mark, so I pull out her chair instead. She thanks me, and I'm sure she'd let me hold her hand if I tried.

Mark gave me a long pep talk this morning, ending with "She's clearly in love with you. Just go for it."

I still can't decide if his appraisal of Martha is realistic or if I'm letting my experience with Betty cloud my judgment. I've done my own assessment, and I'm almost convinced. Martha's eagerness to work with me on *Janesville Presents* . . . , her willingness to stick with me when we were left with *The Classy Homemaker*, her jealousy when I agreed to help Betty—it's all too familiar, that kind of unrequited love. It'd be so much easier if I could love her back. What's wrong with me?

"You guys ready?" she says to both of us, wiggling her eyebrows.

"Yup. Even wrote my speech." Mark flashes a set of note cards.

"Impressive." Martha takes a glass of wine off a waiter's tray. "The Small Market categories are stacked this year. I bet WKBT or WAOW will win. Actually, I'm counting on not winning. If we do, the speech is on you, Greg."

I know she's teasing, but my throat tightens at the idea of speaking in front of professionals from across the Midwest in this gigantic ballroom. The crowd is full of serious journalists, newsmen, and writers. Heroes of mine. They've been to Korea, Cambodia, Vietnam. I'm just some kid sitting behind a camera safe and sound in Janesville, Wisconsin.

"I'm kidding." Martha slaps at my arm, and I take a sip of my drink to calm my buzzing nerves. "I wouldn't do that to you."

"I would. When I win, I'm calling you up to give my speech." Mark razzes me and then excuses himself to get another drink.

"I think Nicole Davenport just walked in with her husband. Won't Mark be disappointed?" Martha searches the table cards for our names. We're seated next to each other, which of course makes sense. She sets her clutch on the table beside her place setting and then gazes across the room at the other clusters of prettily dressed men and women.

"I'm going to introduce you to some people tonight, so do what you gotta do to loosen up a little. Here. Take this." She gives me her wineglass, half full, with the shape of her lips imprinted on the edge in lipstick. She encourages me to drink as she grabs two more.

"I'm not sure alcohol is the answer . . ."

"Humor me," she says, pulling me to my feet. I take her liquid prescription, regretting it almost immediately as my head starts to spin. "Now, hold on to this one." She hands me a third glass and I take it, determined it's just for show.

"Barry. Hey . . . Barry . . ." she calls to someone behind me. A medium-height man in his thirties, balding prematurely and wearing dark horn-rimmed glasses, hugs Martha with one arm, giving her a polite kiss on the cheek.

"Smith. Look at you. Belle of the ball." He twirls her around with a natural flick of his wrist that I envy. Her dress spins out at the bottom, and she does look like she's from a fairy tale.

"All right. All right. We don't want to make Lila jealous now," Martha says, a little winded. She slows herself down, but the hem of her dress continues to swing from the momentum. She's so good at talking to everyone.

"Too late," Barry says, taking out his wallet and retrieving a picture of a fair-faced twentysomething woman and a chubby, smiling infant. "She's home with the baby and is green as eggs and ham that I get a night off."

"Oh, my heavens. Yes. The baby! Congrats, Barry. My goodness, never would've imagined you two crazy kids settling down and having a whole human child, but you proved me wrong." She claps happily. "Greg. This is Barry Montague. He was a grad student at UW when I was there and swept my poor, unsuspecting roommate off her feet. Until very recently they traveled the world together. Barry now works for KSTP. Barry, this is Greg Laramie. We work together on that housewife show I told you guys about at Easter."

"Greg? Like *the* Greg? Fellow videographer, right?" Barry shakes my hand. I stutter as I process everything Barry and Martha have said.

"Well, camera operator for now. And Martha is the boss. I'm just another set of hands."

"Not true. None of that's true. He has an eye," Martha says, giving me a hard stare. I'm struggling to pick up on the intricacies of this conversation after having so much to drink so quickly with no food in my stomach.

"So I've heard," Barry says. "Martha showed us the segment you two worked on together. The tornado story. You've got some balls, man. I was impressed."

"I'm glad . . . I'm glad you liked it."

"Like I've told Martha a million times over"—he leans in and lowers his voice as though he's concerned someone may overhear—"when you get tired of small-town news and wanna broaden your horizons, I always need a good eye over my way." He finishes his drink and adds, "We have a crew heading out next month to do some in-the-field stuff in Vietnam. Nothing super dangerous, but you never know over there. One of our guys came down with mono, and I'm looking for a late replacement."

Vietnam. The word sounds like a funeral bell ringing. It's the last place my brother walked this earth, the soil tainted with his blood. But I've often thought that the journalists over there, the ones showing the world what this war is truly like, are the only way to spare more young men, mothers, and brothers from the same fate. I've thought of going, of being one of the brave ones, using my camera for something that really matters.

Barry takes out a business card and passes it to me. I accept it without hesitation and place it in my inner coat pocket, noticing Martha watching me closely. I'm about to ask a question about KSTP and Barry's experiences in the field, when a flash of gold catches my eye.

In the doorway of the banquet hall Betty stands alone, dressed head to toe in a curve-hugging gold lamé gown that pools around her thin-strapped heels. My breath hitches in my chest as she looks into the crowd like she's lost and alone. My feet urge me to go to her.

"Thanks," I say finally, sure of my reply, "but I'm invested in WQRX."

Barry nods and shakes his tumbler, rattling the ice resting at the bottom.

"I get it, man. I get it. You're comfortable there." He pats my arm, and I bristle at his condescension. "I gotta get a refill before dinner. You've got my card. And you, pretty lady"—he turns to Martha, who seems to have also noticed Betty's entrance—"the offer still stands. Minnesota is lovely at least six months out of the year, and we can get you on the road for the rest of it."

"All right, Barry. Kiss Lila and the baby for me," she says with less oomph than she started the conversation with. As we walk away, she doesn't say anything about Barry or the job he referenced. And by the time Betty and Hollinger make it to our table, Martha's glow is beginning to dim.

I nod a hello to Betty, which she timidly returns. She's all decked out, but her nerves are showing. She must not realize it's unlikely she'll win. Her hands shake with each sip of wine, and when dinner is served, every time she takes a bite of her broiled cod, it almost slips off her fork.

Martha's my date, I remind myself, making a concerted effort to ignore Betty and focus my attention on my companion for the evening. Thankfully, Martha makes it easy to be her partner. We whisper back and forth for much of dinner, Mark joining us in boisterous laughter over an inside joke as the president of the MWBA takes the stage, starting the evening's awards program.

When the presentations start, I sneak a glance at the other side of the table. Betty bites her lip nervously, and Hollinger is locked in to every announcement as though we're all nominated for the Nobel Peace Prize. I turn to ignore him again, but when Will Barnett and Mark are passed over for their categories, Hollinger's mood turns stormy. At one point, he tosses his napkin onto his empty plate and complains about the slow service before finally taking it upon himself to return to the bar.

I shift in my seat. I couldn't hate the man more. And to think Betty is going home with him. If we lose, if she loses, what will that look like for her?

"This is us." Martha grabs my focus again. The emcee announces the next category, and when *The Classy Homemaker* is mentioned alongside other nominees, including serious news programs, it's a bit embarrassing. I'm proud of our work, and I believe Betty is incredibly talented, but do I think what we do is newsworthy and deserving of an award? No.

When our names aren't called, I'm relieved. I think Martha secretly hoped we would win, but she also seems to understand why the series about war widows was chosen instead of our homemaking show.

"Well, that was thrilling," she says, letting out a long breath and blinking her fake lashes several times like she may have had tears in them at one point. Tipsy from a steady supply of white wine, champagne, and very little else, I squeeze her hand where it rests on the table and quietly tell her what I really think.

"You deserve more than this, Martha."

She puts gentle pressure on my fingertips. "You do, too."

Her touch doesn't burn like Betty's, but it still has an effect. I've grown to care about this woman. I know she cares for me more than any person outside of my family ever has. For a sliver of a second I think I might be able to fall in love with Martha if I didn't feel such a magnetic connection to Betty.

"And the winner is . . ." The award for Best Personality is announced in the distance. It's almost like the speaker is reading a cue card transcription of what I have on my mind when he says: "Betty Wilkens, *The Classy Homemaker*."

Hollinger, back from the bar, whoops. Betty sits frozen in her seat, astounded. Her confused gaze meets mine. I slip my fingers out from Martha's grip and join in the applause. The movement seems to snap Betty out of her daze, and Don lifts her to her feet, ecstatic. I wonder how much of his happiness is for his girlfriend and how much is about his own personal clout.

Betty nearly trips over her floor-length gown as she winds through the tables toward the stage. She looks so glamorous up there, poised, ready for anything. I watch her accept the plaque, and my heart races like I'm the winner.

After thanking the station, Hollinger, her family, and so forth, she ends with one final word of gratitude. "And thank you to my producers, Martha Smith and Greg Laramie—my lifeline. I couldn't do this without you. Here's to many more years together!"

She holds up the prize and exits the stage as the bigger markets' awards are handed out.

"Can you believe that?" I ask, turning to Martha, but I find the seat beside me empty. Her clutch is gone, her wrap is gone, and as I stand to survey the rest of the hall, I find that Martha is also gone.

She can't have gotten far since I drove her here. I abandon my seat and the dry piece of chocolate cake I've been picking at for the past twenty minutes and dash toward the coat check. My feet are clumsy from a night of drinking and there's not a lot of grace to my pursuit. I catch a glimpse of blue, green, and white slipping behind an accordion partition that separates the banquet hall from the ballroom.

I make it through the sliver of an opening and find Martha halfway across the empty parquet dance floor. The deep bass of the presenter's voice announcing the final award of the night—Best Station—echoes through the speakers and into the empty space and nearly drowns out my call.

"Hey! Wait!" I shout. Martha freezes, stopping before the exit. She lands in a pool of cool white moonlight that brings out a gossamer shimmer from her gown like the printed flowers are covered in a delicate frost.

"What do you want, Greg?" Her question is icy, and I stop by the partition.

"Nothing. I just . . . I just thought you wanted to stay for the party." Martha made me promise to dance with her at the party after the awards ceremony.

"I'm not really up for it," she says, swiveling around slowly like she's standing on a turntable. The announcer in the other room reads the nominees for the Best Station in a Small Market award.

After some paper crinkling, he shouts "WQRX!" But I hardly notice because Martha starts to walk away again.

"You should stay, though. Clearly, it's a big night." She points to the speakers in the ceiling. Cheers and applause fill the room and pound at my eardrums.

"Come back. There's champagne and"—I stammer—"and you promised to dance with me."

The corners of her mouth lift into a half-hearted smile that drops immediately like she's remembered something tragic. "I don't think so, Greg. You go. Have fun."

"Do you . . . do you need a ride?" I'm not in any condition to drive, but the least I can do is get her a cab.

"Ha, no," she laughs grimly. "I'm perfectly capable of arranging my own ride . . ." she says, clearly referring to Betty's panicked call nine months ago.

The unspoken part of the sentence hangs between us as Hollinger starts his acceptance speech by quoting the dictionary. "Webster's dictionary defines a leader as . . ."

Normally, I'd roll my eyes and make a few snarky comments to Martha, but she's not listening to his victory address, her cheeks glistening with tears. I consider striding across the room, taking her in my arms, drying her face, and kissing her passionately like I should have that September night at my apartment.

But instead, she drags the back of her hand across her face, drying her own tears, and I stay fixed in place.

"See you Monday" is all I can think of to say.

She steps out of her moonbeam spotlight and exits without another word, and I let her leave. There's heartache in her echoing footsteps but also relief. As wonderful as she is, I don't know how to love Martha. She doesn't deserve a half love story like that.

I slip back through the partition where Hollinger is still speaking. Betty is back at the table, and I observe her as he speaks. She's watching him with the same plastic smile she wears on *The Classy Homemaker*. The rest of the room looks impatient, ready for the Best Station announcements for the bigger markets and then to celebrate or console themselves at the after-party.

Hollinger finally starts to wrap up.

"And though I'm thankful to God for this blessing," Hollinger says, taking on the pious persona EBN requires of him, "there's one gift from on high that's more valuable than money or earthly accolades." As he pontificates, I snake through the aisles. "Thank you to the one woman who knows how to make every day like heaven on earth." He holds his award out toward us at table seven.

As the meaning of his words starts to sink in, he leaves no question. Don Hollinger, a man I do not like, much less respect, a man I'd rather see behind bars before seeing him awarded with anything, especially the hand of a good woman, says her name. "My fiancée—Betty Wilkens. I love you!"

The crowd cheers, and the room swirls around me. Betty blushes handsomely. I notice a gold-banded diamond ring has appeared on her finger like some kind of magic trick. When the awards officially close and the folding wall opens with a thunderous crunch, the crowd slowly migrates to the ballroom. But I am stuck to my chair.

My date is gone, and the woman I love is engaged to the wrong man. My head spins with alcohol and outrage, and I'm sure of one thing—someone needs to call out that asshole Hollinger. My hand gathers into a tight fist. And I think it should be me.

CHAPTER 27

Charlie

Present Day

"Dad!" I call out, entering the house without knocking, clutching my phone, the screen still open to an image Cam sent me.

The inspector's truck was gone when I pulled up to the house and so was Ian's car. I paused to check my email in the driveway and read through an update from the inspector and a recap of the meeting from Ian. A handful of items need to be addressed before the next cleaning phase begins, and Ian's message promised me he was on it.

Then, Cam's text came through. A picture of a marriage certificate from 1971 with my mother's name on it. 1971, not 1976. I was already determined to have a word with my dad, and with this additional piece of information, I'm even more resolute.

"Dad! Where are you?" I shout, listening for a response. Papers rattle in the corner, likely rodents, and I follow the now familiar goat path to my parents' room. His car is parked outside. He's either trapped beneath a collapsed tower of belongings or he's hiding from me.

The back and side yard, only viewable through narrow slats of exposed window, show no signs of life. I'd easily hear anyone upstairs through the old floor and creaking support beams. He's not there. When I break into the bedroom, the Tiffany-style lamp over my parents' bed is on, and I can finally see the impact of our weeks of work.

Though we've only made it through about three of the six feet of stacked items lining the perimeter of the wall, the room now seems vast compared to when I first entered it. The newest layer is made up primarily of scrapbooks. I've started to look through the articles and handwritten letters pasted onto pages with recipes, book suggestions, and crafting instructions, like a Pinterest page in physical form. Now I know what they were for—my mom's show and her book. Why didn't he just tell me?

"Hello, Lottie," my dad says from behind the bookshelves to the right of the doorway. The house phone is plugged in there, and I can tell by the stony look on his face when he emerges from the cavern he's had a call from Shore Path and he's not happy about it.

"There you are." I reflect his expression.

"Whose blood is that?" He points at the stained shirt I forgot was still around my waist.

"Mom's." No reason to lie. "She's fine. There was a little misunderstanding."

"I heard," he says, his posture slumped, thumbs threaded through his belt loops. "Lottie, I appreciate your help but . . ." An exquisite pain expands in my chest realizing what's about to happen. Rejection. Again. He doesn't want me. Again. He's picking her over me—again.

"You better not be mad at *me*," I say defensively before he can finish disowning me—again. "When will you see that I'm not the problem, Dad?"

"I'm not saying you're the problem, Lottie. But your mom isn't in a good place right now."

"Mom? You think I'm saying *Mom* is the 'problem'?" I put air quotes around *problem*. "No. I'm not the problem and neither is Mom. You, Dad. You are the problem." I spit out the allegation that's become clearer to me the longer I've been here.

"I'm certainly not perfect and you have every right to be upset, but . . ."

"No buts. None. Mom was sick, is sick, but you—you chose to get rid of me. And you're doing it again."

"I'm not trying to get rid of you, Lottie. I just think it's better for your mother if you keep your distance. You keep insisting on pushing, pushing, pushing. It's upsetting to her."

He crosses his arms, standing to his full height, a rare sight. Defending my mom—that's my dad's greatest talent. He could have been a famous musician or photographer or expanded his business beyond the small main street of Lake Geneva, Wisconsin. He could have been a father and grandfather, but he was too busy being my mother's keeper, protector, enabler.

"You're right. It is." I untie the stained shirt and toss it on the bed, queasy at the thought of wearing it any longer. "And I don't want to upset her anymore, but you know what I realized?"

He looks at me blankly, and I point the phone I'm still holding in his direction.

"You're the reason we had an incident today. You could've answered at least some of my questions without playing little games, dodging the real answers. But you let me keep collecting my breadcrumbs and taking them to Mom for dead end after dead end. You let me find answers on the internet and in libraries and courthouses instead of telling me yourself. I'm not the reason Mom is upset. You are."

I repeat my accusation, and my dad shakes his head, deflating after his very brief moment of puffed-up defensiveness.

"You don't know what you're talking about," he says, a deep sadness in his voice, but I'm not in a place of compassion.

"Exactly. I don't know. So tell me. Tell me about Janesville and WQRX and that damn show and"—I wrestle the picture out of the waistband of my yoga pants and drop it on the bed—"who the hell she married in 1971, 'cause I know it wasn't you. And how all of this happened." I reference the remaining hoard that towers above and around us.

My dad looks at the picture on the bed and then looks away immediately, like the image causes him pain. When he responded that way before, I thought it was because he found it excruciating to see my mother at a wedding she didn't remember anymore. But after Cam's text, I know that's not why.

"Who is Donald Hollinger?"

Letting out a weighty sigh, his knees crumple, making him slump onto the bed, head in his hands.

"I know it's hard to understand, but there are some things your mother wants to remain"—he clears his throat, looking at me through the crook of his arm—"personal."

"What could be so important that you need to hide it even now? From me?" I clear a spot next to him and sit. My nerves are still prickling with anger and frustration, but a full-on attack will get me nowhere.

"Aren't there things you don't tell your daughter?" His question hits home. Of course there are things I've kept from Olivia—this house is one of them, her grandparents, the problems with Ian.

"She's too young . . ."

"Is she?"

I think of my beautiful daughter, her first steps, her first heartbreak, her first time driving, her graduation cap, her prom dress, her dorm room, her face when she showed up here chasing the secrets of my life.

"It's different."

"Is it, though?" he asks, hands on his knees, looking at me and nodding slowly. "All right, then. Don Hollinger was the man your mother married before me. We met at WQRX and Don was our boss. He died suddenly a few years later, and your mother never fully recovered from that loss. I loved her so much that I thought I was helping her, and things got . . . out of control in the house. I never wanted to lose you, Lottie. I love you, but after a while I realized your life would be better without us in it. I couldn't abandon your mom, and this house was no place for a child. And then everything happened with your career, and I thought it was proof I was right."

"You weren't right, Dad. I needed you. I mean, I needed Mom, too, but if I couldn't have both a mom and a dad, I at least needed you."

His head bobs, and he pushes off of the bed, clearing a shelf of old books and placing them in a large cardboard box for sorting.

"Life is always easier when looked at backward, I guess."

"It's not over—life, that is. You don't have to lie down in your grave and erase the past just because Mom is sick. I'm still here. Olivia and Ian's boys are amazing kids. You'd love them. It doesn't have to be like this anymore."

Greg clears another shelf, picking a few papers out of the cover of one of the books and placing them in the "save" pile.

"You're a wise one, Lottie Laramie. Always thought you were an old soul," he says, which is kind to say but also a handy way to avoid engaging in the confrontation. "And for now, how about we let your mom rest up? No more visits for a bit, huh?" He places another line of dusty books in the cardboard box.

The seemingly friendly suggestion sends a flash of heat up my neck. He wants to stop me from seeing my mother after I've spent the past thirty-odd years without one. I sit in my feelings of rejection as he continues to putter around the room. He's not asking me to leave or halting the next phase of our renovation. He didn't immediately step up and become the father I need after witnessing my much-rehearsed confrontation, but he did say he loves me. I can keep pushing, screaming, fighting and get nowhere, or I can endure my father's avoidance and finish at least some of what we've started.

I guess I can live off breadcrumbs for now.

"I'll stay away," I say to his back as he leafs through a stack of papers inside a collection of manila folders. "From Mom. I'll give her some space."

He thanks me and says over his shoulder, "I'm sure she'll be eager to see you again soon enough."

Irritated but resolved to hold my tongue, I roll my eyes at the back of his head, stand, retrieve my sweatshirt and the picture on the bed, and put my phone in my pocket.

"I'd better go change and check on Olivia. I'll be here bright and early tomorrow for phase two." I stop at the foot of the bed when he says his goodbyes as though we hadn't just had an argument. He's cooled off from the protective anger I walked into, and I'm sure my ban won't last very long. His forgiving nature is something I definitely didn't inherit.

I consider asking him to join us for dinner, but a force field of resentment stops me, and I walk out of the room instead. And as I exit the house, slamming the old door closed hard enough to shake the support beams, I remember why I'm not passive like my dad. There's something dangerous about being too forgiving. I'll follow his rules, I'll play nice, I'll let him love me in his flawed, distant way, but why should I let him into my life when he keeps me out of his? No. Tonight he can eat alone.

CHAPTER 28

Greg

May 8, 1971
Midwest Broadcasters Association Awards
The Venetian Club
Rockford, Illinois

Don Hollinger has his arm wrapped around Betty's waist as if he owns her. Betty is all smiles and laughter, but I can't help but think of what she looked like the morning I woke up next to her in the front seat of my car, no makeup, heartbroken, real. And it was all because of one man—one singular villain who rejected and punished her as soon as he found out one of her many secrets. My nails dig into my palm, my knuckles aching.

"That was unexpected," Mark says, his statement accurate in more ways than one. He joins me in watching Betty and her new fiancé. "He's a lucky SOB," Mark continues when I don't answer. I chug the rest of my drink in one gulp, glaring now.

"He's a son of a bitch, that's for sure." I slam my glass on the table as the profanity explodes out of me full volume. Hollinger seems to notice, and Betty definitely does. Mark's eyes bulge and he looks shocked but also a touch entertained.

"Whoa, buddy." He pats my back and urges me away. "Let's get you some water. I think someone's been having a little too much fun."

"I don't need water," I grumble, still moving toward the couple, easily freeing myself from Mark's grip. I sound like an insolent child, but I'm finding a blistering satisfaction in speaking freely.

"Fresh air, then? Coffee? Wait—" He looks around. "Where's Martha?"

"She left," I say, hyperfocused on my target.

"She left?" he repeats, stunned, catching me again and forcing a fresh glass of water into my hand. "Why?"

As I continue to watch Betty and Don, Mark seems to understand.

"Hey. Let's go to the Oasis. We could skip this whole dog and pony show and grab a burger instead." He's being a good friend, I know it. He's paying me back for all the times I've dragged him out of a bar after he's hit on some guy's girl or gotten in a row about Bears versus Packers or said the wrong thing to the wrong guy about Vietnam. But this is different. I'm not blowing off steam or looking for an adrenaline rush—I loathe Don Hollinger, and Don Hollinger is our boss.

"I'm not going anywhere till I've had a word with that guy." I lower my voice or at least attempt to. "He's all holier than thou, but he should be arrested for what he's done to her."

Mark stands in my way, talking low and urgently.

"Don't do this, man. I know you've got a soft spot for her, but it's not gonna happen."

I grind my teeth.

"Don't you think I know that? I'm not the kind of guy to end up with a girl like that, but that doesn't mean she should end up with that asshole. There's stuff you don't know . . ."

"Listen. Let's go get drunk somewhere else and you can tell me all about it. Oh, shit," Mark growls as Hollinger skirts around the perimeter of the table, headed in our direction. I sniff, loosen my tie, and prepare myself for the confrontation I've been planning in my mind since I walked through broken glass in the parking lot of the Playboy Club-Hotel.

He seems steady, like he's sober even though he's been drinking steadily throughout the night. Maybe the high of winning and having an up-and-coming star on his arm, wearing his ring, eager to take his name, counteracts the alcohol.

"Big night, eh? You fellas sticking around or heading out?" If Hollinger heard any of our conversation, he doesn't let on. I tower over him, though he's got enough muscles to snap me in two if he wanted to. There's no aggression in his question. No wonder Betty keeps falling for his "nice guy" act, especially when diamond rings and fancy cars are involved.

"I'd like to talk to you," I say, raising my finger and swaying enough to show I've been drinking.

"I'd love to hear your thoughts." Hollinger steps up, clearly sensing my aggression. Mark moves in defensively to keep us from getting too close. "Outside?" He raises his eyebrows in a challenge, like we're going to meet with pistols at dawn in the OK Corral.

Damn, it'd be fantastic to slam a fist against his smug face. Will I get fired? It's likely. But so what? Why should I stay here and watch a woman I love sign on for a life with a man I've come to abhor?

"I don't think that's a great idea—" Mark interjects, but Hollinger cuts him off.

"This is between me and Greg, isn't that right, Tin Man?" His eyes lock on mine, and I read the truth in the steadiness of his stare. He knows I know. Maybe she told him or maybe he just guessed, but he knows. He's probably wanted to get me under control for a while now. He's setting me up to make a fool of myself. I should calm down, listen to Mark's advice, but I don't know how to stop now. I don't want to stop.

"Don't call me that," I answer, the room spinning when I take my first step. My feet are burdensome, as if my shoes are filled with gravel or lead. Mark tosses his hands up and leans against the back of one of the gold-leaf ballroom chairs with an unlit cigarette between his lips, giving up on an intervention. I follow Hollinger toward the exit, every step demanding intense concentration to keep me walking in a straight line.

Just short of the broad set of double doors that lead to the lobby, a soft, familiar hand takes mine and yanks me back.

"Ask me to dance," Betty demands as I stop and stare down at her. Her brow is slick with sweat, and the thick foundation on her face accentuates its lines. The blue eyeshadow on her eyelids is creased and fading, and the cord-like vein in her neck pulses rapidly. "Ask me. Right now."

"I . . . I can't," I say, watching Hollinger disappear out of the room. She crushes my hand and speaks through gritted teeth.

"Ask me to dance, Greg." Her eyebrows crunch together, and the corners of her wide blue eyes pinch.

It's not a request or even an order—it's a plea.

Hollinger is gone. I'm sure he'll come looking for me once he realizes I'm not following him. But with Betty in front of me, the haze of hatred begins to lift. I clear my throat and focus on the dreamlike sensation of her hand on mine. The sound of "Groove Me" rolls through the banquet hall from the ballroom like it's carried on a crisp, clean breeze.

"Would you like to dance?" I ask.

"I would love to," she says as relief smooths the lines on her face.

It's much easier to follow Betty to the ballroom than to follow her fiancé to the exit. We make it to the wooden dance floor just as the playful rhythm of King Floyd shifts to a slower tempo, accompanied by the rich baritone of Elvis. I expect Betty to change her mind now that couples have begun to sway. Instead, she positions herself in front of me, placing my right hand on her waist and my left hand in hers, while her other hand rests on my bicep since she can't reach my shoulder. Even with her heels on, her head barely reaches my chest. To speak, she would need to crane her neck, and I'd have to hunch over to hear her.

So, we don't speak.

We dance to the King singing "The Wonder of You." With Betty in my arms, my feet suddenly know what to do. We step and turn in slow unison without words. I cherish having her safely against me, and the scent of her perfume acts as smelling salts, bringing me to near sobriety. Barry Montague stands to the side of the crowd and raises a glass in a sort of hello, and I nod back.

Mark isn't dancing. He isn't even talking to Nicole Davenport or any of the pretty women here. He's watching me and Betty with a look of bafflement, sucking on his cigarette and blowing large clouds of smoke into the upper atmosphere of the room. I can't guess what he's thinking, but I'm sure he'll have a few words for me later, or more than a few based on his stormy demeanor.

As the song repeats its chorus for one final time, I'm nearly dizzy from our turns about the room, the greens, golds, oranges, silks, polyesters, and brocades melding into a surreal tapestry. Betty finally speaks.

"You promised you wouldn't say anything," she whispers, leaning in so her entire body is pressed against me. I take her in and spread my palm against the small of her back where her skin peeks over the zippered closure, holding her tightly.

"I know, but he's a sadist. And just so . . ." I search for the right term, the one that represents how brazen Hollinger comes off. "Unrepentant." My molars clench together as I imagine him handing her the keys of a new car when the only reason she needed one was because of him.

She sighs and nods without attempting to defend her fiancé. "I know you must judge me, and I don't blame you."

"I'm not judging." It's not the time to spill my feelings for her. It's likely I'll never speak those words out loud—they're a private, bittersweet secret that only a fool like me would understand. I find the next best explanation. "I'm worried about you."

"I know, but I'm all right. I'm . . ." She looks up at me as the song fades to an end and a new one begins. "I'm happy."

She smiles, that big, beautiful smile she shines into the camera every day as she talks to her viewers. It's a shield so well fortified that I'm certain most who see it believe it. I don't. I haven't for some time now, but does the truth matter at this point?

"Well then, I'm happy for you," I say, releasing her and sliding backward. A rush of air flows in like a river, dividing us. My palm still tingles, and I'm chilled without her warmth. But it's time. It's been time. "And I'll keep my mouth shut. I promise."

"Thank you," she says, her voice thin and unsteady. She starts to say something else, but the music has changed to a disco song and the floor is now filled with gyrating bodies and flailing arms that encroach on our quiet conversation. She fades into the crowd, and I think she says goodbye, but I don't really want to hear it.

"You still up for a burger?" I ask Mark when I free myself from the dancing mob. He's leaning against the side wall watching the dancers, sipping on a cup of coffee. I can't stay here, but I'm not ready to go home, not ready to be alone with my drunken thoughts, my ridiculous, aching heart.

He gives me a searing look like he'd like to take me in the alley himself. I hold up my hands in surrender. "And a beer. On me."

"You're an idiot," he says, placing the mug on a nearby decorative table and straightening his suit coat.

"Agreed." I wipe at my brow, eager to get out of this place with or without Mark. "So. You coming?"

"Let's go," he says, forcefully moving past me, beelining through the crowd toward the empty dining room. I go to follow him but allow myself one look back. Betty is watching my exit. Behind her, a path clears through the wild mass of dancers, like a predator swimming through a school of fish. It's Don Hollinger, without his jacket, his sleeves pushed up, and his jaw flexed and firm. He reaches Betty and spins her around. I bristle and hesitate, watching for any signs of distress. Part of me wants to go back, take the microphone, and spill the truth to the crowd cheering for him, but as Betty comes out of her rotation, she's laughing.

"Damn it. Let's go," Mark shouts across the abandoned banquet hall.

"Coming," I say, not looking back to check on Betty and Don or anyone else in that room. Whether I believe her displays of happiness or not, I can't help someone who doesn't want to be helped or love someone who doesn't want my love. It's not right for me to convince Betty she isn't happy.

"She's not worth it," he says when I slide into his car, the spring night air chilling my sweat-drenched shirt and back. "They rarely are."

"I know," I say, staring out the window at the sprouting fields as we speed back toward Janesville, not believing a word either of us says.

CHAPTER 29

CHARLIE

Present Day

"I'm sorry that took so long. I hope you found something in the fridge . . ." I call out to Olivia, tearing off my sweatshirt and sweatpants as soon as I get inside the house. I need to get out of these tainted garments, spoiled both by blood and by the fight with my dad.

Right now, I want to put on my pajamas, have dinner with Olivia, and text Cam the information my dad told me about the name on Mom's 1971 marriage license. There's clearly more to the story and more I need to know before my interest will be satiated. There are two more boxes of films, and I'm sure they hold some answers and probably will spark more questions, but I don't know when I'll get to them.

Using my toes, I flip the pants off the living room floor into my arms, preparing to scurry to the bedroom, when a low cough mixed with a laugh comes from the kitchen. Startled, I swerve around to see Ian standing in the corner by the painted gray circular pedestal table. He's dressed in a full suit—blue single-breasted jacket with a white shirt unbuttoned at the collar and a tan belt. In his hands he holds an oversized bouquet of white tulips. His beard is neatly trimmed, and his hair is cut in a tight taper up to a sharp part on the right side, held in place with pomade.

My heart skips a beat like it always used to when I saw him on set, before he asked me out for drinks seven years ago. Who am I kidding? The heart thing never went away. I've always been insanely attracted to my husband, even when I don't want to be.

When Ian's formal attire registers, I squeal and clutch the crumpled sweats in front of me, remembering I'm standing in the hallway in my underwear.

"Ian! What the hell are you doing?" I shriek. His rich laugh fills the room, and he doesn't even pretend to avert his gaze.

"Olivia let me in. Call me crazy, but I thought you'd be dressed when you walked in the front door . . ."

"Olivia. Of course." I roll my eyes, saying her name like a curse word. Her meddling is growing untenable. "Where is she?"

"Took an Uber over to visit your mom, I think. Also mentioned something about going out with one of the nurses afterward, a local girl."

"Let me guess. She said she'll be out late, and she knew about—this." I gesture at his impeccable hair, pressed suit, polished Italian leather loafers.

"She dressed me."

"She's lost her mind," I mutter, unsure of my next move. "Turn around. I need to change."

"Do I have to?" he asks with a flirtatious smirk.

"Ian McFadden. Yes. Turn around."

"Yes, ma'am." His southern upbringing comes out, and I can't help but smile. Once his back is to me, I run into my room, but inside I find another surprise. A red dress in a clear garment bag hangs from the overhead fan, and a shoebox sits on the bed. "Shit."

My phone buzzes. The messages are from Ian in the living room.

Ian: The dress was my idea. Let me take you out.

Ian: Please.

The gown is a beautiful halter dress with a pleated skirt. Not cheap and my exact size. I lift the shoebox lid and peek inside. The shoes have six-inch heels, and I think of all the times I've dressed up and stood beside Ian, held his hand, felt proud to be his wife.

My left hand is still bare, my heart still sore, but instead of tearing the dress down and telling Ian to back off like I would've a week ago, I caress the silky material and consider the offer. Ian made a mistake, but unlike my parents, he didn't give me away. He apologized, he begged for forgiveness, he showed up here. He is choosing me. I think of Olivia, the twins, and all the years we've given to one another, and type a response.

Charlie: Where are you taking me?

Ian: It's a surprise.

Ian said our reservation was at six thirty, and that's all I knew until we turned into the front gate of the Grand Geneva. The road winds past smaller hotels, patches of budding trees, and a palatial par-72 golf course. Thankfully, the drive took only fifteen minutes, and we spent most of it talking about the twins and generalities of the renovation. As we pull under the pavilion covering the entrance, Ian puts the car into park and turns to face me.

"Thanks for saying yes," he says genuinely. Recently, I've felt like something's missing from our off-camera connection. Every interaction plays out like we have a lens shoved in our faces, even when we're alone. Tonight, that's all stripped away. There's something alluring about wearing a dress he chose for my body and trusting Ian to drive us to an unknown destination. As he helps me down from my elevated seat in the SUV, I let his hand linger on my waist. Chills run up my spine as his thumb grazes a bare spot between my wrap and dress on my lower back.

"You look so beautiful," he says as the valet drives away with the car and we stride through the automatic sliding doors.

"You dressed me," I say back, taking in the two-story lobby. My eye is drawn to the floor-to-ceiling tan brick fireplace, hunting lodge chandeliers, white furniture, and a long bar on the main floor. A pianist plays the grand piano. A glass wall offers a view to the busy Ristorantè Brissago on the second floor. It's not the most glamorous place we've stayed or the most memorable, but it's perfect.

"I love this," I say, running my fingers over the roughcast stone that lines the walls as we take the short flight of stairs to the next level.

"I knew you would. It reminded me of . . ."

"Frank Lloyd Wright." I finish his sentence in a synchronicity I haven't felt with Ian in a while.

"Yeah, exactly. Inspired by Frank Lloyd Wright. Prairie style. They kept a lot of the original design details," he says as we approach the glass-encased restaurant.

We're led to a table against the window. From here we can see the bustling lobby bar, but the sounds from below are muted other than the tinkling of the highest notes floating up from the grand piano. I'm reminded of how publicly perched our relationship is. Our every move draws the public eye, and they watch with fascination, as though our lives exist solely for their entertainment. I turn away from the hotel patrons, a little dizzy.

Ian orders our drinks and grins at me across the table, his smile stabilizing me. It looks like he's going to say something important, something he's been rehearsing in his mind.

"Did you know my mom worked here?" I blurt, dodging his serious topic. "There was a picture at Thumbs. Sorry, Thumbs Up is a bar in town. I went with my friends on one of my first nights here, and it was like Bunny night. Everyone was dressed in corsets and ears and the guys in smoking jackets . . ." I babble, trying to explain everything at once, and Ian's eyebrows rise.

"You wore a Playboy Bunny costume to a bar?" Our drinks are delivered, and I giggle at the misunderstanding.

"Oh, God, no. No," I say, taking a sizable sip of my lemon drop martini and enjoying the nearly immediate headiness of the first taste. "Lacey had no idea—just a friend reunion kind of thing. And there was this wall of pictures from when this was the club. They had a picture from the first group of Bunnies, and my mom was there right in the front row. Almost didn't recognize her, but I'd found this name tag in her things that matched the ones in the picture . . ."

I'm rambling, and Ian doesn't wait for the rest of my story before asking, "Is that where you saw Cam? Cameron. Your 'friend'?" He bristles at his own mention of the man he left in my house a few nights ago.

I wondered when this would come up. I take a deep breath and search for the right approach. Honesty couldn't hurt. I start poking at my newly delivered salad, no longer hungry.

"We ran into him there, actually. He was with some guys from high school."

"Ah, simply getting wasted at a bar with his buddies on Playboy night," he says, sounding uncharacteristically judgmental. I cock my head and narrow my eyes.

"No, actually. He was the designated driver. And he's not some barfly. He's a dentist."

"A dentist. OK. Happily married?" His jealousy becomes very obvious as he ferociously chews a bite of lettuce. He doesn't even like salad. More of a meat-and-potatoes kind of a guy, but today he's eating salad. Clearly, he's experiencing something. For a moment I feel disloyal, like I'm a cheater. But then I remind myself that Ian and I are separated. Even if we weren't, it's not like I crossed any lines with Cam.

"He's divorced," I state flatly.

"And you?" he asks, looking at my left hand, my ring still absent. I fiddle with the utensils and then clasp my hands under the table.

"I don't know, Ian. I don't know what we are."

A substantial weight sits on my chest as I gaze through the glass at the full lobby. I should've worn the ring in case people recognized us and posted photos on social media. I should act like my half of the happy couple, but I don't know how to hold it all inside anymore. I feel like my mother's house, bursting at the seams, threatening to collapse under the pressure of all the retained pains and memories. I should've learned by now that if a mess is ignored for too long, there will be unexpected consequences.

Caleb, our waiter, approaches during my pregnant pause. He's figured out who we are and is trying not to let on. He brings Ian's T-bone steak and my barramundi. He replaces my martini with a fresh one and slides a full glass of scotch across the table without asking if we'd like another round. I can't imagine eating right now, but I pick up my fork and go through the motions as Caleb leaves.

"Are you in love with him?" Ian asks in a low mutter.

Love. I almost laugh—not because I haven't felt anything for Cameron, but because it's difficult to understand how Ian could imagine love developing so quickly. It took me a year and a half to say "I love you" to Ian and to let him meet Olivia. Love is a matter of substance. It takes great effort and time to build and needs a strong foundation. It requires constant tending. It's not made of sticks or straw. I don't want a house that can easily be blown down.

"I could ask you the same question about your friend." I stare into his eyes, coming closer to confronting him than I have since the night I found those messages.

"Hell no," he says, pushing his phone toward me across the table, and I shove it away. I already did a full deep dive into his phone before I left for Wisconsin, and anything I'd see now would be a curated version of the past month, not the reality. "You can look through anything you want anytime you want. The passcode is your birthday. It was one stupid conversation."

We are having *the* confrontation. Here. In a room full of strangers sitting nearby. My mouth is dry, and I gulp down half of my newly refreshed drink.

"It was one conversation that could've ruined everything." I lower my voice to emphasize the seriousness of the situation that could have unfolded if that woman had taken screenshots. I insisted he unsend every message and block her, not only out of jealousy but also for damage control.

"I know. It all happened so fast. I don't even know why I responded."

"Well—why did you?"

"I don't know. I really don't. I'm so happy with you, Charlie, with our life."

"Clearly not totally happy. If there was nothing wrong—why would you talk to her that way?" Then I ask the most painful question of all. "Am I not enough for you?"

"You're more than enough. It's about me. I started therapy. I'm completely dedicated to fixing things—" I interrupt him with another question that's been rolling around in my mind, brushing past the revelation of his new foray into therapy.

"But if you could flirt with a woman on the internet, let her talk to you like . . . that . . ." I lower my voice again as I reference the sexually explicit texts I read in horror while sitting on our bed as he showered in the other room. I can't erase those words from my mind—the shock of seeing his eager responses and the pain of seeing him react to images sent by a woman whose body hasn't changed with age or from carrying a life inside of her. "What about in person?"

"Never, Charlie. I never met her or anyone else in person, and I never want to."

Ian leans across the table to touch me. He sounds so sincere, and until this situation, I never questioned his loyalty. I thought Ian was disgusted by women who flirted with married men. Even when he was a single dad with his DMs full of messages from horny fans, he said he felt violated by their propositions. He claimed my insistence on taking things slow was a huge turn-on. But now, I don't know what to think.

I glance around the room and out the window and then back at Ian. "Can we not do this here?"

He swallows a bite of steak and washes it down with his drink, wipes his mouth, and drops the cloth napkin in his lap.

"Yeah, yeah, of course. Of course. I wanted tonight to be special, a new start." His jaw clenches, hand curled tight on the table. "I'm sorry. It's just—I've been going crazy since you left and stopped answering my calls. And then when Olivia and I got here and I saw you with that guy . . . I nearly lost my mind."

Ian is not a man who easily gets jealous. Women are drawn to Ian and his burly, muscley, "I can fix anything with my hammer" quiet strength. Fame has brought unwanted attention my direction, too. But my husband has always brushed it away with a long kiss, a hand on the waist as a reminder that we belong to each other. But tonight, I'm seeing jealous Ian. I shouldn't like seeing this side of my husband, I shouldn't find satisfaction in knowing that I could move on, that he could lose me and it'd be his doing. Cam isn't some pawn in our marital conflict, and I wasn't trying to beckon the green-eyed monster, but now that it's here, I don't feel as alone in my struggle.

I snake my arm through the landscape of plates and glasses and place my ringless hand over his coiled fist. He clasps it tightly as though he might miss the opportunity if he doesn't act fast.

"Can I try to fix this? Please?" he asks, the intensity of his gaze fading the rest of the room to a blurry haze. His calloused fingers are familiar and reassuring, like his smile when we first sat down and his caress on my lower back as we entered the resort. My body hasn't forgotten how to trust him. I want to believe it's this easy of a fix, that all I need to do is choose to forgive, trust, start over, let him do the work, and stop running away.

I don't have the right words to say that mean "yes" and also "it'll take time," but he somehow knows when I bite my lip to hold back the tears that will come if I say too much.

He nods, his signature grin tugging at the corner of his mouth. He places a lingering kiss on my hand, and I let him, which is as much of an answer as I can muster right now.

Just then, Caleb appears out of nowhere, his squeaky, hyper voice asking about desserts, cutting our conversation short. But we've said enough to know that we're going to take on a new rehab project: our marriage. Tomorrow, I'll tell Cam we're meant to be friends but nothing else. I'll let Olivia think she's properly "trapped" us. And then I'll let Ian meet my mom.

Ian rejects Caleb's dessert offer and asks for the check, explaining that he's already planned our next stop. After he excuses himself for a bathroom break, I lean back and finish the last bit of my drink.

The calming endorphins from Ian's touch and the buzz from the martinis mingle together and make it like nothing bad ever happened in my marriage and never could in the future. It's comforting, this attempt at forgiveness, at moving on. I get to reclaim my life, my family, my stability. It's what I always imagined it'd be like to have my dad show up on the doorstep of the foster home with Mom sitting in our sky-blue Subaru parked on the street, telling me the house is clean and they want me to come home.

I sit in the bliss. I must look like a fool, smiling dreamily. Then Ian's phone vibrates on the table, face down where he'd left it earlier as an offering. The sparkly daze of perfection evaporates, and a warning siren starts a low squeal in my ears.

I could flip it over. I could look. He said I could. But do I want to? What if I see something incriminating? What if all my renewed faith falls apart as quickly as it was restored?

The phone buzzes again and then once more. Those are definitely text messages.

Shit.

The ringing in my head crescendos. The phone, in its industrial-strength black case, calls to me. He'll be back in a second. He'll be able to delete anything he doesn't want me to see. He could lie to keep me locked into this relationship, to keep me, period.

I turn over the phone and tap the screen. A line of notifications shows up, and I type in the password.

The first message is from a number I don't recognize. Several messages appear from today. They look as though they're part of an ongoing conversation, though none of the previous texts are intact. He must have deleted them. Red flags flash in front of my eyes as I read the messages one at a time, starting at the top of the conversation box.

TBB: You're asking her tonight? Fill me in asap.

Hell no. Who is this? I pull the phone closer. TBB? I think through all the possible names that might match the initials but come up with nothing. As I scroll up it looks like the next text is from an hour ago, checking in with no reply. And another two below that make my head spin.

TBB: Did she sign the papers?

TBB: It has to happen tonight. I can't stress this enough.

Papers. My head spins. Divorce papers? Ian clearly wasn't going to ask for a divorce tonight, but do these texts mean he was telling some girl he's leaving me—just like those scummy cliché cheaters always do while trying to keep two women on the line?

I will not be one of those women.

I tap the reply box on the screen and quickly type out a message as Ian—giving the girl on the other end a dose of truth that might save her from falling for any further lies.

"Ian": I'm on a date with my wife right now.

Ian walks across the dining room, rubbing his hands together like he always does after washing them. I hold my breath, waiting as bubbles appear, disappear, and reappear again. He's only a few steps away when a sixtysomething woman with dyed brown hair and a sparkling top stops him and asks for a selfie. He smiles, always so gracious with fans. He urges me over to join as a line of text appears.

TBB: Good idea. Soften her up. Her dad too. Don't get distracted, though. Crews will be there to start shooting on Wednesday. Don't screw this up.

I read it twice quickly and then once slowly before grabbing my purse, wrap, and both phones, slapping his into the palm of his outstretched hand as I walk out of the restaurant without stopping for a picture or worrying about what anyone might think. The only thing running through my mind is the image of that last text, the one that stole any remaining hope I had for trusting my husband, any assurance that we could go back to the way things were.

I know who's texting my husband and it's worse than some floozie on social media.

TBB. The Big Boss. Our boss. The boss of all HFN—Alex McNamara.

CHAPTER 30

Greg

April 20, 1972
Caravelle Hotel
Saigon, Vietnam

The tile floors of the Caravelle Hotel, where nearly a hundred war correspondents are housed in Saigon, is wet from the afternoon humidity. It's monsoon season and I've never felt damp in so many ways.

Reaching my hotel room, I peel off every centimeter of wet clothes until I get down to my socks, which strip away from my waterlogged feet with a sick slurping sound. My body is worn, and the landscape of my ribs is easy to see through my skin, which is tanned dark brown from the days in the sun. Yet, lying in my underwear inside the only air-conditioned building in Saigon, I find I can't complain.

I've seen too many living and dying in worse places than this—both soldiers and the Vietnamese who are left homeless, starving, injured, and ragged. The young soldiers we interview tell us their honest perspective about the war. Some are here out of patriotic service or proud family military tradition, but many of these men didn't choose to be here and wish nothing more than to go home. They are young men like my brother, who had an unlucky birthday drawn and no money or connections to get out of being shipped overseas.

I, like the patriotic soldiers who volunteered for this hellish war because of moral and political beliefs, chose to climb onto that plane out of Minneapolis ten months ago. Martha and I resigned from WQRX on the same day, and Don Hollinger lost his ever-loving shit as we cleaned out our desks.

"When you crash and burn out there, don't even think about crawling back. You're dead to me."

Martha had a few choice words for Don, but I'd already packed away my bitterness after almost unleashing them at the MWBA banquet. It'd been Betty who'd convinced me to keep quiet, who'd reminded me of my pledge to her, but she had no idea how far away I'd need to go to keep those promises.

"What do you mean, Vietnam?" she asked from behind me as I sorted through the standing toolbox in the studio after escaping Hollinger's tirade, collecting a few screwdrivers and wrenches I'd brought from home.

"I was offered a job with KSTP. They're a part of a group of some Midwestern stations headed over there. They lost their other camera guy."

"I thought you hated the war," Betty said, the sound of her foot tapping increasing my anxiety.

"I do," I said. "That's why I'm going—to show people what's going on over there, to make a difference."

I tossed a screwdriver into my canvas bag and faced Betty. She stood with her arms crossed over the buttoned bodice of one of her Classy Homemaker dresses, the hand with her engagement ring tucked under the bicep of her right arm. I couldn't see it, but I still knew it was there.

"It's not safe," she said with tears in her eyes, like she was really worried, like I was her sweetheart or her brother rather than a coworker. I was ready to leave WQRX and I was ready to leave Betty, mostly because it hurt far more to stay, but I never thought leaving would make her cry.

"Listen, I'll be fine," I said, wiping some grease off my fingers with a rough towel. I wanted to reach out and touch her one last time but stopped, knowing I'd ruin her show-ready look.

"You don't know that."

"None of us knows that," I said, hiking the canvas bag over my arm, thinking of Pop's heart attack when I was twelve, Ma's lifeless body three months after finding out about Jim, her grief too great to keep on living.

"True," she said falteringly. "So, you'll write?"

"Sure," I said as though I didn't care either way, even though the idea of receiving even one letter from her brought me near euphoria. "I'll write."

"Good. And I'll write you back."

Then, as I was about to leave, she did something I've been replaying in my mind ever since. She dove through the space between us and collided with my torso, her arms encircling me in a crushing, lingering embrace. When my initial shock wore off, I dropped the bag and wrapped my arms around her. My God, if she'd asked me to stay while I held her that way, I'd never have been able to say no.

We stood like that for what seemed like forever, her tears soaking the front of my shirt and my lips finding the top of her head. I inhaled her sweet, powdery scent, forcing it into my memory. Intoxicated by it all, I kissed her hair once and then twice. When she leaned back to look at me with tears still wet on her cheeks, I wiped them away with the side of my thumb, running my fingers up into her hair from the back of her neck. To have her that close, to touch her with such freedom, it was nearly worth all the torture I'd endured.

"Kiss me goodbye," she whispered.

Usually, I'm a man of inaction, of hesitation, but in that instant, I was all the things I'd always wanted to be. I dug my fingertips into the flesh at her waist and deeper into the velvety depths of her bobbed hairdo, yanking her into me, pressing my mouth against hers. There was no tentative start—from the second her mouth met mine, a fire erupted between us. She shivered under my touch, opening her mouth to take me in, our tongues reaching for each other, her hands wrapped in the fabric of my shirt so desperately my knees went weak.

And as suddenly as it started, it was over. She broke away mid-embrace, her hand covering her mouth as though she'd been sleepwalking and awoken to find she'd nearly walked off the roof of a tall building. Without a word, she ran out the studio door, leaving me vibrating with passion and dizzy with confusion.

I didn't see her again before I flew out. I donated my mother's piano to the local school, put all my belongings in storage, and drove to Minneapolis with one suitcase in the back seat. Martha was the only familiar face at KSTP, but I was only there for a few days before I left with the team. She stayed behind, as KSTP's newest news operations manager, also promising to write. No lingering embraces there. I broke Martha's rose-colored glasses the night of the banquet, which ended up being a blessing. Now that she knows how useless I'd be as a boyfriend, we can be friends.

Martha wrote to me right after I left, sending me six double-sided pages about all the new experiences at KSTP, her coworkers, the still uphill battle she faced as a newswoman, and then a whole narrative of how they decided what shades of orange to paint their new set. The letter was waiting for me in Saigon when I arrived back from my first assignment.

After twenty hours of nonstop travel, we dropped our belongings in the shared hotel rooms and then hopped on a helicopter that took us into a combat zone, where we bunked with the grunts for a week.

I'd been warned by Scott O'Neil, the correspondent I'd been paired with, that the trips into the field had two speeds: boring and deadly.

"Avoid anyone with a radio," he said when giving me tips on staying alive. "And keep low. You're so damn tall you're like a walking target for the VC."

We didn't end up seeing much "action," as they call it, on that first outing, but I did lug around my heavy camera and bag. I spent the days recording O'Neil interviewing men who wanted to send messages home or say their own two cents about the war and what it was like out there in the "rice paddies." I didn't talk much on that first trip. I had no reason to. I was a facilitator, a means to an end, a silent witness, but that didn't mean I was unaffected.

When O'Neil and I returned to Saigon, I craved distraction, and finding a stack of mail on my bed was just what I needed. Besides the letter from Martha, I also had one from Mark, who wrote me about his new Playboy Club key and his repeated attempts at convincing Lucy to let him take her out for dinner. As a sign-off, he included one very graphic and impressively accurate drawing of breasts.

And I had two letters from Betty.

"I got your address from Mark," the first line in her letter read, which at this point I've reread so much it's close to falling apart, the folds of the off-white stationery reinforced with Scotch tape. "He said you're doing well and I'm sure that's true, but I thought I should probably find out for myself."

The pages smelled of her perfume, and her tight but loopy handwriting looked so feminine that it made my pulse rise, making me feel like some kind of pervert. The first letter was one full page, front and back. She detailed how the show had been taken over by an import from EBN, resulting in Martha's more feminist segments being trimmed down. She also mentioned that she was writing a book, though she wasn't doing it alone. A team had been assembled to help her shape it according to EBN's views and agenda. She included a lot of talk about work and even a small paragraph about the weather, but I didn't care how bland her narrative was. I was delighted to have something she'd held in her hands and taken the time and effort to send.

The second letter, though, took me by surprise.

In it she told me about a mistake she made on air. She said it made her remember her tenth-grade music concert, how her voice cracked during a solo. It was the last concert her mother attended before she went missing. "For two years I would always think about how I wish I'd sung for my mom one more time before she left so she didn't walk around living the rest of her life embarrassed by her daughter."

She went on to explain that her obsession with that mistake went away when a neighbor's hunting dog uncovered her mother's body buried in the woods near the main road. Her stepfather, Bill, was arrested but, with all the evidence erased by time, he took a plea deal for a lesser charge, leaving Charlotte alone for the next three years. Stunned and pregnant with their second child, she was easily brainwashed into believing his innocence. After that, he was in and out of jail for petty crimes, fights, and a few DUIs.

"I'd send Charlotte money when he was incarcerated and stop when he was home. Every time he got locked away I hoped she'd wise up, but she always let him come back. Over the years I started to realize my mom wasn't turning over in her grave thinking about some note I missed in a tenth-grade concert. She was heartbroken I couldn't get Charlotte free."

It's a quality that's always drawn me to Betty, the vulnerable soul underneath the outward beauty, the sister who wants to protect and save by any means necessary, the sad girl who has no one to protect her. I wish she could see herself the way I do, the way she really is. I'd give anything to be her safe harbor.

After that letter, I've received at least one a week from her.

I write back every time, speaking very little of my daily life, especially not of the dangers I see and experience firsthand. I don't tell her how we know we're lied to in the nightly press briefings, how many soldiers don't want to be here and how clear it's becoming that this war is unwinnable.

In turn, she never mentions Don or her wedding, even though Mark keeps me apprised through his correspondence. But when he sent me a copy of her wedding announcement cut out of the newspaper, I hate to admit I burned it. Now, to maintain the illusion of Betty's devotion to me, I wait to open his letters until after I read any I've received from her.

One letter from Betty started "Dearest Greg, I got my first television today. It's a ten-inch black and white with bunny ears, but I get all the local stations, which is why I wanted it. I watch every news broadcast I can get on my little set and wonder if you're the one behind the camera whenever they report on the war. It makes me feel closer to you, but some nights, I can't sleep with worry. I hope you come home soon."

All her letters start that way, like I'm the only man in her life, like she's waiting in a little bungalow for me to return to her and fill it with children and a future we'll build together. It's not true, I logically know that, but being so isolated, so surrounded by terror and death, I let myself pretend. A lot of the guys out here live like this, putting their girl up on a golden pedestal which keeps them motivated to live long enough to get home.

I've made it ten months and filmed more tragedy than I knew existed before climbing onto that plane last year. The injuries, the fear and disillusionment—it's all palpable and nearly as poisonous as the napalm I was warned about.

And the stories, damn. Most of what we film will never be seen, I know that. No one wants to know about a soldier's dying words or the heavily racist views of some of the men when it comes not only to the enemy but also to the native population they're supposed to be protecting. To say nothing of the nonstop pot use that's almost as pervasive as smoking cigarettes.

"We gotta do something to keep from remembering what we've seen," one twenty-year-old from Dubuque told O'Neil when asked on camera about the drug use. "I didn't fucking ask to be here."

The cursing and unsavory details would prevent that clip from being broadcast, but we didn't shy away from the truth. I really respected that about O'Neil. He had integrity. He wanted to show things the way they were. And for the first three months, I went where he told me and shot what he wanted. We made a good team. But then he was hit in the leg in a combat zone and sent home for limb-saving surgery. I was placed with an older reporter, Dick Zan. Dick prefers to stay in Saigon for the military briefings, nicknamed the Five O'Clock Follies. He only goes into the field for a day or two to get some fluff for a feel-good segment every few weeks.

I've had the chance to leave twice already and chosen to stay.

Zan is going home for the summer, and the network offered to fly me back at the same time, but I've decided to stay a little longer. The work is hard but rewarding. I'm finally living a life rather than letting it happen all around me. What's waiting for me back home, anyway? I feel closer to my brother here where he took his last breath than I ever did behind a camera on a soundstage in Janesville, Wisconsin. Betty is more my girl here through her letters than she'd be as Don Hollinger's wife back home. I could go back to KSTP and tag along on Martha's rapidly ascending coattails, but even that connection has waned. I have four letters in total from Martha, who has moved on not only careerwise but also romantically, her last letter announcing her engagement to a nice banker she met at a disco on ladies' night.

A pang of jealousy rushed through me reading that letter, I'll admit it, but it's not the same as the torturous spasms brought on by Mark's mentions of Betty. I care about Martha, like her profoundly, but the surge of emotion I felt came from a place of envy at the forward motion of her life rather than a desire to be with her.

Vietnam is my self-appointed purgatory. I stay here as an act of penance, to redeem the shame I feel for being the only survivor in my family, for somehow escaping the draft, for not going back to stay with my mom after Jim died, for not taking her call that night she chose to join him instead of staying alive for me.

And here in Vietnam I have Betty. I have her picture, the one from her wedding to Don, taped up on my headboard, and I have her letters in my hands that end with the words "Love always."

"Damn, she's a real looker," Leon, the CBS cameraman says, dropping onto his bed next to mine. I look up from the powder-scented letter I just slid out of one of Betty's signature pink envelopes. "That's your girl?"

I consider telling the truth or saying something vague or un-incriminating. But I don't. I tell everyone here the same thing. It's my favorite lie.

"Yeah," I say, smiling. "That's my wife. Betty."

CHAPTER 31

Charlie

Present Day

"Men. Always causing trouble," Betty says over the phone after I tell her I'm still dealing with a broken heart. It's our second conversation today. I had a call from Nurse Mitchell yesterday morning saying that Betty had been asking for me incessantly—well, asking for Laura—and she wondered if I'd be up for a phone call. Feeling desperately alone, I took her up on the request.

I can't tell Betty about the texts I found on Ian's phone and our altercation on the stairs of the Grand Geneva, where he tried to talk me into staying. But I'd seen enough, and it felt almost worse than if I'd uncovered some long-standing salacious affair. My husband was secretly working with Alex McNamara to get my parents' house rehab on HFN. Ian didn't come here simply as part of Olivia's *Parent Trap* plans; he came here to further his career—to exploit my family's trauma to enhance his fame and increase his bank account.

"Screw you," I shouted in his face on the landing of the main staircase overlooking the busy lobby. Everyone's heads snapped toward us like we were performing on an elevated stage. Phones popped up in the crowd, and whispers passed through the mass, likely identifying the noteworthy couple having a very public spat.

At that, Ian let me go. After I explained the need for privacy, the manager let me hide in the front office until a car could be arranged to take me home. Once he realized why I was so angry, Ian began sending me a barrage of texts. His messages quickly turned into calls, but I haven't answered a single one. Over the past three days, I've avoided most human contact, except for Betty. I've never had a mother to turn to during a breakup, and though this version of Betty is more like a friend than a mom, it's a novel sensation.

"I thought I could trust him. I really did," I say into the receiver, repeating myself, but Betty doesn't notice, as if she's experiencing the conversation for the first time.

"Yes. They'll let you down, now, won't they?" Most of Betty's responses are general and airy. This time, I'm not digging for hints at her past. This conversation is just two women on the phone, simply enjoying the comfort of each other's voices. What a strange twist—my mother's voice is comforting to me.

But where else could I turn? My business colleagues are all far too busy or too willing to side with HFN and Ian. Lacey would help me hide a body, for sure, but she's a bit of a gossip and was far too eager to pass Cam my number when I told her about my separation during my first week here.

And Cam. I've muted his texts, which mostly relay what he's found at the library or the city clerk's office, but he's also sent a few asking if he's done something wrong. I had to force myself not to answer. As much as I want to confide in him like I did after reconnecting at Thumbs, it wouldn't be fair to vomit my marital issues onto a man I know has growing feelings for me. Somehow, I know that if I lean on him now, when things are such a mess, Ian would see it as the ultimate betrayal.

And then there's Olivia, working her butt off to fulfill some kind of magical movie moment with me and Ian. The night of our fight she came home sometime around midnight and peeked into my room as I pretended to sleep. She was gone by the time I got up in the morning, sending a little text telling me she was going to meet Ian for breakfast and inviting me to join. I didn't respond, burying myself in my covers, listening to self-help books on "finding my true self" and "learning to be alone." I haven't seen her since, though she still updates me on her plans. Today, she's headed to the library. When she returns, I need to figure out how to tell her my side of what's going on with Ian. She's flying back to California in the morning. I can't believe how much of our time together I've wasted.

"Will you come visit me today?" Betty asks in her shaky voice, pulling my mind back to our conversation. "We could go to Ike's." She brings up the diner for the tenth time during our call. I wish I'd never mentioned the place, a detail from her past that she fiercely hangs on to.

I've stayed away from Shore Path, honoring my dad's request. I need to warn him about Ian's plans for the house, but he hasn't answered his home or cell phone, so I'll have to put on a stoic face and go to the house in person today. My lawyers, agent, and manager all agree—the only hope for stopping this is my dad. I don't trust Ian alone with my dad and the house. After those two-faced texts with Alex, I don't trust Ian at all—period.

"I'm very busy today, but maybe tomorrow," I tell Betty, unsure when I'll be able to see her again and if she'll even be happy to see me by then.

"Oh, that's too bad. I have a new dress for my date. I'd like to look for some shoes and make a day of it."

I smile, thinking of the time I did her makeup as we listened to the Beatles and talked about her days in front of the camera for *The Classy Homemaker*. Though they aren't the childhood memories most people cherish of their mother, I'm filling in a few blanks in my emotional canvas.

"That sounds like a lot of fun. What kind of shoes are you looking for?" I ask, letting the conversation drift away from the heavier topics of love and betrayal.

"I don't know." She pauses, making *mmm* sounds as she thinks. "Black ones with a buckle?"

"That sounds very pretty," I say, knowing Betty loves pretty things.

"And a dress for the baby. Pink to match my skirt."

The baby? I sit up straight. *Me?* She's talking about me as though I'm still an infant.

"Your baby?"

"Yes, of course, my baby. She's very little and pretty. I think she's sleeping right now." Her anxiety seems to be slightly triggered at the realization that her baby isn't by her side.

"I'm sure she is. She's sound asleep in her crib."

"Oh, yes. Yes, she is. She needs a bottle when she wakes up. I'll go find one . . ." And the phone line cuts off as Betty leaves on an impossible errand from her past. I put the phone on the counter and whisper "Goodbye, Mom" before taking three long breaths and two short ones like one of the therapy podcasts suggests. Looking down at the frumpy, stained shirt I've been living in for the last two days, I sigh.

Well, I can't go anywhere looking like this.

Showered, shaved, brushed, and makeuped, with some carbs and coffee in my stomach, I make the walk over to Lake Shore Drive. Olivia still hasn't returned with the car. The weather is unpredictable, as warm as summer some days and flurries littering the air on others, but this morning is cool and sunny. The rebirth of all things green and colorful makes the walk a rejuvenating one.

I will not cry today. I will not cry today, I chant internally with each footfall, then switch to *You are a badass bitch. Don't let anyone walk all over you.* First, I check Time and Again for my dad but only find Natty, his shop manager, who says she's been flying solo all week.

At the last minute, I decide to take the shore path to the back of the house instead of the longer route around Lake Shore Drive. The unpaved parts of the path are muddy, and I arrive at the side yard with ruined shoes but in half the time it would've taken to go around.

Blue tarps are pinned down throughout the yard like a plastic patchwork quilt, with tall open-air tents perched over each one. Some tents are already filled with boxes and piles of clothes, shoes, books, and papers. The sorting process is starting to feel so futile, and there are times I wish we could trash it all. But Dino continues to remind me that the entire procedure is essential for a positive outcome, and so does the social worker assigned to my parents' case. So we keep putting all of my parents' belongings—their treasures and their shame—on their front and back lawn to be gawked at. At least the boat tours aren't up and running yet. Hopefully, we can get a privacy screen installed before the summer season hits.

As I step onto my parents' property, I see Dino on the back deck, calling out orders to the crew below. I approach genially, but as I climb the slope of the backyard, the rest of the deck comes into view. I see a camera operator, camera loaded on his shoulder, boom mic hovering in the background. Among the crowd I notice two more cameras directed toward him.

Jordan Kelp, the producer of *Squeaky Clean*, stands to the side, holding a clipboard and wearing a World Window baseball cap pulled down to his eyebrows in what I've always believed is an effort to hide his bald head. A terrible realization hits me when I see who is standing on the other side of Dino. It's my father.

"What the hell?" I growl, blind rage flaming inside, burning away my mantras and making me run the rest of the way, waving my arms.

"Cut! Cut! Turn that off." I say, pointing to the camera operators, who I recognize now as Mike and Wendy, crew members from *Second Chance Renovation*. In fact, everyone is here from our show. I also notice the host of *Squeaky Clean* comforting my father.

I sprint up the back steps, causing one of the more delicate slats to splinter. Out of breath, I lunge in front of Dino to block the shot.

"You turn those cameras off. I told Alex and Karen we are *not* signing off on this." I point a shaking finger at Jordan, my breathing unsteady with rage. He looks annoyed but not totally surprised at my outburst.

"Alex bypassed you on this one. Hadley will host it if you won't play ball. We can still patch you in, but we had to get started," Jordan responds coolly, like he's trying to manage me.

Dino jumps in. "We're not trying to take this over, Charlie. It's a special project and you should be in charge, but we've been sitting around for a day already, so we had to get something going."

"I'm not blaming you, Dino, but I don't care what Alex said—this isn't right. I didn't sign off on this. My parents didn't sign off on this."

The crowd below has started to disperse, murmuring among themselves. A single camera continues filming as Dino, Tina, and I form a tight circle. I call for my dad to join us, and Mike tries to follow with his camera.

"Don't you dare. Now turn that thing off." I cover the lens with my hand.

"Charlie, you can't touch the cameras. Mike, keep rolling," Jordan directs the camera operator, who gives me an apologetic look.

My fight isn't with the cast and crew—it's with Karen at World Window, and HFN's legal department, Alex McNamara and my own freaking husband. I reluctantly remove my hand.

"Fine, but this isn't consent."

"Noted," Jordan says, clearly irritated.

My dad joins the circle, looking stunned and ashen.

"Is everything all right?" he asks like he has no idea why I'm losing my shit.

"No, it's not all right. Are you OK with this?" I gesture to Jordan and then to Mike and his camera.

"Well, I don't know. I suppose so," he replies in his wishy-washy way, like my explosive response is irrational.

"Dad," I say, not caring that everyone here used to believe my parents were dead. "Did Ian make you sign something?"

"Ian? No, hon. No one made me sign anything."

Jordan interjects, "Who do you think we are, Charlie? My God. You need to take a minute and get your head on straight. Alex and Karen presented Greg with a very—and I mean very—nice offer. Being a man of vision, he recognized the benefits of the deal. I got the signature, not Ian, who is also AWOL, by the way. I assumed he was with you."

"He's not with me," I say matter-of-factly, not believing Ian has nothing to do with this circus in my parents' yard. I turn back to my dad, sure he's been manipulated in some way. "Even if you signed something, you don't have to do this."

"Well, that's not exactly true . . ." Jordan interrupts.

"Shut the hell up, Kelp," I blurt, glaring at him.

"Lottie," my dad says in a calm, almost patronizing tone. "They're gonna do the whole house for free, hon. I trust Dino and Tina to do it right. I can use the money to help pay for Mom's care."

"Dad, I told you—I can help you with that."

"Honey. You're busy. This way, you won't have to put in so much of your time, and I know you've been using your own money for everything. Now, I can pay you back. It's time. You've already been here for a month. I know you can't stay in Lake Geneva forever."

He tucks a strand of hair behind my ear and grazes my cheekbone with his thumb, as if he's telling his little girl the truth about Santa Claus or the Easter Bunny, as though he's signaling that the fantasy of the past few months is over. I have to leave—again.

"Plus," he adds, "your mom needs some stability. All this has been hard on her."

I back away from his touch as if it's covered in razor blades, the dark camera lens following me, the boom mic positioned low enough to catch my dad's words. I know he meant to comfort me, but it feels like rejection. He wants me gone because of my mom. The coffee in my stomach turns as a gust of wind brings up the dusty, mildewy smell of my parents' belongings from the piles down below. My head spins, and I grip the railing to keep from tipping over.

"Whoa, there. Whoa. OK. Emma," Jordan calls to a production assistant, "get me a chair. No, not that one. That one. Yes." He shouts orders, holding me by my upper arm. An old folding chair is dragged out of one of the piles and opened beside me. "Sit down. Head between your legs," he tells me, guiding me into the seat, whispering urgently to the PA, "Get medical over here."

"No, no. I'm fine," I say, sitting up and regaining my equilibrium, an arch of faces leaning over me in concern, the constantly aware camera just behind them. "I need a little air."

In near unison, they all shuffle back, letting in a breeze.

"Let's all take five," Jordan shouts to the cluster of people on the porch, the declaration repeated via walkie-talkies through the yard like a game of telephone. The cast and crew disperse in different directions, leaving only Jordan and my dad with me on the porch.

"You know we want you and Ian in on this, right? Hadley is nothing compared to you two. I know Alex is willing to talk some big numbers if you are interested. Think about it," he says, leaving me to take his own five-minute break.

I should be furious at the pressure and the wads of cash dangled in front of me and my dad like a carrot before a starving horse. But my father's reasoning for accepting the deal eliminates any protective instinct I might have had. This is my parents' house, their mess, their relationship. I haven't been a factor in their decisions in a long time. How can I expect anything different now? When it seems like everyone has lost interest in my panic attack, I sneak out the same way I came in, leaving them to deal with everything on their own.

Out of breath, I stop at the tiny public library on Main Street but find neither Olivia nor my car. After running away from Jordan and the whole film crew, my daughter is the only thing on my mind. She goes home tomorrow, and now I'm sure I'll follow her soon thereafter, leaving my whole life and career in flux. Olivia gave up her first college spring break, and I've done nothing but push her away the whole time she's been here. I have one last day before everything falls apart. I'd like to spend it with her.

Charlie: Where are you?

I text as I walk east down the main drag. Likely, Olivia is at home, wondering where I am after spending yesterday in bed.

A response comes through almost immediately.

Olivia: I'm in front of you.

I stop abruptly on the sidewalk. A young mom, dressed in Lululemon head to toe and pushing a designer stroller, nearly crashes into me.

"Sorry," I mutter, gazing past the disgruntled woman as I look for Olivia. Suddenly, a car horn sounds kitty-corner to my location, making me jump. My car is stopped at the intersection, Olivia behind the wheel.

I jaywalk, running toward her. She pulls over and rolls down the window.

"Get in!" she calls.

I grab the passenger-side handle and slide in, slamming the door behind me. Olivia rolls up the window and slams on the gas.

"Olivia!" I gasp, bracing myself on the dashboard with one hand and buckling my seat belt with the other. "What is going on?"

"We're going out to lunch," she replies, the needle on the speedometer flying above the speed limit.

"Where? Canada? Did you rob a bank or something?"

"Eh, kinda," Olivia says with a grimace-like smile as we pass out of Lake Geneva into Como.

A shuffle and a sound like a giggle come from behind me, and a familiar scent fills the car. Guerlain Shalimar—my mom's favorite. Turning so quickly that the belt locks and digs into my side, I check the back seat. There, lying on her side with her favorite blanket pulled up to her neck, is my mother.

CHAPTER 32

Greg

June 16, 1973
Harry's Antique Haven
Lake Geneva, Wisconsin

"Good afternoon," Harry's gruff voice calls out to a customer entering the shop. Hours into a piano rehab project, I don't leave the small work area off to the right of the main showroom. I rarely work the counter. Harry's better with the browsing tourists, the small talk and sales part of the job. He should be. Harry's worked at this store since his parents ran it as a general store back when the train still dumped tourists in Lake Geneva on a regular schedule.

I find solace in the workroom's solitude and in checking price tags and arranging the displays. When I'm not in the shop, I'm on the road, searching estate sales, garage sales, and auctions for inventory. Harry, the father of one of my brother's friends who died in Vietnam a few months after Jim in '68, says I've gotten good at identifying a find. I study *The Complete Antiques Price List* and have learned how to negotiate. In this job, my reserved nature works more in my favor than against it. When we make a big sale to one of the rich people from the big houses on the lake, I get a rush. Unlike the dread and terror that comes with war journalism, this is a fulfilling rush, wholesome, like I felt behind the camera in my early days at WQRX, chasing storms with Martha or on *Janesville Presents* . . . or even Betty's show.

I haven't picked up a camera since I got home three months ago. By home, I mean, back in country, because nothing really feels like home anymore. In my twenty-one months overseas a lot of things took on a sense of unrealness. Maybe it was because I watched the world through a lens for a little too long and surrendered to fantasy a little too fully.

When KSTP pulled out their crew permanently after the Paris Peace Accords, I had no choice but to return to the States. Well, that's not entirely true. A few weeks ago, CBS offered me a new position that included the option to return to my self-appointed mission in Vietnam. If CBS had made the offer while I was still there—while I was still staring at the black-and-white picture of my fake wife, still used to the early morning helicopter rides, smoke-filled rooms of frustrated reporters begging for the truth every night—I probably would have taken it.

But once I said yes to Harry's offer of a job and the room above his store and felt the magic of objects that were once treasured by people who are no longer in this world—I quickly found I preferred looking through this dusty, backward-facing lens. I stay away from television in general right now. It's too hard to watch images from the war I just left behind, a war that's taken too much from our nation and continues to consume us hungrily.

I close the lid of the upright piano I've been working on and pull a chair up to the keys to check my handiwork. My thumbs meet over the worn ivory of middle C, and I consider what to play. My mom's favorite song comes to mind: "Que Sera, Sera." After my dad died, she'd spend most of her nights listening to Doris Day's record as she caught up on her mending next to the fire. It seemed to be a way to comfort herself, convincing herself that she was a passenger in her life, that she needed only to close her eyes and let the stream take her wherever it may.

I think Jim's death made her open her eyes, and she didn't like where the current had taken her. So she made the first strong-willed decision of her life. My fingers falter when I reach the chorus for a second time and close the key cover, reaching for an off-white price tag and wax pencil.

"I love that song," a woman's voice says from behind me. "How much?" I finish writing numbers on the tag and then tie it to the music stand.

"Fifty," I say, which is a lot. I got it for ten, but Harry taught me to start high to leave room for negotiation.

"Do you deliver?"

"Depends on where," I say, wiping off a missed patch of dust, hoping she didn't see it.

"Janesville," she says with a familiar smile in her voice. I spin around, an immediate brightness lifting the gloom left behind by the memory of my mother. There she stands, in an oversized pea-green coat buttoned at her throat and a large white purse clasped in front of her, hair pinned up in a tight twist, her lips red as the day I first met her.

"Betty?" I exclaim, stunned at her miraculous appearance in my workroom. "How did you . . ."

"Mark told me. My last letter came back, and I was worried sick that something happened to you. Then, you didn't come to Mark's wedding, and I know how close you both were, so I had to ask."

"I . . . I had to work." It's the same lie I told Mark, claiming I was out of town searching for new inventory at a big auction. The truth was, I chose to leave town that weekend to avoid seeing everyone from WQRX again, particularly Don and Betty together. It was selfish. Mark had been such a steady friend and now he was finally settling down, but I wasn't ready. I planned to never see Betty again, to count her as something I sacrificed in Vietnam.

"Yeah, that's what he said. You always said Mark and Lucy were right for each other. Thought you'd be there to gloat."

"Believe me, I've gloated plenty."

"You doing all right?" she asks, looking me up and down, probably noticing how baggy my pants are and how the buttoned sleeves of my shirt are loose on my wrists.

"I'm adapting," I say, not mentioning the panic attacks and the light I keep on in the corner of my room to quell my new fear of the dark. "And you? You doing all right? Marriage all it's cracked up to be?"

She shrugs. "Not exactly, but things rarely are."

It's a nebulous response, perhaps meant to goad me into asking more, but I don't. My new negotiation skills are keeping me steady. Even if she's miserable with Don, there's nothing I can do about it. She's married to him, she chose him; I can't be the opium that dulls her pain, not when it hurts so much to do so.

"That's true," I say simply. Betty cocks her head like she can't make sense of my withdrawn responses. Perhaps I'm not all she thought I'd be, either.

"So, do you think you might come back?"

"To WQRX?" I chuckle a little at an idea that seems so audacious to me now. "No."

"We sure could use you. Things have been kinda tough since you left." Her forehead ripples with an emotion I can't identify. Mark already told me about some of the problems—money is tight, tempers are flaring, and Don is no longer the golden boy. He said Betty will soon have to choose to stay with the station and her show or leave the station with her husband.

"I've moved on from Janesville," I say. I'll never set foot in that town again no matter who offers the invitation.

Her lips twitch, and I think about the last time we were alone together—a memory that kept me brave when bombs, bullets, and troop movements were the terrible truths of my every day. I focus on a spot over her head where an old cuckoo clock leans against a wall waiting for a new set of weights.

"Greg, why didn't you tell me you were back?"

I keep my gaze fixed above her. All I'll see in her bright eyes is disappointment and all I'll see on her left hand is another man's ring. I've come to terms with this loss, but that doesn't mean I like seeing her standing in front of me while she's wearing Don's ring and carrying his last name.

"I didn't think it was a good idea. Letters are one thing, but . . ." I shrug, leaving the rest of the sentence for her to finish. She nods as if she understands exactly what we've been doing the past two years, what grew between us, though unintended at first, and what we stoked with our kiss and our communiqués.

I love her more now than when I flew halfway around the world to escape my feelings for her. I love the person she shared with me through hundreds of pages of stories, thoughts, and memories. I love the real Betty, and she knows it. It's cruel to expect me to stand by and watch. A part of me wants to call her on it, but the more rational side knows it'd only serve to hurt us both.

"I don't know how to not write to you anymore. These past months, I feel like a piece of me is missing," she says, a sorrowful vibrato at the end of her sentence causing a sense of panic to rise inside of me.

"Me too," I reply, and I mean it. I let myself look at her, a lump forming in my throat. This is the end, the final curtain, the cherry on top of the melted sundae.

"Mm-hmm," she hums in response. She senses it, too. But what else could she expect? "Well, I should go," she says with a sigh. "I'm meeting one of my girlfriends for lunch. I thought I'd stop by and check on you, but you seem fine."

"I am." It's not one hundred percent true, but it's all she needs to know. If I let her into my heart at all, I won't be able to let her walk out that door without begging to see her again, settling for half a life.

"I'll see the man at the counter about the piano, then?"

"Yup. Actually, bring him this." I retrieve the tag. She takes it, gripping the stiff paper as I hold on to the tag longer than I should. She's so close I could lean down and kiss her, and by the needy look in her eyes, I think she'd let me. My God, I want to hold her again, let the desire swell between us, see what happens when two years of yearning are realized. But then the purse she's been holding in front of her slips down her wrist, leaving her midsection uncovered, snapping me out of the trance.

My eyesight blurs and then focuses. I release the ticket, striding away to the opposite side of the workroom like I remembered an important project, running my hands through my hair. I'm not sure if she says goodbye, because I'm overwhelmed by what nearly happened. It would've been so easy to forget my resolve if she hadn't dropped her purse, because what I saw there changed everything—more than the ring or a wedding or the label of Mrs. Don Hollinger.

Betty is pregnant.

CHAPTER 33

Charlie

Present Day

"Mom!" I shout, and Betty gives me a confused look but doesn't correct me, still caught up in a conspiratorial snicker. My head swivels to Olivia. She doesn't look nearly as entertained as Betty, her eyes focused on the road. The navigation on her phone dings and gives directions.

"Olivia. What the hell is going on?" I demand as I unbuckle and climb halfway over the seat to help Betty get out from under her blanket.

"Laura's taking me to Ike's," Betty says, lying on her side, her arms too weak to push herself up.

"Ike's? In Janesville? Olivia. What are you thinking?" I scold, frustration weighing heavily on my frame. "Pull over. Now."

"Mom, I can explain," she says defensively as she guides the car to a gravel shoulder.

"Yeah, you sure better." I leap out, swing open the back door, and help Betty sit up before buckling her seat belt. I notice her new-looking pink dress and low black heels.

I'm out of breath when I get back to my spot beside Olivia. Sitting up seems to have energized Betty, and she's chirping requests from the back seat. "Let's roll down the windows and listen to the radio. Get the wind in our hair."

I reach across Olivia to activate the child safety lock on the windows and then flick on the radio, scanning through the stations until I land on an oldies station. "Your Song" is playing, which seems to satisfy Betty.

"Turn around. We're taking her back," I say to Olivia once Betty is settled.

Olivia taps her thumbs against the steering wheel. "Let me explain," she repeats, as though there's anything she could say that would make this caper seem logical.

"Explain. Now. Quickly." The road isn't busy, but I know if we stay here too long, someone will call the police or stop to see if we need help—this is the Midwest after all.

"I went to visit her this morning since I'm leaving tomorrow. I got her a new outfit from Lucca and some new lipstick, and I wanted to give them to her before I left. You didn't seem up to it," she says, shrugging in a way that stirs up feelings of failure and shame. "And she kept going on about wanting to go to lunch and she was so happy, you know? I think she thought I was you or Laura or whatever she calls you. Nurse Mitchell said I could take her on a little walk by the lake since she doesn't like the courtyard, and I have experience with this kind of thing."

The memory of the incident in the courtyard flashes in my mind. Betty's nails dragging against her thin skin till blood flooded down her arms and wrist. Yes, I can understand why Betty would avoid that place, even if she can't remember why.

"But when I got her outside, she went to the first car she could find and grabbed the handle, saying we were going to Ike's. That one was locked, but the second one wasn't, and she tried to get in. I don't know—I panicked. So I took her to our car and put Janesville in the GPS hoping I could get her to settle down.

"At first, I thought I'd drive her around town, but when we saw you, she hid under her shawl and laughed about surprising you. I thought it might be an adventure for the three of us. I thought it might cheer you up and fix things with you and Grandma a little. I'm sorry," Olivia says, her eyes filling with tears. "I . . . I got carried away. Not only with this but with everything. I shouldn't have come."

"Oh, honey. I know you meant well. It's just—this is adult stuff. You shouldn't have to deal with it." I never was a "my daughter is my best friend" kind of mom. That always seemed like a conflict of interest. A kid needs a mom far more than a best friend. I may not have been the best mom, but I didn't dump my emotional baggage on my child for her to carry, and that has to count for something.

"I'm nineteen, Mom. I'm not a kid anymore."

"I know, but you should be allowed to focus on your life, school, and friends and all that. When I was your age, I had so much on my plate . . ."

"I know. When you were my age, you were on your own. But I'm not on my own. This is my family, too."

"It is, and no matter what happens with Ian and your grandparents, we'll always be a family," I reassure her, quoting all the things I'd learned in the "broken family" divorce books I'd read when she was little.

"Don't give me that BS. Dad isn't your family anymore. He's my family. Please, Mom. Please let me in."

I know this experience of knocking on a sealed door that has no doorknob, as I've experienced it while trying to connect with my dad. Now, here's my own child, begging to be let into my inner world. I want to welcome Olivia in; I want to be a different kind of parent than my mom and dad were. However, understanding how to open up in a healthy and safe way is complicated. My dad is right—there are things I don't want my daughter to know. Ever. But why? I tell myself it's to protect her, but is it really? Or am I trying to shield myself from those feelings all over again?

"What . . ." I cough and glance at Betty, who is nervously straightening her skirt over and over again. "What do you want to know?"

Olivia's flushed cheeks lose color, and she licks her lips before asking, "Are you and Ian going to break up?"

I knew she was going to ask me that. I flinch and reply honestly, "I don't know."

"He told me about the messages."

"What?"

"He told me about the messages on Instagram, and I understand why you're upset."

My list of reasons for being mad at my husband is growing longer by the minute. "He shouldn't have told you that . . ."

"Well, he did. And I'm glad, because if you can't forgive him, at least I know why. I . . . I understand if you can't trust him anymore. It doesn't seem like you've had a lot of people you can trust in your life."

She's talking about my parents, I think. I glance back at Betty to see if she's listening. She's conversing with her reflection in the glass as if she's made a new friend. I take a deep breath and tuck Olivia's hair behind her ear.

"My parents' house, the way it is, uh . . . that's how it was when I was a kid. You know that, but I don't really talk about the rest. I, um, well . . . I went into foster care when I was fifteen, and my dad promised . . ." I choke up, remembering the sincerity in my father's eyes when he came to see me for visitation. "He promised they'd fix the house, and I could go home, but . . ."

"They didn't?"

I shake my head. "And my mom," I say, looking at Betty and biting my lip, "blamed me for everything. She hates me."

"Really?" Olivia's brow wrinkles. She's only met Betty, her confused but sweet grandmother.

"Yeah, hon. Well, maybe not hate, but when she remembers who I am, she's pretty pissed."

Olivia seems stunned. "And you came back anyway?"

I roll my eyes at myself.

"I was running away from the Ian stuff. Then, when I visited Betty, she opened this window to the woman she must've been before me." I flash back to those first days, the "bad days," when she didn't know my name but also didn't bristle with rage at the sight of me. I think about the woman in the films and pictures, what it felt like to hold her past in my hands. "I thought if I knew what happened to her, what triggered this disorder, it wouldn't be my fault anymore."

"See, I get that. Coming here, seeing where you grew up—it wasn't just about you and Ian. I needed this, too. Like you did with your mom."

Defensiveness coils inside me. "I'm glad you got something out of this trip, but this is different than what happened with my mom. I've always been there for you."

Her lower lip trembles. "OK. It's not exactly the same, but I barely saw you for like five years other than at some school things, crazy busy vacations, and a few weeks in the summer."

I open my mouth to argue, wanting to tell her that we made the best of what we had and that she was the one who wanted to move in with her dad, but I stop myself. My daughter thinks I abandoned her. Though the details of our stories are different, some of the main themes are heartbreakingly the same. And despite all that, she came here to help, to fix things for me, and as a bid for connection.

I calm my stirred-up guilt and regret, and instead of explaining her pain away, I say what I'd love for my parents to tell me.

"I'm sorry, Olivia. I'm so sorry I've made you feel like that."

"I should've said something sooner," Olivia says, trying to take on the blame. I correct her, thinking of my conversation with my father a few days ago.

"No, no. You were a kid. I was so wrapped up in my own life that I let myself believe you knew exactly what you wanted."

"I had a good childhood. I know I shouldn't complain, but I just—I don't know—I've missed you. And it used to make me so mad at you, like all teen angsty, you know? You've always been so freaking strong and independent and successful, like . . ." She searches for a comparison, then blurts, "It's like you're this goddess, and I'm your mortal offspring. But now, with the Ian situation, and things with Grandma and Grandpa, I've seen the human part of you."

Human. I'm no longer a mythical creature, the immortal, infallible creature called "mother"—I'm real. I discovered that dissonant truth about my own mother and father at a far younger age, but the revelation wasn't like this. It was more like finding out at the end of a movie that the villain was the hero's best friend.

"I'm definitely not mythical," I agree, rubbing her arm, wishing I could go back and fix the parenting mistakes I've made, when another hand is laid on mine. The nails are painted pink, the skin translucent and spotted, the joints swollen. It's my mother's hand joining me in comforting Olivia.

As I've gotten to know Betty, I've come to see my own mother's humanity as well. Seeing my hand sandwiched between Betty's and Olivia's, I feel a bit more accepting of my mother's flaws.

"I love you," I say to Olivia and maybe a little bit to Betty. "I will do better. I promise."

"And I'll stop acting like a character in a Disney movie," Olivia says, smiling tearfully.

"We're a little too screwed up for Disney."

"Hey," Betty says from the back seat, patting my hand. Olivia and I wait, assuming she'll add her own *I love you* and put a heartwarming cap on our multigenerational bonding. Instead, she asks, "Are we going to Ike's?"

Olivia and I break into laughter at Betty's one-track mind. I hold my mom's hand and encourage her to sit back in her seat so the belt doesn't lock up. I finally understand what came over Olivia in the parking lot of Shore Path. It's our last day together, us three.

Tomorrow, Betty might not remember a trip to Janesville or a lunch at Ike's, but we will. My dad might be furious, but you know what—screw him. He never had to deal with my rebellious phase. Anyway, he's been tiptoeing through life, tiptoeing around my mother. If the day turns toward reality for my mother and she remembers my name and her house—if she stops loving me—it is what it is. At least we had today.

"Hey, switch places with me," I tell Olivia with a conspiratorial tone. She raises her eyebrows at me but trades spots without asking for more information. Once we're all buckled, I roll down the windows, turn up the radio, put the car in drive, and pull onto the empty highway.

"Faster!" Betty calls from the back seat. I press on the gas until the engine revs and the wind slaps the ends of my hair against my cheeks.

"Faster! Faster!" Betty, Olivia, or both chant. I push the gas pedal to the floor, and Olivia whoops from the passenger seat as I slide into the westbound lane toward Janesville.

The smooth road, newly plowed fields, and cheerful baby-blue sky make for a pleasant ride, and Betty dozes quietly for most of it, the bunched-up blanket wedged beneath her head and the window. I turn down the music to allow her to rest, and Olivia takes the opportunity to dig deeper into our freshly exposed issues.

The miles fly by and it's a relief to leave Lake Geneva behind me for a bit. My father made it clear this morning—my days there are limited. I need to get used to the idea of leaving it behind, closing this unfinished chapter, moving forward with my unwritten ones. My parents' house and story are for a different book than mine—it will be told whether I share in the telling of it.

CHAPTER 34

Greg

August 15, 1973
Betty's House
Janesville, Wisconsin

By the time Harry arranged the delivery of Betty's piano, I regretted the little temper tantrum I threw in my bedroom after she left. I took out all her letters, ripping off the length of silk ribbon I'd bought at B⊠n Thành Market to keep them together, and started rending them into pieces one at a time, destroying the physical evidence of the delusional love story I'd lived through them. As I worked through the stack in a frenzy, the picture of Betty I'd slid into the wooden frame of a small, cloudy mirror hanging over my desk stared back at me. Betty, looking down on me in her wedding dress with that TV show smile, flowers she probably arranged on her own, and the ring I first saw in that banquet hall, the impetus for my escape to Vietnam.

I dropped the letter I was about to tear apart and grabbed the faded photograph, which was sticky in the corners from where the Scotch tape had kept it on my headboard in the Caravelle. It needed to go, even more than the words she'd written. This picture of my fake "wife" needed to be shredded into pieces.

Turning the photograph over so I didn't have to look into Betty's eyes as I destroyed her, I held it tight, closed my eyes, and willed my fingers to do the rest, but I couldn't. No matter how many times I gritted my teeth and cursed, or how many tears squeezed out from my crunched eyelids, I just couldn't shred it. Eventually, I let her drop onto the desk, intact, and then put my head down on the pile of letters and wept.

"Knock it off with those tears," my father used to say. When I fell off my bike and scraped my knee so severely that the blood turned my tube socks red, he told me to suck it up and be a man. When at six, I sniffled from grief at my beloved grandmother's funeral, again, he told me to be a man. And when the boys at school called me a sissy for playing piano and Pete Hachette broke my nose behind Food Queen for calling him out on shoplifting, he told me there was no use in crying about it, that next time I should punch them in the nose. Maybe that's why I didn't cry at my father's funeral—because he would've been ashamed of those tears. He taught me to hide my emotions—he masked his feelings with anger, and I boxed them up and stored them away somewhere deep inside.

I didn't even cry for my brother or my mother. I didn't cry for the nineteen-year-old boy from Iowa who died right next to me after stepping on a mine. Yet, there I was, crying over pretty pages that'd kept me safe and hopeful and a picture of a woman I had to give up.

The tears were for more than that. They had to be. They were for the man inside me who'd never been allowed to feel, now overwhelmed by a flood of grief. It was like the monsoon season in Vietnam, where the rain pours endlessly, as if the sky itself is mourning the loss of life, compassion, and humanity.

It took all day to get my emotions reeled in. I repaired Betty's letters as best I could, then placed them in a box with her photograph. I put the box in the corner of my room, hoping this act of containment might help dry my eyes and remove the suffocating weight of sorrow that felt like an elephant pressing down on my chest day and night.

Lost without my fantastical obsession, I immersed myself in work, researching rare items. In the past, I would've locked myself in my room to look through Betty's letters. Now, I took to walking the shore path around the lake, studying the mansions and imagining the impressive lives unfolding inside the massive edifices. I dreamed of a day when I might find my own piece of land to settle on—a home I owned where I could watch the lake come alive with summer adventurers and then grow still with the winter frost.

Two months after Betty placed her order for the piano, Harry called me into his office and handed me a delivery form with Betty's name on it. It'd been so long since she made the deposit that I assumed she had changed her mind.

"It's a bit of a drive, but they paid extra for the delivery," Harry explained. "It's a two-man job. Take Toby."

By this time, I've locked my emotions away, and though I'm wary of driving to Betty and Don's home, I don't let on. Toby and I load the piano, cover it in moving blankets, secure it to the wall of the truck, and head toward Janesville.

When we pull up to the two-story white house with black shutters, a one-car garage tucked up under the second story, and a red-brick path leading to a glossy ebony front door, I leave Toby with the truck.

"I'll do a little recon. See what the plan is," I say, swallowing the lump in my throat repeatedly. My mouth is dry, and anxiety buzzes in my extremities as I walk up the front path. I need to find out who is waiting inside without Toby in tow. As much as I loathe Don Hollinger, a part of me would rather see him on the other side of the door than Betty.

But when the door swings open, it's neither Don nor Betty but a nice-looking, dark-haired young woman in capri pants and a loose short-sleeve blouse.

"Hi, uh, we have a delivery for"—I'm about to say Betty's name but catch myself—"Hollinger. A piano."

"Oh, yes. Yes. Come in," she says, waving me over the threshold. "If you want to wait a sec, I'll go grab Mrs. Hollinger."

The woman excuses herself as I step inside. Alone in the entry, I spin slowly, taking in the details of Betty's house. It's everything I expected: warm, earthy colors and polished parquet floors. To the right is a teak dining table with eight orange upholstered chairs and not a spot of dust. Through the dining room, I glimpse a stylish kitchen with an avocado-green top-of-the-line refrigerator and stove, the smell of a roast filling the house with an inviting scent. To the left is a sitting room with low-profile furniture, a drink service in the corner, a large stone fireplace, and a blank spot on the far wall where I'm guessing the piano will be placed.

Directly in front of me, a long, curved stairway covered in a dark-orange shag carpet rises to a line of doors at the top. This is the house, *the* house, the one she probably dreamed of as she wrote her book, the one she promised her viewers they could have if they simply followed all the rules of etiquette and homemaking. I feel a pang of inadequacy. This is what she's always wanted, and it's something I definitely couldn't give her.

If I want the best for Betty, then I should be happy for her, I try to convince myself.

"Greg," Betty says from the stairs, and the sound of her voice thwarts my well-laid plans. The Betty standing on the stairs isn't the one from the diner, or from WQRX, or even from the picture she sent me. This is the Betty from the morning I woke up beside her in the car, the day I met her family. She's plain faced, dressed in jeans and a loose sweatshirt, with her hair tied up in a scarf. To me, this is the most beautiful version of her.

"Where would you like the piano?" I ask.

I don't greet her or act like an old friend or someone who knows what it's like to get lost in her embrace. She jogs down the last few steps, her bare feet hitting the herringbone flooring with a slap.

"I was thinking that wall," she says, pointing to the exact spot I'd predicted, biting her chipped nail as she watches me.

"As long as it's an interior wall you should be fine."

"The garage is on the other side. Is that a problem?"

"I don't think so," I respond, though I'm not sure of anything right now. Betty leans against the back of her fancy tangerine leather Cassina sofa, and immediately the room goes from looking like a show set to a home. She lives here with her husband, lucky bastard.

"It'll take a few minutes to get it prepped. Do you mind leaving the door open?"

"Nope, that's fine. Need anything else?"

"Nah, you're all set," I say as I step outside, taking a welcome breath of fresh air. The words I truly want to say are suffocating me, like a hand over my mouth.

Toby and I get the piano inside without a dent in the mahogany or a single scratch on her flooring. While Toby collects the dolly and blankets to carry them back to the truck, I run my fingers across the familiar keys, playing scales from one side of the keyboard to the other. I discover a few off-tune notes and make some adjustments, repeating the scales until the chords sound right. I'm playing through a few simple songs when Betty speaks ups with a request.

"Play 'Bridge Over Troubled Water,'" Betty says from the couch. I turn and see Betty and her friend sitting there, listening intently. The dark-haired woman cradles a bundle of soft pink blankets, a sleeping baby nestled inside.

"Gosh, I'm sorry. I didn't know. Was I too loud?"

"No, no. She likes it," Betty's friend says, swaying slightly from side to side. "Been crying all day till now. You're a miracle worker."

"I don't know about that."

"Greg likes to pretend to be humble," Betty jokes, eyebrows raised at me, "but we know better."

"Greg?" The friend's eyes bulge, her head tipping toward me like she's pointing. Betty nods and I wonder what she's said about me. It can't be good. I make one last tweak and then start to put the piano back together. "So you're Greg, huh?"

"Yeah, I am." I close the key cover.

"Sorry, I should've done it all proper. My head is a little all over the place since . . ." She indicates the baby that couldn't be more than a month old. "Greg, this is my college roommate, Laura. Laura, this is Greg."

Laura is holding a baby, and my hands are dirty from the delivery, so I just wave. She smiles at me conspiratorially, but I'm not in on the message held in her dark eyes.

"Nice to meet you, Greg."

"You too." I close the top lid and push in the piano bench, dropping the last of my tools into the large red box with a clank that makes the baby jump, her little face scrunching as Laura's bouncing intensifies.

"Shoot." She stands, pacing the room. Betty's calm, motherly expression ripples, revealing a sheen of desperation beneath. She leaps up, putting out her arms.

"She's probably hungry."

"She just ate. It's colic. Little Betty had it when she was this age," Laura says, keeping the baby close to her chest and lowering her voice. "I've got this. You need some rest before he comes home."

Betty glances at me and then back at Laura, who has shifted the now-wailing baby up to her shoulder, worry visible on her brow.

"I should let you go," I say, hefting the toolbox, wishing instead to sit at the piano and pluck out a calming melody to give Betty some support, but it's not my job to protect her anymore. God, it never was, as much as I wanted it to be.

"Are you sure you can't stay for dinner?" Betty asks, and even as she says it, I know it's a hollow offer. She knows I'll decline, but strangely, I appreciate the invitation, though I can't accept it.

"Thanks, but we have other deliveries." It's not true, but she doesn't need to know that. "It was nice meeting you, Laura."

"Same here," Laura says as though we're old friends, and she bounces her way into the kitchen with the colicky baby, leaving Betty and me alone. This time, however, I'm more centered.

"Sorry, Laura can be a little fussy," Betty apologizes.

"Fussy?" I snicker. Laura seemed a little snarky but mostly helpful. "She looks like she knows what she's doing."

Betty gives me a confused look and I swing the toolbox into my other hand, my arm aching from holding it so long.

"Oh, God. No. Laura is my baby's name." She points to the kitchen, where things seem to have calmed down. "They're both Laura. We promised we'd name our first girl babies after one another. She has a four-year-old named Betty, so I'd be kind of a creep if I didn't fulfill my half of the deal."

We laugh together at the mix-up until the humor is sucked out of the room by the sound of a car pulling into the driveway. Her face falls, and a deep dread tugs at me like a magnet, sucking me back to the safety of the truck and the haven of my new town, my new home, my new life.

"If there's ever a problem with, you know, the piano or you need something else from the shop, you can reach me here," I say, handing her a business card. My name is written on the back, and on the front the name of the shop along with the address and phone number.

"I'll keep it handy," she replies, tucking it into her palm as the sound of the automatic garage door echoes through the house, sending the baby into a fit.

I hurry across the lawn, the sharp metal corner of the toolbox scraping against my calf in a painfully welcome distraction as she closes the door behind her, the faint echo of Don's voice chasing me back into the truck.

"I think I've seen that lady on TV before," Toby says excitedly as we drive away.

"Me too," I agree. "Me too."

CHAPTER 35

CHARLIE

Present Day

The red neon "Open" sign is lit up in the window of Ike's Diner. It looks untouched, like it could be part of a movie set, and Betty seems to recognize it immediately. We rolled up the windows after a few minutes of singing and driving, the chill getting to Betty, though she didn't seem to realize it, her fingers turning a little blue, jaw chattering. We've had the heat pumping since, and after using a small brush from Olivia's bag, Betty seems ready for the visit to the café her mind hadn't let go of.

It takes both Olivia and me to help Betty out of the low back seat, but her physical limitations don't dampen her excitement. If she could run, she'd sprint to the diner's door. It's like this is the first thing that's made sense to her confused mind in a long time. At the curb, we have to remind her to lift her feet one at a time to climb up the edge.

Initially I thought the hour-long drive would be the biggest obstacle, but the walk from the car to the restaurant is proving far more challenging. It takes a full fifteen minutes to get to the chrome-and-glass entry of Ike's Diner.

Inside, the establishment's age is apparent: cracked floor tiles, booths with taped vinyl seats, and one topless stool with a handwritten cardboard sign saying "BROKEN" in wobbly black letters. A flat-screen TV in the corner over the counter displays a local news station. The neon lights that run around the perimeter of the diner are mostly intact, although the line nearest the painted crimson kitchen doors flickers as if it's on its last leg. The smell of chicken soup mixes with the sour scent of old fryer oil, making me both hungry and nauseous.

The diner was far more magical in my imagination, like the soda shop scene from *Back to the Future*. A middle-aged waitress shouts to us from behind the counter to take any seat as she collects plastic menus from the side of the gray cash register. I scan the tables. They're all open.

Olivia excuses herself to use the bathroom.

"Where would you like to sit?" I ask Betty, checking her reaction to the underwhelming scene. I expected disappointment, but instead, she lets go of my arm and takes several solo steps, holding up her finger like she's counting.

"This is Ike's?" she asks.

"Yeah, it is."

She looks first at the entrance, then the booths and the counter, and then finally lands on a booth in the back corner. She lets out a little breath and smiles.

"Over here," she says, walking in the direction she's pointing, folding into a clumsy crouch when she reaches the table. I sprint across the room to catch her before she lands on the floor.

"Whoa, there, missy. You almost missed." The waitress, whose name tag reads "Taylor," swoops in to offer help. She's dressed in blue jeans, an oversized white T-shirt, and a red apron with "IKE'S" printed in white lettering. She tucks a pen behind her ear and tosses the menus onto the table.

"Thank you. I think we're all right," I say, helping Betty move away from the edge of the vinyl bench seat to avoid any further risk of falling.

"I'm fine. I'm fine," Betty mutters, and I sit next to her as a human guardrail. Back from the restroom, Olivia settles across the table, claiming one of the plastic-coated menus for herself.

"I'll grab you all some water and utensils, give you some time to look at the options."

"I don't need it," Betty says, shoving her menu away. "I'll have a number two with coffee instead of a Coke and a baked potato instead of fries." The order spills out of her like a line from a script, and Olivia looks at me with raised eyebrows.

"A number two is . . ." Olivia says, projecting her voice as she reviews the interior of her open menu, "country fried chicken steak. Does that sound right?"

Betty's nose crumples, making it clear that's not the number two she remembers. "No, no. It's a turkey on rye, and I'll have the soup of the day, please. They have the best soup here."

"It's chicken and wild rice today, if that's all right."

"Oh, yes. One of my favorites."

"Sounds like you've been here before," Taylor says to Betty with a patient grin that I appreciate. I glance at the menu, my nerves masking my appetite.

"I have."

"She's been asking to visit every day for a week. She used to work around here. We thought it'd be a nice girls' day," Olivia explains.

"Oh, yeah? Where did you work?" Taylor asks Betty, but Betty is distracted by straightening the fabric of her skirt.

"I have a new dress." Betty smooths her long baby-pink skirt over her legs. Taylor tells her how nice she looks, and I answer her question.

"A small television studio. It was in the old bank down the street."

"WQRX?" Taylor spouts the call letters like it's nothing, and the fact-finding part of my mind lights up.

"You've heard of it?"

"Of course I have. It was on in here nonstop when I was a kid." She pats her chest, making her name tag wobble. "My grandpa is Ike. I think the studio was bought out in the eighties and moved to Madison or something. Some of the crew over there were regulars. That's how my mom met my stepdad, actually."

"Your stepdad also worked at WQRX?" I ask, putting down my menu.

"Yeah. Back in the seventies. My stepdad, Mark, opened a car wash in '81, but we used to have some of their autographed pictures on our wall. But I . . ." She hesitates and then admits, looking a bit bashful, "I took them down when he passed and Mom moved to Tampa with my sister."

"Makes sense," I say, after giving a few courteous condolences, remembering what people used to tell me when they thought my parents were both deceased.

"She was on a Martha Stewart kind of show. The . . . something . . . *Homemaker*," Olivia says, passing Betty a brush, which she drags through the ends of her short hairdo, oblivious to the conversation about her.

"*The Classy Homemaker*," I fill in.

"I totally remember that show, but I heard . . ." Taylor glances at Betty and then back at Olivia and me like she's trying to decide if she should say something else. "She's your mom?"

"Yeah. I'm Charlie, this is my daughter, Olivia, and this is Betty," I say officially. Taylor takes us all in, sweeping her gaze around the table twice before speaking again.

"Never mind. I think I'm confused." She scribbles something on her pad and gives a tight, fake smile. "I'll get those waters and that coffee." She starts to walk away, but I leap out of my spot, following her fluorescent gym shoes to the counter.

"Wait. What did you hear?" I ask, after adding two more turkey on ryes to our order.

"Nothing. Just gossip," Taylor says, setting out a coffee cup and saucer and grabbing the half-empty pot of coffee from the warmer. She seems uncomfortable, but the part of me that's been chasing Betty Laramie's ghost is begging me to keep pushing. Just a little. What could it hurt?

"I don't mind gossip," I say, leaning against the counter.

"I mean—you don't already know?"

"Nope. I left home when I was pretty young and now my mom's memory is bad. I promise you won't offend me," I say like we're having some casual girl talk.

The pot's glass clanks as she returns it to the warming plate. She sighs and puts her hands on the linoleum on either side of the steaming cup.

"When I took down the pictures before Mom moved away, she showed me your mom's picture, asking if I remembered her show, which, of course, I did." She slides the coffee in front of me. "She told me the show was canceled 'cause something crazy happened with her house and . . ." I hold my breath, wondering if my mother's hoarding started so long ago, perhaps it was discovered and discredited her title of Classy Homemaker. "I'm sure it's mean talk, jealous people."

She puts three cups of soup on a tray and stops in front of me to grab the coffee. I look at her with raised eyebrows, my need to know the decades-old rumor intensifying.

"Fine," she says. "People said she lost her mind and killed her husband and daughter. She was never arrested, but . . ." Taylor shrugs. "It kinda ruined her TV career." She picks up the loaded tray. "But it can't be true 'cause"—she tips her head to me and Olivia—"you don't look so dead."

Taylor sways to the corner booth, leaving me frozen next to the broken stool with the cardboard sign, my mouth suddenly sticky and dry. Killed. Husband. Daughter. Not dead.

It wasn't the gossip I expected, and the words don't make sense.

Killed. Betty Laramie may not have been a perfect mother, but she never laid a finger on me. And my father—she may have buried him alive with her belongings, but she also kissed the nape of his neck when she thought I wasn't watching, dreamily listened to him play the grand piano in the back room of Time and Again as though he was a virtuoso, made sure a hot dinner waited for him on the table every night and that his clothes were clean and pressed no matter the state of the rest of the home. My mother was mentally ill, but a murderer?

As I quickly type a message to Cam, filling him in on the gossip, certain words stand out to me.

Husband. Until three days ago, I had no idea my mother had a first husband. Cam found the marriage license. Dad said he'd died tragically.

Daughter. I always wanted a sister or brother, someone to play with, to share the responsibility of being Betty's child. Though I haven't considered myself her daughter in a long time, I am Betty Laramie's only daughter, or so I thought.

Not dead. Nope, I'm definitely not dead, so much so that I've passed Betty's genes to my daughter, who sits with her grandmother, sipping on soup and checking my position across the room. When Taylor slips back into the kitchen, I hit send on my text and return to the table.

"Careful. The soup is hot—" Olivia starts to say, but I talk directly to Betty, sitting beside her in the red vinyl booth.

"Mom," I say in a steady voice, trying to remain calm. "Do I have a sister?"

Olivia looks at me, confused.

"What?" Betty asks, like I've snapped her out of a trance. "Who are you?"

"Did you have any children with . . ." I search for the name my father said, the one Cam told me over the phone. "Don. Did you have any kids with Don?"

"Mom, what are you talking about?" Olivia says, a line forming between her eyebrows. I don't let her question distract me.

"Did you have a baby with your first husband? Don."

"Don?" she says. It seems like she recognizes his name and my curiosity swells.

"Yes, Don. Your first husband." I push a little. I know I'm breaking the deal I made with my dad but I can't stop myself. When I found out she was a Playboy Bunny, I let it go. When I found out she was on a whole-ass TV show and wrote a book, I let it go. When I found out she was married before, I let it go. But a sister? I can't let that go.

The bell above the door rings. Betty's eyes dart to the entrance as a family of three—husband, wife, and their teenage son—walks into the diner.

"He's always late," she says, disappointment abundant in her voice.

"Who's late?"

"My husband," she says. I lean in. "He's late. He's always late. I call and call and call, and he never comes home."

"Don?" I ask, encouraging her to provide more details.

"It's a girls' day today," Olivia says sweetly, doing a better job at noticing Betty's growing agitation than my tunnel vision allows. "No husband talk."

"He's supposed to call when he's late. Where is he? Doesn't he know I'm home all day with the baby?" Betty's temper flares as she pounds against the table, and I see the outrage of her motherhood years rise in her body, her shoulders tossed back like they carry the weight of the world. And as always, when the mother version of Betty returns, so does the hurt child inside of me, only adding to my already heightened emotional state.

"What's your baby's name?" I ask, convinced she's on the verge of telling me. A sister. Can I possibly have a sister?

Olivia talks over me, opening a packet of crackers.

"Mom. Stop. I think her blood sugar might be crashing." She offers Betty a packet of saltines, which she bats away, sending them flying across the room, and that's all I need to snap me out of my line of questioning.

Betty's not okay. She's agitated and disassociated from reality. This isn't just blood sugar. She's spiraling.

"Betty," I say, reaching for her shoulder. At my touch she lets out a blood-curdling scream.

"Don't touch me! Don't touch my baby," she wails, swatting at Olivia and me as though we're kidnappers holding her at gunpoint with zip ties and duct tape at the ready.

In her frenzy, Betty sweeps the plates and bowls off the table. The boiling hot soup and coffee splatter onto her hands and spill onto her lap, eliciting an ear-piercing scream. I reach out to stop the spill, my forearm catching on a jagged edge of the table. Olivia, who escaped the flood of hot liquid, pulls me out of the booth, and I notice my own hands are covered in red welts and small white pustules that grow as I stare at them. Blood pours down my arm from a deep gash and my head spins. The room grows blurry.

"Hot! Hot!" Betty cries as Olivia and Taylor help her out from behind the table. Her new pink dress is soaked with yellow and brown splotches. I can only imagine the vulnerable skin underneath, remembering how easily her flesh tore when she grew frantic in the courtyard.

"Take it off. You have to take it off," I say, lurching forward to unfasten the buttons running down the front of the garment, when a nice woman from another table holds me back, wrapping my hands in cool, wet rags.

"Tim's an EMT," she says, referencing the tall, middle-aged man she'd walked in with, encouraging me to sit down. Tim speaks calmly to Betty, who is still screaming.

Taylor emerges from the kitchen, carrying pitchers of ice water with a phone pressed to her ear. Tim's partner introduces herself and asks if there's anyone she can call to help us. Taylor retrieves my phone, dries it off as best she can, and holds the screen for Face ID. The lock screen shows a picture of me, Ian, Olivia, and the boys on the beach, taken during our last family vacation.

"Oh, my God, I knew you looked familiar," she says as sirens wail, mingling with the heartbreaking sound of my mom's cries.

CHAPTER 36

Greg

February 4, 1974
Lake Geneva, Wisconsin

"You'll need these," Harry said a few days ago, dropping quilts on the end of my bed.

The attic room has no heating or air conditioning, making it hot in the summer and freezing in the winter. During the summer, I would open the windows, sleep in my underwear, and sprinkle the bed sheets with a fine mist of water before bed to help keep me cool.

After spending twenty-one months in Vietnam, my internal thermostat recalibrated to guard against the heat. Then fall hit and the cold cut through the layers of bedding like a frozen blade. I found an old space heater in the junk pile in the basement, and with a few scrap parts, I got it working well enough to keep the water from freezing in the glass on my bedside table in the frigid winter temperatures.

So when the phone in the office starts ringing at 2:36 a.m., I ignore it. The first set of rings wakes me, the second makes me think it must be a wrong number, the third makes me sit upright.

Something must be wrong.

I drag myself out of bed, my skin crawling with anticipation. Lincoln, a young sergeant we interviewed, used to call it the "gut punch." Claimed it's what kept him safe, even though he'd already been injured twice and awarded two purple hearts. His nickname was Hero.

"You want Hero with you out there. He'll keep you safe," a private said, the camera focused on the scrawny twentysomething from Hart, Michigan. "Pulled me out of an ambush last week. I'd be turned inside out without him." The kids weren't wrong. Jeremy Lincoln did keep us safe; he tossed his body over O'Neil when a land mine went off. Neither man was injured thanks to his "gut punch." But I wondered if it only worked to keep others safe, 'cause not long after I got back to the States, his mother sent me a letter, thanking me for the footage of her Jeremy. Said they used it at his funeral. Three purple hearts.

I remember a time when Betty called me a hero, but what did I do? Did I save her? Did I sacrifice myself for her safety? Did I do anything other than fumble around like a lovesick puppy desperate for her regard? I'm no hero.

The cold wooden planks send goose bumps prickling up my legs through my bare feet. I shove on my work boots, keeping a patchwork blanket around me as I stumble groggily down the narrow staircase to the office.

"Hello?" I say into the receiver, my nerves blasting warning alerts through every cell of my body.

"Greg?"

"Betty. Is that you?" I already know it's her. She said one word, but I knew. The panic grabs my lungs and squeezes till it feels like they might burst.

"I need your help. Please."

"What's happened?"

"Don. It's Don . . ."

She lets out a sob that makes me think of the call she made so many years ago from a pay phone at the Playboy Club-Hotel—a night of blood, broken glass, heartbreak, and, on my part, outrage. It's rising inside of me again. If he hurt her, I don't know what I'll do. I might—I might kill him.

My neck flashes with a heat that fills my face and burns a path to my hands clutching the phone.

"Where are you?"

"Home."

"Are you safe?"

She doesn't answer, and instead she pleads, "Come. Please. Please."

I look around the room for the keys to the store's truck, my only transportation option, and lift them off a hook by the door. I'm supposed to sign the truck out when I use it, but in my fury and panic I ignore protocol. It's instinct, an autopilot system I have little control over.

"Damn it, Betty. Are you safe?" I ask, and she cries again on the other end of the phone. "Listen, hang up. Call the cops and get you and the baby out of the house. I'll be there soon."

"Uh-huh," she says in a small, childlike voice. "Thank you for coming. I didn't know who to call. I didn't know what to do . . ."

"Call the police. You hear me? Get in the car and park down the street. I'll be there as fast as I can." She mumbles a response, and when the dial tone comes through the receiver, it sounds a bit like the heart monitor that flatlined when an injured soldier passed away while I sat waiting for O'Neil to have his leg wound dressed.

Plenty warm now, I bolt out the door, climb into the truck, and toss the blanket I've been wearing into the front seat. I have on sweatpants and two flannels over a tattered Beloit sweatshirt. It's not exactly a knight in shining armor, but the many layers may help in case Betty or the baby need them. Hopefully, the police will be there when I get to the house. Hopefully, she listened and left. Hopefully, Don doesn't cause a scene. Hopefully, I can keep Betty and her baby safe.

As the heavy diesel engine roars to life, I check Harry's house across the street for any sign of life or lights but see none. I sneak the truck, lights off, out of its spot, turning them on only after I've reached Main Street. Pausing there at the intersection, I lean across the front seat and lift the latch to the glove compartment with one finger. It falls open with a thud, and I reach inside and grab a metal object wrapped in a stained orange rag.

"When you're carrying cash, you can't be too safe," Harry said when he showed the gun to me before my first big acquisition. He clicked out the magazine, checked the bullets inside, and loaded it again. "I'm assuming you know how to use it," he said, handing me the weapon. I took it and went through the same motions, pretending the cold steel against my skin wasn't a sickening reminder of the Smith and Wesson 1911 I'd carried at my hip after an attack on the Caravelle Hotel.

"I sure do," I said confidently, dumping the weapon in the glove compartment as soon as Harry walked away. I hadn't touched it again until now. I flip back the fabric to reveal the gunmetal barrel, then wrap it up again, placing it on the front seat. Foot pressed against the gas pedal, I speed down the darkened highway. I'm an hour away, at least, probably more, but when I get to Betty this time, I won't stand by like a helpless little boy like I did the last time she called me for help.

Tonight feels different.

Tonight, I feel different.

CHAPTER 37

CHARLIE

Present Day

When I close my eyes, the red and white lights of the ambulance flash against the back of my eyelids. It's been nearly two hours since the paramedics pulled up to Ike's, sirens blaring. Betty was crying on the floor, head on Olivia's lap when they arrived. I knew I should be the one petting her hair, saying calming words, but the dripping wet towel around my burned hand and my guilt kept me at a cautious distance. Once the medics took over, Olivia found her way to my side.

"She's gonna be fine," she said, as if she knew I felt responsible and wanted to reassure me.

She drove me to the hospital, where they dressed my second-degree burns and stitched up the cut on my arm. After being administered a dose of pain medication, I told Olivia I'd be fine on my own and asked her to check on Betty. As soon as she was gone, I looked at my phone. Plenty of texts and calls from pretty much everyone in my life, but there was only one I decided to respond to—Cam.

Within fifteen minutes of my text, Cam bursts into my treatment room, pulling me out of my regret-filled thoughts.

"You didn't have to come," I say. I didn't ask him to come. I just filled him in on the intense breakdown at Ike's, and when he asked where I was now, I told him the truth. I should've known he'd rush in to help if given the chance. Maybe somewhere deep inside I did.

"You came all the way to Janesville—the least I could do is stop by for a visit," he says, attempting a joke that falls a bit flat before growing serious. "I canceled the rest of my day."

"Cam, you're the best," I say with a slight slur from the medication.

"I don't know if you noticed, but I've been trying to get in touch with you," he says, politely reminding me of how I've basically ghosted him as he sits in the chair next to the hospital bed.

"Oh, Cam, I'm sorry. It's been a shitty few days."

"I get that, but . . ." He takes out a photocopy of a record of some sort. "I have some information that might help. I don't know about the rest of the story, but that waitress was right. You do have a sister."

"What?" I pick up the paper and lean in to examine the faded lettering, finding it difficult to read in the dimmed light, especially after a dose of pain medication.

"She was born in 1973. Her name was Laura."

The revelation hits my body like a cannonball in the gut. That's the name my mother has called me from the first day I walked into her room at Shore Path.

"So it's true? The murder thing—it's true?" I drop the incriminating document, unsettled by the loss of a sister I never knew.

"I don't know. This was as far as I got. I'm sure we can look for more information . . ."

My mom's cries and Olivia begging me to stop pestering Betty with my questions play in the back of my mind. "I should've let sleeping dogs lay—or lie, or sleep, or whatever."

"I see the painkillers are working," he jokes, this one funnier than the last, probably because of the morphine. "But seriously, Charlie, I don't agree. 'What's past is prologue' is also a saying, a better one than the stuff about dogs, I think. I could pull every tooth that had decay, you know, but then you'd end up with no teeth."

"It's not *my* decay," I rationalize. "It's my parents', my mom's."

"I'm dropping the tooth metaphor, but whatever this rot is—whether it's the house, the trauma, or the past—it's also a part of you. It shaped you. Take my parents, for example."

"Sue and John? I love them."

"I know. Everyone does. They seemed so happy forever, perfectly matched. But what no one knows is that they're moving to Florida because my dad got caught in another affair."

"What?" My mouth drops open. I thought his parents were perfect. "What do you mean 'another'?"

"Another. As in he's been having affairs for their whole marriage. I found out about it like a year after you left. My mom considered leaving him and moving in with her parents in Milwaukee. She said she stayed for us, to keep the family together. I always felt guilty about that—her choice to stay with a philanderer 'cause of her kids. But even when Sammy and I moved out, he kept cheating and she stayed."

"I had no idea," I say, reaching out clumsily for Cam with my unbandaged hand. He secures it with his, covering both of our hands with the scratchy hospital bedding.

"Yeah, no one did. All families have the rot, Charlie. You know, it's OK to want to understand some of it, keep what's healthy and dump the rest."

Emotion tickles at my tear ducts, my vision blurring.

"Hey, come here," I say, tugging at his arm until he's close enough for me to see his eye freckles again. I caress his cheek, realizing it's smooth, his light beard shaven. Amid the haze of painkillers, I grapple with the ache of everything that's transpired today. I'm comforted by the familiar face of Cam, someone who knows about my rot because he was there when it started. "I think you're one of the things I want to keep."

Cam, the boy with the spotted eyes who made me feel loved when I felt like another piece of junk in my mom's house, brushes my hair back from my forehead and places a soft, lingering kiss there. He takes a long look at me and shakes his head as he speaks.

"Here's the thing, Lottie. I read your book, the one about you and Ian." I groan and start to protest, but Cam continues his thought. "Are you two over? Like, for good?" he asks.

I want to explain everything—the messages, the fight at the Grand Geneva, the demands from Alex McNamara—but that's not what he's asking. He wants to know if we're getting divorced, and I don't have an answer for that yet. I shake my head.

"I didn't think so." He lets out a heavy sigh. "I like you, Lottie. I like you a lot, but I don't want to mess you guys up."

"You're not the problem—" I begin to say, but he hushes me.

"I'm not the solution either. I can't get in the middle of your marriage. I know how divorce works. Even if you break up, that's a major life change. I think . . . I think right now you could use a friend." Even with my woozy head, I know he's right. I can't run away from Ian and jump into Cam's arms, expecting all my problems to disappear.

"You should be a dentist and a therapist—a dental therapist," I suggest, and he laughs softly, though the moment is anything but lighthearted.

"That one was definitely from the drugs," he jokes to lighten the mood. He gently releases my hand and folds his arms across his chest as if he fears he might change his mind.

We don't dig any deeper into "what might have been." Instead, we watch funny videos on his phone until my eyes grow too heavy to keep focused.

Eventually, the nurse brings in the final paperwork, and I'm released shortly after. Cam escorts me into the waiting room, where Olivia is sitting in a corner with her laptop open on her thighs. We're instructed to wait here for news about Betty.

Still drowsy from the medication, I doze off with my head resting on Cam's platonic shoulder. It seems like only a few minutes have passed when a familiar voice jolts me from a dreamless sleep filled with red and white flashing lights. I raise my head and see Ian's face looming over me, a stormy hue contrasting with his naturally bright complexion.

"Ian," I say, bolting upright. My head is clearer now, although the pain in my hand and forearm is becoming more nagging. The clock on the wall reads 4:37—four hours since the accident.

It's strange to see Ian standing in front of me instead of being the one sitting beside me, his arm around me, eager to help and trying to ease my pain. He's the one who drove me to the ER after our miscarriage, the one who stood up to a particularly aggressive paparazzo camped outside our house in LA. He's the man who showed up to fix my parents' house, even though we might be getting a divorce. And here I am, sleeping—quite literally—with another man.

"What the hell happened?" he asks, directing his question at both me and Cam, his tone dripping with blame.

"It's fine. There was an accident with my mom."

"You don't look fine," Ian says, glaring at Cam as though he's the reason for my bandages.

"Just some spilled soup and a little cut. It's silly really," I try to explain, but Ian doesn't find anything silly about the moment.

Cam senses the awkwardness of the situation. He leaps out of the seat and pats his scrubs pocket.

"It's second-degree burns and a laceration to the right antebrachium, uh, forearm. They said the burns aren't serious, but she needs to change the dressing every day or so. Here are her prescriptions." He hands Ian a folded stack of papers, which he doesn't take.

Ian looks between me and Cam in the same way he did on the porch when he inadvertently interrupted our first kiss—our first kiss that never happened. Then he storms away, swerving to the right to join a tall, hunched figure at the nurses' station. My dad.

"I don't know if you sensed that, but I *think* he might be mad," Cam says, making an exaggerated grimace that I'd normally find funny. "I should probably go."

And though I don't want to lose my one ally in this situation, I agree. I haven't seen Ian for three days, and he looks worse than when he first arrived in Lake Geneva, if that's even possible. He's deeply upset, and my dad—well, that's not gonna be any easier. It wouldn't be fair to ask Cam to stay and buffer the fallout.

"I'll call you later," I say as he helps me up from the uncomfortable upholstered chair.

"I live ten minutes away if you need me."

"Thanks," I say as we embrace. I rest my head against his shoulder one more time, a touch of homesickness washing over me when he lets go.

"Don't forget," he shouts as he walks out the sliding glass doors. Everyone looks, including the police officer posted at the door, whose hand reflexively goes to the spot next to his firearm. "You still haven't accepted my friend request. I'm waiting . . ."

His voice fades away as the doors shut behind him, and his absence is palpable immediately, especially when I catch Ian grouse, "Funny."

The hairs on my neck prickle and stand on end as I realize he's beside me.

"Hello, Charlie," he says. I wait for him to ask why Cam was here and what his intentions were, but he doesn't. Instead, he says, "You ready to talk?"

I fill my lungs and consider all the ways I could respond—all the daggers of truth and criticism I could hurl in his direction. But getting a glimpse at my father, weary eyed, hand shaking as he signs paperwork fastened to a clipboard, I hold back my words.

I nod, pulling my sweatshirt tighter around my body.

"Good," Ian replies, following my gaze to my dad, who is talking to an official-looking woman in a suit jacket and dark slacks. "Because I'm not the only one with questions."

My dad joins us and says "Your mother is unwell" for the millionth time in my life.

I want to say, *No shit, Sherlock.* Damn it, I'm so tired of hearing those words.

"I know, Dad, I'm sorry. We didn't mean to cause any harm."

"Yeah, Grandpa, it was my fault," Olivia chimes in from behind us, taking full responsibility, which is wrong.

"It wasn't her fault. It was mine. I drove us to Ike's and I made Mom upset. She seemed so happy to be there again, so awake, you know?"

Greg unfolds the handkerchief from his front right pocket, wipes his nose, then folds it to dab his eyes before returning it to its place.

"I know you girls didn't mean it," he says, agitated but still soft spoken. "But, Lottie, I told you to leave her be. I told you it was painful for her."

I scowl. Yes, he warned me, but he's been asking me to tiptoe around my mom's fragility since I started walking.

"I told *you*, Dad. I just want to know the truth. You invited cameras into your house, signed papers, but you won't tell your own daughter some basic facts about you and Mom."

"It's better to leave some things in the past," my dad says, which I've always known is his mantra. It's probably what he expected me to do—leave things in the past like Mom's neglect, Dad's abandonment, and their absence from my life all these years.

"I tried, Dad. I tried to leave you and Mom in the past, but then *you* called and asked me to come home. You needed me. You know where you'd be if I hadn't come? The social worker said you're about to lose guardianship of Mom. If it weren't for the work I've facilitated on the house, you'd lose that, too. You're willing to use me to help Mom, but when I want a few answers—it's too much. Damn you, Greg. Mom isn't the only one with trauma, OK? I have trauma, too. I was in goddamned foster care. I lost both my parents, but they didn't die, they chose not to be with me."

My voice is loud, and the nurse sitting at the reception desk is definitely listening. If I were anyone other than Charlie McFadden losing my shit in a hospital waiting room, I'd likely be asked to leave.

Ian, who's been withdrawn and irritable since finding me with Cam, is beside me now, his arm around me. I lean into him, melting against his solid chest, wishing it could be this easy.

Inside the shelter of Ian's embrace, I wait, hoping my father will apologize like I did with Olivia. At the very least, I wish he would offer an explanation to fill in the missing pieces of our family's story, which feels like a chaotic Mad Libs version of our lives. However, he doesn't get the chance. A middle-aged doctor, nearly as tall as my father, approaches, his scrubs top carelessly tucked into one side of his drawstring pants beneath his white coat, and calls out my mother's name.

"Betty Laramie. Is Betty Laramie's family here?"

As messed up as we all are, the label seems to fit. Ian signals to the doctor.

"How is she?" Olivia asks, her toes bouncing against the waxed tile floor.

"Hello. Yes. Uh, Betty Laramie. You're her . . ."

"Granddaughter," I jump in for Olivia. "And I'm her daughter, this is my husband, and my dad." Ian's embrace tightens when I call him my husband, and I can't deny it—saying it feels better than I expected.

"Ah, I see. Well, she's stable now. Obviously, there are some complications because of her mental state, but her injuries are mostly superficial." Olivia and I let out a sigh of relief at the same time.

"Thank God," I say, grateful not only because I put Betty in this situation and allowed Olivia to be a part of it, but also because as hard as I've tried not to, I care about my mom.

"That being said," the doctor continues, adjusting his glasses and flipping through the chart, "your mother has an untreated bacterial infection in her urinary tract that I'm fairly certain she's had for a while." He must sense our increased concern because he quickly follows up. "It's a simple infection. We started her on antibiotics and should see some improvement shortly."

"Well, that's good," Greg says, his fists in his pockets. "Can we see her?"

"Soon, but here's the thing with bacterial infections and patients with your wife's medical history: Even a minor UTI can cause increased delirium for those already struggling with dementia. Have you noticed a rise in erratic behaviors, mood swings and such?"

I think of the recent outbursts, both in the courtyard and Ike's, and the way she tried to run into the cars in the parking lot with Olivia. I nod, and my dad adds some additional insights, asking a few more questions as if he's dealt with this complication before.

"We've got her on IV antibiotics. While not all of her erratic behavior over the past few days can be linked to this infection, some of it could be. Time will tell."

As the diagnosis sinks in, I realize there is a possibility that with treatment, we might start seeing more of "good day" Mom instead of "Betty" Mom.

I sink into one of the maroon chairs. I might not get to see Betty again, say I'm sorry, say goodbye. If I visit her before leaving town, Betty might be my mom—the mom who abandoned me, the mom who hates me.

I suppose I deserve this. I've been playing around with a sick elderly woman's mental state for far too long—I should've known it would eventually catch up with me.

"I'd like to let her rest for a bit, but I'll have one of the nurses take you up to her floor and we'll call you back when she's awake."

He leaves, and Ian makes a pizza order through an app on his phone. I consider whether to sit around in a waiting room with my dad or help Ian. I quickly stand up when the elevator doors open and leap inside.

"Whoa. Hi," he says as the elevator closes again. He hits the LL button for the lobby.

"I need a breather," I explain, crossing my arms and leaning against the elevator wall.

"And you thought helping me was a better option than hanging out with your estranged dad? Thank you?"

"You should take that as a compliment."

"As someone who has been trying to get you to talk to me for days, I'm not going to complain." His tone is teasing, but he has a point.

"As someone who has been the victim of your selfish choices, you probably shouldn't," I reply in a singsong voice.

"Victim? Seriously?"

"Yeah, seriously, Ian. I mean, how dare you act like I'm overreacting?"

"How dare I? Damn it, Charlie. I've been trying to fix things, and you keep cutting me off and then flirting with other men."

"Men, plural?" I scoff, disgusted at the accusation.

"Fine. Other man. Is that better?"

"I told you Cam is a friend."

"Yeah, you sure did." The doors open and neither of us get out, even though it's our floor. They close again, and Ian pushes the highest number on the button panel. I don't stop him since it's probably our best option at privacy right now.

"This isn't even about Cam or the stuff on Instagram. I'm willing to . . ." I grit my teeth and say what I'd decided before seeing the messages from Alex on Ian's phone at Ristorantè Brissago. "I'm willing to try and work through that in therapy."

Ian's jaw clenches. I thought he'd have a bigger reaction—a hug or a "thank God"—but he just looks at me expectantly.

"What is it about then if it's not about the stuff on Instagram and Cam?" he asks finally.

"The texts from Alex. Obviously. What do you think?" The doors open on the fourth floor, and a hospital employee walks in and we go silent. She gets off on the next floor, and Ian spits out his response.

"I'm not a part of that. I told him no, Charlie. Just like you did."

"I don't believe you. They were at the house this morning, filming with Jordan Kelp."

"Yeah. With Jordan—not me. I spent the morning on the phone with Carol, Phil, and our attorneys, trying to find a workaround. I was on a Zoom call when your dad called me. I tried getting through to you, but you weren't exactly answering your phone. Olivia filled me in, which, by the way, I don't love that our daughter has to be the messenger between us."

"You're the one who dragged her into our stuff," I say, my head spinning as we reach the top floor.

A couple gets on the elevator; the dad is carrying their new baby in a car seat, while the mom is in a wheelchair, accompanied by a nurse in colorful scrubs. By the time we make it back to the lobby, the husband recognizes Ian and asks for a quick selfie. We take a few pictures and congratulate the new parents. When we get back into our mobile fighting room, we've both cooled down and I'm buzzing from the interaction. Ian and I are good together. I want his promises to be real. I want to make this work.

After the doors close and we start moving in whatever direction it decides, Ian pulls me close.

"How many times do I have to tell you—I'm on your side."

"It's not about telling me. It's about showing me."

"How can I show you when you keep closing your eyes?" he asks, staring down at me as if he wants to kiss me.

"My parents gave up on me, Ian. And then Ricky did the same. At some point it's easier to . . ."

"Run away?" he suggests.

"Leave first. It hurts less. I just don't want to hurt all the time anymore."

"I don't want that either. I promise," he replies. I raise my eyebrows at another promise, and he corrects himself. "I'll *show* you, I mean."

"And I'll try to keep my eyes open this time."

"Deal," he says. We shake on it, and Ian yanks me in for a kiss that lasts until we finally arrive back in the lobby where our pizza driver is pulling up. It's frightening to say yes to a second chance. It's like I'm standing still while someone takes aim, but I know how to escape if I need to. I've done it plenty of times. I might as well give staying a try.

By the time we get to the third floor, where Olivia and my father are waiting, we have a large pizza, cans of soda, and a bag of overpriced snacks purchased from the gift shop.

"My God, did you buy all the food that's ever existed?" Olivia asks, laughing, glancing between us, catching on to the change in our vibes.

"I'm sorry, I'm hungry," Ian replies.

"Wait, where's your grandfather?" I ask, noticing Olivia is alone.

"Grandma's awake. He went back, like, fifteen minutes ago. She was asking for you."

"Me or Laura?" I ask as Olivia opens the pizza box and snags a triangle.

"You," she says, talking while chewing. "She asked for you. Grandpa said to send you in when you got back."

The nurse seems to pick up on our conversation and chimes in.

"You're the daughter? She's waiting for you. Room 312. I can buzz you through." A deep *zzz* emanates from the wall dividing us from the patient rooms.

"You OK, Mom?" Olivia asks, wiping a splotch of sauce from the corner of her mouth.

Mom. What a funny word. It seems so natural coming out of my daughter's mouth, yet it's so awkward to say as a daughter myself. Which mom will I see when I walk through that door—the one who raised me, loved me sometimes, and bit me like a coiled snake at other times? That mother is the one who blames me for our estrangement and is the same person who chose her hoard over me, the one who kept her secrets buried not inside her house, but deep within her mind. She resembles a sweet woman named Betty—a person I could have had as my mother if life had treated us both differently.

"I hope so," I say, diving through the door to the other side before I think better of it all.

CHAPTER 38

Greg

February 4, 1974
Glen Oak Drive
Janesville, Wisconsin

As I approach Betty's neighborhood, I have the gun resting on my lap, prepared for any confrontation that might await me. But when I attempt to turn down Glen Oak Drive, I'm stopped by a man in a uniform, hand up, flares blocking the road. With shaking hands, I slide the pistol back into the glove box and slam it shut as the officer gets to the driver's side door.

"This road is closed," he says when I get the window rolled down.

"What's going on?" I ask, leaning out to look down the street filled with police cars, ambulance, fire trucks, and groups of neighbors in bathrobes. Unfortunately, I can't see beyond them or the line of trees that obstructs my view around the turn. The scent of fireplaces burning to combat the February chill fills the air.

The officer looks irritated by my question, as though the unfolding events in this neighborhood are the only reason he isn't back at the warm station, drinking coffee.

"A problem in one of the houses," he says, looking at me and then the lettering on the side of the truck, one eyebrow raised. "What you doing out this time of the night, anyway?"

Driving around with a gun in my lap fantasizing about killing a man, I think, keeping my hands visible so he has no reason to suspect anything shady. "I worked for a guy on this street." I point in the direction of Betty's house, not mentioning her name just in case the officer got the wrong idea about our relationship and decided whatever Don did was justified.

"On this street? On this street where?" he asks. I tell him the address, and he checks something on a notepad before glaring back at me.

"You worked with Mr. Hollinger? Doing what?" The mention of Don's name makes me dizzy. Shit. Shit. Shit. What did he do? I readjust in my seat, the springs creaking beneath me.

"I was an assistant producer and cameraman at WQRX. I've been overseas for the past two years." The officer writes something on his pad, and the last shred of my patience slips away. "Listen, are they OK?"

He doesn't answer my question. Instead, he asks a follow-up. "What's your name again?"

"Greg. Greg Laramie." He jots it down, clarifying the spelling, then continues his asinine line of questioning.

"Did someone ask you to come here tonight, Mr. Laramie? What you got in the back of that truck?" He tips his hat, narrowing his gaze at me as the flares reflect in his eyes, painting them an unholy crimson.

I think quickly and answer as simply as possible. Taking a breath, I remind myself that this man isn't the enemy. I haven't done anything wrong. I'm offering to open the cargo area and let him take a look when a red and white ambulance crawls to a stop a few yards away, waiting for me to move. I freeze, staring at it. Who is inside? Why is it moving so slowly? Where is Betty?

"I'm gonna need you to go ahead and park around the corner and unlock the back." He points to a spot past the stop sign at the intersection leading back into the subdivision.

"What's with the ambulance?" I ask as its lights spin and swirl together into a blur, resembling an impressionist painting.

"I need you to back up, sir," he repeats, this time with an edge to his voice that means business, but I also mean business. I slap the exterior of the door, and the officer's attention snaps back to me, away from directing the ambulance through the flares and crowd.

"Is somebody hurt?" I ask, ready to jump out of the truck and rip open the doors of the ambulance to check for myself.

"Somebody is *dead*," he responds sharply, as if he's scolding me. "Now get the hell out of the way." He motions me back with his hand near his gun like I'm pushing him past his boiling point. Dizzy and stunned, with a tinny ringing in my ears, I throw the truck into reverse, working through the fear like I learned to do in the jungles of Vietnam as bullets flew and airplanes and helicopters hovered overhead.

Leaving the truck behind, I stumble past the shouting officer and wade into the crowd.

One woman is holding a tissue up to her reddened nose, and another is turned into her husband's chest, his glasses flickering orange as he stares into the distance. As I pierce through the throng of bodies, a burst of intense heat brushes against my exposed skin, bringing with it a sickening familiarity that conjures images of burning villages.

"God no," I mutter as a mist of water hits my face, followed by embers carried by the wind and smoke that stings my eyes. I rub them, hoping to change the image in front of me, but nothing shifts.

Betty's house is on fire.

Men in fire-resistant suits and helmets surround the scene, pointing long hoses at the burning structure. Arcs of water pour into the second-floor windows, seeming to do little to stop the hungry flames. I turn to the couple next to me, desperate for answers.

"What . . . what happened?" I think of the ambulance driving away slowly, as if there were no reason for concern, and the officer's proclamation.

"Don't rightly know yet," one of them says, staring at the fire, enthralled. No one seems to share the urgency coursing through me, which is far more painful than the drifting embers that settle in my hair, burning my scalp.

"What do you mean you don't know? Who does know? Who's in charge?" I sound frantic, but I can't restrain myself. I charge toward the fire trucks, the hoses, and the fire, grabbing at the first firefighter I see and begging for answers. "Did anyone get out? Anyone? Anyone?"

My voice strains as I shout above the roar of the fire, the orders from each of the men in the crew, the whoosh of the water from the hydrant. The firefighter breaks away from my desperate grip when I'm yanked backward roughly.

"There you are." The officer from earlier catches my arm, and another in a similar uniform does the same on my other side.

"Wait. Wait. They're inside," I scream, pointing at the crumbling home. "She's inside."

"Come on, buddy. This way. Let's go," one officer says as they work to drag me away. One of my loosely tied boots pops off and is abandoned in a puddle of cast-off water, left behind to bear witness. Still wild with terror, I find myself handcuffed and shoved into the back seat of a cruiser while Betty's dream house crashes in the flames, a sickening shriek erupting from the onlookers.

I lie on the back seat of the cruiser, shivering uncontrollably. I sob, muttering as the officer drives. He checks on me every so often through the grated divider. At one point, he says he's heard about my time in Vietnam and tries to find out if we ran across any of the same soldiers or officers, but I don't have the energy to respond. When we arrive at the station, he leaves me alone. The cold intensifies until I'm shaking so hard my joints ache.

"All right, bud. Let's go," he says. I sit up the best I can through my body's jerky movements, my tear-drenched face chilled by the sharp breeze. As I exit the car onto the dark asphalt of the police station parking lot, the officer orders me to turn around. He unlocks the handcuffs and works them off my wrists before offering me a blanket with a hint of kindness this time.

"I'm having Officer Franklin bring your truck over. Your story checked out, but we still have a couple of questions. We've got coffee inside. You seem a little shaken up. Why don't you come in, warm up, and then you can go."

I nod and start to follow him until I consider what that last word meant—go. Where would I go? Betty's house is gone. Is Betty gone? Nothing makes sense. I just need something to make sense.

"But . . . what happened?" I ask for the millionth time, stopping in my tracks.

"Let's get you into a room," he urges, trying to move me forward, but I would gladly be handcuffed again if it means getting the one answer I need more than my freedom.

"Are they OK? The family? D-Don's family?"

"Your buddy, Don?" He puts a friendly hand on my shoulder, just like the officers did when they came to tell me about my mom. "Sorry, man, but he's dead."

Dead. Just a few hours ago, I was considering killing the man myself, but his demise feels like being socked in the face.

I cover my mouth, already knowing there must be more to the bad news. Betty's fate is tied to Don's. How could she survive if he burned to a crisp?

"Yeah," the officer added, giving me a meaningful pat, "and the kid."

My eyes fill with tears again thinking of the tiny figure in Betty's arms when I delivered the piano to her house—her little baby, the one she held inside her when she came to see me at the shop. Dead. My God. How did this happen? We just talked. She promised to leave the house. She promised.

"And the wife?" I ask, knowing the truth has to come out at some point. "Betty?"

He shrugs. "That lady is a bit touched, if you know what I mean. My wife watched her show. Always thought she was a looker, but damn,

I'd take someone who's a little less good looking and a lot saner any day," he says with a locker-room-humor tone to his comment. It's rude and sexist, especially considering the circumstances. Then again—he said *is*, not was. Does that mean . . . ?

"Wait. She's alive?"

The officer darts his eyes from side to side, nodding. "Yeah, she's alive. She's inside."

"Here?" I ask, wanting to break through the doors and see the miracle for myself, when another realization hits me. "Why is she here?"

"Uh, because the crazy lady killed her husband and baby and set the house on fire."

"That's—that's impossible."

"No, you know what's impossible? A house burning up that fast without some help. You know what else is impossible? Getting out of a house on fire without so much as a sunburn. But murder? Now that's totally possible. You know what I mean?"

I don't know exactly what he means, but I do know this: Betty is in big trouble, such big trouble that I don't think she can get out of it without some help—any help, *my* help.

"But she didn't start the fire," I say, my body no longer shaking.

"How would you know that?" he asks, his eyebrow lifted suspiciously again.

"Because Don called me. That's why I was there." I clear my throat and prepare to tell the biggest lie of my life—one that could either save Betty or condemn us both. "Don told me there was a problem with their furnace. He couldn't get it to light. Said the place smelled like gas. I told him to get out and I'd be right over, but I guess . . . I guess he didn't listen."

The officer looks at me, a flicker of understanding beginning to show on his face. I'm uncertain if my lie will hold or if it will turn out that Betty, or Don, or someone else poured gasoline on the house and lit a match. But this time, I had to actually do something to help Betty. If it meant lying—lying a million times over—I'd do it. Today, tomorrow, and for as long as she needs me.

CHAPTER 39

Charlie

Present Day

"I heard you were here," Betty Laramie says as soon as I step into her hospital room. She's attached to beeping machines and long tubes, with bruises starting to form on one of her cheeks and bandages wrapped around both of her hands. A jolt of remorse fills my chest.

My father, who is sitting in a chair at Betty's bedside, chimes in. "Lottie's been here for a month now, Bets. She's a real help. Her girl, Olivia, is here, too. A smart kid. She did your nails, I think."

"I don't remember any Olivia," Betty says, glaring at me. "You haven't let them in the house, have you? You know how I feel about that. If Charlotte wants something, she can come ask me herself, but no one else can go inside."

"I know, dear," he says, working to calm her with a pat.

She'll forget her house and belongings soon—my father knows it and I know it. It's strangely easier this way. If her memory were intact, we'd have to fight her tooth and nail to clear out the house. In fact, if her memory were intact, I don't think I'd be here at all. Nurse Mitchell says some people turn from sweet to bitter with dementia, while others turn into a more amiable version of themselves. Then there are those, like my mother, who swing back and forth between both extremes.

"When are we going home, Greg? I want to go home." She sounds different when she talks to him—sweet, as if she remembers that he's her husband and that she loves him. You know what, good for him. He's invested more into Betty Laramie than any other person or endeavor in this world, so he deserves the bursts of kindness when they come.

"You had an accident, dear. You need to stay in the hospital for a bit. They need to help you get better." He speaks slowly and clearly. Even though she's only a few hours into her antibiotics, I swear I can see a slight difference. She's confused about time and struggles with recent memory recall, but she seems to have access to some more well-established neural pathways.

"Is the baby all right? I had her in the car seat," she says, and I wonder which baby she's referring to.

"It wasn't that kind of accident. Everyone's safe. You just need some medicine and some rest," my dad reassures her.

"Well, you don't seem all right," she says, noticing my bandages. I haven't said a word since I walked in the room, but she's completely focused on me.

"It's nothing," I say, attempting to deflect her attention. She scowls at me as if I'm annoying her.

"Don't lie to me, Charlotte," she says, using my real name. Anxiety spikes inside me so high I'm sure it's affecting my blood pressure. A little woozy, I search for a chair and end up settling for the rolling stool on the other side of my mom, usually reserved for the doctor or nurse.

"See? You're not fine. You're hurt. Come on, get over here," she orders, urging me closer. I don't know what to do. I've been repeatedly told not to argue with a person who has dementia. I've been taught to placate and then change the subject if necessary and encouraged to remember that they're not truly themselves because of the disease. But in this case, I'm worried that she is indeed herself and I'll regret letting her get so close to me.

I scoot the stool across the floor until I'm next to the bed, but not touching it.

"Now, tell me what happened?" she says. "Show me."

"Like Dad said—an accident." I lift my bandaged hand, where I was both burned and scratched.

She glances around the room critically and says to my dad, "The lighting in here is perfectly dreadful. Greg, open the curtains, will you? I need some sun." It's growing dark outside, so there's no way to bring in natural light, but Greg dutifully opens the curtains and turns on every light he can find. With every bulb burning, I flinch against the eye-aching brightness.

My mother sucks in a breath through her teeth.

"I'm sorry," she says, "I thought you were my daughter, Charlotte. I can see I was mistaken. Could you tell her I'm waiting and ready for her to come in?"

She doesn't recognize me, but it's different this time. Instead of thinking I'm Laura or an old coworker, she's looking for her daughter Charlotte but can't see her in me because she's looking for the fifteen-year-old girl who left her house thirty years ago.

"I *am* Charlotte," I say.

"No. No. You're not Charlotte. Charlotte is a little girl. She's got blond hair and blue eyes and . . . and . . . Greg, where is Lottie? Did she run away from home again?"

"No, no. This is Lottie, honey. She's back. With her daughter, Olivia," he repeats, knowing that only some of what he says sticks.

"You are Lottie?" she clarifies, her eyes softening, a mix of young Betty and my mother Betty. She tries to touch my face, but she can't because of the gauze wrapped around her hands.

"I am."

"Goodness," she says, shaking her head, "I thought that nasty woman took you away, but you came back. You came back, and now everything is fine."

I can tell my dad is holding his breath, wondering if I'll explode with pent-up resentment like I did a few days ago. I look at his anxious face and back at my confused, frail mother. I want to tell her they did take me away and that she did nothing to get me back, but what good would that do at this point? I'd just be beating up on a sick old woman for my own satisfaction.

"Yes, Mom, everything is fine."

There's something peaceful about that mantra: Everything is fine. In some ways, it's true. I have a beautiful life—it's not perfect, but it's mine. I have my own children, house, career, and family. And over the past several weeks I've gotten something I never thought I'd have—a relationship with my mom. I've found a way to love her again. Betty Laramie can't apologize for something she doesn't even remember, and I don't really need it. I think I'm starting to forgive her.

But strangely, the more I've come to care for Betty, the more I wish I could really know her. I can research news articles and court records, but without Betty's perspective, I'll never know what it was like for her to work at the Playboy Club-Hotel, whether she experienced the same kind of stage fright I do every time I start a show, and if that fear turned into steady calm once the cameras started rolling. I won't know if she loved her first husband, what color my big sister's eyes were, and if she killed them both.

"You look sad. Why are you sad? Are you in pain?" she asks, sounding more like the nurturing mom I remember from my childhood than the one who turned against me during my teenage years.

"I'm not in pain. I just . . ." I glance at my dad, who is refilling my mom's water cup from a pitcher on the nightstand. I don't want to upset Betty again, not after everything that happened at Ike's, but I can't help but tell her the truth about what is on my mind. "I was thinking about Laura."

The pitcher slips out of Greg's grasp, splashing water everywhere. He curses under his breath, and I pass him a towel to sop up the mess, giving him a reassuring stare.

"Laura?" Betty asks, looking to my dad and then back to me. "Who told you about Laura?"

"You did," I reply, which is the truth. She called me Laura the first day I was in town.

"I did? Now, how could I possibly have thought that was a good idea?" she muses.

"And you showed me a picture of her as a baby." I recall the first photograph I put in the "keep" box from my parents' bedroom—a woman holding a baby with the name Laura written on it. My sister, Laura.

At first, she seems a bit dazed, but then she grasps onto a memory. "Baby Laura."

Greg offers Betty a sip of water, staring at me with a look on his face that says *Be careful.*

"Dad, maybe you'd like to chime in here since Mom's a little confused. Tell me about Laura," I prompt.

"Stop, Lottie. This is not necessary," Greg says with finality, and I think of the argument we had in my parents' room a few days ago.

"I agree, Dad. You could've told me a long time ago, and none of this would've happened."

"It never should've happened," Betty agrees, and I know she's not talking about the current conversation.

"Don't do this. You'll only upset her. There's no reason to—"

While I've been learning to forgive my mother during my time here, the resentment toward my father has grown. The more he retreats, the more blame I find to direct at him. He could fix all of this and leave my mother out entirely.

I take a breath in through my nose and speak again, calmly this time. "How about this—I'll gladly step outside, and you can answer all of my questions honestly."

"I don't know. Your mother wouldn't like it."

"Mom, do you care?" I ask, aware that she isn't following our conversation.

"You both talk too fast. You always talked too fast. I don't know what you're saying."

"There," I say, gesturing to Betty, who is starting to look irritated. I roll the stool down to the end of the bed and loudly whisper to my father. "Now *please* tell me what happened to my sister."

Greg glances at Betty, then back at me. He picks up the remote for the mounted television, clicks through the local stations until he finds a game show that captures Betty's attention, and then he sits on the edge of the bed right in front of me.

"If I tell you this, do you promise to leave your mother alone and never mention it again?" he asks, which doesn't exactly make me feel great.

"Oof, ouch. I promise to never come back, if that's what you want. You've got the crew and the contract; you don't need me."

"No. No, that's not what I mean. I want you to help. I want you here. I never wanted to upset you, but they promised they'd fix the house so your mom can come home again. With the money from the show, I could get her a full-time nurse. She always wanted to live out her last days in that house."

I hold back a groan. "You're moving her home? Dad, she's gonna flip when she sees the stuff is gone, and then she'll start hoarding again. Don't let them fix the house only to have it ruined again."

"This is the clearest I've seen her in a long time, and these bursts are happening less and less frequently. I want her to be somewhere familiar when things really go downhill. I want her to spend her final days in our home."

"You really do love her a pathological amount," I say, envious he never loved me that way.

"I do love her. I do. And I know we failed you as parents, Lottie, but I tried. I swear I tried. Not hard enough, but I did. Back then, the social worker arranged a hard clean of the house, and they started to do exactly what Dino's doing now. But halfway through, your mom had a total breakdown, and I was afraid . . ."

"Afraid of what, Dad?" It's hard to imagine something more terrible than losing his child.

He bites at a hangnail and then rubs a thin spot on his jeans. "You don't know this, but my mom took her own life after my brother died." I slide back a bit, shocked by the revelation. "And your mom—well, remember how Dino said that's common for people dealing with your mom's affliction?"

"Wait, your mom was a hoarder too?"

"No. No. Not at all. But I knew what it was like to lose someone that way," he says, being careful not to say the words *hoarder* or *suicide*. "I was afraid of it happening again. You were safe in foster care, and whenever I talked to you—you said you were happy and fine. I thought . . . I thought a different family would be better for you, at least until your mother got better."

"I was lying," I say, sadness swelling in my throat and tears burning my eyes. "I wanted to go home. I prayed for it and begged for it every single day until I turned eighteen. Then I realized—you weren't coming back and so I had to let you go. I had to let my hope go. I wasn't OK. I don't think I'm OK now, believe it or not," I add with sarcasm. Nothing about my behavior lately seems like that of a totally stable woman.

"I see that now, but your mother read your book. I told her not to, I thought you'd say something about how you were raised or about the house and your mother and me. As much as it would've hurt to read those sad truths, I think it hurt her worse to be erased."

"I was erased, Dad. You both erased me from your lives. For what? For a house full of junk? I never wanted to be like her, so I used to throw everything out if I'd had it longer than a year or two. I did the same with relationships, ditching them before they could do it to me. And then my own kid—I let her go live with her dad without putting up a fight. Turned out like you guys after all."

Greg's brow furrows. He pats my head and gives me his signature shoulder squeeze.

"Oh, honey. No. You're not like us—at least, not in that way. You have to understand that your mom had a reason for being like that with the house." He refers to her hoarding disorder in generalities again. "You saw her books and her show. Every woman who watched her show wanted to be her, and every man wanted to marry her. She was all that, until . . ." He glances at Betty, who is completely absorbed in the TV show. I think I know what he's going to say. It's starting to make sense, at least a little.

"The thing with Laura?" I ask, bringing up the topic of my sister again.

"Yes," he replies, pausing again to ensure Betty's not listening. "It was a fire. It burned her house to the ground and took her husband and baby with it. A . . . a furnace malfunction."

I raise a skeptical eyebrow. "I heard something far more—upsetting," I go on to share what Taylor, the waitress, told me and then ask, "Is that what it was? Murder?"

Greg's face is pale, and he looks miserable, as if an ancient worm lodged in his stomach is trying to climb its way up through his esophagus and into the light. He peeks over at my mom and then back at me and blinks slowly, staring at the speckled hospital tile as he finally—finally puts my desires in front of my mother's.

"She called me the night it happened, crying and asking for my help. Her husband was a real piece of work—my old boss at WQRX—and I knew he was bad news. Your mom and I were . . . close. So, I drove to Janesville, but when I got there, the whole place was on fire and she was the only survivor."

"Did they conduct an investigation?"

"Yup. Never found any evidence against her. Don and the baby died from the smoke, and Betty was only spared 'cause she was waiting outside for me to arrive. But it was in all the papers. She lost everything, her family, her house, her job. She got me, which doesn't seem like a fair trade on her part." He lets out an odd kind of chuckle at the self-deprecating comment.

"But when we started over, I couldn't bear to ask her what really happened that night. I just couldn't. Whenever it came up, she'd freeze or break down and—why dig it up? Why make her relive it all? I simply wanted to fix her life at that point, start over. We built the house. Got married. Then you came around, and it all seemed good. At first it was a bag or two of supplies, a box of clothes she'd bought or made. Then it started to get out of control, like a snowball rolling down a hill, and then it was too late and—we lost you, too."

His voice cracks and he wipes at his nose with his shirtsleeve. I wonder how long he's been holding this inside. I have to give him credit, as basic and trusting as his retelling is, it's also the most open I've ever seen him. He's obviously been wearing blinders for so long that he's lost the ability to see clearly, but the fact that he's trying helps.

I tilt my head and cautiously ask the question that's been tickling the tip of my tongue.

"But what if she did it? What if she did start the fire? Were you ever worried that she'd—"

My dad starts to answer, but Betty interjects.

"I didn't start any fire."

"I know, dear. I know," he says, moving to her side, patting her arm lightly, clearly mortified she's heard our conversation.

"Stop fussing over me for a minute so I can be heard," she snaps, waving him away, and Greg listens, as always. He steps back, folding his arms and leaning against the darkened windows on the far side of the room where he watches as I slide the stool to the head of the bed. Her eyes are clear and focused as she speaks.

"I didn't kill them. I didn't kill Don, and I didn't kill my baby," she says, her voice growing warbly when she mentions her firstborn child. My father flinches like he wants to comfort her again, but I raise my hand, urging him to let her finish.

I take her hand in mine and she continues.

"My husband came home that day, and he was drunk, drunk and mad, mad and drunk. I'd seen him that way before, he was like that more and more since the baby and . . . and . . ." She trails off, seemingly losing her train of thought.

"Don. He came home from work the day of the fire," I remind her, and she starts again.

"Oh, yes. Don. He was tall but not as tall as Greg. Greg's a boy I work with—a kind man, good with tools," she says. For a split second, I can envision him as a young man: a handsome, scrawny guy with big hands, curly hair, and a nervous smile. "That night Don and I fought because he wanted to leave town and leave our house." She closes her eyes and winces as if she's replaying the argument behind her eyelids. "I went to bed. I woke up in the dark and . . . and there was a strange smell in the house."

"The fire?" I ask.

"No, no. This was a different smell. This was . . ." She opens her eyes, fear evident in them. "Exhaust. Car exhaust. I ran to the garage and I found him in the car. It was running. I opened the automatic door and dragged him out. He was still breathing just fine. He confessed that he was in trouble at work, and he thought this would solve things. I could get the life insurance instead of a husband in prison for whatever it was he'd done." She brushes the detail aside as if it's nothing and then focuses in closely. "He was fine—worked up and still a bit drunk, but fine. I made him coffee and sat him on the couch. I went to check on the baby to make sure the outburst hadn't woken her, and . . ."

Betty explodes, not into her usual fit of anger, but into a sorrowful flood of tears. Greg rushes across the room to her side and I can't stop him this time. He sits next to her on the bed, his arm around her, dabbing at her tears, shushing her sobs. He gives me a pleading look asking me to let her be done.

"Of course," I say, emotional myself at my mother's retelling of Laura's last night on this earth, but as I start to pull away, she shakes my hand to get my attention. The eagerness in her eyes tells me that it's not me forcing her. Betty finally wants to tell her story.

I give her a reassuring squeeze.

"The garage was below the nursery," she says, sniffling but stable. My father stays by her side, the look on his face telling me he's never heard this part of the story before. "Somehow, maybe bad insulation or another flaw in the building was to blame, but when Don tried to take his own life—the exhaust had risen up into the room above it and taken my little Laura instead."

I inhale sharply. What a tragedy. What a horrible, horrible loss. What a—totally valid reason to lose your ever-loving mind and burn shit down. I lean in, eager to know what happened next.

"I tried to get her to breathe, but she wouldn't. Then Don tried, and he couldn't either. He screamed and screamed, and I had to run away from his screaming or it was going to shatter my mind into a million pieces. I called Greg, asked him to come, and went outside to wait for him, but while I was sitting on the front porch, I smelled something new. This was not exhaust. This was burning. This was fire. I went to open the door to go inside and get Don and Laura, but the handle was already red hot, and I knew there was no way to get in. I ran to a neighbor's house and called the fire department, but by the time they got there—it was too late. It was all gone."

She finishes the story, holding up her bandaged hand as though she'd just burned it on a superheated doorknob and starts to cry again. I release her other hand and step away as she turns into my father, burying her face into his chest. He pats her arm, soothing her gently, whispering sweet words to her that I try not to listen to, feeling like an interloper.

"Promise you'll stay," she begs my dad. "Promise."

"Of course I will, darling. Shhh. Shhh," he replies, curling his body around hers, murmuring, "I didn't know. You never told me."

In the hallway, I find a nurse and explain Betty's emotional state. A few minutes later they add a sedative to her IV, and soon she begins to drift off to sleep. I gather my belongings and stand by the door, waiting for my dad to notice so I can say goodbye.

He'll stay here tonight, probably until she's ready to return to Shore Path, which means the project at the house will be on hold for a few days. That's just enough time for Ian and me to get up to speed and make a few important decisions.

"I'm sorry," I say to my dad when he looks up, hoping the apology covers all the mistakes I've made since I stepped foot in Wisconsin.

"It's all right. We're all right," he says calmly, chant-like, rubbing large circles on Betty's back.

Though Greg Laramie stayed by Betty's side without needing to know what happened, I like to imagine he's grateful to know the truth—or at least what this version of Betty claims is the truth. I can search records to confirm her story the best I can, but even with that, I don't think we'll ever really know for certain.

But I got enough of what I needed today.

My father cracked open his locked door just a little and whispered to me from inside, and my mom, she gave me a tiny glimpse into the tragic origin of her compulsion to hoard.

It's likely she won't remember this in the morning—she won't remember him or me or even why she's in the hospital. But I'll never forget the sight of my father holding my mother as she weeps for the daughter she lost to death while talking to the other daughter she lost to life.

As I'm about to slip out of the room, I hesitate. I watch my father tenderly kiss my mother's cheeks and pet her hair, and suddenly I see them as they once were: young, broken, and living this life like we all do—without instructions.

I rush across the tiled floor and lean down to kiss Betty on her head, just like I used to do with Olivia when she was younger, and as Betty did with me when I was a little girl, feeling a sense of coming full circle in this moment.

As I walk into the waiting room where Ian and Olivia are sitting, I'm grateful not only for all I've gained as I've faced the pain of my past but also for all that I've started to purge. Sometimes I forget that the first step of renovation is demolition. It's not easy to look trauma in the eye and have a conversation with it, but I'm learning it might be the only way to not become captive in a prison of your own making.

We are not healed by any means, not me and my parents or me and Ian or even me and Olivia, but one month ago I thought our family was too damaged to repair. And now I think maybe we're finally ready to try and put the pieces back together—one truth at a time.

CHAPTER 40

Greg

June 12, 1976
Lake Geneva, Wisconsin

"Do you, Betty, take Greg to be your lawfully wedded husband? To love and cherish him, in good times and in bad, in sickness and in health, for richer for poorer, for better for worse, and forsaking all others, keep yourself only unto him, for so long as you both shall live?" The reverend stands between us on the swaying wooden dock that juts into the lake. Behind us, our freshly painted house sits up the hill, while a small gathering of guests is seated on rows of mismatched chairs brought over from the shop.

Pink ribbons line each side of a makeshift aisle Betty just walked down. It's covered in pink rose petals, and the rows are marked with hanging vases of daisies. Pink ribbons are strewn through the towering willow branches, and rose petals float in the water by the dock. The strands dance in the warm summer breeze above us, and little bells tinkle with each gust, as if fairy kings and queens are attending our union.

As magical as the decor is, the most mystical sight is that of my bride. Her long hair cascades nearly to her waist, and her antique peasant-style dress flows from her neck to the ground and covers her wrists, with her skin visible through the lace at her neck and down her arms. A wreath of flowers and garland encircles her head, ribbons pouring down her back like she too is part of the canopy. I watch her pink lips repeating the same vows I just completed, in awe of her, of us, of the future we're building together.

Betty hasn't left my side since the day I brought her back to Harry's store after that terrible night where she lost everything. As I washed the mud from her feet with warm water and a soft terrycloth towel, I told her what I'd said to the police—how I claimed that the call they would eventually trace from her house to mine came from Don.

She listened quietly, and as I patted her feet dry she agreed to adopt my storyline. I didn't ask what really happened, thinking it'd only cloud my ability to tell my version of the truth. And I already knew the two most important details: First, there's no way Betty is capable of murder, especially not of her own child and husband, and second, whatever she did inside that house that night she must've done out of desperation. Those two facts are enough. I've seen what desperation leads men to do, and it isn't always simple or morally black and white.

We soon moved into a little apartment a few blocks from the shop when Harry expressed concern about the scandalous nature of our cohabitation, especially with the rumors about Betty spreading nearly as quickly as the fire that'd engulfed the Hollinger home. My name was cleared immediately, and after a six-month investigation, Betty was cleared as well.

However, it took longer for the public suspicion to die down, especially when people heard about the insurance payout—more than a quarter of a million dollars. The car was insured and was in the garage when the house burned. The house was fully covered, and of course there was Don's life insurance.

I suggested we move far away, somewhere no one knew her name or face, and where no one had heard the story of her husband and daughter's demise. But Betty didn't want to leave. She wanted to stay close to Charlotte and her nieces and nephew, hoping that one day an opportunity would arise to spare her sister from the same tragic fate she had suffered due to an unhappy partnership.

Betty almost got her wish. Soon after she received her insurance payout, Charlotte called to say that Bill had been arrested again and that she was ready to leave. Betty promptly sent her sister a significant sum of money, enough to pay off any debts and provide a fresh start.

A week later, we made the drive to Kegonsa to help Charlotte pack up her kids and move into a small house in Lake Geneva. When we arrived, the house was empty with a "For Sale" sign at the end of the driveway. It'd all been a ruse to get some of the insurance money. Another gutting loss for Betty.

We searched for Charlotte and the kids for months, and then Betty suddenly stopped. "I can't keep what doesn't want to be kept," she said. The next day, she purchased a piece of land on the lake, and we never spoke of Charlotte, the kids, baby Laura, or Don again.

From that point forward, she put all her energy into building her dream house, using the same plans she used to build her home in Janesville, only with a detached garage and a large deck in the back looking over the lake. Had it been my choice, I would have opted for a new design—something that symbolized her fresh start, but it was her money, and the project came at an enormous cost. I wasn't her husband yet, not even her fiancé, when she broke ground on the new house.

That all changed once the house was finished. She handed me a key and finally said yes to a question I'd asked nearly every day for two years. Yes, she'd marry me. Yes, we could build a family together. Yes, she felt safe entrusting me with her future.

And I feel the same. She *is* my future. She has been since she walked into Ike's with her red lipstick and misplaced keys. She was my missing piece, and I felt it—the gaping hole where she belonged and the urge to fill it with her presence. Now, it's official: in good times and in bad, in sickness and in health, for richer for poorer, for better for worse . . . for so long as we both shall live.

"I do," she says as I slip the band around her left ring finger, mine already in place, my promise already made.

"You may kiss your bride," the officiant declares. Her hands are clasped in mine as I lean in to kiss my *wife*. Her touch still brings me the same thrill it did in the dark studio when I was about to leave the country and she was about to marry the wrong man. It's not her beauty or fame, nor is it her body or the clothes she wears that I love. It's the resilient, creative, resourceful person inside her. It's because of her painful past that I feel honored to try to shield her from any future loss.

As we pull away, Lucy, Mark, their two kids, Harry and his wife, and a few of our regular customers and neighbors explode in cheers loud enough for a crowd ten times their small size. They toss confetti into the air, where it swirls between the pink silk tendrils fluttering in the wind.

We run through the deluge, laughing as the handful of people we still have in our lives after losing so many cheer us on. Out of breath when we reach the deck, we stop for one more kiss—a dramatic dip. Our lips linger against one another, our heartbeats pounding in our necks and vibrating through our chests in sync.

I hold her there, suspended backward in my arms.

"So beautiful," I say tearfully, overwhelmed with gratitude for both my bride and the stunning scene she planned and curated. "How the hell did I get so lucky?"

"I told you," Betty whispers, pecking my lips gently before standing up. "You're my hero."

She squeezes my hand, my new ring pressing into my finger in a way I'm sure will become second nature.

"And you're mine." I clutch her against me, kissing the top of her head, wanting to memorize every second so I'll never forget it. "You're mine."

CHAPTER 41

Charlie

Five Years Later

"Dad? You in here?" I call from the entry, using my key to unlock the smooth navy-blue front door. I texted him when I landed but he didn't respond, so he's either gone on a walk without his phone and is unaware we're about to descend upon him, or he forgot to text back. The twins wanted to stop at the beach before coming to the house, so I dropped them off with Ian.

"We'll walk home. They'll get cold in, like, ten minutes," Ian said like an old pro. You'd think he grew up here now after coming here every summer since we finished my parents' house. He even claims KC's ice cream is superior to Annie's, which is sacrilege.

"OK. Don't forget we're supposed to meet everyone at Hogs and Kisses at six," I said loudly so Mack and Bradley could hear the deadline from me as well as their dad. Lacey and her husband, Finn, and Cam and his girlfriend are meeting us for dinner and drinks. It used to be weird for Cam and Ian to hang out when we came to town, but over the years they learned how to be friends. "Lacey will freak if we're late."

"We will not be late, right, guys?"

The fifteen-year-olds nodded in unison.

"Love you! Be safe!" I said, playfully stern. They chanted "I love yous" back and then ran off wildly toward the lake.

Closing the door, I can hear my dad in the back room now, playing the piano. I drop my bags by the stairs and follow the sounds of "Bridge Over Troubled Water," my parents' wedding song, to the den.

The floors are a gorgeous ash color throughout the house, the kitchen counters a white Italian marble. I remember a time when I couldn't see the floor, much less the walls, and there was a risk of collapse at every turn. That's when the house seemed a total loss and so did my relationship with my parents. If I could go back and tell old me that one day I'd be happy to be in this house, I'd have laughed in my own face. But instead of anxiety and worry, fight or flight, I'm grateful to be here.

I watch my dad play, his eyes closed and his knobby fingers dancing over the keys, effortless. I've learned so much about my father since we first set out to clean this house. His amazing musical talents, of course, but also as we finished cleaning this room, we found not only Mom's history but his as well.

"Dad, what are these?" I asked when I happened upon unmarked canisters of 16 mm film. I'd decided to have all of Betty's *Classy Homemaker* episodes digitized and thought I might have found more to add to the collection.

"Oh, let me have a look," he said, putting on his reading glasses, holding up the cans to the hanging Tiffany light. He fidgeted and slid off his glasses, and I could sense he was battling something inside of himself.

"You can tell me," I encouraged him. He was working on opening up more, and he couldn't argue with the positive effects on our relationship. He coughed and sat on the bed, giving me back the film.

"Those are mine," he said simply. I waited, sure he'd tell me to toss them or give me some placation, but then he added, "We . . . we can watch them if you like."

When we loaded up the film on the library projector I still had at my rental, what I saw took my breath away. Footage from another land, another time. Footage from war.

"You filmed this?" I asked, stunned. I found out through my search of Mom's stuff that he'd been a camera operator at WQRX, but I had no idea he went overseas as a war correspondent. I don't think I ever would've known if Betty's story hadn't found its way out from the dark.

"I did," he said, not saying much else as we watched side by side on the couch and it grew dark outside. We put the films away, and I made a mental note to also have them digitized. But it wasn't until we were at the house last summer that I showed them to Ian and the kids, and from the armchair in the corner of the family room, my father told us the stories of his time as a video journalist in Vietnam.

Greg Laramie sold his antique store a few years back, and since then he's come to see us in LA, visited the Eiffel Tower, walked the Great Wall, and even taken up biking. His life has expanded now that he's let it.

"Hey, Dad," I say, walking into the now spotless den where Mom spent her last year. It was once my parents' prison.

"Oh, hon. There you are." He turns slowly on the low piano bench. He's aged visibly since the last time I saw him, and it concerns me. He's had a few of his own health challenges in the past few months, needing home health care of his own. I will always pick up his call when I see his face on my phone, and the kids have bonded with him, Olivia over photography, and Mack and Bradley over fishing and his war stories. We don't know how long he'll be with us, which summer might be his last, but we're making up for lost time.

"You sure know how to play," I say, leaning against the doorjamb, arms folded, remembering the days in his shop when he'd play the same song for Mom.

"Nothing special," he says, still as humble as ever. "Are the kids here? I have some surprises for them."

He's always finding treasures for his grandkids, a special fishing lure, an antique camera, an interesting book he found at a swap meet. It's touching to see my kids, who grew up in the age of new, new, new in a privileged home, learn the value of the unique items he finds for them.

"Ian took the boys to the beach, and Olivia is about an hour away." Olivia is flying in from New York, where she's working on her first documentary.

"I come from a family of storytellers. Thought I might as well give it a shot," she told me when she broke the news of her change in majors. I didn't need Olivia to follow in our footsteps, she could've become a waste disposal engineer and I'd have been proud of her, but I get why this path has called to her, and I'm watching each step she makes with great reverence.

"I hope we're not too much trouble," I say, squeezing my father's shoulder, noticing the darkness under his eyes.

"Heavens, no. I'm overjoyed you're here," he says, patting my hand. "This is your house, too."

I kiss his head and help him up from the bench, opening the French doors on the back wall that lead to a private patio. He sits in his favorite chair, my mom's favorite, and looks out on the lake that's dotted with boats, and I breathe in the fresh lake air.

He's right. This is home. A home away from home. The kids have come to call it home even though it's only for a handful of weeks every summer.

Second Chance Renovation went through with the crossover show with *Squeaky Clean*. My dad wanted the show to happen, and my dad rarely got what he wanted, so I sucked up my concerns and took the opportunity to get involved in the project.

With the full power of HFN behind us, in two weeks we had the house emptied, and we were able to watch the fireworks over the lake on the Fourth from my parents' deck. I thought it'd be awkward, that I'd want to leave as soon as we stepped inside the fully renovated, state-of-the-art, wheelchair-accessible house.

"We should rent a place down the street, just in case," I told Ian as we got on the plane in LA.

"Let's give it a try. You never know. If it's bad, we can leave."

But it wasn't bad. Olivia and the twins fell in love with the lake, Ian and I remembered how much we loved one another, and I got to watch my parents love each other in a way I never had as a child. We went home with sand in our shoes and a sense of peace that called us back to the house again the next summer.

That summer my mom sat in her wheelchair, not my mom or Betty any longer, but a confused version of both who stared at the lights in the night sky like she was watching a miracle from God himself.

The crossover episode was a hit, as Alex had predicted, and all the major networks and magazines covered the story of the house renovation guru restoring her parents' home. It was a vulnerable time for me, weathering plenty of online criticism about how I abandoned my parents while others said I never should've forgiven them. I could see both sides in the aftermath of the show and press tour. But in the end, it didn't matter what people said.

I'm grateful for the time I got with Betty.

As her memory continued to wane, she faded away from all of us over the next year. She occasionally seemed to remember her missing treasures or the baby she'd lost or even her daughter who was taken from her house, but she spent most of her last days staring out at the lake through the large windows in her bedroom while my dad played for her on an old Steinway he'd restored.

The repairs and the paycheck he received for letting strangers into his house made it possible for my mom to live in a safe home with round-the-clock nursing care. And one June evening in a rare instance of lucidity, she asked my father to hold her, and she passed quietly in her own home.

We spread some of her ashes in the lake, the rest remain with my dad.

There was a time in my life I thought I'd never step foot in this town again, and now I can't imagine losing this part of myself and my history. We considered selling the house and putting Dad into the assisted living side of Shore Path. He was willing, saying he didn't want to be a bother. But, like today, when I watch my father in this house, a home he built with the woman he loved, a home they nearly lost, and a home we restored as a family, I know he belongs here. We belong here, and I'm glad I finally found a way to come home again.

ACKNOWLEDGMENTS

First, a warm thanks to Lake Geneva and Janesville, Wisconsin, residents—my visits to your towns were informative, entertaining, and filled with hospitality. I never crossed paths with someone unwilling to answer my (enormous amount of) questions or without a helpful resource or story to pass on.

Thank you as well to the Grand Geneva Resort & Spa for allowing me to explore your facilities and pointing me in the right direction for answers to all my curiosities. Also, thank you to the waitstaff at Ristorantè Brissago for sharing their personal and passed-down experiences from when the Grand Geneva was the Playboy Club-Hotel.

I'd like to express my heartfelt thanks to the friends, family members, and caregivers who have generously shared their experiences with loved ones affected by dementia, memory loss, and Alzheimer's disease. Your stories of love and the journeys you've navigated through this challenging situation have inspired and deeply touched me.

Thank you as well to Nicholas Greco, president of C3 Education and Research, for his dedication to Crisis Intervention Team (CIT) training, where I've had the chance to work as a scenario actor on the NAMI Kenosha County CIT training team. Thanks also for allowing me to participate in Dementia Live with the Lake County Sheriff's Office CIT program to gain perspective on living with dementia. Your work saves lives and hearts, and I'm proud to be a part of it.

A huge thank-you to those who were willing to meet or talk with me about their experiences with hoarding disorder. I respect your request for privacy, so I won't mention your names. However, I want you to know how impressed I am by your openness and resilience. I could not have written this book without your valuable perspectives.

My dear author friends (you know who you are)—I appreciate your guiding light, impressive example, and unwavering support. Any messages or calls from one of my siblings-in-arms brings me a sense of solidarity I cannot find elsewhere. I look forward to returning the favor in your future endeavors.

Thanks to my found family at Improv Playhouse. I enjoy creating with you all onstage and living life with you offstage. You expand my imagination with every rehearsal, show, and scene.

I am deeply grateful to my original editor, Melissa Valentine, for believing in this book, and to my new editor, Chantelle Aimée Osman, for approaching this story with such enthusiasm and trust. I would also like to thank my developmental editor, Jodi Warshaw. You not only understand my stories but also me as a writer. I value your feedback and appreciate how you've helped me build confidence during the revision process. Thank you all!

To my agent, Marlene Stringer—your guidance, tenacity, and care have positively changed my life path in many ways. Thank you for being my partner throughout these years.

As always, much love to my parents and siblings for their unwavering support and encouragement. A special thanks to my mom for giving me a book on homemaking many years ago. That book inspired me to write this story and sparked my interest in exploring the concept of the perfect home.

And to my sister, Elizabeth—you deserve an award for enduring all my texts about plotlines, excerpts, and self-doubt. I couldn't write a book without you (please don't make me try).

All my kids—you have no idea how much you inspire me daily. I love seeing your imaginations explode as you grow. I watch silently in awe as you all mature into remarkable individuals. Being your mom has been the most incredible honor of my life.

Sam, I can hardly remember life without you, and maybe that's because I don't want to. Thank you for shooing the kids away while I'm working, for preparing food so I don't get grumpy, and for listening to me (or the robot voice on my computer) read my book out loud on repeat—all while you continue to pursue your own artistic endeavors. I can't wait to see what's next for both of us. I love you endlessly!

ABOUT THE AUTHOR

© Organic Headshots

Emily Bleeker is the bestselling author of nine novels, including *When We Chased the Light*, *What It Seems*, *When We Were Enemies*, and *The Waiting Room*. Emily is a former educator who learned to love writing while teaching a writers' workshop. After surviving a battle with a rare form of cancer, she finally found the courage to share her stories, starting with her debut novel, *Wreckage*, and the *Wall Street Journal* bestseller *When I'm Gone*. Emily lives with her family in suburban Chicago. For more information, visit www.emilybleeker.com.